"Maurice Broaddus has an all to capture the flavor of the streets. This is a wild, imaginative journey grounded in a gritty reality so compelling that you'll swear these characters must live in your own city. Put this on your must-read list!"

*Brandon Massey, award-winning author of*
*CORNERED and DON'T EVER TELL*

"This is really a great idea for a series, and I would recommend it to anyone. An interesting new voice in urban fantasy, and one that deserves your attention."

*Civilian Reader*

"This book is a triumph. Maurice Broaddus has created a masterpiece of original, compelling and thought-provoking drama, irresistible and unforgettable."

*SF & Fantasy UK*

"An Indianapolis ghetto might not be the first place you'd think to look for Arthurian knights. But in the run-down Breton Court neighbourhood they need all the knights in shining armour they can find. The earthly violence is shocking enough, but Maurice Broaddus adds and edge to the horror by introducing a number of fantastic characters who put this tale of gangland tensions into the context of the eternal struggle between good and evil… It's ultimately a very uplifting novel."

*Warpcore SF*

# MAURICE BROADDUS

## *King Maker*

### THE KNIGHTS OF BRETON COURT
### VOL. I

**ANGRY ROBOT**

ANGRY ROBOT
A member of the Osprey Group

Lace Market House,
54-56 High Pavement,
Nottingham
NG1 1HW, UK

www.angryrobotbooks.com
Dragon rising

Originally published in the UK by Angry Robot 2010
First American paperback printing 2010

Distributed in the United States by Random House, Inc., New York

ISBN 978-0-85766-052-7

Printed in the United States of America

9 8 7 6 5 4 3 2 1

## THE PLAYERS

### THE CREWS

*Breton Crew Folks*
Night
Green
Dollar, Prez

*Phoenix Apartment People*
Dred
Baylon
Junie, Parker

### THE CLIENTS
Tavon
Loose Tooth
(aka CashMoney)
Miss Jane

### THE POLICE
Det. Octavia Burke
Lee McCarrell

### THE ROGUES
Omarosa
Michaela &
Marshall

### THE KNIGHTS
King James White
Lott Carey
Wayne
Merle
Lady G.
Rhianna
Percy

# PRELUDE
## *The Fall of Luther*

*Indianapolis, Indiana. Back in the Day.*

The streets have their own legends, their own magic, and for a brief moment, Luther White was the heir apparent to both.

"Listen here, keep that motor running." Staid snorts of smoke poured from Luther's nose and mouth like a dragon's exhalations as he puffed on a cigarette. Cutting his eyes at CashMoney's rayon shirt as if he were ashamed to know him, Luther slid along the gray vinyl car seat with the coolness of shadow. His twin Caliburns glinted in the moonlight as he tucked them into his waistband.

Everyone knew there was a street tax to be paid if they wished to operate in Luther's neighborhood. If rent wasn't paid, he came a-calling with his Caliburns. Costing a fortune, the 9mm Springfield Armory custom-ported stack autos – with the frames, slides, and some other parts plated in 24K gold, with gold dragons rearing up along the contrasting black grips – were his trademark. He rarely had to do more than brandish them for his point to be made. Tonight a stronger counter argument was called for.

CashMoney drummed his fingers along the steering wheel of his Chevy Nova. He wore what barbershops called the Perfecto cut, his hair like sculpted topiary with its precise parts and molded crown. His drawn face held an air of sadness, his brim pulled low on his head to shade his dull brown eyes. The car's cassette player was broken so he rolled the dial on the dash, getting mostly static. As if there were any other choice for music other than WTLC, unless you wanted some of that easy listening rock garbage.

Luther ground the cigarette out with his heel, the sparks skittering into the slight breeze. Little set the rundown four bedroom house apart from the other rundown homes in the neighborhood, yet Luther strode toward it with determination and purpose. His brown leather jacket remained opened enough to reveal the gold chain along his black turtleneck. Life was all about façades and impressions and Luther took extra care to make sure his appearance remained slick. His brown eyes brimmed with ambition. Sideburns, thick but tight, framed his wistful sneer. He could almost see his reflection in his polished knobs.

Fall Creek was a natural ley line that helped carve up Indianapolis, one of those tracks your mother warned you about that people crossed at their own peril. On one side were large historic homes, one-time summer houses for those who lived in downtown Indianapolis; the playground for old money. On the other, around 30th and Fall Creek Parkway, a neighborhood spiraled downward with streets which ought to be named after local reverends and civil rights activists. Luther knew nothing about ancestral memory, his imagination not given to neither fancy nor spiritual stirrings. The idea of ley lines or connecting high places of power or sacredness was the stuff of superstition. It definitely wasn't part of his world at all. His world was gray and concrete and real as the dollars that fueled it. Light from the open door of the old house swathed him and he disappeared inside.

Barely old enough to drive, though rumor had it that he was one of the best getaway drivers for rent, CashMoney viewed himself as half an apprentice to Luther. Truth be told, his admiring eye transparently masked a covetous gleam. Barely in his twenties, Luther had already earned the rep and done crowned himself king of the streets. He lacked the ruthlessness and deep hatred for women that made career pimps, but he loved the street hustle. His resume stretched back to his early teens when he ran numbers, setting up a string of pea shake gambling houses using his uncle's reputation for muscle.

CashMoney's less-than-ambitious thoughts idled around trying to figure out how to get Yolanda Jenkins to give it up. He squirmed uncomfortably in his seat, regretting his last three beers. Fishing a joint from his pocket, CashMoney kissed it and hoped they could stop off at Burger Chef later. A hot minute later, he butted the remainder as shots touted a break in the evening's festivities.

Luther backed out the doorway with as casual a stride as possible for a man as cautious as he. A high yella, stone-cold fox flickered into his peripheral vision. Her large breasts pushed her shirt straight out, exposing her flat belly over her tight jeans. With Asian eyes and long black hair, she would have stood out anywhere; however, here, she almost made Luther trip over himself. Their eyes locked on one another, her haunting beauty captured him in its spell. He shook himself to stay focused on business. Luther clutched the bag full of money and tumbled into the passenger's seat. Maybe he didn't have to push up on Green's people, but a message had to be sent.

"Floor this motherfucker."

Luther banged on the front door of the rowhouse apartment then stepped back. Cupping his hand, he blew into it to check for any telltale smoke or drink on his breath. Getting with one of these church girls required some effort; still, it was worth it to have the proper woman to raise his future. He'd changed clothes twice before coming over, because Anyay's mom was no joke. A serious Christian woman – in church every time the doors were open and was known for falling out with the Holy Spirit every Sunday morning – she wasn't about to put up with a trifling fool showing up on her doorstep. Her massive forearm shoved open the storm door, but she kept

her other hand on the knob of the house door. A
florid woman with a body more brick wall than brick
house stood between him and the fresh face of
Anyay who peeped from over her shoulder.

"Hello, Mrs Watkins. I was wondering if Anyay
was in."

"She is." Mrs Watkins pulled the door closer behind her, further shielding her daughter from his
gaze.

"Would it be possible to speak to her for a
minute?" His voice strained with politeness, not used
to asking for anything, much less the added tone of
deference. He hoped the gesture would be noticed.

Tilting her jowly face at him, her expression
locked in stony inscrutability, Mrs Watkins weighed
her options. She had dropped her guard once around
him before and Anyay had a newborn to show for
it. The situation twisted her heart since she knew it
wasn't right to keep a daddy from his own son. Too
many men simply ran at the prospect of fatherhood
and at least this boy seemed to want to put in the effort. Not that she'd give him an inch. Even the rakish
angle of his cap screamed that this man-child was
too cocky for his own good. When he relaxed, he favored his father, not that he'd know since he never
knew the man. However, Mrs Watkins came up with
the boy's grandma. He was four years old when he
went to her, and even then she knew he had an
anger in him only soothed by running wild. The poison of the streets sopped up into him like gravy into
a biscuit.

"You ain't coming in my house and Anyay ain't leaving the porch. The baby's asleep and you got ten minutes."

"Thank you, Mrs–" he said to her back, the slamming porch door cutting him off.

Anyay lowered her head as her momma passed, hiding her excitement while appearing properly repentant for past indiscretions.

The stairs creaked in protest as Mrs Watkins climbed them. "Ten minutes," a dismembered voice reiterated.

Anyay opened the door and slipped out.

"Girl, check you out. Your momma ever going to give you a break?"

"Not as long as we're living under her roof." Anyay leaned against the porch door. Her thin arms crossed in faux impatience. Her face caught the moonlight, rekindling her freshness, as if unsullied by his, or any, hands. Reddish-brown braids cascaded down to her shoulders, a T-shirt draped along her lithe body. Though longer than most dresses, she still had to wear pants around the house, much less to come to the door. Momma's rules.

"I'm working on that."

"I'm serious, Luther. We need a proper home. You need a proper job, not all this rippin' and runnin' you call a life."

"You knew I was in the game when you got with me, baby." Luther trotted out his tired defense. Tonight, with her looking as beautiful as she was, searching him for more, he knew she was right.

"I know, but still… we got responsibilities now." The glint in her voice matched her no-nonsense eyes. Anyay dared to dream of a better life for them, her words a fine razor of guilt. She had no interest in changing him, she only wanted for them to be a family. And get away from the streets.

"How's he doing?"

"King is great. Misses his daddy."

"Can I see him?" Luther's face lit up despite his cloak of cool nonchalance. Even the idea of the boy broke him down in ways he couldn't explain – not to CashMoney, not to his boys, and barely to himself. Good ways.

"Can you be quiet?"

"Ain't that how we came up with him in the first place? Your mom's at her prayer meeting, but decides to come home early."

"Guess the Holy Spirit was whispering to her that night," Anyay said, her large eyes glancing up at him as her head nodded down. It was a look, a meaningful gaze, reserved only for Luther. She was his in ways she couldn't explain – not to her momma, not to her girls, and barely to herself. Good ways.

"Yeah, the Holy Spirit's got a mouth on Him. But I wasn't 'bout to leave before I got done. Man puts in the work, he expects his paycheck."

"Luther…" she said in her "you're terrible" voice.

"Where is my little man?"

"Come on."

Luther trailed Anyay into the house. Around her, the bravado he wore as armor melted into meaninglessness. The desperate gasp his life so often became reduced to a measured breathing. He could relax. Even a king had to rest his head some time.

His mouth open, head turned to the side while drool leaked from him like an untightened faucet, King James White slept blissfully unaware on the couch. A coordinated outfit of a light green set of pajamas – matched down to his socks. Luther couldn't have his son crawling about in hand-me-downs. The infant had a purity about him that swelled Luther's heart with the knowledge that he was a part of making him. King was his legacy and he had to do right by him.

"I was about to take him upstairs. We expected you earlier."

"Yeah, I had some unexpected business that needed straightening out." He stuffed a handful of yards into her palm. If he couldn't be present in their lives the way either of them wanted, the hundred dollar bills would make sure they wanted for nothing.

"How much longer will you have… business?" Despite the sad, disapproving quality to her voice, Anyay folded the bills and slipped them into her purse. In the end, she was a practical woman with bills to pay, but she hated herself for accepting the money. Luther came up behind her and wrapped his arms around her.

"One more matter to settle and I'm out, I swear. If I can't hand things off in the proper way, everything will fall apart. I'm trying to put together something that will last."

"I know, baby. I know. The important thing is that you're here now."

"I gotta book."

"But you just got here." She pulled from his embrace, facing him but backing away. Only when she pouted like this did her young age reveal itself.

"My ten minutes are almost up."

"Go then, you'd rather be with the streets than with me, anyway."

Luther rolled his eyes then sighed to himself. "Come here." True, his duty was to the game. There was magic in its call, a magic he had long ago embraced. It was as if his Indianapolis had two sides to it: the day-to-day world only the squares knew and the magical underbelly, the world of wonder he knew. She may never share in his world, but he could one day join her in hers.

Anyay turned around. "What?"

"Come here." He folded her into his arms and kissed her. "I'll be back, you hear?"

In front of the shopping strip which housed Preston Safeway, the Crown Room, and Nell's Beauty Salon, Antwan X, with his militant Afro and corduroy bell bottoms, passed out flyers to the next meeting for those interested in the ever-in-the-offing revolution. Sure, he'd done a stick-up or two in his day – hell, last week – however, always with The Cause in mind. Like the griots of ancient Africa, he knew the history of the neighborhood.

The rivalry between Luther and Green was the topic of many a corner conversation. Luther ran wild with robberies and number running, setting up pea shakes in the neighborhood. Green's trade leaned toward whores and drugs, leaving the occasional body in his wake (but only of those in the game, such was his code). How the two came to cross each other, no one was quite sure since their respective business interests rarely intersected. Probably little more than professional jealousy, the battle of street reps. The latest reports were not found in any paper, not even the Indianapolis *Recorder*, the city's black newspaper. No, for the discerning ear, word of their exploits traveled the vine from barbershop to barstool.

"Now, Speedbump was the craziest brother I ever knew." Antwan X ironed the freshly pressed stack of flyers with his hand.

"Speedbump? I never heard of no Speedbump." CashMoney, still sporting his red Chuck Taylors, was all about getting some of that herb. He had been a legend on the ball court – the tales of his athletic exploits grew in the retelling – until he messed up his knee over some nonsense after a game. Money. A woman. Drugs. One of the usual suspects.

"Old school cat. Used to run the streets with Bird and Green."

"Hard to believe Green's still around."

"Green always around. He eternal," Antwan X reassured him.

"So why'd they call him Speedbump?"

"Cause the fool would run into the middle of the street every time he got chased. Always get hit, bounce off people's windshields. Get up like it was nothing."

"What about Bama?"

"Now he was country crazy. He'd walk straight up to a fool and pop him. Did that shit on some police once. Folks kept their distance from him cause they never knew what he was going to do next or what would set him off." Antwan X smiled at the memory of the story. The roll-call of street kings; their exploits burned brightly but briefly. The smile curdled on his lips as he recalled their all-too-eventual fates.

"It's a small neighborhood." CashMoney offered a hit off his joint to Antwan X, who waved him off. A sadness fastened itself to the times that begged a drug-induced numbing to get through. Anyway, if he was to get to philosophizing, he preferred to do it in the throes of a high.

"What you mean?"

"I mean, we got Luther and we got Green." He leaned his head back and released a puff of smoke against the backdrop of the moon and away from Antwan X. "These two are running wild and the streets ain't big enough for 'em both."

"Green's no joke."

"Neither's his girl." CashMoney flicked his tongue along his teeth then spat.

"Morgana?"

"Fine. Ass. Sister. If I'm lying, I'm dying."

"I don't see how you can work for Green," Antwan X said.

"Baddest mother this side of Nasty Mike. Even Bama don't cross him."

"Bama ain't Luther." Antwan X nodded over CashMoney's shoulder. "Speak of the devil…"

"Be straight, baby." CashMoney booked inside without turning around, as if a student not wanting to be caught smoking by the principal.

The confidence of Luther's gait suggested that if he stopped, the neighborhood's orbit would have spun off its axis. Every day brought changes to the neighborhood he loved so much. Neto's Bar closed up, another bit of his childhood devoured as shop owners who'd built up a life moved out. Woolworth's, Roselyn Bakery, Meadows Music – they were here now, but for how much longer as working people left the area? No one owned anything in the neighborhood anymore. No ownership, no stake. But his name rang out and everyone beckoned occasion from him. So fuck everyone else, he had to go for his.

"All right now, brother, all right now." Antwan X clasped Luther's hands.

"Brother, Antwan." He crossed some Panthers because he had no interest in their revolution. Antwan X was neither a Panther nor Nation of Islam, choosing to call himself an independent intelligencer. He read a lot, spoke a lot, and spread a lot of the same "power to the people" bullshit. However, Luther still stepped lightly – nuff respect due and all that. Luther's rueful eyes followed the back of a man crossing the street. "Who was that?"

"One of Green's people. You been making a lot of noise with them. Here you go, brother." Antwan handed him a flyer. "Check us out when you get tired of having the man's boot on your neck. Can you dig it?"

"Right on. How's your boy?"

Antwan X raised his gloved hand. "Live righteous."

Luther returned the clenched fist and disappeared behind the black-tinted windows of the Crown Room. The darkened back room of the Crown Room was Luther's home away from home. A lone light hovered over the pool table and created an optical illusion. Until their faces or hands leaned into its protective glow, they were shadows in the darkness, voices from the spirit world for all any other knew. It was the way he preferred to conduct business. CashMoney chalked his cue stick, cocky but already high. Merle, already full of drink, shifted his eyes from the scene to the barkeep. Luther knew his days running the streets were coming to a soon end if this were the class of consigliere left to him.

"Damn." Luther's ball pulled up short.

A mild smirk on his face, CashMoney always took Luther's money on the table but never talked crazy about it out of respect. A cigarette dangled from his lip, the last inch of which was ash waiting to drop off. How CashMoney managed to smoke so much of his cigarette yet keep his ashes from falling remained a mystery. Everyone had their own gift. CashMoney leaned in for his shot. "Couple o' cats in here looking for you."

"You know them?"

"Nah."

"What'd they look like?"

"They had heat on them."

"Green's boys. Green like Spring. Green like dollars. Dollar bills. Cash money." Merle folded his arms and laid his head down next to his drink. He drooled into his craggily auburn beard. A black raincoat draped about him like a cloak and his huge bald spot reflected like a chrome cap.

"So what you think?" Luther asked CashMoney.

"Maybe sit him down for a parlay."

"Parlez. It's French," Merle interjected.

"Why you even let him in here?" CashMoney hated the crazy-ass white boy, yet Luther listened to him more than any other member of his crew. "He smells like piss."

"That's cause I had to pee. And my gentlemen's gentleman is shy. My drawers are like his... home court advantage."

Luther stumbled across Merle during one of his Thanksgiving turkey giveaways. Every so often, Luther gave back to the neighborhood he called home. It bought him a measure of goodwill – positive PR never hurt – but it was also his responsibility. Part of the code he lived by. Hundreds of hands reached up to the back of the truck – anxious, desperate, and greedy – then a ragamuffin of a white dude hops in to help hand out the frozen birds.

"They won't fly, you know. Even if you drop them from a helicopter."

"Get the fuck out of here, old man. We got this."

"Green's penumbra falls even on the Pendragon. And a squirrel's always got to get his nut."

CashMoney was ready to lay a beat down on him then and there, but Luther stayed his hand. In some way he couldn't explain, he was drawn to the homeless man. Like they were meant to be together, Merle always having advised him. Luther suspected the man knew more than he let on, the mystical gleam in the man's eye dancing with delight in its secrets.

Plus, Merle made him laugh.

"So what you think, Merle?"

"When you put the toast in the toaster who pops up? Jeeeeeeeeesus." CashMoney slammed his cue stick into the table, his patience nearing its end. Merle didn't acknowledge his outburst. "I think you can have a truce if you play things right. Too much noise on the streets brings the man down on all of us." Merle turned to CashMoney. "Makes it hard for Sir Rupert to find his nuts."

"Why you listen to this Hee Haw-lookin' mother-fucka? He better not be still talking about his–"

"Sir Rupert's his squirrel," Luther insisted.

"That's not any better."

"Go on."

"That's all." Merle leaned out of the ruinous light. "You want the streets calm, call for the parlez. That's the best play."

Luther, too, stepped out of the light. The image of the vaguely Asian-looking black lady crept into his mind, unbidden, like a spell of enchantment. Passion stirred in his loins at the idea of her, pushing aside stray thoughts of Anyay and King. "His girl's awful fine."

"Who? Morgana?" CashMoney asked.

"Morgana." Luther repeated the name in little more than a whisper, savored the sound of it, caught up in the spell of her.

"Best to not think too hard on her," Merle said.

"She's always had a thing for you," CashMoney said.

"For real?"

"It's what I heard."

"What about Anyay?" Merle sat up, lucid eyes fraught with concern.

"What about her? I'm not saying I'm trying to lay the broad, just rap with her for a minute. See where her head's at. Get in Green's head a bit. Where she stay?"

Merle sighed with resignation. "You have the Pendragon spirit, true, true. Betrayed by yourself or those closest to you, such is your curse. Father, son. Son, father. The path is unclear."

"There he go with that crazy talk again," Cash-Money said.

"I'll tell you this plain enough: if you get with her, there will be no truce."

"You tell me where she stay and won't be no need for a truce. I'll book," Luther said.

"She stay on Sussex Avenue, over by the Meadows Apartments." Merle cocked his ear as if listening to a voice on an unfelt breeze. "Hmm, that might not have been in my best interest."

"I dunno. Maybe I will sit down for a parlay."

"Not the right man," Merle muttered. "Not the right man, indeed. He falls before his own nature. Perchance the son." Merle staggered into the light then back into the shadows before departing the room entirely. "Coming, Sir Rupert."

The lure of the city was that there was always something new to conquer. One last score, then he was out, Luther swore. His weakness was that he had a way of making things fall apart, of never being strong enough to hold things together. The spade King Midas, but whose touch turned everything to shit.

CashMoney, his spirits raised with the departure of the drunken would-be soothsayer, exchanged skin with Luther then chalked up his cue stick. "My man. Always finding yourself in situations, usually involving some tail. You got your hands full there, boy."

"What's up on the score?" Luther had been planning the bank heist for a while. True, it was a neighborhood bank, but money was money.

"They pick up the money once a week."

"Cash money?"

"Like my name."

"Guards?"

"Four. Two in front, two in back. Three revolvers, one 12-gauge." CashMoney studied him. "Think you can take them?"

"I still got my Caliburns." Their weight grew heavy in his shoulder holsters.

"Welcome to the revolution," CashMoney said.

"Save the militant bullshit. After the parlay and the score, I'm out."

Luther had little more than stepped into Morgana's pad before their lips met. Women weren't hard to get. His rep was whispered on the lips of those in the know and he flashed just enough for folks to know he had money. Events careened at him. Half the time he was the sole conductor of his life. The other half he felt caught up in circumstances beyond his control; at least, that was the lie he told himself when he found himself in situations he knew there'd be severe consequences for. He preferred to live in the minute.

"What about Green?" He asked not out of any worry about being discovered, but wanting to know that his conquest was complete.

"He out of town. Besides, Green don't own me. Would it matter if he did? Wouldn't you simply enjoy taking me even more if I were his?" Morgana issued a small smile. Being around her intoxicated him. Though he had never touched the stuff before, they did a line of cocaine. He hated the muddle-headedness of it, the slow creeping nausea and the lack of control that came with not being focused. He thought nothing of her then, breaking up a bud and rolling a fat, tight number.

The sounds of rutting animals soured the night. Their bodies pressed together, unbridled. Their passions flared with little thought for the next day. With each thrust he erased himself. Other than CashMoney and Merle, all the people he came up with were gone. In his heart, he knew his time was almost done, but as long as he breathed, there was time to rekindle his old fires. From the confines of her warm embrace, he answered the siren song of the streets and hoped to get out before his ship crashed against the rocks.

Piercing a fog of memory, Luther slowly recalled the past evening as the unfamiliar surroundings alarmed him. Already the spirit of regret churned in his belly. It took a few moments for the figure who loomed over him to coalesce into view.

"Baby, you gots to go."

He hadn't felt Morgana stir nor heard her get ready. Her back to him, she fitted gold hoops into her ears. Her hair styled into Afro puffs, she wore a gold one piece jumpsuit dotted with maize colored swirls. Turning, she revealed a cruel smile, a cat in the afterglow of finally devouring a mouse it had long toyed with. Whatever spell last night held him in sway had been a heady one. She slipped on a pair of sunglasses to hide her cold, calculating eyes.

"What's happening?" Luther asked.

"Green on his way over."

"Shit. I thought you said that fool was out of town?"

"He was. But he just called. Said he'll be here in a few."

*Shit shit shit,* Luther thought as he threw on his clothes and tucked his Caliburns into his shoulder holster. Not that he was afraid of Green, but he hated needless drama. A deal gone bad, a confrontation on the street, those were the cost of doing business. Emotional stuff – and Lord help him if Anyay heard about this – exhausted him to no end. And no matter her protestations to the contrary, another man in her bed would drive Green to... emotional stuff.

His leather jacket wrapped around him, he rammed his probing tongue past her dispassionate lips. Her kiss was dismissive at best.

The first rays of dawn punctured the night, the closest thing to a peace time the streets ever knew. Freaks finally called it a night and young ones scrambled about to get up in order to tune into *Cowboy Bob's Cartoon Corral.* Going over plans for the heist, he thought of King and pulled a pack of Kools from his inside pocket. He had barely drawn out a cigarette when he noticed the car. A brand new two-door Cadillac Coupe DeVille – red with a white vinyl top – its 454 big block with a four barrel carburetor idled loudly. The door was open, displaying its opera lights. A lone figure leaned against it.

Green.

Luther stifled a grin. There were few things more dangerous than a young man with a loaded gun, light trigger finger, and nothing to lose. His blood raced. Adrenalized. He finished firing up his cigarette, cocksure and slow, as he sized up the man with the hint of a goatee and his dark skin. Green had the look of a dude who'd done a couple bids in prison, not some county lock-up. His suit was cross-checked with gold and green stripes. Emerald silk lined it and his matching cuffs. Gold rimmed shades encompassed much of his face. A gold, minky velvet coat rested on his shoulders, leopard fur trimmed it from his collar to the bottom and around to the back. A matching fedora angled on his head.

"If it's not the Spade King." Green's voice was like bark being scraped.

"Green." Luther walked up to him, hands in plain sight, but unafraid.

"Here on business?"

"I'm not on a hustle. Just visiting a friend."

"A man needs to be careful of the friends he chooses. They may not always have his best interests at heart." Green sauntered toward him, inexorable and deliberate, yet heavy with promise. "You're a soldier in a war you don't even understand. You fight just to be fighting."

"What you trying to lay on me? What about you?"

"Live for the Spring, die in the Winter; in between, I soldier."

"Business as usual."

"It's never personal." Green stepped closer, his breath smelled of freshly mowed grass. "I heard you wanted to parlay."

"I'm getting out of the game."

"Just like that?"

"Just like that."

"Mm-hmm." Green took a moment to mull over things.

Luther wanted to read the man's eyes but only saw his own image darkly reflected in the shades. Green's thoughts, like so many of the deepest players, were ever his own.

"I'm looking to tie up a few loose ends before I move on."

"You really think that's how it ends for soldiers like us? That we get the wife, the kids, the white picket fence and the happily ever after? You don't get to just walk away. You get till you get got. Blood simple."

"That so?" The weight of his Caliburns pressed against him, begging to be used. He desperately wanted to end this farce and draw down on Green.

"You drawing on me violates the parlay," Green said, though unafraid, as if reading his thoughts. "A man is only as good as his word."

"I have a simple proposal. I turn the pea shakes over to you for a taste. Ten per cent off the top, consider that my pension."

"That'd all been fine except for one thing."

"What's that?" Luther asked.

"There are always consequences to our choices and the friends we choose to make."

"We're still at parlay."

"I know that. But I can't help things if a man can't control his own troops."

The shot ripped through Luther's side like a molten thrust of a blade. He spun, drawing a Caliburn in the same balletic movement. CashMoney stood there, gun in hand. Luther squeezed the trigger, with only a resounding click in response. Unsure of what to expect, CashMoney flinched at first but with the click, returned a knowing grin. Luther scuttled to the side, but CashMoney fired off a quick three shots, the first two hitting him in the chest, the third going astray.

It caught Green in the arm.

CashMoney's face blanched in response, lowering the gun immediately.

"Oh shit, Green, I–"

"Chill, little man," Green said. His flesh began to re-knit itself, thin vines extending out as if covering a house then assuming the appearance of flesh. "No harm done, but you owe me for the cost of fixing my coat."

"You still staking me?"

"Done." Green reached into his Caddy and tossed CashMoney a small duffle bag. He inspected the contents, finding the cash and product to his liking. "Welcome to the game."

Morgana watched the street pantomime of police and ambulance lights while people scampered back and forth in vain, attending to the fallen king. As promised, CashMoney retrieved her gifts before anyone arrived on the scene. Opening her keepsake chest, she placed in it the twin Caliburns, joining the bullets she had removed from them.

Such a disgraceful and ignoble death for a king.

She patted her belly with the knowing of an expectant mother.

Long live the king.

# CHAPTER ONE

"It ain't even right," King said to stave off the impending silence. He drummed his fingers along the steering wheel. Absently noting the recently closed or unoccupied stores in several strip malls along Lafayette Road, it was as if blank spaces pocked his neighborhood. Even the newly opened Wal-Mart struggled, though neighborhood lore held that within its first week it had to let fifty of its employees go for excessive shoplifting. He hated driving, preferring to walk when he could, but Big Momma asked him to pick up her son and even loaned him her car to do it. King hardly knew Prez – as he was known around the way, though born Preston Wilcox – but Big Momma was a neighborhood fixture. Her word that he was a good kid was all King needed, despite the boy striking him as just another neighborhood knucklehead.

"I know." Prez had a just-shy-of-amiable half-smile on his face. The wisps of an attempted goatee sprouted along the sides of his mouth. Eyes fixed on the road, he nestled into his oversized Kellogg's jacket, a picture of the Honey Smacks frog danced on the back. Though late in the summer, the temperatures remained fairly mild.

"You should have your own spot." King heard the lecturing tone in his voice, but chalked it up to wanting to mentor the boy. The streets had their lure and anything he could do to inoculate Prez to their madness, well, he couldn't help himself. His street, his responsibility – that had always been his way.

"Ain't no shame in it." A sullenness quilted Prez's face, man-child struggling with independence but having to retreat to his moms. Grandmoms, technically. His moms turned him over to Big Momma so that raising a child wouldn't slow her down. He knew full well that he'd have to hide any of his foolishness from Big Momma because she would have none of it.

"I know. Big Momma ain't gonna let her baby sleep out on the street."

"Shit, I'd still be on my own if this dude who I stayed with had let me know that he was moving out and his cousin would be taking his place. But his cousin wasn't trying to pay no rent, and it wasn't like either of us were on the lease. So, boom, the landlord kicks us out. We only had till Monday to get our stuff out of there before he puts it out. And the cousin ain't even started to pack his stuff up."

"Yeah," King said without commitment, part from having nothing to add, part due to distraction. He eased off the gas as they passed a row of apartments.

A little girl skipped into an open door while a woman struggled with pulling a basket of clothes from the backseat of her car.

"What's up?" Prez asked, noting King's focused attention.

"Nothing." It wasn't as if King was going to say "That's my baby's momma's place. Look at her. You know she be having men all up in there all hours of the night. In front of Nakia."

Prez spied a buxom, dark-complexioned woman walking in the front door of her apartment carrying a load of laundry. "Pretty girl."

"Reminds me of someone I used to know."

King flipped through radio stations, though Black radio in Indianapolis only came in two flavors: hip hop and adult soul. He loved hip hop, but he really needed something with a melody right now. His mom called his taste in music the legacy of his father. King had no true sense of who Luther White was, only the legend his mother made him out to be. It was easy to be a legend when you were long dead and gone.

As if Saturday afternoon traffic in front of Meijer wasn't going to be bad enough, they crept the last mile to the Breton Court townhouses due to construction on the only street leading there. Prez eased back in his seat and put one of his Timberlands on King's dashboard. A half-muttered "my bad" and the foot lowering followed a stern gaze from King. Kids today, King thought, no respect for anything.

Sliding into one of the parking spots, one assigned per townhouse, King grabbed the two bags of clothes from his trunk, to which Prez nodded in appreciation, and carried them toward Big Momma's. Already outside holding court, she slowly fanned herself with a tattered magazine. Her usual courtesans, the neighbors from across the way, sat around the plastic table. King couldn't quite remember the name of his neighbor who lived across from Big Momma, though they seemed like a nice family. Every Sunday they dressed up for church along with their two kids. The neighborhood kids (half of whom Big Momma ostensibly babysat) played with a garden hose, spraying each other and turning the center of the court into a mud slick, a dirt-floored "slip'n's-lide". The white-haired candy lady, who had lived in the court longer than anyone else, stood on her porch passing out popsicles to any kid who took a break from the hose. Her cats keened against the front storm door like children denied the chance to play with their friends.

"Damn," he said to himself, as Prez left him with his bags to hook up with a couple of neighborhood knuckleheads who were setting up shop on the corner. Their fixed gazes dared him to do something about their presence. His face flushed with heat, but he wasn't about to return a hard look for each one he received, nor could he afford to get bent out of shape every time some fool stepped to him wrong. Attitude and anger came in shorter supply for him these days so he chose his spots rather than exhaust

himself on every bit of drama. However righteous
his rage.

Merle never imagined that a Timberland boot in his
midsection would be the defining moment of his day.

The abandoned shoe factory on the south side of
downtown had been declared a historic landmark, but
neither the city nor any foundation knew what to do
with it nor wanted to put up the money to restore it
for modern use. The owner languished with the alba-
tross of high property taxes, unable to sell it, so the
building existed in a state of limbo, between being and
not being, and thus was the perfect place for Merle to
break into and lay his head. With a flattened refriger-
ator box as his mattress, visions of dragons, mist, and
silver-armored knights filled his dreams.

Waking with a start, disturbing the rats which
scurried along the broken bits of crates and skids,
Merle knew he had to make his way to the west side
of town.

"Sir Rupert?" he called out. A brown and black
squirrel, with a gray streak along its back, poked its
head through a hole in the bay door of the building.
"I had the dream again. I think the time has finally
come. He has returned."

The squirrel sat back on its haunches, eagerly
working at an acorn.

"I know, I know. There have been several false
alarms, but this time I know it's real." Merle
wrapped his arms loosely around his knees and gathered his wits while Sir Rupert ate.

The squirrel finished with the nut, turned, and ran out the hole in the door.

"You're right, you're right. We mustn't tarry." Scooping up his backpack and his black raincoat, Merle slipped between the still-chained doors. The raincoat doubled as his blanket, though its winter insert had pulled free and with a few teeth missing from the zippered lining, he was unable to reattach it. Not much of a clothes horse, he kept his attire simple. A furry hat, the kind a Russian soldier languishing in Siberia would wear, a tattered black sweater with matching jeans, and black socks with no shoes. He had the most difficult of times keeping shoes and suspected Sir Rupert, prankster that he was, of nicking them at night. He pulled the raincoat tight around him, buttoning it only at the middle where a belt might fall. He already missed his normal routine that had him checking in at the Wheeler Mission, then panhandling outside of the Red Eye Café – whose owner often let him push a broom for a meal – and avoiding the police eager to sweep him under the city's rug. It would be little more than a three hour haul to the west side that awaited him.

Merle kept to the bank of the White River which was unusually low due to the lack of rain. Though the White River was a natural ley line winding its way through the heart of the city, another one lay closer to Eagle Creek Park, along Breton Street. Whatever called him, he knew his destiny had to lie there. After three hours, he climbed up the embankment to follow 38th Street west.

The Breton Court housing addition had changed considerably in the quarter of a century since it was established. Once a solidly all-white not-quite-suburban enclave, it now languished as a neighborhood in decline. Street lore attributed this to two things. For one, the first black family moved in a decade or so ago. Their white neighbors, not wanting to let a bad element gain a foothold in the neighborhood, harassed them to the point that a U-Haul truck was soon being loaded. Unfortunately, they had made a slight miscalculation. The black family was also seeking a respite from bad elements and had more in common with their white neighbors than not. And though they moved, they never sold their town house in Breton Court. Instead, they rented it out. They found the worst of the "bad elements" they could find and let them live there rent-free for six months. The white flight was more of an exodus of Biblical proportions.

The second factor? The townhouses had since been bought up primarily by three owners who, in an act just shy of collusion, opted to let the property run down, renting to Section 8 tenants or anyone who had cash in hand. While the word "gentrification" hadn't been bandied about, their goal was to sell off the whole piece for development and by "development" they envisioned razing the entire lot.

Merle plodded along the creek line which ran the length of Breton Court from 38th Street. Sir Rupert had long scampered off, perhaps to survey the scene from his own vantage point. No matter, Merle recognized layabouts and ne'er-do-wells when he saw them.

"What you need, old timer? You look like you need to get up." A young man, more boy than man, stepped toward him. His slightly faded blue jeans had rolled-up cuffs and sagged just below his blue and white striped boxer shorts despite the presence of a skull-buckled chain through the belt loops. Rhinestones dotted his black shirt.

"All's not right in Who-ville," Merle said.

"What you got, Dollar?" Another young man sported a formidably sized pair of black Timberland boots, smothered in a hooded jacket with a frog across its back. Merle couldn't help but think of the cartoon with the frog singing "Hello my baby, hello my darling" when no one but his owner was around.

"Don't know. You up?" Dollar asked, never one to let any potential sale slip past. The court had been a quiet stretch of real estate until Dollar built it up into a profitable venture. He was due to be moved up the ranks soon, climbing the corporate ladder, to get away from actually handling product.

"No, no. Just passing through," Merle said while he fished in his pockets as if he misplaced his wallet.

"What? We some sightseeing stop? Get right or get gone."

"I'm tired of these ghetto tourist types. 'Let's see how the po' folks be living.'" The Timberland-booted man stepped nearer, a hulk of aggression needing to be vented.

"Come on, man. Green said no drama less we had no choice." Dollar understood that in such stark economic times, fiscal responsibilities demanded certain precaution. Ever-present muscle was the cost of doing business. But some of these young bucks were too eager to make a name, thinking that being crazy was the surest route to success. It was a headache he didn't need.

"Green?" Merle had hoped to never hear that name again. He buried the gleam of recognition too late.

"You know Green?" Dollar tilted his head with piqued curiosity.

"Yes. Uh, not really. Maybe I've heard the name."

"I bet his country ass is a snitch." Mr Size 12 Boots gave him an exaggerated sniff. "Yeah, he smells like a snitch bitch."

Merle waved his fingers in front of him as if with a sudden display of jazz hands. "These are not the droids you are looking for."

"Are you making fun of me?" Before Merle could respond, the young man punched him in the gut with such force that Merle crumpled to the ground. With blood in the water, the Timberland boot slammed into his side three or four times for good measure before the man bent over to grab him by the lapels. "Yeah, I'm gonna give you a name to re-member."

"My man." Dollar backed up a step or two, looking over his shoulder for Green, instead spying another approaching figure. "Ease up."

"We got a problem?" Tall and straight, visibly muscled, but not with the dieseled artifice of prison weight, the man had the complexion of burnt cocoa. His eyes burned with a stern glint, both decisive and sure. Hard, but not in a street tough way, his walk was street savvy, with a hint of the swagger of someone who knew how handsome he was. Carrying himself properly was a survival tool. Level chin, squared up, not moving too fast which betrayed fear. The streets hadn't changed much in the years Merle had wandered them. If your body language portrayed you as scared, you became nothing but prey. Despite the oversized black T-shirt with a Jackie Robinson portrait, the young man wasn't much older than the other man-boys. He cold-eyed both Dollar and Mr Size 12, though not so hard as to give Mr Size 12 a challenge he'd have no choice but to respond to.

"Nah, we ain't got a problem. Simply a misunderstanding," Dollar said.

"He in the wrong place at the wrong time," Mr Size 12 said. "He needed... directions."

"He's just an old man." The man turned to Mr Size 12 with a weary disappointment. For a moment, the two seemed to square off, an untold story between them, but Mr Size 12 without displaying a measure of backing down, withdrew nonetheless. It was as if his spirit, if not his bearing, deserted him. "Come on, man, he isn't even worth the hassle. Things that slow out here?"

"Come on. Fun's fun, but we still on the clock," Dollar said.

The Timberland-booted man cocked his hand like a gun, fired off a shot at Merle, then trailed Dollar.

"You all right? You know them?" The man's gaze followed them, disappointment rife in his eyes as he helped Merle to his feet.

"All jackals and hyenas… without a lion in sight." Merle brushed the leaves and loose dirt from him, though his many-stained jacket reeked of grime.

"Uh huh."

"Who is my would-be savior?"

"My name's King. King James White."

"Merle."

"Merle what?" King asked.

"At your service, oh King." Merle bowed before King's steady gaze.

"Great."

"Damn, son. You broke him off a piece for real." Dollar laughed as they made their way back to the spot. Brief distraction aside, they were still on the grind, though he always had his eye out for new talent. "You ready to step up to this here game?"

"I'm here to put in work. I'm tired of playing out here." Prez knew what he was going to hear from Big Momma. Not even in her house and already he'd found the streets. But he'd been watching Dollar from way back, a few years at least. Steady slinging, always in fine clothes and just enough bling to set it off. It was either the game or continue to attend Northwest High School. Though the ladies were fine up in there, ladies could be had just as easily out here. No point in wasting everyone's time killing time and taking up space in school when he needed to be out here doing dirt.

"Anxious to make a name for yourself."

"Something like that."

"I feel you. Look here, you hang with us for a minute. Think of yourself as an apprentice or some shit. See how we do. We got our eyes on you and we'll see how you handle yourself."

"Yeah?"

They bumped fists. A new day, same as it ever was.

Ultimately stemming from the nearby Eagle Creek reservoir, creeks bordered the Breton Court condos along the south and east. Not too long ago, several kids had followed the tributaries back to the reservoir and drowned. The tragedy was still repeated at supper time to children who dawdled too long after the street lights went on. The main drive of Breton Court was laid out like a horseshoe with elongated tips. As one went down either side, individual courts of townhouses faced one another. King lived at the base of the horseshoe. A few townhouses were still owned and rented out by people who simply refused to sell to the three owners even if they didn't live there.

King stayed in one of those. His condo overlooked the southern bend of the creek, now overgrown with weeds and filled with discarded shopping carts from the nearly vacant strip mall on the other side of it. It was better than living out of a car which he had done for months. Clumped between his court of condos and the next were trash dumpsters. A black raincoat and a pair of jutting legs dangled from one. Merle fell from his perch, a tangle of legs and arms in an awkward sprawl, then drew the collar of his black trench coat up about his neck, though there was no chill to the air. The aluminum foil helmet was a nice touch.

"What's the good word, Merle?"

The old bullshit fool gave a clenched-fist salute, though he didn't pause from his rummaging activities. Merle had a familiar spirit. Maybe he was one of those faces, those strangers you bumped into on a bus or train and instantly poured yourself out to. Maybe he was one of those neighborhood peripheral figures who seemed to travel in the same circles he did, even if the two had never officially met. Thinking back on those times, King felt a certain comfort about the man, as if the shambling bearded tramp were a filthy protective shadow. If he were the Merle he had heard people whisper and laugh about over the years, by most accounts, he appeared better, younger, now than he did back in the day. Maybe he cleaned up from drugs and such and was now merely homeless. His breath smelled of pork rinds and Funyuns.

"Signs, signs, everywhere are signs."

"I heard that." King plopped down on the curb, withdrew a burrito from his bag, and offered it to Merle. "Somehow I'm not really surprised to see you here. You seem to get around."

"That's me. The bad penny." Merle pinched off bits of bread and scattered them about him. He shooed away the birds, making way for a squirrel to come collect as he will. Without a warning, Merle suddenly bowled over, gripping his head as if trying to keep it from exploding. His face flushed an agonized shade of red, his mouth locked in a silent scream. Collapsing on the ground, he waved King off from helping him. When he next spoke, his voice had the weak rasp of a sick kitten.

"You alright, man?"

"I'm fine. I suffer from spells."

"You ought to see a doctor. Get that checked out."

"I'm past the concerns of a doctor. What say you, good King? Caught twixt the knights of Dred and Night?"

"Nah, they just jawing. They needed to show their teeth some."

"The Night's too long. Night's daddy was a crackhead. Got hit in the head with a shovel."

"Do what?"

"He was sitting on a curb, people acting stupid. Crackhead just bopped him straight in the side of the old noggin." Merle tapped the side of his head, dislodging his aluminum cap. He sprayed food with each sloppy bite, losing almost as much as he ate while he spoke.

"My daddy was crazy, so I hear," King said. He fought to be legally emancipated from his mother years ago. She had two little ones at home and he was old enough to live on his own so that she could concentrate on providing for the young ones. According to his grandma, she was never quite the same after his father's death. Whenever she spoke of him, it was with a mix of awe and sorrow, as if either she had been betrayed or her idea of him had been. At any rate, he had to get his social security benefits transferred into his name but to her address so that she could spend it. They'd make it without him. As would Nakia. More family he'd abandoned.

"An OG OD'd on the streets. Brought down in a fight over a woman. He had to have her, though."

"My pops wasn't no drug addict."

"Never said he was. Heavy is the head… and all that." Merle wiped his hands in the grass. "Prisons and graveyards are full of fools who wore the crown."

"Truth and all, I didn't know my father at all to speak of. I just sort of fill in the blanks here and there, the way I'd want them." King froze, not understanding why he gave up that bit of personal information at all much less to a stranger. A white stranger at that. Like he thought, maybe Merle had one of those faces. Before he could speak again, the homeless man spoke.

"Can I tell you something?" Merle leaned in, still chewing on too big a bite of his burrito.

"Sure."

"Last night, I dreamt of the dragon."

"You sound like that's supposed to mean something." King had an air of being trapped in himself, of not knowing who he was, that came off as rather petulant. "You act like you ain't right in the head and yet you seem so…"

"Content. I am what I am. I know who I am. I accept who I am."

King heard a bit too much bite in his tone. "What does that mean?"

"You war with yourself. You're the 'should've' man. You–"

"Should've finished high school. Should've gotten involved in something larger than myself. Should've let myself fall in love," King said.

"Instead you hide, afraid of betrayal. A spectator in your own life."

"Until lately. I don't know how to explain it."

"You felt the call."

"The call?"

"To action." Merle thrust the remaining bread into the air, a makeshift sword jabbing at clouds. He turned the jousting loaf toward King and engaged him in a one-sided duel, waving the bread about in strokes and feints. "Feelings overtook you. Who you really are wants to take over."

"And who am I?" King kept turning to face the loaf-wielding man. As much as instinct might have told him to, he couldn't write Merle off as either a bum or a lunatic. He had too much gravitas, too much presence, to be easily dismissed.

"That is the question. I can't answer it for you. Some people are built to lead, some to follow. Which are you, lion or lamb?"

King inspected the stretch of Breton Court like there were parts within the sphere of his influence and the hinterlands, those areas on the outskirts, out of his influence. Prez. Damn. What happened to that brother? Everyone seemed infected with the same sickness, on edge. King saw the fear, the frustration, the cauldron of terror and rage with life reduced to desperation and survival. So many stood by and did nothing; sick of gangs and violence, yet suffering in silence.

"You get off on knowing the rule book without having to share anything."

"Knowledge," Merle tapped his aluminum foil helmet with the loaf, then returned to feeding the birds and squirrels, "is power."

"Power is power, too."

"Ah, the first lesson in ruling. That wasn't so hard, now was it?"

"What wasn't?"

"Making a decision. Making the hard choices is a gift."

"What do…" King didn't know why he sought Merle's advice, or approval, nor could he explain the strange sense of kinship between them. "What's my next step?"

"Take hold of your destiny."

"How do I do that?"

"Either you seek it out or…" Merle stood up as if dismissed. "Here come your boys. Anyway, I have places to be and fey to annoy."

"What?"

"You're the right guy, my guy. If you were another guy, you'd be the wrong guy."

Evenings were made to sit out and King relished the few quiet moments. He had grown up in the area though now he spent some time away, maybe to come into his own. His boys were still his boys. So they drank some, listened to the sounds of kids playing, the occasional car horns, and dogs barking from the fenced back patios of the rowhouses.

"Ain't nothing changed," King said.

"Look around you. Why would it change?" A hard-faced man, with a scar on the back of his neck, Wayne had the build of a defensive linesman, stocky and chiseled, with the swinging step of someone who knew how to use their size should the necessity warrant. Thus also explaining why the plastic chair wobbled every time he shifted his weight. A mane of long dreadlocks furled down to his shoulders. Wayne was King's case manager down at Outreach Inc., a ministry that worked with homeless and at-risk youth. He'd helped King with his emancipation and got his benefits straightened out. Even though Wayne was four years older, the span of attaining his college degree, he hung out with King now out of true friendship as much as anything else. King had a spark about him that drew folks to him.

"You know what your problem is?" King asked.

"What's that?"

"You pessimistic. Now me, I'm a glass half full of Kool Aid sort of man."

"Just something in the air." Wayne carried his sur-vival instinct, too. The eyes in the back of his head that let him know when something was up. King re-spected and depended on it.

"I know. I feel it, too. A vibe. Like a whole lot of anger bubbling out there waiting for an excuse to blow up."

"Yeah, something like that," Wayne said.

"Want another one?"

"Nah, I'm good with this one. Don't need to be set-ting a bad example for you young 'uns."

"Sure."

"What about you?" King raised a beer to Lott.

Lott bobbed his head to beats and rhymes only he heard, keeping his own counsel. He was a week past getting his hair tightened up and his large brown eyes drifted with the activity of the court. His FedEx uniform – a thick sweatshirt over blue slacks, his name badge, "Lott Carey" with a picture featuring his grill-revealing smile, wrapped around his arm – girded him like a suit of armor. Lott put on his pimp-roll strut for all the eyes to see as he moved toward an open seat, a puffed-up exaggerated gait with a cool blank stare, his face locked into a grimace of put-on hostility purposefully designed to make old ladies clutch their purses and white suburbanites cross the street if they were in his path. A row of faux gold caps grilled his teeth. He was a wrong time/wrong place sort, always getting caught up in situations he didn't start but felt compelled to finish, with jail being the typical finish line. These days he

kept his dreams simple: dreaming of holding a job
and breathing free air, not like some of the other
talkers on the block.

"You know I don't drink."

"It's still polite to ask."

"And where would we be without politeness?"

King nodded then popped open the beer. There
were too few evenings with anything approaching
peace, so he opted to enjoy the time he had.

It was a glass half full of Kool Aid evening.

A nest of fine braids lined Omarosa's head, not a hair
out of place as if she had just stopped from the
beauty salon. Hers was a cultivated beauty, but
where would her kind be without beauty? With skin
like heavily creamed coffee, almond eyes that missed
nothing, and the high cheekbones with accompanying aquiline nose of a European aristocrat, her
pointed ears were the only tell of her mixed fey her-
itage. The pair of handcuffs clicked in her hand as
she spun one spindle through the rest of the cuff.

Invisible to all, she strolled along the court side-
walks. Only three kinds of people generally
remained invisible: fiends, homeless, and pros. Such
a station in life supplied invisibility because as fixtures in the neighborhood, most folks averted their
eyes from them either in sympathizing shame or due
to the desire to not be approached by them. Folks
tended to assume she was a pro, though few dared
ask her for sex. She allowed them to carry on in their
assumptions, for her kind also valued the power of

illusion. After all, few suspected the need to be on guard against the sawed-off 12-gauge that rarely left her side.

"The game begins again." She didn't turn her head to address him nor otherwise betray any surprise at his presence. Few managed to sneak up on her, with her battle-hardened senses keen as the edge of the blade strapped to her thigh. However, Merle had a way of appearing when least expected. "All the players are almost in place."

"Indeed," he said. "They've woken the dragons."

## CHAPTER TWO

Juneteenth Walker wanted more. Trapped in the corner of the fevered nightmare of his life, he suffered from the epiphany of a fuck-up's resignation: he was never going to rise higher. Baylon kept him on the crew out of what passed for goodwill, but Dred was the main man and if Dred got word of his latest fuck-up, he was done.

The slow growth of keloided needle tracks trailed along his arm. Too many black moles dotted his skin. The spike rested in his vein though he'd already pushed the plunger. His head lolled back and the heroin rush took him to dark places. Images of a flesh-stripped baby sucking at the damp skin of the elongated tits of an emaciated old woman with too much paunch and lank hair danced in his mind's eye. The resounding closeness of the dark thundered in his ear.

The picture of this scene froze like a bootleg DVD in need of cleaning before resolving into his present or at least not-too-distant past. Half-formed shadows entwined in the night. The dirty mattress stank of liquor and blood, the close squalor of rusted pipes and cracked plaster walls around him. A woman with a large nose and a numb smile gazed up at him in the approximation of a come-hither stare that at one time might have been sexy. Her body remembered her poise and flirting coyness despite her now-sagging skin and dusty complexion. Her toothless mouth wrapped around his engorged member, still mewling from his lap for a taster package. A transaction of flesh for a free dose. As if electric wires stabbed into his thigh, he convulsed, her filthy fingernails digging into him as she bared her gaping mouth full of his seed. Far from pleasing, the entire concerto of writhing flesh played out with the pleasure of him crawling along a hill of razor blades. Anything to divert his attention. To numb him.

Junie tripped over a body in the debris-littered corridor. A series of doorless rooms lined the hallway. Alone with the ritual madness and his thoughts, a long drag from the cigarette helped him to ride down his high. It was almost time to get back on the clock and start grinding, if he still had a place on the crew. In a straight-up dope fiend move, after he screwed up the count, he blamed it on being jacked by a notorious street thief. He knew he had better keep hiding the truth because if Baylon knew, goodwill notwithstanding, they'd beat his ass before putting him out of his misery.

Back in his spot, he set down the controller for his PlayStation and spat out the last of his sunflower seeds when Parker Griffin hit him up on his cell for them to do a run. For appearance's sake, he wanted to appear busy or, if nothing else, at least not at the immediate beck and call of Baylon as, after all, he was no man's errand boy. He told Parker to be at 30th and MLK and he'd pick him up in a half-hour. Nearly an hour later, practically punctual in his world, he saw the skinny man with a boy's face, with his eager eyes and teeth too large for his mouth. It was his hair, a Mohawk with the hair on either side of it braided into corn rows. Five-O would always be picking him up if he worked a corner.

"'Sup, Junie," Parker said.

Junie hated the nickname, but it wasn't as if he were in love with his given name, either. "'Sup, big man. You still got that hair."

"What took you so long?" Parker changed topics. The last thing he wanted was to become one of those nondescript fools. He envisioned himself like Samson in the Bible; his strength, his image, was in his hair and he'd be damned if he'd cut it for a woman, much less a dude.

"You interrupt a man while he's in mid-stroke, you should expect him to take a minute to get his rhythm back."

"I heard that." Parker reached out to give him a pound.

The easy acceptance of the lie pleased Junie. It meant that his rep was set. Truth be told, he already had five kids by five different baby mommas, none of whom he bothered to know. But he had rather informally taken Parker under his wing and enjoyed the way Parker clung to his words. Junie was over-protective of him to the point of being too quick to take knucklehead bullshit to the next level.

For his part, Parker, though young, was anxious to prove himself both to Junie and to Baylon. It was just like Parker to admire a no-heart pretty boy with too much flash and too much to prove like Junie. He rolled with Parker's older brother – "Griff," as the right of the firstborn included the claim to his own name – and Parker worshiped both of them. It had been three years since Griff was killed.

"Where we heading?" Junie asked.

"Over to Breton Street. Night's boys playing our corners a little too close."

Junie held his fingers up like a gun and squeezed off a few rounds.

"Nah, nothing like that," Parker said. "Yet. He said we should just make our presence felt."

"A'ight."

Jonathan Jennings Public School 109 – named for an early governor of Indiana – was a no-tolerance zone for the drug trade, not that the fact stemmed things beyond creating a neutral zone of sorts between the two major crews, Dred and Night. Dred's lieutenant, Baylon, had been tasked by Dred with establishing a west side beachhead which started with control of the Breton Court condominiums. Night's crew, helmed by Green, Baylon's equivalent in Night's organization, held down the Breton Court corner along with three of his boys and staked a claim to much of the west side of Indianapolis. Boys was the right word: all of the street games were run by would-be men who had "teen" in their age. Except for Green. Green was eternal. It was rare for a higher-up such as Green to be seen on street level, though if anyone would, it would be him. There was no getting in Green's head, he simply was who he was.

Junie pulled his car into the parking lot of PS 109 and adjusted the rearview mirror so that he could get a full view of the situation. He had barely gotten Green's crew into sight when Green's baleful stare locked onto him. It was almost as if Green's grim countenance, his haunting eyes in particular, filled the mirror. Junie snatched his hand back as if burned.

"Everything all right?" Parker asked.

"Yeah. I just wanted to get up before we do what we do." Junie reached under his seat and pulled free a rolled sandwich bag thick with chronic. Two pre-rolled blunts sat on top. It was well known that Junie always held a bag filled with weed at almost all times. By his account, he simply liked to carry enough to have a party any time. He was a sharing kind of guy. Truth be told, he lacked the patience and dexterity to roll a simple blunt and often had folks roll him a couple as thanks for his generosity. Junie sparked one up then and without hesitation, passed it to Parker. "Pass me my business and pop that glove box for me."

The act itself, being treated as an equal by Junie, got Parker up as much as the weed itself, but he retained his sense of cool. He handed him back the blunt and reached across to the glove box. It fell as open as Parker's jaw at the sight of the Taurus 85. "That live?"

"They all live, remember that. You better tuck that away if you're gonna step with me."

"Baylon said no beefing, just be a presence."

"Then we'll be a strapped presence. I'm like a Boy Scout up in here. Always prepared. If shit jumps off, I want to be able to hold more than my dick, you feel me?"

Cognizant of ever-present eyes, Parker kept the gun below the window line and slipped it into the large pocket of his oversized jeans. The pair exited the car escorted by a cloud of smoke. Parker's stride changed immediately. More than just the newfound weight in his pocket altered his gait. No, his entire bearing was different, like he'd gone from boy to man for real. He imagined himself as taller, harder, like one of those dieseled brothers in lock-up. His eyes narrowed as if daring any passing motherfucker to fuck with him. Yeah, the gun juiced him like he'd been popping Viagra all evening, and when he glanced over at Junie, he realized he'd found the secret to Junie's reckless, Chief Swinging Dick stride.

Decorative red posts lined the curb in front of the entrance to the Breton Court rowhouses, now seats for Green's men. Green stood, a proud tree shading his men under the umbrella of his presence.

A Mexican family had purchased the gas station/convenience store as well as the restaurant beside it. The convenience store doubled as a fast food kiosk and, knowing their demographic, served Hispanic and Jamaican dishes. Marbles, two stores down in the mini-strip of shops, catered to folks' soul food needs. Strolling down the sidewalk fresh from a run to the convenience store for some burritos and Jamaican patties, King's steps hitched as he came upon the panorama. His street-smart eyes analyzed and broke down the scene.

The name of the older of the two who crossed the street from the school's park eluded him. They walked toward the Breton Court condos from the east side keeping pace with King's approach from the west. No one needed reminding who was at the center. Green had been around as long as anyone could remember and stayed in because he had three things working in his favor: he was smart, he wasn't greedy, and he wasn't ambitious. Green always seemed to be someone's lieutenant, the shadow advisor/enforcer to whoever wore the crown. Yet he had little interest in the throne itself. Despite the warmth of late summer, Green kept a regal demeanor. A chinchilla fur coat rested atop his suit, gold like leaves in fall, which matched his pair of Robert Waynes. The duo passed Green's crew without comment, slow-stepping in front of them, chests puffed out in a preening dare to action. Like a fine conductor, Green's sole reaction was to hold out the palm of his hand; his well-trained orchestra didn't so much as flinch.

Suddenly, the name of the older one came to King: *Juneteenth Walker.* They'd come up together, though Junie ended up doing a nickel in juvey rather than complete high school. Whether he realized it or not, Junie had the fallen crest of a man who'd been broken by time lost, reminding King of the man who was too old to be in the club: he had the right dress, talked the right talk, but had the air of being rather... pathetic. He stopped directly in King's path.

"You on my corner," Junie said to King, but for Green's benefit. King remained close-mouthed as if too good to speak to them. "I'm talking to you, motherfucker."

"Excuse me?" King neither broke his mild stare nor stepped away.

"You heard me, motherfucker. Do you know who I am?"

"I know who you are, Junie."

Junie's heart swelled despite the use of the nickname, part with pride as he believed his name had began ringing out on the streets and part jacked up on adrenaline and weed. He spared a glance at Parker to see if he'd heard the same thing. Parker's hand itched, wanting an excuse to pull his newfound manhood. King displayed no emotion other than his eyes saying that he could care less what they thought of him. He was mindful of the territory boundaries. Gray zones were the most dangerous. To the west, Dred. To the east, Night.

"I heard there was a misunderstanding over real

estate over here," Parker said in a poor man's stage-whisper.

"You heard wrong," Junie said. "We expanded into unclaimed territory. Think of it as a market correction."

"Excuse me." King pushed the cold, coiling temper of his down to a deep place. Well, a deeper place. Unlike them, he had real responsibilities and folks who depended on him and didn't have the time or patience for machismo posturing so he moved to step around them. Green glared with baleful and empty orbs.

"Punk-ass bitch," Parker said to King's passing side. "That's what I thought."

"We'll finish this later," Junie echoed.

"I highly doubt it," King said.

Life came down to crossroad moments. Staring at Junie, waiting, eyes heavy with contempt, King had no interest in this little street performance, no matter whose benefit it was for; however, he wasn't going to be pushed around in his home court. He neither sought the street nor any of the foolish sense of self it engendered. But he could and would handle his business.

"What'd you say?" Junie asked.

"If I have something to discuss," the cold thing slithered up King's gut, through his throat, and found a home in his mouth before he could control it again, "I doubt I'll take it up with some scrub nigga. Your boy here talks too much shit. Ain't got no call to be talking to me like that, but now you done had your say, you want to be a man, you free to step to me any time." His back stiff with resolve, King waited for Junie to make the next move though he hoped for a quiet resolution. He just wanted to put his head up for the evening. The younger one had the natural youthful swagger brought by easy access to guns and leading to reckless courage, but Junie was a punk and would always be a punk.

"You going to be seeing me later on." Though his voice was unconvincing, Junie brushed his hand against his shirt and revealed the outline of his piece.

"We got a problem?" Green asked as if bored with the entire affair. His voice grumbled like branches snapping in a storm.

Junie stepped forward, Parker stayed back and to his left. Green's men withdrew a few paces, backing up Green. Junie thought about stepping to Green, but a voice in his soul cried out knowing better. Junie waited a moment too long. Fear lit his eyes as he searched for the right mix of bravado and wit. "Nah. I think we understand each other."

The French described the feeling he would experience for the next few days as l'esprit d'escalier: all the shit you thought of to say on your way down the stairs after your butt had been clowned in front of your boy. Junie couldn't meet Parker's eyes.

"Too many eyes on us now anyway." Parker revealed the gun butt above his waistband. "You didn't see nothing."

"You don't want me to see shit, don't do shit where I can see it," King said, the cold thing slowly wrestled under control before it pushed its luck in the calming situation.

"Come on, man. I think our message has been sent." Junie hoped sheer attitude would be enough to stanch the wound of bleeding pride.

Parker turned on his heel, glanced back and then spat at his feet. He'd have pulled his piece and dusted that fool in front of Green to show him they were men to be taken seriously, but he backed his man's play. They might think they punked him, but they'd soon know what it meant to cross Baylon's men.

The chorus of barks from the Rottweilers stirred with his passing, Baylon walked his prize bitch, an American Pit Bull Terrier. She never barked, the "surgery" saw to that. From a distance, she was a beautiful dog, but upon closer inspection, she was a stalking hematoma of a brute. A network of still-healing scars latticed her head and legs, with recently cleaned-out puncture wounds, she was a picture of barely suppressed rage spoiling for an excuse to explode.

From his back patio, it was only a matter of getting to the end of the row of apartments – shielded from the prying eyes of the street by a row of perpendicular facing apartments – to confront the figure waiting for him. His lawyer wanted to look down his long nose at Baylon, but couldn't. In fact, he could barely meet his eye. Baylon studied him with his harsh squint, waiting for the payoff. It was barely perceptible, but the slight movement of his small Adam's apple came: the swallow of fear. He knew he had him.

"Things are looking good, Baylon," he said, with his high-pitched, tense voice.

"That a fact." Baylon approached with his flexing gait. Not quite the full pimping stroll, but enough to convey the fluid movement of his prison-built bulk. "Hearing's coming up."

"It was only a juvey charge."

"I'm not trying to see the inside of any jail."

"I wouldn't worry about it. The DA's entire case hinged on one witness."

"My nosey-ass neighbor."

"Exactly. Word around the court steps says that your neighbor's up and vanished on them."

"Word?" Baylon asked, nonplussed, eyes half-closed in on-setting ennui.

"Yeah, I figure that they'll be dropping formal charges shortly." The lawyer skittishly glanced about. "You got anything for me by way of payment?"

"Yeah, I got you." Baylon reached his hand out to shake. The lawyer took his hand, palming his future fix, then backed away quickly from the bared teeth of the dog. Baylon smirked. "Do you know how you turn a perfectly tame pet into a ruthless fighter?"

"Not really."

"You chain it up, beat it, starve it, tease it, then beat it some more. That's the way life is. The sooner it knows it, the sooner it's ready to handle it. Then it's ready for the fight every time out."

"Um, OK, then I guess I'll see you at the next date." His lawyer swallowed again.

"Whatever, man." Baylon turned on his heel in a casual dismissal of the man. He had some fools to sit down with. A row of Rottweilers' snouts protruded from under his patio. They seemed every bit the innocent dogs seeking a petting hand. He'd seen those same snouts rip apart cats thrown their way. He walked past them, short, heavy chains attached to thick collars held them at bay. He usually kept them hungry, lean for the fight, but he spoiled them the other day. Other neighbors may have seen the feeding; hell, he wanted them to see. Even if no one did, he'd spread the rumors himself, building his rep, instilling fear, and quieting any other would-be heroes or nosey-ass neighbors.

"That's a good bitch," he said to her.

But she said nothing.

The houses were piled on one another, barely a few feet between them, with their fenced-in small yards. Every now and then, one of the houses had a boy sitting absently, bouncing a basketball between his legs. Two cars couldn't pass one another on the cramped streets if anyone was parked on either side. Junie kept his head low, his eyes darting from side to side, studying the mess of kids hanging out on corners. The low bass from a passing car roused his attention, so he scuttled down the sidewalk then crossed the street abruptly. If he were worried about being followed, he needn't have been. Everyone knew where he was heading. Junie knocked on the door of the two-storey home.

"It's me."

Parker opened the door. Excruciating silences and averted eyes shadowed their interactions – Junie hadn't spoken to him since the incident with King James White.

Baylon stood down the hall in the living room and glared at them with drooping, yet condescending eyes. Abandoned by family – they gave up on him long ago – his people had been scattered by the game. His friends were either dead or in jail. His life was transitory, with him moving often. Cash up front, no name on anything; as far as the system was concerned, he swam underground. Junie reached out for a hand clasp, but Baylon glanced down at the expectant hand as if it were leprous, then found a seat in the living room. All of the furniture had been pushed back against the walls for maximum room to navigate. Junie and Parker turned at the clack-clack-clack of paws on hardwood floors. Baylon's dog trotted past the open doorway. Junie couldn't help but think of a shark swimming in its tank.

"What's the matter? You afraid of a little bitch?" Baylon asked.

"Dogs make me nervous is all," Parker said.

"Look here, Sideshow Bob." Baylon focused on Parker's Mohawk, so ragged it looked like a small village of crows nested in it. He snapped once and then pointed to the ground next to him. The dog came and laid down where he aimed his fingers. "You just have to know how to handle bitches."

"What's her name?"

"What the fuck I'm going to name a bitch for?" Baylon demanded. "Now, someone mind telling me what the fuck is going on?"

"I'm a-tell it to you straight." Junie tapped his fist into his open palm. The loudest one in the room, by Baylon's reckoning, was usually the weakest one. Junie was too quick to step to a man and jump into foolishness, which usually led to a bigger mess and a greater headache. He was out of his depth and long overdue to be demoted. "Me and Parker went down to represent, just like the man said to."

Parker nodded. Young and inexperienced, but he had potential. He was smart, anyone could see it in his eyes. If he put that mind of his in some books, he could be an engineer or a scientist of some sort. Not into a lot of the flashy bling nonsense, not overly ambitious, he took the long view on situations. Rarely speaking unless he had something to say, he also had a streak of crazy to him. It danced in his eyes, ready to step up, when needed, as needed.

"So you went down to the school to scope out what's what…"

"And it was just like you thought. Night's boys be out there grinding. Green his self out there overseeing."

"Green? No shit?" No charge ever stuck on Night because Green took them when the police thought they had a case to make. Green's was the same old story: soldiers fell on their swords and the king survived. After his bit, and because he stood tall, Night promoted him to his number two man. *Promote* wasn't the right word. If the rumors were true, Baylon didn't understand Green at all. Green could step out on his own any time, but he preferred to defer to someone else when he could. It was like he was beyond ambition and was in the game strictly for the love.

"True, true. Now, we's about to step to them when your boy comes up the street," Junie continued.

"Who?"

"King."

At the mention of the name, Baylon's face tightened. A more perceptive eye might have noticed the slight hitch to his breath as if suddenly troubled by an old, dull pain he thought he'd learned to live with. "Go on."

"I'm not saying King stepped into it, but he got caught up in some back and forth."

"Even though you were there to deal with Night's boys." Baylon knew Junie thought all of his fast talking would save him. He wanted to tell Junie to save the bullshit, but he opted to indulge the little performance.

"I done said Green was there."

"So you...?" Baylon's voice trailed.

"Sent a message to them through King."

"And this... message... how do you think it was received?"

"I would have to say... mixed," Junie said.

"A mixed message?" Baylon lowered his head and rubbed his eyes as if that would stop the migraine that threatened to crush his skull in a vise. Speaking

of skulls, he wanted to crack Junie's open if only to
see what passed for brains in him.

"I'm just saying, it wasn't as clear as I would have
liked."

"Are you trying to be cute with me, motherfucker,
or just trying to piss me off?" Baylon got up and
paced. Junie opened his mouth, but Baylon's curt
gaze shut him up. "So what I'm thinking is that since
our message may have gotten muddled in the delivery, we need to send a stronger message."

"Parker and I are already on it."

"You two sit still. I'm gonna need to think on this
for a minute, see what's what with Dred, and get
back with you."

"Maybe if I was to explain it to Dred…"

"You don't get to speak to the man." Baylon knew
his control on the men was constantly being tested.
Despite their failings, they had the nerve to question
whether he could still run things. The shit stopped
with him and it was only a matter of time before
someone took him for weak and made their move. Or
Dred would. So Baylon damn sure couldn't leave his
fate in the less-than-capable hands of the Junies and
Parkers of the world. Experience beat youth every
time, and right now, their crew was way too youthful.

"I think what Junie's getting at is that we want a
chance to handle this ourselves," Parker spoke up.
"Without bothering Dred. Show him, and you, that
we can handle our own end. Like men do."

"Like men do, huh? Is that it now?" Baylon itched
for a drink, nothing alcoholic or anything like that.

Just something to steady him. He imagined something civilizing, like a hot cup of tea. Something a gentleman would drink. He stood, his prize bitch cocking her head in trailing attention, anticipating his command. "Everyone had their say? Now let me tell you *men* something. Business is good. We have a quality product and a quality pipeline. We will always have competitors, but we don't need to escalate things to knucklehead level without cause. The right statement, the proper show of force should be… elegant. You two aren't suited for elegant, but that's all right though. You don't send a bull into a grocery store for eggs. But I tell you what, I'm gonna let you prove me wrong. Within reason, step up and move up. If not, I'll bring in someone, or someones, who can."

Though quite likeable and charming most days, Baylon had grown quite disgusted at Junie. At the quality of soldiers in general, these days. If he passed for their muscle, that meant their shit truly was weak and Baylon hoped Dred hadn't concluded the same thing.

"Where is she?" Dred asked. This world could not contain him, yet it managed to hide her. The room was thick with smoke as he needed to get his head up, to reach the next plateau for his thoughts. Stoking the dragon, like a distant furnace, he needed to sow terror, to bury teeth of hate to raise an army. For now, he was at war and his immediate enemy had revealed himself, but Dred knew she also remained a loose end.

The room had grown hot with closed-in heat. Thick tufts of smoke issued from his mouth. His mahogany skin glistened with perspiration – the cloying scent of chronic barely covering his mild BO – from the exertion of summoning. His vacant eyes viewed a dream, bending and reshaping it to suit his needs. That was the true magic, sculpting dreams and calling them forth. Which was why he loathed interruptions, preferring the clarity of his own thoughts.

"You got a minute?" Baylon hated dealing with him when he was like this and hated entering the room even more.

"I know she's out there."

"Who?"

"My moms. I know she's out there and she has one lesson left to teach me."

"What's that?"

"That's between a boy and his moms," Dred croaked, his voice cracked as it grew distant. "I'm conjuring."

"I can see that."

Dred rolled into view. The sight of the once so vital man strapped to a wheelchair never failed to alarm Baylon. He bent over for the forearm-to-chest hug. Dred's wheelchair notwithstanding, the ring must be respected and kissed. The chamber, bereft of any furniture, seemed more cavern than room; steep shadows gave the illusion of it being deeper than it was. Bay windows faced the moon, yet the light didn't seem to much penetrate beyond being a dim glow. An ethereal swirl of the smoke coalesced above the mounds of uncut heroin mixing with their product.

"Word has it Junie and Parker have made a royal mess of things," Dred said.

"Not to hear them tell it, but yeah. Worse, Dollar and 'em will have to come back on them. On us."

"Worse still, we're going to be seen as incompetent. Weak." Despite being confined to the chair, Dred had a better read of the streets than those who traipsed in them. His arithmetic of the situation arrived at the same unfortunate conclusion Baylon had.

"We just don't have the soldiers. We've got to have more bodies. Parker has potential, but not if he keeps up with Junie. All he's learning is to be bold to the point of crazy. Sees everything as a test to make sure he's ready to go to the next level."

"First things first. It's time for a leadership shake-up."

"What do you mean?" Baylon felt the tremor in his voice even if his ear couldn't pick it up. Maybe Junie wasn't the only one overdue for a demotion. Suddenly the same anxiety of being called to the principal's office overswept him.

Dred waited a few extra heartbeats to let Baylon stew in his discomfort.

"Junie and Parker have fucked up one time too many. More than even they realize." Junie, like no other, made Dred miss the use of his legs. He wanted to rise up and kick the living shit out of him.

"How so?"

"Assuming Green leaves Dollar to handle things, that's one thing; but he may want to get involved personally on top of things. That's two fronts if Night truly wants to push back. Then our own fools brought King into the mix, which drew the attention of the mage. He may not be what he once was, but I wanted more time before that happened."

"What does King have to do with it?" At the mention of the name, a pain shot along the base of Dred's back, a lightning bolt which faded to nothing as the pain rippled to below his waist, a black hole of sensation. Dred remembered when it happened and thinking "My God, did everything just change for the rest of my life?" He rolled his chair backward and inhaled. "I'm calling in the Durham Brothers. They'll be reporting to you. They'll be our new hitters. Put Junie and Parker on some corner work, cool them out for a while. That solve your problems?"

"The trolls? That's all you had to say."

"Don't let them hear you call them that."

# CHAPTER THREE

Wayne got the phone call at 7:30 in the morning. A wave of unruly locks fell onto his face as he reached for the phone. His mattress groaned in protest as he rolled over. Typically, he didn't take calls that early because clients had to respect the boundaries of his life. As much as he might have cared about them, he wasn't at their beck and call nor was he their taxicab, nor their nursemaid, nor their errand boy. Their lives were steeped in (mostly self-created) drama and he had to carve out rest from it or be forever caught up in it. Kay sniffed at the back door, pawing quietly to be let out. Wayne poured food into his bowl and refilled the water bowl. He opened the back door and stared at his phone. "One missed call. Parker." He always checked the messages left on his voicemail. The frantic-edged voice of Parker Griffin trembled through the poor connection of the cell phone.

"Hey man. You got to ring me back. Someone dropped a body on my block."

Wayne sighed. He wouldn't have time to run into the offices at Outreach Inc. and his mouth watered for the taste of too-strong coffee sweetened with honey if he was lucky (donations were down and they hadn't been able to buy sugar in a while). Two phone calls later, and he was on his way to the address Parker gave him. The other call had been to the office to let them know it was going to be one of those days.

The battle for Parker's soul had been waged in earnest for the last year. Parker was one of the many boys on the cusp of manhood who could go either way. Extremely intelligent, Parker's laconic drift through his daily routine belied his eyes which little escaped and keen mind which analyzed street scenarios with the acumen of a political strategist. Wayne only wished that Parker could imagine himself as anything but destined for street soldiering. Wayne would get him into a GED program; Parker would nearly finish, then drop out. He'd get him into job training; he'd nearly finish, then drop out. He'd get him a job, he'd nearly get through probation and then quit. Yet there was something special about Parker – a desperately clung-to innocence or the measure of something salvageable or maybe he simply saw a bit of himself in the boy – that made him keep trying. All Parker needed was to sink his hooks into the straight life and not be tripped up by the lures of short cuts and the promise of easy cash.

Every war demanded an enemy and in this war the enemy came in the form of Junie Walker. As

Wayne approached, Junie smiled stupidly, high on whatever he'd managed to get a hold of that morning. The skin of his face stretched tight over his skull. Wayne took the measure of the man in one meeting. A would-be soldier not nearly as competent as he aspired to be. If Wayne could spot that Junie was losing his own battle with the needle, surely Junie's employers had to know that he was a catastrophic fuck-up waiting to happen.

Parker led Wayne down the alleyway, the path suffering from the erosion of green as grass sprouted in the many cracks of the sidewalk. Bushes – more branches than leaves, brown and long unpruned – overtook fences. A gap-toothed grin of missing slats, the remaining posts of the wood fence were either broken or spray-painted with the latest gang tags. ESG. Treize. The letters ICU within a circle. Merky-Water. Non-stop traffic ground along the road, dogs marked their trespass in harsh barks, and air-conditioning units barreled along like over-worked engines. Wayne stalked the too-familiar scene as if he were home.

"He's in there." Parker stopped short and pointed to a trash can.

"He?" Wayne asked, still studying Parker. He was troubled, though neither Parker nor Junie set off any survival alarms. However, Parker's posture bothered him. The careless shrug of his shoulder. The faux deference to Wayne. No, there was something calculated about this performance.

"The dead dude."

Wayne pulled the lid free from the bin. Arms and legs sprouted up, a potted plant of limbs. He jumped back, holding the lid as a shield. Inching forward again, as if at any moment the limbs might snare him, Wayne risked peering into the garbage can again. A naked black man was folded into the container. His head cocked at an unnatural angle, a small entry wound dotted his forehead. Bruised purple with a burned black rim, a small-caliber gun had done its work close up. Wayne couldn't help but note that his knees were ashy. Funny the things the mind chose to lock on to. A hard heart had to have walked up on this man whether he was in the life or not and ended him. Wayne searched Parker's eyes, but no longer saw any hope in them. Only a deadened hardness.

"The police are going to have some questions," Wayne said, not knowing what to do with the lid. He needed to make some phone calls, yet he didn't feel right covering the man like he was inconvenient trash. Nor leaving him exposed to all passers-by.

"You got my back though, right?" Parker asked.

"As long as you didn't have anything to do with this." Wayne continued to stare into the trashcan.

"Cool."

Junie skulked off, fading into the background of the alley, a rat scavenging for food in a dumpster then scuttling for cover when exposed. Suspicions aside, Wayne wouldn't give him up. To be known as a snitch would cost him the trust of all the kids he worked with. Every day he'd wonder if it'd be worth it if only to rid the world of a Junie or two.

Tying them up for hours, the police had plenty of questions for both Wayne and Parker. They had more questions, more for Parker especially, but were satisfied enough to let them go. Wayne had time to make the afternoon drop at Outreach Inc., a ministry for homeless and at-risk teenagers, so he swung by his house to get Kay. On the television – which he'd left on so that Kay wouldn't get lonely – the news reported that on the other side of town, six year-old Conant Walker had been shot while standing in front of his kitchen window. The day just kept getting better and better. He pushed past the crowd flanked by IMPD officers; onlookers – though not witnesses, as the interrogating uniforms found out – to the latest murder scene. The intersection of 10th and Rural marked one of the city's highest crime areas, yet he ambled about as if he wasn't a walking anomaly against the neighborhood backdrop of decay and violence. Kay tugged against the leash to get a better sniff of the area, but Wayne kept it taut. He knew better than to let the Rottweiler stray too far or to let him get past his guard. Even as he selected him from animal control, he was warned that the dog had no hope of being socialized. He'd been rescued – if *rescued* was indeed the proper term – from a dog-fighting ring. Abused and taunted for as long as he drew breath, his personality was mercurial on his best days. No, his fate was his scheduled euthanasia, for his sake and the public's. Wayne adopted him without hesitation. If Wayne didn't believe in redemption and hope, there was no point in him taking another breath.

Wayne graduated from Indiana University with a major in Computer and Information Science and a minor in Psychology and joined the staff of Outreach Inc. right out of school on the recommendation of his Bible study leader. As a case manager, he did a little bit of everything, but mostly what he did was build relationships with the teens and early twenty-somethings who were his clients. Drop night was when Outreach Inc. provided meals and activities for their clients to get them away from their situations. It was a safe night off the streets for the kids. Funny how they still thought of themselves as kids even though most were in their late teens.

The Neighborhood Fellowship church building offered free space for Outreach Inc. The burnt brick façade, once a public school with the design sensibility of a penitentiary, overlooked 10th Street onto an abandoned gas station with a gravel lot.

"All right everyone, I need twenty seconds of silence," Lady G bellowed. The room fell silent, to everyone's surprise.

Lady G stood tall and proud, a commanding dark-skinned beauty if one could see past the layers of clothes with which she wrapped herself: a T-shirt under a long sleeve thermal shirt under a grimy, faded blue hoodie, under a jacket that had seen better days. No matter the temperature, she carefully selected her wardrobe in order to hide her shape. And wore gloves with the fingertips cut off.

A cell phone rang, strains of Soulja Boy Tell'em's "Crank That", Rhianna Perkins' fave, echoed as if muffled. Rhianna clutched at her buxom chest before plunging her hand into her bra – no longer capable of supporting her engorged breasts – clearly visible through the threadbare material which stretched over her protruding belly. She fluffed her breasts after fishing out her phone, her voice a little more than a rasp. "I forgot to check my 'luggage'."

The room raised up in cries of "aw" and "nuh-uh", faux disgust at being silenced for such a phone search, protesting a tad too much to believe over Lady G and Rhianna's latest antics. Rhianna was a foot shorter than her cousin, with more curves, even when not carrying a child, though this would be her second in her fifteen years. She slept with anyone who could provide a roof, with her babies fulfilling her quest to be loved. Having a baby wasn't so hard, she often said. The fact that her mother actually raised the child and likely the second was an irony which eluded her.

"I'm so sick of that song," Lady G said.

"That's my joint," Rhianna said.

"I'm tellin' you, no one older than sixteen can get with it."

"How are you doing, ladies?" Wayne asked. Kay lay at his feet, unassuming yet on guard.

Lady G slipped on earphones, retreating into herself, her hair slicked back and shaved underneath her lengthy ponytail. Despite being seventeen and having already been shot, stabbed, and beaten in the last year, she carried herself no different than her younger cousin. She tugged at her gloves before thrusting her hands into her coat pocket, hiding her scars well.

"Fine." Rhianna turned away.

Wayne was inured to the various armor the ladies donned to protect themselves. It was like this every week, the intervening days between Drop nights allowed the bricks of their walls to fall back into place. Each conversation needed to re-establish the semblance of trust.

"How's the baby doing? We still on for me to take you to your doctor's appointment? That reminds me…" Wayne pulled out a bottle of vitamins. "Those are for you."

"Thanks," Rhianna said. It was only one word, but the thawing had already begun. Appeasing her "what have you done for me lately?" defenses was rarely difficult.

"If you come in next week, we can get you enrolled in food stamps."

"What good are food stamps when you got no place to cook?"

"We're working on that, too. Things improve with your mom any?" Wayne knew there was no point in asking about her father.

"Nope."

"You still see the baby's daddy anymore?"

Lady G balled her hand and punched her thigh repeatedly, drawing their attention. Familiar with her case file, Wayne didn't press her. Her life didn't start easy as her mother tried to cut her out of her stomach while pregnant with her. Despite being born addicted to crack, her mother took to beating her, the worst typically coming at Christmas time when the Christmas lights became an improvised whip. After a house fire, she fell into a pattern of moving from house to house, becoming a couch surfer before she hit her teen years.

"No, I don't see him anymore," Rhianna lied, more to Lady G than Wayne. She planned to meet Prez later on that day.

"Don't waste no time with petty niggas," Lady G said with a sing-song lilt as if along to the words of a new joint.

"I know, I know. 'Do better'."

"I'm just saying, no dude better touch me, much less hit me over no butt. Do better."

"I ain't gonna trip." Rhianna's whisper sounded even more hoarse.

"You stand by yourself, you stay by yourself."

"Girl," Rhianna searched for a retort but found none, "...boo." Then she upticked her chin toward another table. The trio's attentions shifted to the large boy sitting by himself.

"What you looking at?" Lady G's tone raised up in the posture of attack that was now reflex. No perceived slight or challenge went unmet.

"Nothing." Nearly tipping three bills, Percy had been watching them as his personal dinner theater. Mounds of food – half already consumed – filled his plate. Sheets of paper lay scattered next to his plate as he doodled while lost in his thoughts. He had a darker knot above his left eyebrow in the shape of a crescent moon, his downcast eyes searched for the television remote. The batteries for it rolled along the table; he'd taken them out after fumbling with the buttons in an effort to get it to work.

"Oh, I know you're looking at something," Lady G said.

"You want you some of this?" Rhianna rose to the sport. Neither of them knew how to react to someone, a male especially, who was always around without the agenda of getting into their pants. Yet Percy was always nearby, trailing them more like a faithful puppy than anything creepy. They didn't trust his faithful protectiveness either. "You are way too special."

"You got to get some game. Can't come up in here looking like Super Mario in black face."

"Look here, Negro Gump…"

*"Jesus loves me this I know, for the Bible tells me so,"* Percy began to sing to himself. He rocked back and forth, contenting himself to wait them out. There was only so much for them to make fun of: he was slow, fat, had yellow teeth, was not especially handsome, and his clothes were secondhand filthy. Though his nose was long numb to it, he knew that he stank. Wayne's eyes filled with pity every time he saw him and it made Percy sad to see him sometimes. Lady G and Miss Rhianna, they'd laugh and laugh and laugh – they had such pretty laughs – but

eventually they exhausted themselves. There were worse fates, he knew, like being ignored entirely.

"Ladies, that's enough," Wayne snapped. He made a production of him clearing his plate in disgust, letting the girls' eyes linger on him, and joining the boy at his table. Percy lowered his eyes even more, his shoulders sank and he leaned his head away from him, the same body language Kay assumed when painfully cornered but not wanting to attack. "They didn't mean anything, Percy."

"I know." The world was a simple place to Percy. There were good people (like Wayne) and there were bad people (like Prez). Better to be born simple and not realize the horrors around you. He looked up at Wayne with complete trust in his eyes. Theirs were a simple little band, assembled by loss.

"Sometimes they go a little too far."

"I know."

"I happen to know they care about you." Wayne placed his hand on his shoulder. The boy flinched at the touch then shied away as if shamed by the contact.

"I know."

"You're probably the safest guy in their world and they don't know how to act around you."

Lady G got up and walked over to the piano that sat at the other end of the room. It had been donated by a family which had no further need of it, but hadn't been serviced in a while. She pecked tunelessly at it. Percy closed his eyes as if enjoying a concert recital.

"They can't trust. When you trust someone only to have them do you dirty…" Percy trailed off as he observed Wayne studying a crumpled piece of paper. He pushed the piece of paper under another.

"Who is she?" Wayne noticed the resemblance to Rhianna but said nothing.

"Just a girl," he said. *"Little ones to Him belong. They are weak but He is strong."*

# CHAPTER FOUR

If the corner were a slave plantation, Dollar was the
overseer, the Negro chosen to ensure the other Negroes performed their assigned tasks. His tall, gangly
frame – like a basketball player with not enough bulk
– filled out his white Notre Dame jogging suit, his
bloodshot glare held the menace of a whip ready to
scourge any who weren't keeping up their end. A
poorly grown goatee outlined his jaw. A black wave-
cap pulled snug under the jogging suit's hood. His
crew were the field Negroes, steady grinding, toiling
away; from the lookouts down the way to the runner
passing product. The fiends? They were house Negroes, come to beg scraps from their master's table.
Some he knew, others were just faces. These broken-
down fools he knew because they ran with his boy,
Tavon. Loose Tooth, the player formerly known as
CashMoney, carried quite a bit of weight to him for a
fiend. Though he had to be pushing forty, his body
hadn't quite given into the wasting yet, but his
mouth hadn't seen the inside of a dentist's office

probably since the mid-'80s. Miss Jane, on the other hand, her dusty ass had to have an eye on her at all times. Always running games, she'd be the one who'd alert the master to any slaves trying to make an escape. In the end, they were all slaves to the game.

Junie studied the scene with the desperation of a man cramming for finals he forgot were that day. He and Parker had waited until Green left. Though neither would have used the word "preternatural" to describe his mien, they knew that Green cast an aura that filled their veins with water. Once sufficient time had elapsed after his departure – his presence still managing to hold court for a time – they were ready to make their move. While Dollar's crew was occupied bullshitting with a couple of fiends, the pair crept toward them. They kept their weapons pointed toward the ground in their loping gait toward their targets. Young, black, and poor, they were the most dangerous men in America, with no hope and nothing to lose.

"They coming up the block, yo," a lookout on a bike yelled as he whizzed by Dollar.

Dollar chose the entrance of Breton Court for a reason (as if he had a choice once Green told him where to set up). Two rows of townhouses ran alongside the main drag of Breton Court, plus outstretched arms from the court proper, each having another row of townhouses facing each other separated by a grassy yard. The rears of the two rows between the main drag and the outstretched arm of condos formed an alley of sorts, the fenced-in back patios providing a series of nooks where bodies could hide or deals be transacted with minimal intrusion. Rising up from one of the posts that served as his seat, Dollar dispatched his boys to the bushes that decorated the ends of the townhouses, wasted landscaping that served mostly to hide stashes and weapons. Guns were also hidden among the concrete bricks used to prop open the back patio doors. With the choreography of a ballet company, their movements swift and sure, the troops were ready for them.

Parker didn't have much more of a plan than to walk up and start busting caps. Their only other real option was a drive-by, but that lacked the personal touch, the demonstration of heart, that would cause their names to ring out. Hitching up his baggy jeans as he broke into a jog – another gun firmly in the waistband of his boxers hidden beneath his black hoodie and trailing white T-shirt – Parker aimed his Glock 17. The fiends and bystander scattered with the first shot, though Miss Jane ducked into the bushes with the presence of mind to use the distraction to raid Dollar's stashes. Parker turned his gun sideways, the way he'd often seen it done in movies, only dimly aware that he wasn't coming close to hitting anything he aimed at. A hot casing popped up and caught him under his eye, the searing pain causing him to clutch at his face and move between the cars parked in the front lot.

Junie fired, not so much aiming as swinging his arm toward any movement. Dollar's boys hid among

the bushes and ran between patio cavities. A couple
ran across the grass yard throwing careless shots in
the general direction of the parked cars.

A car window exploded over Junie's head. He
crouched down even further, both hands instinc-
tively covering his head to shield him from the
rain of glass. Guns still in hand, he accidentally set
off a round, blasting out another window. Dollar
ran into the open, figuring the safest place to be
was right in front of them. He fired at the cars,
then ducked behind the car furthest from them.
Parker threw his arm around the corner and
peeled off a few more shots. Junie's heart pounded
so hard his chest hurt. The taste of copper pennies
filled his mouth, a mix of adrenaline and fear. No
one admitted that they didn't want to die, though
truth be told, Parker no longer cared much either
way.

Dollar's boys could've penned them in at this
point, were they not too busy cowering in their
nooks or bushes, throwing shots without bothering
to see where they were landing. Parker calmly re-
loaded while crouched behind a car bumper. He
nodded to Junie and pulled out his second gun so
that he could fire off both as they backed out. He
saw that in the movies, also. No control, no discipline, it was no mystery why no one caught a
bullet. Little boys playing cowboys having a
shootout to prove their manhood to others. Un-
doubtedly the story would grow in the re-telling,
with tales of derring-do and uncanny accuracy.

No matter how many bodies anyone would claim to have dropped, the only casualties this day were innocent cars and the neighborhood tranquility.

"No one saw dick."

Lee McCarrell's hard-boned face was all jaw and forehead with mean green eyes that bore through folks. A street-wise knucklehead all about kicking down doors, he did one year of patrol, did some time as a part of a special detail out of the mayor's office, and now slummed in Gang Crimes until he could move on to do SWAT work. Lee tired of being the white cop, the presumed racist out to lock up more *brothas*. His thoughts bubbled with their familiar boil. It wasn't his fault so many brothers were up to no good. He'd be just as happy locking up Koreans or being unemployed entirely if it meant no more bad guys. You'd think these people, if not being grateful, would at least save their anger for the... animals (yeah, he thought it), their own that preyed on the rest of them. No, they protected them, hid them from the *cracka devil* out to take away their freedom. Hell, they deserved what they got.

Detective First Grade, Octavia Burke sipped from her bottled water, constantly scanning the streets with her large eyes. She wore her brownish-black hair naturally. Freckles dotted her medium complexion on either side of her wide-ish nose. She shifted her broad shoulders along the seat, getting comfortable, her thick frame part of her "100% po-lice" bearing.

"Not much here either," Octavia said, adopting a rather Zen attitude about her presumed status of police House Negro. The residents of the Phoenix Apartments had closed ranks once again. As bad as they wanted the crime stopped, they didn't want the label of snitch put on them. For every one criminal arrested, that left plenty behind that the good citizens had to live with. So when chased by the police, the greater of two evils, suspects found plenty of open doors and places to hide. Word on the street was that there was even a buried stash of community guns. The "cracker devil" and "house nigger" faced little co-operation. "Seems once the shots started, everyone scattered. No one got a good look at anyone. Can't even get a consistent number of participants."

"Actual detective work. I like this." Maybe it was a trick of the light, but Lee had been letting his hair grow out and it now threatened to become a full-blown mullet, a hairstyle choice which did not combine well with his porn-star mustache. "Deaf, blind, and dumb. No wonder criminals make a home here. What more could they ask for than such cooperative neighbors."

"Take it easy." Octavia slowly grew accustomed to Lee's rhythms and how tightly wound he got about the job. Tilting her angular face, she revealed the hard lines of her profile. She couldn't let him go off half-cocked and ill-tempered, running roughshod over citizens. He'd become his own self-fulfilling prophecy: the boogeyman white police everyone warned about.

"How am I supposed to take it easy?" Lee slammed the steering wheel. "We're nowhere. That many bullets flying and we're nowhere."

"You being upset and making the both of us miserable isn't going to make it any better. Things are what they are."

"Practicing for your television appearance?"

Their lieutenant had tapped Octavia to do the press conference updating the good citizens of Indianapolis on their lack of progress on the case. Not that Lee was jealous, since public relations wasn't his area of expertise. It would have been nice, however, to have been considered.

"Now you're going to break bad on me?" she asked.

"I'm just saying. I don't want to slow you down, have you slumming with us actual investigators when promotions come around."

"Why don't you calm your ass down. Just because a captain's slot opened up doesn't mean they're going to offer it to me. Or that I'd take it."

"Bull and shit. Bet you can't wait to be a bigger boss. Go to all those lunches, rub elbows with the politicos. Sure beats actual police work. Don't open your mouth to me."

Octavia tired of always having to nursemaid her partner, tip-toeing around whatever latest snit he wound himself into. His provocative tone was the last straw. "I'm sorry. I mistook myself for your superior officer. But I guess I'm not a boss, but a *black* boss to you, so you can talk to me any way you see fit."

"There we go. What'd that take, fifteen seconds, to make this a racial thing?"

"With you it's always a racial thing. A black thing. Black junkies. Black skels. Black police. All dirtying up your *Leave it to Beaver* world."

"You can kiss my *Leave it to Beaver* ass."

"Sure, I'm just your black boss."

"You can kiss my *Leave it to Beaver* ass, *ma'am*. Feel free to jam me up any way you feel."

"Yeah, cause we're all out to get you. Watch out now. One of my 'homies' is coming up behind you. He may want to screw you out of a promotion." Octavia turned to study the passing cityscape through her window, feeling the onset of yet another headache. Part of her understood his frustration, shared it, though now it was impossible to commiserate about it. They drove back to the station in complete silence, both their thoughts drifting to what it would take to break the grip that silenced so many tongues. Maybe it boiled down to who folks feared more: the police or the predators.

Most good police work amounted to waiting and paperwork, so one had to learn how to wait. Patience was her gift. Unlike her partner. Reading between the lines of his risky jacket, and listening to the gossipy sewing circle known as the Indianapolis Metropolitan Police Department, rumors of suspected corruption dogged him. The rumor mill gave him too much credit. Lee was more of a soldier, not bright enough to pull off true corruption, though he occasionally found extra money from a drug dealer. Nothing serious, little more than keeping the change found between couch cushions. Still, it was nice to be married to a city councilwoman's daughter, even better, a councilwoman on the budget committee. He would die "100% po-lice" long before he'd ever be fired, no matter how badly he screwed up.

"Traffic stops or domestics?"

"Domestics. Doesn't matter who's in the wrong, you never know when your victim will turn on you once you threaten to lock up the other." Lee sighed, letting his anger go along with the silence. "Going through the door or clearing the attic?"

"Attic. I seen too many horror movies, so sticking my head through a dark hole? No thanks."

"Come on, now. These days a black woman in a horror movie has to make it to the end. It's affirmative-action Hollywood these days." Lee lived to push her buttons. Octavia did three years of patrol work, moved to vice, prostitution decoy, and then moved to Gang Crimes. After the Pyrcioch case, she was promoted to detective. He could read a jacket, too. All that and she still walked as if she had to prove her worth on the job.

"I see your diversity training has paid off." Octavia coolly glanced at him sideways.

"I've learned a heightened respect for others. An appreciation for other cultures and worldviews. I can only hope to use my newfound..." He stumbled for the right word.

"Sensitivity?"

"Yes, thank you," he continued in his faux-polite manner. "My newfound sensitivity in order to facilitate others in moving forward in the job."

In the end, she tolerated her partner's half-a-cracka antics. Too often a cop's prejudice got the better of him, aimed at the poorest community in which he served. Today it was blacks. Tomorrow he'd forget about blacks and hate Hispanics. "You're full of shit. And you shouldn't burn through so much coffee. You'll be up and down to piss all night."

"That's why God created partners. And," Lee pointed to a man approaching the corner in order to cop, "why He created junkies too stupid to pick out cops obviously sitting on a corner."

"Lookie here, lookie here. Poor dumbass Tavon."

They had set up on Night's crew and had the beginnings of an outline of his organization worked out. They knew about Night who operated out of the Phoenix (all they had on him was a name, which was more than they had on his rival). One of Night's operations, Green's actually, was a red, two-story house known as The Shack, a pea shake house offering neighborhood games similar to Hoosier Lottery's Pick Three or Pick Four games. Since the money didn't flow to the state, they were illegal. Everyone knew it, hustlers, cops, citizens, and politicians, but that activity never led to bodies dropping and lined too many pockets, so a convenient blind eye was turned.

The police currently attempted to get up on Night's lieutenant Green – as high up on the food chain as they had worked – and, right now, Green's boys were doing sloppy work. Probably the reason Green was on the streets as much as he was. The detectives waited because before long someone had to pick up the count. However, Tavon Little provided them an opportunity they couldn't pass up.

Tavon paused on the corner with an eye on the car parked in front of a nearby house. The trunk, left agape while the owner ran stuff into the house, called to him with a sultry seduction, open and inviting. Wiping his mouth, he double-checked to make sure the coast was clear, Tavon hitched up his pants and nonchalantly strode toward the car.

The pair of detectives skulked from their car to intercept him. He veered off his beeline to the trunk like a gazelle who'd picked up the scent of hyenas. Half-throwing his hands up in a "why me/why now?" declaration, he moved out of sight of his would-be suppliers. The last thing he needed was to be seen with black police old enough to be his mother, and worse, this redneck fool who'd love to see him dangling from a noose. Or a bumper.

"Tay-Von Little." Octavia started in, emphasizing his name. Conversations were a finesse game and she hoped she had at least imparted that much to her erstwhile colleague. "Tavon, Tavon, Tavon."

"Officer Burke." Tavon shrank against the tall wooden fence separating the prying eyes of neighbors. Burke and McCarrell crowded him. He chewed on a black-tipped fingernail, his bony body retreating further into his grim-stained, one-time-gray hoodie.

"Detective," she corrected.

"My bad. De-Tec-Tive Burke." Tavon addressed only her. "What can I do for you?"

"Just looking for some information. A name really. Someone in Baylon's crew."

"Baylon's crew? They ain't around here."

"We know that, Tae. We didn't want to put you in the awkward position of dealing out your hook-up. Every organization has a weak link and if anyone knows about spotting a weak link, it'd be you."

"I don't know if I can help you, Detective Burke."

"Tavon, you watch Bugs Bunny cartoons?" Lee grabbed the man's jaw and turned his face to meet his, having grown a little hot about the casual disrespect shown by this bit of junkie trash. He decided he needed to get his attention.

"Yeah." Tavon muttered through his clenched jaw.

"You remember the ones with the coyote?"

"Yeah, Road Runner."

"Nah. The other ones, the ones with the sheep dog. You see, every day was the same. The sheep dog and Mr Wile E. Coyote would ride to work together, break for lunch together, but when they were on the clock – you know, once that work whistle blew – it was all business. Coyote would try and steal sheep. The sheep dog would drop an anvil on his head to handle his business."

"Tavon," Octavia, picking up on Lee's thread, pointed to him, "this here's my anvil."

"A name or maybe I should let you ride up front with me," Lee said.

"Huh?" Tavon said.

"You know, all cozy like. Take a tour of the corners."

"No need to go to any trouble." Tavon raised his hands.

"Let your boys see you riding in style with po-po. Maybe drop you off on one of your favorite corners. How does that sound?"

"Juneteenth Walker. Folks call him Junie," Tavon said with a quickness.

"Junie? He like folks calling him that?" Octavia asked.

"What's that matter?"

"I'm just saying. His momma, all proud of her beautiful baby boy names him after a black holiday, the celebration of our emancipation, but he turns around and the streets call him Junie. Junie... like he's some kind of bug."

"That's the point," Tavon said. "You don't get to choose your name. Those with power over you name you."

"That's a fucked-up way of looking at things," Lee offered.

"It's a fucked-up life."

"We'll check this out. If you on the level, there'll be something in it for you down the road."

"This here's America." Tavon's eyes grew wide with the lucidity spurred by capitalism. "We believe in credit, but with all of this economic uncertainty – downturns and shit – we also a cash down payment sort of people."

Octavia fished out a twenty dollar bill. She held it up when he snatched for it. "Your info better be straight or else my anvil will have an excuse to drop all over you."

"We're cool." Tavon grabbed the bill and ducked out of their little enclave before he could be seen.

"What you think?" Octavia asked.

"Be nice to find out where this motherfucker lays his head. Hold on, I got something so that this night's not a total waste."

Lee pulled some firecrackers out from under the backseat of their car. Octavia rolled her eyes and slipped into the driver's side. Lee tossed the lit firecrackers into some nearby bushes. Watching folks jump into each other's pockets wasn't her idea of entertainment as the touts and lookouts scurried for their covey holes, a few soldiers, hands on weapons, popped their heads out to see what was what. Lee grinned with the glee of a kid kicking over an anthill.

No one knew where Green lived. When folks needed him, they caught up with him on his cell.

His coat hung from a nail lodged in a bullet hole in the wall. A series of cracks in the plaster filigreed his wall. The water-damaged ceiling and floorboards trapped mildew within their spaces, so thick at times, breathing was a chore. Or would be to any but Green. The rest of his place was unfurnished for all intents and purposes. Surrounding a card table were mismatched chairs, from a broken La-Z-Boy to a lawn chair, not that he entertained often. Plywood covered the window creating the darkness of a cave which obscured the stained walls. A bare bulb dangled from the ceiling. Radiators filled the abandoned house though they, too, were long-stilled. From the bathroom came the stench of excrement and urine from a paper-clogged toilet, though the clawfoot bathtub next to it remained bone-dry. No electricity, no gas, no water. Burn marks trailed along the window sills from previous squatters. There was no bed or mattress to be found in the bedroom. For all practical purposes, the room was a walk in the closet, wall-to-wall with suits, coats, shoes, and brims.

Green stood.

"How's business?" Merle asked.

"Steady mobbin'. People always want to get their head up." Green's voice was dry as kindling. "What do you want, mage?"

"Can't two old friends share a moment?"

"Is that what we are now?"

"Depends, do you still have that thing for heads?" Merle asked.

"I see you haven't tired of your word games."

"Chop, chop, fizz, fizz. Oh what a relief it is."

"He's returned, hasn't he?" Green said, still not turning to meet Merle.

"He's been here a while."

"It's really him?"

"Slowly finding himself. Here, there be dragons, or so I hear." Merle ran his finger along the edges of the jutting sconces as if performing a white glove inspection. "How's the old lady?"

"In seclusion. Well guarded. What do you want?"

"A name. What's in a name? Bercilak. Bredbeddle. Bernlak. I guess it depends on who you ask."

"I won't ask again." Green remained rooted to his spot, unflinching, yet his gaze followed Merle.

"Really? Third time's a charm."

His gray-flecked red sideburns straggled out from beneath the aluminum foil helmet he'd crafted. The voices of the dead or else gone were getting harder to sift through. His body aged one way, his spirit the other, he thought, though he couldn't remember which aged which way. "Damn it, Mab. Can't you be quiet for a moment?"

"I see Dred is not the only one haunted by echoes of his mother."

"You can be reached," Merle said.

"And you can be killed."

"A year and a day. A year and a day. The challenge comes full circle."

"Bah."

"A year and a day. Nothing is evergreen. Do what you always do."

In a thought, the flesh of Green's hand stretched and tore, raking the shape of a shorn branch, with one side beveled to form a close approximation of a blade. He swung the slicing hand in an arc directed at Merle's neck, but the mage had already vanished into the night, abandoning the elemental. Which was just as well. He'd grown restless and still had an errand to run.

• • •

Inside the Phoenix Apartments, the woman had a name. A mother of three whose baby daddy walked out when the pressures of taking care of a family proved too hard to shoulder. She worked two jobs to make ends meet, refusing to go on welfare. Not so much due to pride as much as never again wanting to be dependent on anyone – a lesson she wanted to pass on to her children.

She let her sister live with them in the Phoenix Apartments, paid half the rent, and bought most of the groceries. In trade, her sister watched the kids after school and read to them before they went to bed. Though honest and hard-working, she wasn't a saint. On weekends she and her sister weaved each other's hair and they got their party on; she deserved to let off steam and have a life. Her body held up fairly well after three kids. Sure, her breasts sagged more than she would have liked and she had a pudginess to her belly that spilled over her too-tight, low-cut jeans; but she had thick thighs and knew how to carry herself in a way to accentuate her assets. The woman had a life.

None of which mattered to Green.

The woman, while out at a party, stumbled across Dollar putting Prez on in the life, overseeing his initiation. He had drawn the joker from the deck of cards and was meant to take out a random mark. His shot went wide of his intended target and had the misfortune to strike Conant Walker through the Walker family's window. The woman had been staggering down the sidewalk when she witnessed the shooting. When Dollar and Prez broke out, she was sure she hadn't been spotted. As the days passed, what she had seen ground on her conscience. She was careful, only telling her sister about the possibility of her going to the police. She was positive she had only told her. Fairly positive anyway.

None of which mattered to Green.

"Snitching is a lifestyle choice." Green circled the woman who was tied to one of her kitchen chairs. Her home was modest and clean. Poor didn't have to mean dirty, she had always instructed her children. The floors were swept regularly, the countertops wiped down and the house picked up. She was in the middle of mopping the kitchen when Green kicked in her front door, leading Dollar and Prez, as he, too, had a mess to clean up. Dollar and Prez brandished guns, directing the kids to sit against the wall. Green forced her to sit in the chair as they used zip strips to bind her hands behind her. Her sister was out for the evening. "Usually a choice to shorten one's lifestyle."

"I'm not going to tell anyone, I swear."

"That we're all for damn sure. What we have here is an opportunity for an object lesson."

His chinchilla coat hung from his broad shoulders like the mane of a lion, Green reached into the folds of his burnt orange suit jacket. The woman flinched, the correct impulse, though he withdrew only a tiny box. The children were a chorus of stifled cries and hitching breaths.

"Open it." Green placed it in her trembling hands. Complying, she found three brand-new razor blades. "Chew them."

The woman's eyes flared open in disbelief. Green stood, fixing his impassive gaze on her. The box shook in her hands.

"I can't."

"No, you *won't*. A distinct, though subtle, difference. You simply lack the proper motivation. Prez, shoot one of the children."

"No!" the woman screamed.

Prez glanced over at him with questioning eyes. The night he shot Conant Walker, his shot hadn't gone wide on accident. While many thought him a stone-cold killer, one stare into Green's terrible eyes... he knew that Green knew different. Prez was in, but he still had to prove himself to Green. The children huddled closer together. The youngest girl burst into fresh tears.

"I didn't stutter, nigga. Shoot one of them," Green reiterated.

"No, wait. Please don't hurt my babies."

"Do what you have to do."

The woman closed her eyes and opened her mouth. Green, dark priest of the streets, placed the blades like a communion wafer on the flat of her tongue. She closed her mouth gingerly around them. Hot tears trailed down her face. Her eyes pleaded with Green for this gesture to suffice, that she'd learned her lesson and her place. She swallowed involuntarily, the blades shifted in her mouth, and she let loose a muffled whimper.

"I said *chew*. Don't make me tell you again."

She lowered then clamped her jaw. With each action the blade sliced through her tongue, sharp knives through the tenderest of veal. She coughed up a mouthful of blood to the raised wails of her children. A blade slashed through her cheek.

"That's enough."

The words echoed from down a long tunnel the way the woman heard them. Still, carefully as she could muster, she let the blades fall from her mouth.

"Good girl." Green knelt down, his coat draped about him like James Brown preparing to be walked off stage. He met her eye-to-eye but spoke loud enough for the children to hear. "You even think about talking to po-po and there is a price to be paid. Gentlemen, can you wrap up this little lesson?"

Prez watched as Dollar stepped to the woman and fired once into her face. Blood mixed with brain matter splattered her clean kitchen walls and her blood pooled on her freshly mopped floors. Dollar took out his penis and peed on her, nodding to Prez to join him. Prez started to turn to Green, but opted to avoid the gaze that bled into an eternity of nights. Instead, he pissed on the woman.

With that, Green led the men out of the apartment. Before closing the door Green whispered to the children: "Tell everyone what you saw here. Everyone except the police."

## CHAPTER FIVE

The floorboard creaked at the scurry of movement from the other room. Percy laid already awake, though never truly asleep. Not as long as there was another man in the house. A jumble of legs and arms, the three babies slept next to him. The family referred to his young charges as "the babies" despite them all being in elementary school. Oblivious to the sounds from the next room, they slept with a hail of snorts and snores, under his guard, sprawled out like Power Rangers caught in mid-action. Percy tried to cover his ears to block the rutting sounds from the next room. The moment itched against his skin and ached his stomach; even his unintended eavesdropping intruded on something private. Something dirty.

It wasn't as if he had snuck into his mother's room and hid under her bed in order to divine why so many "uncles" stopped by to stay the night. Or the hour. Or the quick fifteen minutes. It implied her having a bed, instead of the stained mattress hauled from down the street after it had been set out for heavy trash pick-up. A "ghetto garage sale" Miss Jane called it, then she convinced several of her fellow partiers – she always called them partiers, with her always in search of the next party – to haul the thing back to where she stayed. They squatted in one of the dilapidated houses boarded up by the city which had long been zoned to be demolished. The plan was to build a few affordable houses, a Section 8 oasis among the older homes in the neighborhood. Those houses too run-down to be refurbished were to be razed. Until the paperwork went through, bids submitted then chosen, and contracts signed, the houses were free game for whoever chose to live there.

And Miss Jane never missed an opportunity.

A man, his voice gruff and low, called out her name as if he were in church and struck by the Holy Ghost. Percy all but pictured him jumping down the aisles caught up in the throes of the spirit that moved him. His mother's name. God's name. A stream of words people shouldn't use. All to the staccato rhythm banged against the thin wall separating them. His eyes squeezed shut even tighter, Percy acted as if that would block out the sounds. He began to sing softly to himself: "*Jesus loves me this I know, for the Bible tells me so…*"

Finally, mercifully, it stopped.

The knob turned noisily, furtive whispers exchanged after the long creak of the door, barely on its hinges, opened. Attending to his final duty, Percy rose and positioned himself formidably in the hallway, his large frame shadowed by the dawn light through the cracks of the plywood boarding the windows. He was a looming shade in a faded Polo T-shirt stretched by his bulbous form and a pair of five year-old jeans, his size carried the day as the man paused upon seeing him. Disheveled, shirt unbuttoned and untucked, pants hastily put on, the man glanced back toward Miss Jane half-flustered. Percy nodded, the way his momma taught him. The man reached for his wallet and peeled off a few twenties.

"Later." The man stumbled toward the door, carefully avoiding Percy's gaze.

"Later, baby," Miss Jane said, an echo of exaggerated seduction to her voice. As easily as she turned it on, she turned it off. "How's my big man?"

"Tired." Percy rubbed his eyes. With the man gone, his body slouched in an exhale.

"Couldn't sleep?" Miss Jane played at naïve innocence, the wisp of a devilish grin at the edge of her mouth.

"What we going to do for breakfast?"

"We got any cereal left?"

"No." Percy had hidden the remaining half of a box before Miss Jane and her parade of would-be suitors returned from their nightly routine of running the streets foraging for highs. He would divvy it up among the babies for dinner, before the idea to sell the box occurred to her. He made that mistake last week after restocking the shelves with food stamp-bought groceries. What her paramours, his "uncles", didn't eat, she sold the next day. Before then, he had to learn the hard way his lesson about letting her have the food stamps card directly. They went without food for a month, getting by on church pantries and neighborhood moms who pitied them and gave out of their own meager food supply.

"Guess we going to have to get to work early this morning." Her breasts peered unapologetically through the flimsy material. She stretched, her shirt raised to expose her belly, fully revealing that she wasn't wearing any panties. A smile with too much knowing inched with devilish glee across her face. "Send them off early, maybe they can catch a free breakfast at school. Then hook up with me at the spot."

Miss Jane slipped into gray sweatpants and a matching jacket and pulled her hair up into a pink wrap which matched her slippers. Schemes already half-forming as to how to raise enough money to not only get right but also to get through the day, she marched out the house with nary a backward glance.

Percy roused the babies and found some clothes which had been aired out for a few days. Maybe to-morrow he would be able to scrounge enough change to make it to the laundromat or perhaps a teacher might do a load for them. He, too, bled a life full of maybes. He walked them to school, many of the children kept a mocking distance from them. The babies without combed hair who smelled funny were easy targets, even from children just as poor and just as crusty-assed. Percy waited until the school doors swallowed his younger siblings, before he was assured they were even somewhat safe for a time.

And he felt tired.

He wanted to go to school. If nothing else, it was a break from the world he knew. Some days, however, he had to put in work. Almost like skipping school to help out on the family farm... if by "family farm" one meant a new way to get over on folks. Percy met up with her behind the Fountain Square Mortuary. She made a few extra dollars as a professional griever. The old man who ran the place gave her forty dollars to wail at funerals, especially when there were only a few mourners in attendance. For an extra twenty, she'd throw herself onto the casket.

"Boy, look at you." Her hands on her hips, she eyed him up and down, a scorn-filled countenance displeased with the measure of the man.

"What, ma?"

"Shuffling around like you got nowhere to go. *What, ma?*" she mocked. "Even when you talk, you sound beaten down. You radiate weakness like you the sun beaming down on all us folks. You ain't ever going to be half the man your daddy is."

"Is?" His voice raised with hope. It wasn't as if he believed his father to be dead or even purposefully absent. Hope gilded Percy's thoughts of the man. With dreams of being wanted but his father being too busy to come around. Too important. Yes, he had one of those important jobs which had him constantly traveling. The word "is" carried the promise that not only was he still around but that Miss Jane knew where he was. Hope was a death of a thousand small cuts, bleeding the life from him in a steady, painful stream.

"Boy, you too slow for words most days. You ain't built for this here game. You have to have hardness. You have to have heart. And you? You so…"

"Soft." Percy sighed, eyes cast downward.

"Look here." Miss Jane sidled alongside him, not putting her arm around him or anything too… maternal. But the boy, despite his obvious deficiencies, touched something within her. Maybe he was so simple, so pathetic, she drew near just to staunch his feebleness. He had a way about him, not his father's way, but a way. A purity, one which shamed her every time she approached. She stepped back. "You see them boys over there." Dollar and his crew stood about gearing up for the day's trade. These days, Dollar oversaw a couple of crews. He might be in line to rise to the next level. As it was, boys buzzed about, attending to him without so much as a word from him. "You have to know a few things about folks. First, everyone is out for they self."

"But…"

"Ain't no buts. This is all about survival and doing whatever it takes to survive, well, sometimes ain't a lot of room for pride left. You get over on them or else they will get over on you. That leads to rule number two."

"What's that?"

"You can't trust nobody."

"Not even you?"

"Not even me." Miss Jane paused, struck by the honesty of her answer. Something about the boy just made folks… simple. "Folks be stupid or too sneaky. Everyone's got an agenda, some angle they working. That's why you have to play or get played."

"I don't think I like this game."

"That's what I'm trying to tell you. Not everyone's cut out for this. See? Look."

They turned to the scene drawn by someone hollering in pain. He probably got his ass caught shorting money, diluting product to squeeze out some side money, or selling burn bags as their product. All variations on the same theme: his hand in their pockets. Dollar delivered the first fisted blow, knocking the man's head back with the sound like a bag of ice dropped to the sidewalk. After the first punch, he seemed to lose interest, giving license to his boys to stomp and pummel the man into senselessness.

"Why'd they beat him up?" Percy asked, mouth agape and eyes lingering too obviously. It didn't pay to be too fastidious to details. Miss Jane turned his face to hers.

"Dude over there shorting them. Someone takes you off, you can't let that shit slide. Never. Once they see you as weak, you done out here. So you have to put a beatdown on them. They do it again, you got to fuck them up for real. So what you learn?"

"Don't let them read you for weak. Or soft."

Miss Jane caught scent of some new-tested package and ambled off. Percy stood there for a moment, watching the boys play at manhood, and hummed to himself.

The day was brisk but sharp, a chill wind under a blue sky. A second-chance day, when one dreamt of doing things right this time: finish school, don't mess with that girl, get a straight job, be about family. Living life without waiting for the click of a hammer to end it all.

Baylon walked along the street of Dred's house at an easy pace. For some reason, the song "Jesus Can Work It Out" kept running through his head: *That problem that I had/I just couldn't seem to solve*. He hadn't thought about that song in ages. The breakdown chant of "work it out" brought to mind a frenzied choir and folks anxious to get caught up in the Holy Ghost. He hated the show of church.

"Baylon!" a voice called out as he walked by.

He returned the slightest of head nods.

A group of boys slung rocks down the street, not trying to hit anything in particular. Simply whiling away the time with casual destruction the way boys were prone to. At Baylon's approach, the flicker of recognition, respect, and perhaps even fear filled their eyes. They stopped their game and parted for him. Their gazes lingered on him in admiration.

"Hey B," a sultry voice sang. Pert breasts tenting her low-cut blouse with no back over some tight blue jeans, stretched to bursting seams by her full hips. "You got something for me."

"Yeah, why don't you hit me up at the spot later on." Baylon waved her off knowing a few years ago, a girl like that would have rolled her eyes in a "Nigga, you can't step to this" way at his approach, much less chase after him. The charge of fame had pipeheads running up to him to beg for a free sample, like fans pining for an autograph. His name ringing out, he was every bit just as much a junkie, hooked on status, on being the man. He paused on the porch and surveyed the neighborhood. Then he went in.

Every time he crossed the threshold he felt transported to another place. Odd symbols etched the doorframe. When he ran his fingers along them, they gave the same sort of tingle as licking a battery. Baylon thought it unusual that Dred rarely kept any soldiers at the house. None were required here, he had told him. The kinds of enemies I've made wouldn't be stopped by thugs with guns. Baylon ignored the irony of him saying that from his wheelchair.

Dred waited for him in the spacious living room. His scraggy goatee never grew in right. He had to grow it. His face had a natural boyishness to it. The softness of retained baby fat which made him appear younger than his twenty-odd years. His nest of hair coiled out in serpentine aggression. The color of cold onyx, he glared his ancient gaze from bloodshot and rheumy eyes. Long wizened fingers propelled his chair with little exertion, his all-white Fila jogging suit matching his brand-new tennis shoes.

"You hear what happened with Green's crew?" Dred asked rhetorically.

"Everyone heard. Lots of shots." Baylon shifted uncomfortably, standing without having been offered a seat and having the distinct impression he'd been called into the principal's office.

"A lot of noise. If the message was 'we like to make a lot of noise and bring down all sorts of unwarranted attention', message received. Those two fuck-ups couldn't be trusted to send a telegram."

"You gonna call the Durham Brothers?" Baylon kept his sigh to himself. Junie and Parker, Junie more so, *were* world-class fuck-ups. Despite congratulating themselves on a ruckus well made, they needed to be sat down. Reflecting a moment, Baylon realized they weren't too dissimilar from him. They all demanded respect, yet none of them could command it. Dred continued as if picking up on his thoughts.

"Call done been made. Remember when a nigga would say 'I'm gonna hold things down' and business got handled?"

"Lots of things change." Baylon ignored the quiet indictment.

"You got something to say?" Dred wheeled nearer. Baylon never had the sense that he looked down at him. Dred created – he didn't know how else to describe it – a vertigo effect. Despite the height differential, it was like they stared at each other eye-to-eye.

"Nah man, I'm just saying. The crew's weak. You up here. I'm up here. Back in the day, we had things on lockdown."

"Yeah, you right. Lots of things change."

Dred backed away from him. He tapped the small box which hung from his arm rest. The lid popped open and he withdrew a huge spliff. He fired it up. The smoke filled the room immediately, its aroma pungent, like earthy though rotted burnt vegetables. "Think back, remember how I found you?"

Alone. Scared. Cold. Wet. Huddled in the door frame. All his friends turned against him. He still had the knife. Pulled his jacket tighter and higher, both for warmth and to not be recognized. Never felt so isolated, abandoned, and betrayed. He had never known such sheer terror. Breathing became a labored process; he was suddenly conscious of reminding himself to inhale and exhale. His heart pounded arrhythmically, hammering an unsure cadence. The girl was little more than an acquaintance, but he liked her spirit. Her light. He hated the little boys drawn to casually snuff out lights simply because they could. Her blood still on his hands. Her innocence... he took it all away the minute he introduced himself to her. She'd have been better off if they'd never met. She'd still be innocent. Safe. Alive.

*How could they think that of me? Did that even sound like the person I was? They know me. They know me. He still had the knife.*

Dred pulled up, the outline of his black Escalade a blurred shadow in the haphazard rain. Its parking light on, it roamed the lot like a leering hyena in search of wounded prey. Dred rolled down the window. A thick issue of smoke poured from his mouth. Like he'd been expectantly waiting. "Get in. You're not safe here."

"I'm not safe anywhere. Not anymore." Baylon's panic ran so deep, he barely recognized Dred.

"I understand. Look, I ain't gonna bullshit you, you in deep. Left quite a mess back there. But we're handling it."

"We?" Only then did he notice Night in the passenger seat.

"You don't need to worry about that. What you need to know is that your crew, your true crew, stands tall beside you." Dred checked his rearview mirror. "I don't mean to press you, but we gots to roll. Get in."

Baylon ducked inside the Escalade as Dred peeled off. He drove a half-mile or so before turning on his headlights. The quiet thickened between them. Jittery-eyed and dry-mouthed, he jumped at every brake, squeal, or car horn. Arguing, a shout, bursts of laughter. They drove aimlessly, taking in the sights of the city. The street's cacophony of life, abrupt, charged sounds which brought only terror. Edgy, he anticipated something bad about to happen. Ware and uneasy, he leaned forward in his seat, drawing Dred's attention in the rearview mirror.

"That girl back there? That was his cousin."

"Wrong time, wrong place. Tragic."

Baylon remained silent not yet knowing his play. Dred's measured words bubbled with import, calculated to appraise him at every turn. Bleak as things seemed, he knew he had options. It was an accident. It had to be. If he just went to King. Explained.

"King was your boy. Took some stones to do him like that."

"I don't believe it. No one would."

"A no-heart nigga like you. I'm saying, no offense, that ain't your rep," Night said to Dred's obvious displeasure. "He didn't have it in him. That's all I'm saying."

"We all have it in us. We just need the right teacher to draw it out of us. Ain't that right."

"Bay?"

"It got done, didn't it?"

"He might be ready to step up. What you think?"

Baylon hated the way they discussed him as if he weren't there.

"Ain't my call. My man has to make his choice. What you think, B? You ready to step up?" Dred asked.

Still jumpy and unhinged, his nerves drained of all resolve, Baylon realized he was a man of fluid loyalties. After the misunderstanding which ended his and King's friendship, perhaps his future interest was with Night and Dred. Every story needed a villain. Maybe it was time for him to embrace his calling. As hollow as that thought ran, at his core, Baylon was practical. The best way to survive was to stick with survivors. Dred, no matter the level of chaos around him, always managed to survive.

"You cursed, you know," Dred said.

"I don't know shit about no curses," Baylon said.

"Death follows you," Night said.

"Death follows all of us." Baylon grew annoyed at their steady rhythm. He felt pressed in and double-teamed. The Escalade became claustrophobic. He stared out the window. He had a self-destructive impulse he wrestled against. Got in a bad way, a dark head space and wants to take a torch to his life. "We born to die."

"Not all of us. Some of us even death won't touch." Dred stared into the rearview mirror until he locked eyes with Baylon.

Baylon fidgeted with the handle of his knife then shifted uncomfortably in his seat. He ticked off the streets as they headed east on Washington.

"Why you want to help me out?" Baylon eventually found his voice.

"The enemy of my enemy..." Dred said.

"So we friends now?"

"Better than that. We're partners."

Baylon nodded. This was the life he wanted, the opportunity he'd been waiting for. It only cost him his friendship with King. They hadn't been close of late, but they were still boys. They'd depended on each other for so long, they had become comfortable. And now it was evaporated. He was dead to King. He would have to find his own way with his own people.

"And then you brought me in," Griff said.

Baylon jumped. The voice was so real in his ear, he searched Dred's face to see if he heard it. He couldn't be here. Not here, not now, not in this memory. Griff came later. Smoke filled the car, a billowing cloud so thick it now obscured the front seat. The smoke's heady aroma disoriented Baylon. Soon, all he knew was the smoke. It isolated him. The world beyond its fringes ceased to exist. All there was, his entire reality, had been reduced to bodiless voices.

"You wanted in. Remember what I asked you?" Baylon asked.

"'Now you want to get your dick wet and do some work?'" Griff quoted.

"Yeah, you were always the first in line to get paid."

The smoke began to clear. The cloudless sky beamed with such an intense blue it hurt Baylon's eyes. The landscape shifted until it coalesced into the familiar. He grew up in this playground. His house was across the street, behind the community center. His neighbors' houses lined the alley which cordoned off the park. Baylon spidered his hands up along the chains of the swing in which he sat until they reached a comfortable height.

"You remember when we used to race swing?" Griff sat idly in the swing next to him as if he had been there the entire time.

"We were damn fools," Baylon said sharply. "Surprised we didn't break our necks."

"You were a beast. Could get higher than any of us."

Baylon smiled at the thought, the secret compliment, and he remembered. Swings different back in the day. Taller, with wood seats. A fool of a boy could stand on the seat, pump for greater height and at the apex of a swing, jump off to fly through the air and land past the scree of pebbles and dirt that filled the swing area.

"I don't know how any of us survived our childhoods," Baylon conceded.

"There were no children here. There were soldiers in training."

"We were fierce though."

"Yeah. We were fierce. It all worth it?" Griff's words hung in the air, the perfect playground bee sting. He was gone. Baylon was alone on the swings.

Then Dred's voice drew him from his brief respite.

"We in this deep now," Dred said.

"I never thought we'd make it this far. Or this long." Baylon stumbled for words, hoping his matched whatever conversation he was having.

"Some of us didn't." Dred smiled, a rueful and wholly unpleasant thing.

"You ever think of him?"

"Think of who?"

"Griff."

"Naw, man. Best to not dwell on things best left in the past. What's the matter, brotha? You look like you saw a ghost or some shit. You paler than a motherfucka."

The weather ought to have been drizzling, overcast at the very least, but the noonday sun dazzled overhead. Lackluster warmth did little for King's mood. He towered over the small plaque. MICHELLE DAVIS. 1984–2004. Another person he had failed. His life had become a litany of failures, of lives derailed, ruined, or tragically truncated by his involvement in them. The swelling sentiment pained him more when it was family. He couldn't even afford to bury her. Outreach Inc. put up the money to cover her burial.

Burial.

His cousin laid under six feet of dirt, a secret kept from the rest of the world for eternity. A secret that didn't have the chance to blossom, to chart her own way, to fulfill her potential. King ached at the hole in his heart whenever he thought about her. He ran the heel of his hand across his brow, then held his hand like a visor. Lott walked up to him. Fleeting eye contact, afraid of what he might see there. A gain, a sorrow, which matched his own. Combined it might create a well of anguish so profound they might not escape. Or worse, they might break down and cry. And neither would admit or want that.

"How'd you know I was out here?" King asked.

"I didn't. Come to see her on my own." Lott adjusted his FedEx uniform. The heat of it didn't bother him. He rather enjoyed the comfort of its cloying presence. The thin skim of sweat, as if girded for battle.

"I don't know what made me think of her today."

"Me either. Something in the air."

"Like we share a special bond."

"We're brothers. Brothers born of tragedy and pain."

"What?"

"I don't know. Something Merle once said about us... before going off about cycles and cursers. You know how he gets." If he held still enough, Lott could still smell her. Could feel her run her fingers through his hair. She liked long hair, so he rarely cut it. "Seen too many funerals."

"I know she meant a lot to you."

"I don't like to think back on it," Lott said.

"It was a bad time. A hard time."

Obscured by clouds, the full moon created a silvery cast to the sky. Wind skirted the rooftop, thickening the deep chill of the night. The layer of rocks on the warehouse rooftop made it difficult for Wayne and King to keep their footing. Tar-like ichor trailed along it. It was why it was so important that they wore old sneakers: they never knew what muck they might step into. Small alcoves which formerly held air-conditioning units, a mix of brick and wood, spaced in a series, the ridged spine of the building. Tarps or blankets were draped across the individual bays, a tent door opening.

Wayne toted the massive backpack filled with bottles of water, an assortment of snacks and materials about contacting Outreach Inc. King trotted noisily beside him, a long flashlight in each hand. With no additional volunteers that week, and Wayne not wanting to miss a week, he asked King to join him. He was proud of the work he did. Having started several programs within Outreach Inc., from their in-school assistance program to the tutoring session and bible study programs on site, Wayne had poured himself into the ministry. A quiet joy hidden by his gruff exterior, he didn't take for granted the rare opportunity he had, matching his passion to his profession. Wayne's realization that working with hard-to-reach knuckleheads was his gift was another revelation. Took one to reach one, he guessed.

Two nights a week, staffers from Outreach Inc. trekked across the city, checking spots known as stops for homeless teenagers. Bus stops. Bridges. Parks. Downtown rooftops. The places varied and morphed. King knew what "street night" entailed. Wayne had discovered him on one such street jaunt. Set him on a course to better himself and realize his potential. Where King went once he got his feet set was up to him, but the possibilities were endless if he could imagine them for himself. That was the rap Wayne gave him, despite there not being that great a gap in their age difference. But it stuck with him.

King glared out the window, angry at the passing scenery, lost in grim thought. He heard rumors about his cousin being out on the streets. Alone. Scared. Abandoned. She might have taken off on her own, Lord knew her mother was no prize, but family should have been there for her. Should have chased after her and taken her in. But family failed her the same way it had failed him and he was determined not to let history repeat itself.

"Outreach Inc.," Wayne called out. A few groans rang out from a couple cubicles, pissed at their disturbed rest. King flashed the beams in the direction of every sound. "Anyone need water or food?"

A few hands poked out from behind the blankets and tarps. A linebacker-sized altar boy passing out communion of water and peanut butter crackers, Wayne made his way along the path. King couldn't help but be impressed with Wayne's easy manner. Not just how comfortable he was, but how gentle. To be around him like this, there was a spirit of nurturing about him, passing through him, that the kids responded to. Wayne spoke of Outreach's services and they listened. He spoke about school options, and they listened. He offered to pray with them and they bowed their heads.

When the two of them reached the last of the outcroppings, Wayne repeated his announcement. A female voice stirred.

"Michelle?" King dared ask.

The rustling within the chamber paused. The blue tarp parted tentatively, a shadow stirred among the deeper shadows. King sensed they were being studied.

"Who that is?"

"King. Your cousin."

"King?"

A baby girl, maybe all of fourteen, stepped from the hovel. Despite all of the hardness she wore like dented armor, the upturn of her head and beaming face betrayed the kernel of innocence she clung to. Her eyes sparkled with something... undefeated. Her smooth round face wasn't haggard, wasn't worn to premature age. Her figure wasn't gaunt nor her manner reduced to hunger. She still carried her notebook filled with incomplete letters to various boys in her class and odd poems she'd started but never finished.

She was safe.

"Leave her alone."

A man rushed from behind the compartment and tackled King. The flashlights clattered on the ground next to him. The man snuck him a few times in the kidney as King regained his breath. Though bigger than his assailant, the man obviously knew how to fight. King shifted his weight and put his knee into the man's side throwing him off of him. King tried to remain reasonable, putting his hands up to show that he didn't want any trouble. Scrambling to his feet quickly, the man warily circled King, shifting his weight from foot to foot, leaving King unable to read his next move. Looking to land a right hand, his awkward stance attempted to work his way inside. A heavy shot from King left him a bit wobbly. King hoped it would be enough to make him re-think his attack.

They squared off again, arms up, ready for the other to make the initial feint. The man ducked past King's blows. An errant elbow pushed King's head back, which left an opening for a flurry of wild punches. Then that cold thing in him erupted. The needless fight was starting to piss King off more than anything else. Snarling as he charged, he lashed out.

Heads popped out. *"He don't give a fuck."* "Knock *that nigga in the head, fool!"*

The little man wrapped King up about his legs and shoulders, leaving him with only one free hand to whale with. The man's shoulder took the brunt of the damage as he gained the footing to tumble King over. He prepared to begin kicking him when Michelle screamed.

"Lott! Stop it. He's my cousin. King. He's not here to hurt me."

Still locked in a frenzied bloodlust, he seemed to not

hear her.

"King! This ain't how we do things out here." Wayne raised his voice and hardened it. That seemed to snap the two of them out of their fugue.

*"Aw man." "That was garbage."* Rejoinders from the crowd dissipated, their evening's entertainment coming to a disappointing end. They returned to their spaces.

"What's this all about?" Wayne asked.

"It's just... word on the street was that someone was looking to hurt Michelle." Lott directed his comments to Wayne, but kept a wary eye on King.

"The Pall?" Wayne asked.

"No. None of the usual pimp suspects. A dealer is all I know. I still don't know what she did..."

"I told you, I didn't do nothing," Michelle protested.

"But someone's pissed enough at her to put a bounty on her."

"Not if I have anything to say about it." King puffed his chest and put an arm around Michelle. Futile declarations, macho preening in front of Lott and Michelle as much as anything else. The words rang with iron and determination. Both King and Lott stood ready to die in her cause for all the good it did her.

King had been the first to find her. Slumped down, legs akimbo, her jeans thick with blood drained out of her. Flecks of blood speckled her cheek. Her melancholy face turned with a faraway gaze, her eyes glazed. He cradled her in his arms until they were numb and he long past feeling or caring.

A trace scent of a familiar cologne clung to the air.

King remembered the words he said to Lott when he found his voice again. "Every man wants to be larger than himself. He can only be if he is part of something bigger than himself."

Guilt had a way of gnawing at Baylon during his quiet moments. He had hurt a lot of people in the past. Not that he intentionally set out to hurt them, but just in the course of him doing his thing. Concerned only about what he wanted and felt with little regard for the feelings of others and the consequences of what he considered to be "my business". How his sometimes stupid and selfish acts altered the courses of people's, too often his friends' lives. Relationships irreparably damaged often without the luxury of making things up to folks. Fixing matters wasn't always an option: what was done was done. Sometimes you just had to carry the weight of your bad decisions and selfishness and hopefully let them shape you into a better person. Though he hoped that some of the people he had hurt in the past might have the chance to see the person he had become.

Though the memories had a way of becoming a part of him.

Griff sat next to him on the couch, though he didn't react. He merely angled his body more toward Dred, hoping his body language didn't betray his burgeoning fear. Not of Griff, because the dead only knew things, but more of him losing his mind.

"You still with me, Bay?" Dred asked. "Look like

you faded on me there."

"Stress," he said, as if that covered the answer to any question Dred might have asked.

"You need to find a way to relax. I think I can help you out there." Dred positioned his chair directly across from him. Growing more solemn, as if overtook by a darker aspect, he began speaking. "Let me tell you a story told by the old people. Among his tribe there once lived a young man, prosperous in all he did. His fields flourished enough to feed his village. His cattle numbered enough for the wealth of ten tribes. All the people knew his name. The only thing missing from his life was a good woman, someone to share his life with and give him a family. Good women, though a rare treasure, presented themselves regularly enough for a man with his wealth. He had the daughters of prominent men and nearby tribal chiefs offered up to him frequently. But none caught his heart.

"One day, a young woman caught his eye. Of course she sprang up from where he least suspected he would find a woman: from his own village. She had grown up alongside him yet never before had he noticed her. In both beauty and intellect, she pleased him and with that, they were married. His greatest fear in allowing himself to fully love another was that she would be taken from him. And in all too soon a course, their time together was cut short as she grew sick and death claimed her.

"The young man became obsessed with her. He

went to her house, but she was not there. He slept in their bed, but it ached with her empty space. He walked the banks of the river where she fetched water and washed their clothes, but the routine of their life together left a sour taste in his mouth.

"His family spoke to him, begged him to find a new wife, but he was not to be consoled. Love, he believed, could only be caught once. To ask for it a second time was to be greedy. Nor did he wish to let go of the love he had. Sitting in his house refusing to come out, his heart was no longer among the living. His friends had another woman brought to his house. They pleaded with him to take her, to end his solitary and dreary existence. 'The past is done away with and you can't return to it. Let the dead stay with the dead and the living with the living. Love remains in the heart.'

"There was truth in their words, the young man recognized, but the time to let go, to give up, had not yet arrived. He examined his fields and cattle and declared them worthless and left his world behind. He walked until he could walk no further, finding himself in a strange land among a strange people. There he built for himself a house. But still he was not ready to return to living.

"After another sleepless night, he decided better to go to the Land of the Dead. Again he marched, this time until he reached a place of total darkness. The shadow chilled him to his very core. He forgot what the heat of the sun as he strode his fields felt like on his back. But he kept walking. Passing through it, he came to a river and stopped. No birds sang out. No voices of man whispered among the trees. No animal disturbed the grass. A crone of a woman sat on the bank, a straw hat low on her face.

"'Why are you here?'

"'I've come to see my wife. Life has nothing left to offer me without her.'

"'You are not a soul. A living man cannot cross.'

"'Then I will wait until I die.'

"'Death won't come for you. You are cursed. All love that enters your life will die. However, because of your suffering, I will allow you to cross for a moment.'

"The crone pointed to the water and it became shallow. The young man crossed without turning around. Whispers came to him like a gentle breeze, the spirit of her an unseen dancer. The brush of lips against his neck. The embrace of the wind. In his heart, he held a song, the song of her, and then fell into a deep sleep. When he woke, he was among his people once more. He reclaimed his cattle and his fields. He began to work because work was all he knew. And then he called upon his friends for he found a life again. That was the way the old people told the story."

"I don't get what you're saying."

"Life is hard, but this is all there is. Bitches die and sometimes you need your boys to see you through. Now you get your head straightened out, your mind back in the game, and then go back to work."

Wheeling himself backward, not breaking his eye-line with Baylon, Dred stopped at his side door. He knocked three times and crossed his arms, waiting with a self-satisfied grin. A woman opened the door and posed in the entrance way, wrapped inside a long trenchcoat. From the judicious way she held the coat, she obviously wore nothing underneath it.

"She's straight-up jump-off, ready whenever you call and has no problem with whatever freaky shit you can imagine. Ain't that right, baby?" Dred ran his hand down her leg.

"You should know."

Dred left the two of them alone in his office for some privacy. Baylon shoved everything from the desk. She spread herself on it obligingly. Determined to lose himself in her, he dropped his pants and climbed on top of her.

And thought of Michelle.

Baylon had no desire to be an everyday brother. He was tired of living in other people's shadows. His paper wasn't as long as he'd like, definitely not enough to be his own man or have his name ring out. Which meant he never had the effect on women that a King, a Griff, or a Dred might've had. Griff was his boy, one of the few who remained by his side and he knew how Griff did: his deep penetrating stare as if you were the only object in his universe and he saw through you; the hard jaw set and resolute, ready for anything to jump off; his head tilted to the side, only slightly, endearing himself enough to make you lower your guard, followed by a quick wink to let you know he had you. It worked every time, girls and dudes alike. Which was why Baylon was convinced to bring him in. It was Griff's turn to step up since he was so convinced that he was ready.

"You vouch for him?" Dred was new on the scene. No one knew much about him. He had a way of being in the right place at the right time and assembled an efficient crew which allowed him to remain in the shadows. All anyone needed to know was that he had the right connect. His stuff was always on point. His cheap prices allowed him to carve out a huge swath of territory quickly, and no one questioned his main two enforcers, Night and Green.

"He's my boy." After the incident with Michelle, Griff was the only one who came around Baylon and he never forgot that. Not that his other friends set out to shun him; they just suddenly came up busy and involved in their own lives. Some afraid of what folks might say about them should they roll through. Griff didn't give a fuck about what anyone thought.

"He don't look like he played no football." Night was a hood rat through and through. He grew up in the Phoenix Apartments, from back when it was called the Meadows. It was all he knew. As soon as he got a little money, he moved his mom out to Allisonville, but he stayed at the Phoenix as if some invisible cord tethered him. Word on the vine told of Green practically raising the ambitious young thug before passing the crown onto him. Though no one understood why Green didn't simply rule himself.

"Did so. For Northwest," Griff said with the sting of

injured pride.

"*Shit*. I thought you said he played high school ball. The only thing Northwest knows how to do is lose."

"Yeah, you won't hear him deny that. Other teams consider Northwest's homecoming game a home game." Baylon tried to keep the mood light. With so many brothers in a room all out to play hard, it wouldn't take but the wrong word, tone, or lingering stare to set someone off.

"What position you play?" Dred asked.

"Running back," Griff lied. He was a kicker, but they would have run him off the block for bragging about being a kicker. "What do I have to do? Shoot someone? Get beat up?"

"You run your mouth too much." Night's eyes bore a thousand-yard stare into him.

"We work at a whole different level," Dred said. "You can put all that gangsta bullshit out of your head. We about real power."

"So he in?" Baylon asked.

"We'll see."

They walked toward Dred's black Escalade. It neared midnight, but the moon burned bright and full.

"What the—" A blindfold dropped over Griff's eyes. He swung his arms wildly, though Night smiled as he bucked. "Showed heart," he would say later.

"Be cool. You want to blow this?" Baylon whispered. Griff stopped struggling. "Once you in, you in. Ain't no backing out later."

The truck rumbled along, the four men riding without conversation. The sounds of traffic faded and soon the settling silence discomforted Griff enough for him to shift toward the door. His hand trailed along the hand rest to the door handle, assuring himself that he knew where it was. The car stopped. The other three doors opened and slammed shut. Furtive voices consulted one another, though Griff couldn't make out any words. Then nothing. Tense. Jack-hammered heart. The sheen of uncomfortable sweat under his armpits. The door swung open and two sets of arms grabbed him and dragged him out.

They removed the blindfold.

They faced a ruined building, the stones of its wall remained as if a wrecking ball had been taken to it. At the center was a clearing where a fire raged, a series of snaps and sputters spat embers into the air. Shadowed figures took post, guarding against all intruders. Wearing a long black and purple robe, Dred threw powder into the flames. A cloud of smoke rose. The isolated puffs took form, morphing into a face which turned to Griff with a mocking gaze then dissipated.

Baylon escorted Griff to a small wall and sat next to Night. On the wall were scrawled a couple of names, only one of which wasn't crossed out. Rellik. Positioned in front of the wall, an oblation of food and drink on a table before a stone with a leopard pelt draped across it.

"The Etai Ngbe. The Leopard Stone," Baylon answered the unasked question.

"What is all this?" Griff asked.

"Call us the Egbo Society. We control the gangs, the

drugs, the money. We've had our eye on you for a while and I vouched for you. We've invited you to join us."

"I don't remember asking."

"We don't ask." Baylon sounded strong and certain. Not to be questioned or denied.

Night wore a low-cut fade. He was one of them black brothers. Blue black. And as dark as he was, he had a darker knot above his left eyebrow in the shape of a crescent moon. Keloids ran along his big chest and huge arms, constantly itching. He rubbed lotion on them.

Dred began to speak, the purple and black robe draped around him like a poorly fitting hoodie. His face fell into its shadows. "Ours is the house without walls. We call upon Obassi to guide and protect us."

Baylon and Night joined with him. "*Okum ngbe ommobik ejennum ngimm, akiko ye ajakk nga ka ejenn nyamm.*"

Dred lowered his robe to his waist. Two yellow rings circled each breast. Below them, a white ring stamped his middle. Underneath it, two more yellow rings; the yellow rings formed a square on his chest. His back had the same pattern emblazoned on him, with the color scheme reversed. Alternating yellow and white stripes ornamented each arm. Dred gestured for Griff to come before him.

"You want to run with us, you need to be marked. Take off your shirt," Dred said.

"What is it?" Griff asked.

"A sigil. It's like a name."

Dred lifted a small bowl and dipped his finger into it. He daubed each of Griff's arms with white chalk. From another bowl, he marked his forehead with camwood dye. Then lastly, from another bowl, he marked Griff with a yellow dye on his abdomen and back of his shoulders.

"And thus, the Ndibu are complete." Dred raised a goblet from the table. "*Medraut*."

"*Owe*," Night and Baylon said in unison. Griff stared at them.

Dred sipped from the goblet, handed it to Night.

"*Barrant*."

"*Owe*." Griff joined Dred and Baylon.

Night drank then handed the cup to Baylon.

"*Balin*."

"*Owe*."

Baylon handed the cup to Griff. He held it with a look of uncertainty.

"*Balan*."

"*Owe*."

All eyes fell on Griff. He stared into the fallow liquid swirling in the cup. Then Griff drank.

"Now you are one of the Ndibu, the high order of the Egbo Society. We are bound to one another and only by our hand are we released."

Waves of heat shimmered off the pavement. Percy wandered the alleyway ticking off his mental checklist Miss Jane had so painstakingly instructed him. He had to be more aware of his surroundings, know the score in order to stay out of trouble; or worse, let trouble find him off guard. He surveyed the alley.

Lone roughneck in a long wife-beater tee, baggy black pants. The beginnings of a beard along each side of his face. Toothpick protruding from his mouth, the man hard-eyed him.

"What you need?"

"How many lookouts do you have?" Percy began amiably enough, then pointed down the way to a group of kids sitting on their bikes with no particular need to go anywhere. "Those kids down there?"

"What the fuck?" Anger flashed, a lifetime of lessons and reinforced habits snapping into place without a thought. "You better quit playing and get on. Simple motherfucker."

"Where's your stash?" Percy examined how the man stood in front of the garage, careful not to wander towards the side with overgrown weeds and an abandoned tire. "I bet it's in those bushes around the corner of the house."

"Boy, what you doing?" Miss Jane yelled at him.

"Do you have a gun? Can I see it?" Percy asked, nearly reaching to pull up the man's shirt.

"What the fuck's wrong with you?"

"Don't mind him. He simple. I was just trying to school him on what's what out here and he wanders off for some… extracurriculars."

"Well, you need to teach him how to watch his mouth. Could get him killed up in this piece."

"I doubt that."

"Why? He bulletproof or something?"

"You know whose boy he is?"

"Who?"

"You better check out that scar on his left eye."

"Oh snap. My bad." The soldier took a step back.

"Yeah, your bad, motherfucker. Now let me get two." Miss Jane shorted him the cash and dared him to rise up on her to collect the rest. He decided she wasn't worth the effort.

He hated watching her inject herself.

"Momma, who's my daddy?"

"Shit, boy, you trying to blow my high?"

"I want to know. Can I meet him?"

"Let me see if I can arrange something. He might as well see the man you turned out to be."

Not that Miss Jane or Night were up for parents of the year, they had both agreed to keep Percy far from the game. Well, as far as possible. The streets weren't meant for people like him. Soft. Innocent. Miss Jane told him as much about Night as she could, but for what he wanted to know, the questions he was ready to ask, he needed a face-to-face.

The naked light of the bar bleached most of the details away. Already stoked in sweet Scotch fumes and liquor-loose, Night slowly drank. Percy studied the man's face, searching for something familiar. Dark as he was, he had a scar about his left eye in the shape of a crescent moon. He fought the compulsion to scratch his own scar.

"You still with that girl?" Percy asked. Apparently there was always some girl, so it was a generic enough question. It wasn't as if Night kept track of any of their names. To hear Miss Jane tell it, Percy might as well have asked about one of his other babies. There was always some baby. Automatic. Impersonal. The wall.

"That what you want to talk about?" Night's sleep-heavy eyes turned to him. He had a power to him, a force of will, much like hypnosis. Part of his way was his ability to suck you into his web of half-truths, deceit by omission, and out-and-out lies. He had a smile. A broken smile, Percy thought. The smile that usually intimidated others into silence.

"No. I..." Percy didn't know how to form the questions he wanted to ask. He half-closed his eyes, a child pretending to be asleep, trying to get through the conversation, unaware that his body language mirrored Night's. He kept his voice light. He wanted Night to like him. Percy hunched over, making himself appear smaller, more the picture of a little boy. He only wished they were a family. The tidal wave of questions slammed against his cautious spirit and he blurted out, "Didn't you want me?"

"Accidents happen." Night read the sting of the words in Percy's heart-sick looking face. "Shit. This ain't going right. Don't know why Miss Jane insisted on this. Just said it was time. Time for what? Me hurting you?"

"So you didn't want me." Percy's face scrunched up, flat and sullen; his voice tentative and mournful.

"Not just you. I always go in bagged. I had the feeling Miss Jane set me up. Wouldn't put it above her to run a pin or some shit through the whole box of rubbers. Look here, kids bind you. Keep you from doing what you want to do. I'm out here hustling, getting it done. and don't have time for all that daddy mess. Can't be the man out here if I'm doing the Cosby thing. I have to be the man because without leadership, folks run in circles and reach into your pockets."

His job was important, Percy thought.

Night tightened his mouth. His gaze roamed about then suddenly fixed on him in a cat's pounce. He scowled, half-disgusted, feeling cornered and uncomfortable. Then his grimace relaxed. Percy had a way about him, one Night secretly wished would rub off on him. An innocence, maybe?

"It's a terrible feeling when you can't stand the sound of your own kids. The little things. Coughs in the middle of the night. Little sniffles, throw up, sick business? That's a mother's job to take care of shit like that. The stink they make, diapers, I ain't got time for that domestic shit. That's bitches' work. I ain't got time for that." As if repeating it would demonstrate the truthfulness of the situation. Touched by his innocence, he owed him the truth. "So you decide to wait till he got a little older. Show him some shit. My world. Let him see what I do and how I do it. Teach him how to be a man. Then you realize you don't know what to show him. Better off not being around. Put word on the street to take care of you. Keep you safe. We look after our own best we can."

Night searched Percy's eyes, hungry for any sort of understanding.

"So you wait a little longer. You get to the point where he was about grown. Don't really need you to show him nothin'. Can barely face him knowing you had no hand in who he became. Can only hope he do a'ight. Maybe better than you.

"Where I come from, we have a code. We carry it like that." Night leaned back and gave Percy some space. He peeled off a handful of twenties, the only thing he knew how to do.

The neighborhood preyed on itself, an ouroboros of poverty. The irony of taking from people with so little eluded Miss Jane to a nearly painful degree. An anguish Percy experienced as he pushed open the window. The first-floor apartments of the Phoenix were better off without windows. To stare at the outside world through bars. They were an "open for business" sign for the local crackheads opting for an easy score. Most tenants occupied the first level only until they could move to a higher floor. But not too high as the stairwells offered their own dangers.

Miss Jane convinced him to break in. Rumors of the household hoarding money and jewelry, eccentric ghetto millionaires. Such tales bubbled up from time to time, excusing would-be treasure hunters their Robin Hood ethos, though the poor who were targeted by their charitable impulse were usually themselves.

Two windows in the apartment, one with an air-conditioning unit in it, though it too was stolen from a first-floor apartment down the street. The bedroom window slid open easily enough. A young girl stirred,

disturbed by the rush of traffic sounds from the outside. Percy closed the window behind him. Pausing,
he bent over the frame in case the girl fully woke and
he needed to make a hasty retreat. He sensed her in
the dark, could hear her breathing. Fumbling along
her dresser, his large, nimble hands found no jewelry.
He ran them along a chalice; inside was a lone ring.
He picked up the ring, holding the metal goblet in
case it clattered against it. He peered over his shoulder. The sleeping figure didn't move.

Percy leaned over her. Rhianna. The warmth of her
brushed against his cheek. He took in a deep breath.
Flowers and powder, a gentle scent. Peaceful. The
ring grew hot in his hand. He lost the heart to continue going through her things. It was a violation. He
ran his finger along her face. Gripped by the panic
that always seized him when around her, that sense
that he might break her, he scuttled out the window.

"Anything?" Miss Jane demanded.

"No, Momma." The ring burned in his pocket. A
memento.

Miss Jane read his face. The boy was flushed to the
point of blushing and refused to meet her eyes. He
was lying about something. His pants bulged in front.
She smiled.

"Come on. Nothing going on out here. Let me see
if I can get you taken care of."

Burger Chef to Hardees to Burger King to Big
Belly; the restaurants which occupied this spot
changed with the neighborhood. Ghetto to projects
to hood. The evolution of poverty. The names

changed but the problems remained the same. Miss Jane leaned heavily against a car.

"What are we waiting for, Momma?"

"Between your father and mine…" She broke off her initial sentence, re-thinking the tack she wished to take with him. "Pussy makes you stupid. Remember that, boy. You can't be in it for love. There's no love in pussy. Only want."

The bad words made Percy turn his head.

"You like Superman."

"I am?"

"Yeah, you know. He all super strong an' all, but he has to go through life all cautious. He can't just relax. He fuck around and break a ho. That's you. Everything you do is so… tentative."

"Tentative." He rolled the word around in his mind. "I like that."

"Here's my girl now."

A woman sauntered toward them in an exaggerated gait. Her burnt almond complexion and high cheekbones framed a generous mouth, with lips filled to an exaggerated fullness. Her blonde extensions twisted into braids. Wearing low-cut blue jean shorts and a green halter top, her full breasts too easily visible, Percy was embarrassed for her.

"Girl, how you been?"

"Still in the game," Miss Jane said.

"You a soldier to the end. Who do we have here?"

"This is my oldest. Percy."

"He turning out to be quite the man."

Percy wondered if he ought to open his mouth and

let her check his teeth, the way horses did when
being appraised.

"Sometimes a momma has to look out for her boy.
Teach him to be a man." Directly in front of him, Miss
Jane unbuttoned his shirt and lifted it over her head.
She beamed with pride at her baby boy. His premature "out of shape with middle age spread" of a body
not all that different from the baby she bathed in the
kitchen sink so long ago. She tugged at his belt, slipping it free from the pant loops. His pants fell to the
ground, but his gaze remained fixed on hers. "He's
always been a shy boy."

"I don't mind the shy ones." Her friend ran her hand
up along the inside of his leg. He was suddenly aware
of two things: one, just how close he had been standing to her, and two, that he had a raging hard-on that
threatened to poke her eye out if she leaned in any
closer. "I wanted to confirm how deep you were."

"Momma?"

"Hush, baby. Momma knows what she's doing.
You'll be all right."

She stripped him to his boxers and thermal knee-
high tube socks – it was cold out and he always made
a point of dressing properly. Folding his clothes, she
set them in a pile next to her. He didn't want to lose
his virginity, especially this way. Percy began to cry.

"Look at this motherfucker here."

"He always had a problem dealing with people,"
Miss Jane said.

"He's obviously not ready to handle all of this." She
passed her hand down her body to show off her

voluptuous figure. "Tell you what, though. I'll suck him off real good."

Her hands encircled the outline of his penis. His eyes fixed on her mouth. Brown lipstick smoldered on lips traced with black liner. A mole dotted her chin on the left. She might as well have drawn a bull's-eye on her face. She took him into her mouth and seemed to hold him there for eternity.

# CHAPTER SIX

Lott Carey woke from strange dreams every hour.
That was when fatigue got to him so much as to
allow him to drift off into the fitful thing he called
sleep. He dreamt of blood and battles, of swords and
death, of love and pain. It was his calling, his destiny,
and his gift. He knew he'd never know peace. So he
flipped through the motel cable channels as if on this
third time through there might be something on
worth watching. Better the perils of late-night television than the visions that tormented him
whenever he closed his eyes lately. A baleful glare
over a reptilian spread of teeth, no more than a
glimpse, but the familiar sensation sent terror
spreading through his soul like embalming fluid
poured into a corpse.

On the outskirts of Speedway, the Speedway
Lodge, formerly a Howard Johnson's, cost just over
a hundred a week to stay. Just off the Crawfordsville
Road thoroughfare that led to the Indianapolis
Motor Speedway, the stretch was tourist-friendly

year-round; but if there wasn't a race going on, the motel was largely deserted. And worse, it offered few amenities to alleviate boredom. Lott couldn't even distract himself with his cell phone as it had been cut off earlier that day. He had let his cousin talk him into sharing a plan with him because his cousin couldn't get a plan on his own. Ignoring the voice warning him not to do business with family, Lott agreed. The first bill arrived and his cousin had run up over three hundred dollars in texting charges alone and offered to pay him fifty bucks on it out of his next check. Lott never even received the fifty. Another in the long list of reasons for him to stay away from family.

His mother was a fiend. Always working an angle, she named him for a missionary in hopes of impressing some deacons at the church. It worked until they caught her breaking into the office to steal the petty cash. They moved into Section 8 housing, his moms little more than an industrious junkie who knew how to work the system. Even now, Lott suspected that her head bobbed up and down in the lap of a neighbor so that she could score enough to get back to sucking on a glass dick. Of his two brothers, one was barely functional and the other in the ground. He was staying with his sister, but she abruptly kicked him out. He couldn't tell if she was bipolar or simply back on drugs.

Turning off the television, Lott decided to indulge his one vice and went out for a smoke. It was needless, too, because he wasn't addicted. There was no physical urge, his brain didn't get the rush others did. He smoked… just cause. It was something to do and gave him time to think. The outside view didn't offer much by way of distraction. His neighbors mostly paid for their rooms by the hour. One glance of his concrete dour expression and they let him be, though he took no joy in appearing hard. At the thought of having to adopt that affectation, he spat on the sidewalk. However, the role of being hard was a community expectation, a fixed mask, though he had no heart for death, his or anyone else's. Occasionally, he forced a smile for one of the regular pros whose faces he'd come to recognize, otherwise he continued the pantomime of armor needed for survival. Thus he rose up quickly on the streets with a reputation for being a loner until he hooked up with King. They had been boys for a minute, though, truth be told, while Lott was tougher and a better fighter, King had greater heart and will. He'd told King to stop through, but the parking lot remained empty and bleak.

His evening's boredom sufficiently broken up, Lott flopped on his bed and opened one of the six books he picked up from the library. Tom Wolfe's *A Man in Full*. Walter Mosley's *Futureland*. Machiavelli's *The Prince*. Sun Tzu's *The Art of War*. Gary Braunbeck's *Destinations Unknown*. And the book which caught his attention this evening, Joseph Campbell's *The Hero With a Thousand Faces*. He remembered his fifth-grade teacher who rarely spoke to him and never called on him in class. She had already written him off as another street tough and had no expectations of him beyond, hopefully, him not disrupting class so that the other students could learn. Public school became a death by discouragement with him, the memory of which often had him wondering how many boys she'd derailed by not believing in them, by teaching them that they had already been written off. College was a dream he clung to as he struggled to pull together ends. Once he passed his GED. After he got his license. After he paid off the tickets from driving his sister's car without a license. There was always some roadblock in his map of plans.

At the moment he was trapped in that cycle: needed money for a car, needed a car for a job, and needed a job for money. He accomplished the first goal and he got a job. The blue FedEx uniform was like a second skin at this point. He used to work down by the airport, trying to save up enough money to get a car and full get on his feet, but his kin were bleeding him dry for ride money, charging twenty-five bucks for a ten-minute trip. Another reason to add to that list. Life would be easier if he could walk to work or if he worked along a bus line, so he had hopes of transferring to a closer branch. Soon he'd be able to apply to school, maybe IUPUI or Ivy Tech, something to get started.

The room lights flickered, interrupting his reading. Briefly he wondered if rats chewed on the wiring, as such was the natural order of things. Finding his place in his book again, he found comfort in the slightly chilly room by curling up and covering himself with a blanket. Fully dressed and it being the waning days of summer, Lott found himself pulling the comforter further around him. A creeping numbness settled into his feet so slowly he didn't realize the deep ache of cold in his bones at first. Movement skittered on the edge of his vision. Against the contrast of the dark blanket he realized he could see his breath. He was ready to adjust the thermostat or call the super when he noticed something else. Smoke billowed in from under the door.

Lott rolled out of his bed. The heavy fog had a measured creep to it, its movement contrary to the laws governing mists. Cloudy torrents seeped under the door and through the slits of the window with nary a smoke detector going off. Rushing to the bathroom, he scooped up several towels, returning to find that the wisps had formed a hand with a raised finger, wagging at him for having any thoughts of stemming it.

With that, the mist dispersed in a puff then coalesced into a screen of sorts. The picture of a woman formed, one unfamiliar to Lott though her beauty – despite the smoky portrait – was quite evident. Tall and proud, hair pulled back into a ponytail, she had a fragility and strength all at the same time. His heart filled with an ecstatic longing. Soon, another shape entered the scene. Clearly it was Lott, the two recognizing each other. They moved like guilty people not wanting to be caught, yet desiring the other all the more. They embraced, cloudy fingers fumbling over each other, probing, undressing. Lott stepped nearer, his hand raised in front of him as if to touch the entwined pair.

Suddenly, the tendrils of mist took hold of him, whip-like cords wrapping around his hands, squeezing him with such force he winced despite his surprise. The fog rope lifted him from the ground, his arms pulled over his head. Lott kicked at the fallen cloud, each kick dispersing it briefly only to have it re-form. It formed a teeth-filled maw, opening and closing, with dark indentations giving it the appearance of eyes as it drew Lott toward it. A tongue lolled out, snaking its way to him, its serpentine undulations writhing up his body until it arrived at his face. It licked about him, its ephemeral touch both cold and light. Lott pulled away from it, straining from its touch as much as its tight embrace allowed. The coil reared up, a cloud cobra, then it rammed itself into his mouth. The coldness seeped into Lott. Its essence pushed down his throat. He gagged as it forced itself into him, filling him. Growing light-headed, unable to breathe, his eyes fluttered as they sank back into his head.

The door buckled as something with a lot of force behind it slammed into it. The crash roused Lott back to near lucidity. He turned his head to see what manner of beast would follow next. Interminable seconds passed as the mist both drained and filled him. With the next blow, the door flew off its hinges followed by King and Merle tumbling in.

King came to a stuttering halt as it took him a moment to get his head around the sight of his longtime friend suspended on tendrils of smoke. Gathering himself, he swung madly to break the beast's grip. Merle stood, near motionless, as if a patron at an art exhibit taking in the beauty and scale of the machinations as only a true connoisseur such as he could appreciate.

"What is this thing?" King cried out as he punched in vain. "Merle?"

Merle arced his hand as if throwing up a mystical gang sign, and an arc of green light struck the room. The tentacles of vapor collapsed, their tethers cut, dispersing like fog under morning rays. Merle's complexion turned suddenly pallid and gray. He reached out to a lampstand for purchase, but missed it, instead falling from sheer exhaustion.

"Merle, are you all right?" King caught Lott as best he could, propping him up until his legs steadied themselves enough for him to bear his own weight. "What was that?"

"Each action costs." Merle gulped air between words. "Someone called the dragon's breath."

"The what? Why attack Lott?"

"Someone wishes to cut off your support before you can assemble it. Nice."

"You can marvel at it later. Let's get out of here before it comes back."


Loaded with hundreds of songs from his father's childhood, doo-wop mostly, but a mix of tunes through the '70s, the music on King's iPod was the last connection to the father he barely remembered. He had no distant memory of his father, only the idea of him. His mother treasured a few items he'd left with her between visits. Of the few records left at her place, her favourite was Isaac Hayes' *Hot Buttered Soul*. She played it over and over, often saying how the record reminded her of him and how out of his own time he seemed to be. An old soul. Only in these moments, between battles and with his music, did he feel like his father's son.

Lott slept, exhausted but otherwise none the worse for wear after being attacked. As if around a campfire taking the first watch, King plopped down on his couch. Merle laid on the floor, head propped up in his hands, and stared at the dancing lights of the iPod with childlike fascination.

"What the hell was that?" King had been waiting to ask but had decided not to open the topic until he had a chance to digest what he'd seen.

"The dragon's breath," Merle said with a matter-of-factness.

"Oh. Well, now that you've laid it out for me, that explains everything."

"It's the same for every hero's journey. You're only told as much as you're ready to accept."

"And what couldn't I accept?" King poured himself a glass of water, tilting the pitcher to Merle who waved off the offer.

"That magic is real. That mystery has power and truth."

"Uh huh."

"This would be you still being not quite ready." Merle rolled over, a mad light in his eyes. Clearing the countertop that doubled as a table, he spread a few coasters along it. "The city, like many places, is swathed by ley lines, what some might call fairy chains. Think of them as lines of force that connect places of power."

"This better not be some Satanic shit."

"No, no. This is older than that. Think of the magic that I describe as energy." Merle traced a line from one coaster to the next. "A natural energy that runs along power lines."

"These ley lines…"

"Exactly. And they connect places of power."

"Like power stations."

"Some people, or elementals, can naturally harness that energy better."

"Like you?"

"Me? I'm an old man in a tinfoil hat. Barely capable of a glamour here or there, though I've got a few tricks left in me."

"I'm having a hard time getting my mind around this."

"We live in precarious times. No room for magic. Or dragons. For the line of the serpent to continue, it must adapt to the age. For now I have it on good authority that we need to wait."

"On whose authority?"

"Sir Rupert's, of course."

"Great." King stared at his empty glass he didn't remember draining and refilled it. It was going to be a long evening.

• • •

A couple of nights a week, volunteers from Outreach Inc. did what they called a street night. Patrolling the streets, they searched for teens who might be at risk in order to inform them about Outreach's services. Tonight, Wayne and a female volunteer wore the vests emblazoned with the Outreach logo and toted the flashlights that doubled as batons if they got into a scrape. As her case manager, he wanted an excuse to check up on Lady G. He couldn't shake the feeling that she was in trouble.

There was a perception that the poor want to live the way they did, victims of their laziness or poor life choices. As was usually the case, the truth was a little more complex, the stark shades of such black and white judgment tempered by the reality of a system that often erected walls against folks when it didn't abandon them outright, and allowed them to fall through the cracks. To fall into that other world of shadow and societal malice, the forgotten places in the shadow of downtown. The survivors – and truly they survived more than lived – made use of any abandoned space to stay warm and carve out the semblance of an existence. It hadn't been so long since Wayne transitioned out of the streets. Other family members pitched in, one, because when they saw someone working so hard to make it they had to help when they could; and two, his charitable spirit put them to shame. Once he graduated from college, he strove to help as many over the wall as he could.

They made a strange pair, Wayne and the volunteer: he with his broad, muscular frame and unforgiving face, a scar on the back of his neck and a tattoo of a pentacle on the front. She, a head and a half shorter than him, with her bookish glasses and chin stud. A study in contradictions. Wayne thought she was the type who had to try out the streets for a minute, long enough to make herself feel better about her place in the greater scheme of things. Young, pretty, and privileged, a typical white girl, ready to get back into her daddy-bought BMW or something parked around the corner. At least she didn't drop her "g"s and put on a slang affectation. That level of condescension would have just pissed him off.

A scree of rocks led up to the railroad tracks used to get to the black-tarped rooftops of the abandoned warehouses. Each measured step tested for soft spots, with Wayne treading first, though in an anxious sweat about whether the roof would support his, much less their combined, weight. Dubbed the Hispanic railroad because of the high Hispanic population typically found there, rotted cherry tomatoes, discarded beer cans, and free floating trash mined the rooftop. Moldy sleeping bags, rugs, and crocheted blankets doubled as doors to block the biting wind, from the smashed-in roof compartments squatters now called home.

A group of Hispanic men sang along to Tom Petty's "Free Falling," their accents delighting in the chorus as they held what they called a "dance contest". The contest amounted to them smoking while drinking beer, bouncing as the music blared from a duct-taped radio. They accepted Wayne's offer of water, but one man fixated on the female volunteer and began proclaiming how "I hate me some Jesus." A couple of the man's friends pulled him away, chastising him for saying such things. Wayne fixed his hard stare on the man, putting himself between her and the homeless man, allowing her to make her way back to the tracks before he backed away.

They next went to West Street and Kentucky Avenue to what was known as "The Tubes". The buildings across from the water station had been tagged. ESG. Treize. MerkyWater. HeadCase. ICU (the letters written within a circle). Torn-up quarry remains littered a field that led from a sanitation workstation to a path down the bank of the White River. Concrete tubes normally used in sewer work had sheets of plastic draped across their ends. A man with dirty blond hair and a week's worth of facial growth sat in front of a small fire. His USA sweatshirt and blue jeans looked nearly new, but he had neither shoes nor socks.

"How you doing, sir?" Wayne asked after having announced that Outreach had arrived with food and water. With a head nod, he sent the volunteer back to the van to grab a few pairs of socks.

"Good, good." The man studied the small dancing flames, his hands absently scouring for more brush.

"How long you been out here?"

"A couple weeks. I'm in the Army and I'm due to be shipped out in a few days. Then me and my wife will be straight." A feminine mumble asking who was there was met with harsh whispers about Out-reach and water. The volunteer returned with some socks.

"Have you seen any teenagers around?" She handed the man the socks. "We're especially on the lookout for teenage girls."

"I hear there's some under the bridge. A group of them. We came up here to have some quiet."

"Thank you." Wayne left the man an additional bottle of water and a few snacks.

Downtown was the medium of rats and lies. A parade of headlights scurried to nowhere, slowed by the occasional horse-drawn carriage, a quaint throwback to an earlier age's gentility. The steam from the downtown grates, shallow graves for the beasts that lived within the bowels of the city. The Bridge meant either the McCarty Street bridge or the Washington Street and they got lucky on their first try with the Washington Street bridge. Not too far from one of the downtown strolls, the tresses under the bridge were used as small apartments: quiet places where folks could stay warm. Not so quiet if Rhianna had her voice raised.

Wayne hated navigating the steep incline, especially at night. Concrete slabs jutted out at irregular intervals forming a make-shift stairwell down the embankment. The thick growth of trees hindered easy movement. He stayed at the top shining his flashlight so that the volunteer could go first then he proceeded down largely in the dark. Funny, he always felt stronger at mid-day; now his movements seemed clumsy. The tall bonfire by the riverside, surrounded on all sides by trees: the scene looked picturesque.

"Nine o'clock in the morning ain't no booty call," Rhianna's rasp strained.

"I ain't gonna trip," Lady G retorted. "Believe what you want to believe. Don't matter what time of day it is, some fool call and all he has is sex on the mind, it's a booty call."

"You just jealous cause Prez don't call you," Rhianna said behind her G-funk nose and slightly bucked teeth. She nursed the pus pocket on her finger from where she got stabbed. They could've stayed with Rhianna's people, but this close to rent day, tensions boiled over, toilet paper sheets counted, and food carefully guarded. Sometimes the drama just wasn't worth it. She'd been couch-surfing with friends who lived over in the Phoenix when she met Trevant. But it was Prez who stepped to her.

Lady G clucked under her breath. "Girl… boo. You stand by yourself, you stay by yourself."

"I'm glad to hear you say that, G," Wayne interrupted.

"What you doing down here?" Lady G gave Wayne a hug.

"Looking for you."

"How you been?" Lady G turned to hug the volunteer. She was awful with names, but the volunteer had been present enough to warrant a hug. Trust wasn't a commodity easily given. Even Rhianna would more easily trade her body than risk trusting someone.

"Better now." The volunteer squeezed an additional time before releasing her. Rhianna moved in for her hug.

"You ladies need anything?" Wayne huffed as he stumbled down the last few steps of the hillside.

"Rhianna needs better taste in men," Lady G offered.

"Oh?"

"She's trippin'," Rhianna said.

"Don't show out cause you hanging around that retarded boy," Lady G said. "He up there, topside, him and his boy, Trevant. Surprised you didn't see 'em. Wannabe dope dealers."

"Rhianna…" Wayne thickly laid on the sound of disappointment in his voice.

"They ain't real drug dealers. They just playing."

"Call themselves ESG," Lady G said.

"What's that stand for?" Wayne asked.

"Eggs, Sausage, and Grits."

"Ain't that some shit?" The words flew out of Wayne's mouth before he received a scolding glance from the volunteer. They tried not to use profanities in front of the clients, trying to walk the line of being real yet being an example. Wayne bristled at the idea of being an example, uncomfortable with the idea of being a role model.

"That ain't the worst. They up there selling burn bags to folks." Lady G still had her "I'm gonna tell" air about her.

"You can get a beat down behind that mess," Wayne said.

"You telling me? That's why I keep telling Rhianna to drop his sorry behind."

A car screeched to a halt above them. The quartet froze where they stood. Slamming doors were soon followed by raised voices. Wayne moved to shield them, as if protecting them from anything that might fall from above. The shouts, the trumpeting of machismo attempting to get the other party to back down, curdled into abrupt screams. Lady G stifled her own scream, then pointed to the trestle above them. Wayne ushered the girls up there, and they scrambled into one of the holes in the bottom of a support structure. The small alcoves formed a series of tiny compartments with the holes acting as the entrance, though it reminded Wayne too much of sticking his head through an attic door into unknowable darkness. Knowing that he stood no chance in hell of squeezing through the hole, Wayne signaled that he was going topside to investigate. The volunteer shot him eyes pleading for him to stay, but realized he was too exposed to whatever was out there. Rhianna thrust her thumb into her mouth and put her other hand against an ear as she began to rock back and forth. Her mother had warned her to quit sucking her thumb before it bucked her teeth.

Wayne slowly lumbered up the hill.

Prez didn't care what you called him as long as he got called. Though Green had brought him on, he felt it was on an interim basis until he proved himself. In the meantime, until he saw some real money, he still had to make ends so he financed what he termed "independent entrepreneurial enterprises": burn bags. Dried-out baking soda passed for crack and stepped-on oregano for weed – the pair had an assortment of burn bags they sold to newbies. After every sale they set up somewhere new should anyone decide to come back on them. Unfortunately, their current location didn't have much by way of foot traffic, but Prez was more interested in hooking up with his girl. Rhianna was all right enough, not as fine as her girl, Lady G, but she had a fat ass and threw her back into her work.

"I wish some fool would try to come up on us." Trevant, all of thirteen years old, still retained much of his baby fat, especially about the neck. Prez thought it apropos to start calling him Turkey because of all of his would-be gangsta gobbling. "I'd tell him, 'It's Li'l Nam, shortie. It's how we do this bitch.'"

Li'l Nam was the nom-de-guerre of the area just south of the Phoenix Apartments. Trevant was an east side nigga who'd come to truck with Prez and some of Night's boys on the west side because no one else would have his dusty ass. Well, Prez's either, which was why they were left dealing burn bags and calling themselves ESG.

"Damn, fool, you can't keep going off on every fiend we deal with," Prez said.

"Why not? It's not like they're going to quit buying."

"Customer service, nigga. Ain't you ever heard of it? It's not like we the only ones selling." Prez might as well have been speaking in Mandarin judging from the vacant stare Trevant returned.

After chewing on his words, and with them spit out his other ear, Trevant continued. "I seen niggas get smoked right in front of me."

"Yeah, you hard, brotha." Prez eyed the street. Knowing he'd been dismissed, Trevant slipped on a set of headphones to listen to the new Nas.

A Ford Focus screeched to a halt. Prez tapped Trevant on his jacket and nodded toward the idling vehicle. They prepared their wares but also checked their escape route should things go bad. Two people, a man and a woman, stepped out the car, the suspension on the Focus squawking in relief at their exit. They couldn't be dissatisfied customers. They'd have remembered selling to these two.

"They must be part-Samoan," Prez whispered.

"Some ugly-ass Samoans, then," Trevant said, not nearly quietly enough. "Nice suits though."

"What you need, money? ESG can set you up with whatever," Prez said.

"ESG? What weak-ass shit you selling?" the woman asked. Well, Prez presumed her to be a woman.

"Don't matter none. Dred don't like it, so the shit's got to stop," the man's voice boomed.

"Free country. Live and let live," Trevant said.

She whirled and grabbed Trevant by the throat and lifted him into the air like so much a sack of leaves. "Move, or worse, make me have to chase you and you'll get what your friend's about to get. We've got a message for Night and you're just the man to deliver it."

"Wha-what's that?" Prez asked.

The woman grabbed Trevant's arm and pulled. The skin around his shoulder stretched, the bones shifted at odd angles until a dull pop freed the joint. The flesh ripped, the last bits of frayed tendons tearing free amidst a spray of blood. The boy screamed over the cries of "holy shit, holy shit, holy shit" repeated by Prez. She waved the bloody stump at him, trying to refocus his attention on her.

"You with me? Good." Blood gurgled out the arm, ribbons of veins and shorn flesh dangled. She fixed her eyes on him and raised the arm to her mouth. Not blinking, she took a huge bite from it and chewed slowly. The smell of piss from Prez let her know she had his full attention. "Tell your folks what you saw. Let them know the Durham Brothers are in town and Dred's done fucking around with them. And just so you don't forget…"

With her nod, her brother upended Trevant and the two of them each took a leg in a hand. Being around bridges always had the Durham Brothers especially enervated. Trevant's next scream scored itself into Prez's mind, even as the image of his flesh unzipping before him would forever scar his psyche. Trevant's insides splayed out in spools as he was ripped from ass to sternum.

"Go." The woman licked her lips.

Prez ran off into the night, forgetting all about Rhianna.

"Fe, fi, fo, fum," the man said and sniffed in the direction of Wayne, who thought himself well hidden by the foliage lining the bridge.

"Leave him, we've made our point," Michaela said. "Besides, the tale will spread faster with more witnesses."

## CHAPTER SEVEN

Only the desire remained.

Tavon Little didn't care that he killed himself a bit at a time. Squatting to eye level with the table, he carefully doled out the powdered heroin; his works spread out like instruments in an operating theater. He sprayed water from the syringe (Evian – he was particular). He loved this part of it, when he wasn't too sick, the dick-hard anticipation of the ever briefly sated hunger. The match's flame caught the bottom of the bottle cap. Slowly he loaded his syringe, the puff of pink in the bottom of his spike confirmed entry. He shut his eyes and slammed it all home, in-different to the possibility of an overdose. So what if he did? It'd be a rush all the way. A high to end all highs.

He leaned against the rotted drywall and let the first wave of the blast crash into his skull. A slight moan escaped his cracked lips. He pulled one side of his old Army jacket over his dirty tank top to try and keep in some heat. Except for the grime and the worn cuffs, it was in pretty good shape. With his red sweatpants he considered himself the height of fashion. Yeah, he was set for tonight. Tomorrow he'd have to come up with a new hustle to set them up, but he wasn't worried. He still had a good head on him – he couldn't survive the game long if he didn't – but he also suffered from a good heart. Anywhere except here and that was probably a good thing. He simply wasn't wired to do what it took to survive, to prey on his own. Hell, he could barely lie to people he knew, so no stick-ups and no moves that might hurt someone. And it meant that he often suffered bad luck, like yesterday, the C-Devils weren't shit.

"You feelin' it?" Miss Jane asked, ever skeptical.

"Mm-hmm," Loose Tooth mumbled.

"I ain't feelin' shit. What about you?"

"I'm feelin' somethin', but it ain't like it was yesterday."

"Product been stepped on so many times, tryin' to make it last till that new package comes through," Miss Jane said.

"Heard they was gonna re-up in the mornin'. Damn, look at Tae. He's gone f'real."

"I swear that nigga could shoot water into his veins an' get high."

Tavon heard them, but didn't care. He didn't want to even open his eyes, but he knew he'd have to eventually, or else Miss Jane might run off with the rest of the stash, convinced that he somehow had kept the good stuff for himself. Both Loose Tooth and Miss Jane had been in deep from when Tavon was a kid. Theirs was a makeshift DMZ. Their spot was on the corner, a bright lime-colored house from the Arts and Crafts era with brown doors and trim; clay-tiled roof, and a wrap-around porch made of stones. Probably a show home in its day, now a board-covered shadow of itself.

One street over, things were downright civilized. A KFC/Taco Bell/Pizza Hut ("Kentacohut" they called it) recently opened. Twenty-fourth and North Penn, on the edge of what some called Li'l Nam, that part of Indianapolis that no one liked to talk about. Almost two hundred properties owned by the same slumlord. Funny, Tavon thought, how one man had the power to run down a whole neighborhood. Rumor had it that the slumlord was negotiating with the city to sell off a few streets' worth of homes and move to Florida. Especially the homes along the main city thoroughfares, like Meridian, Pennsylvania, and Delaware Streets so that rush-hour commuters wouldn't have to automatically check to see if their doors were locked every time they drove past the houses.

Tavon slipped his stash and works into his Crown Royal bag and stuffed it into a hole behind him, past the slats that kicked up a cloud of dust (hopefully not asbestos, he heard that shit was cancerous) every time he bumped against it. He could feel the toll of the hunger. Everything grew more difficult. Ideas. Words. Slower, fewer, simpler. A dope-fiend lucidity. He fell into a nod, not caring about the drool oozing out the side of his mouth.

Tavon's eyes fluttered open, squinting in the sun-
light, taking in the familiar surroundings. The dirty
mattress cushioned the floor of his room. He kicked
his soiled sheets from him in disgust. Not at his condition, but at the fact that since he had help getting
to bed, his stash that he'd saved to get started this
morning had probably already launched Miss Jane.
Only half-awake, he rested his head between his
knees, hunched over in the dance of the dry heaves.
He hated the nausea, even more than the pounding
of his head.

The hunger called.

A bottle of lotion wouldn't have helped the dryness
of the cratered alligator skin of his needle-scarred
hands. Even his scabs had scabs. He soldiered on, another gaunt, dark-skinned fiend in service to the
hunger. The hunger that squirmed its way through
his intestines pulled at him in a relentless assault. He
shuffled with his hunger down to the front porch, sitting on the steps and tamping out a Kool cigarette.
Blankets nailed over closets; kung fu posed Power
Rangers stood guard over their clothes. The landlord's
fix-it guy had patched drywall by nailing a door to
the ceiling. Opaque Plexiglas windows partly blocked
the wind and might've done a better job if they
hadn't been only stapled over the open frame. People
actually lived here only a few months ago, but even
Section 8 housing said enough was enough as even
government housing could only sink so low.

"The hawk is out." Loose Tooth sauntered over toward him in an Izod T-shirt with holes in it.

"You know that's right. Winter'll soon be here."

"Why ain't you in school?" Loose Tooth asked, strictly to give him static.

"Half-day. Teacher conference," Tavon joked without missing a beat. So black he was practically blue, with his long arms and bowed legs, he looked like an awkward praying mantis. He attended – well, attended was a strong word, but he made a pretense of going to – Crispus Attucks High School as a held-back senior. He couldn't even get a social promotion. The system simply waited for him to drop out. School meant nothing to him, his future even less. Playing at being "gangsta" until he started fiending his own product, he fell to the lure, the allure, of the streets. Now he was half a tout, a one-man walking billboard for new product.

"Ain't this the third conference this week?" Loose Tooth joked. "You got another one o' those?"

"Nah, it's my last one," Tavon said, guiltily tucking the rest of his pack deeper into his pocket. Give away one, might as well give away the whole pack. If Tavon had been holding some candy, he wouldn't have bothered with the lame lie. Loose Tooth – born Earl Anderson, one-time prince of the streets who called himself CashMoney – would've sniffed it out. Though he probably knew that Tavon had some more squares, he didn't press the matter. He was a one man 411, old for the streets – well, over forty anyway – and quick to remind anyone "look here youngblood, I'm the last of these cats out here."

"Got a quarter?" Loose Tooth asked, obviously hoping to score a single cigarette down at the Korean's store.

"Please. I'm out here hustlin' just like you." Tavon put his cigarette out in the crumbling cement.

No one flinched at the reports of a few gunshots: too far away to be concerned about. Not as bad as New Year's Eve when that shit sounded like the 4th of July. The shots, however, drove a light-skinned and freckled young man down the street toward them. With a slight limp, his half-strut and Harlem Globetrotters gear was recognizable even without that pinched reserve the bow-tie-wearing set had.

"Ah, hell," Loose Tooth whispered when he saw him.

(120 Degrees of) Knowledge Allah. "Brothas."

"What's up, Knowledge?" Tavon asked.

"That's right, today's mathematics is knowledge. Let me break it down for you: know the ledge." Knowledge Allah was a fixture in the neighborhood even if no one knew much about him. When he first started coming around, all Loose Tooth offered was his theory that "Black folks always thinkin' they superheroes or somethin', needin' a secret identity."

"Here we go. Why you even got to say 'boo' to him?" Loose Tooth asked.

The problem with Knowledge Allah was that you had to know the code of his language before he made any sense. And it was too difficult to decipher codes while high, or looking to get high.

"You don't know who you are," Knowledge Allah said. "Take on your true name. Arm. Leg. Leg. Arm. Head. You are the original man. You are gods. Yet you sit here, blind, deaf, and dumb to your potential."

"I sit here wanting to get high," Loose Tooth growled.

"They set snares that have been prepared for you. Snares meant to lead you from your path of righteousness. You've let them cave you."

"They who?" Tavon asked.

"Don't ask him questions," Loose Tooth chided. "If you ignore him, he'll bounce sooner."

"Your so-called grafted government's behind it," Knowledge Allah continued undeterred. "The next phase is to destroy us. You think it stopped with Tuskegee? No, they just got slicker. We don't have poppy fields. We don't have planes. We don't have labs. They put chemicals in everything, destroying you cell by cell. Turning you."

"Sounds like we don't have shit," Loose Tooth said, nudging Tavon. But Tavon listened intently, a little too polite for his own good. He enjoyed the way Knowledge Allah spoke. He loved the idea of big ideas, even ones that he didn't agree with or didn't get. There was something about the way Knowledge Allah appeared. Maybe it was a by-product of his high, but if he caught Knowledge Allah out the corner of his eye, he looked different.

"Don't get caught in the game of the eighty-five It didn't stop with Tuskegee," Knowledge Allah said, either out of steam or wishing to move on to a more receptive congregation. "It's all about the third eye. Remember who you are. G is the seventh letter made."

Before Knowledge Allah had strolled even partway down the block, the slow roll of the squad car – once a half-hour – paused their conversation. Timeout. The officers, that cracka devil and house nigga pair, engaged them in a mutual eye fuck, challenging their right to the corner. Their glare read contempt, but it, too, was part of the game.

"What's all the drama about?" Loose Tooth asked.

"Someone probably shot Trevant," Miss Jane said. Her breasts hung like floppy hound ears, the nipples poking through her grungy golf shirt. When times got hard, she was the neighborhood ho, but times were rarely that hard for her. She had a hunter's instinct and had been known to run game on folks. Only in her late twenties, practically fifty in street years, she was the picture of a haggard party girl, partied out. Rail thin, many wondered if she had the bug.

"Who would waste a bullet on him?" Tavon asked.

"Probably got shot up over selling burn bags. Everyone told him to quit sellin' that Arm & Hammer shit so often," Loose Tooth said.

"Yeah, he'll be back on it in a few days." Miss Jane focused on Tavon. "Tae, lemme hold twenty for a minute."

Tavon did the ghetto math. A minute in CP time was bad enough, but in fiend time, shit, that money was hitchhiking to Neverland. Besides, it was time to go. He could parlay aluminum cans into vials with the industry of a fiend. "No need. It's time to go to work."

Negotiating the minefield of broken bottles, newspapers, cigarette butts, stray couch cushions, and burnt-bottomed bottle caps, Tavon and Loose Tooth stalked through the alleys that were the arteries of Li'l Nam. The hunger drove them. Tavon didn't even know he had a habit until the first day it wasn't around. Now all he had was the hustle, the part of the game that had its own adrenaline rush. Always thinking of the latest dope-fiend move and its accompanying childlike thrill; like when he was a kid and used to boost Star Wars figures from Toys "R" Us or smuggle comic books out of Lindner's Ice Cream Shop to read then sell.

They scanned the streets for any house undergoing any kind of remodeling. Their hopes were dashed after their escapades on Talbot Street. Rumors of the city's plans to redevelop the area had already made it fashionable for young yuppie couples and homosexuals to buy up the old, stylized homes. Talbot was now a show street – a well-patrolled show street – but when it was first being gutted, fiends were all over the place. Contractors couldn't walk into a house for thirty seconds without all their tools being stripped from their trucks. Copper piping grew legs and walked off every night. The discriminating fiend, such as Tavon, even took off with antique fixtures.

But niggas got too bold.

The story went that some contractors spent the day putting up siding on a house. They came back the next day and the siding had been stripped off and by strange coincidence, the Jenkins' place a few blocks up had about a day's worth of new siding on their house. After that, lockdown: constant patrols and overnight guards.

After a half-hour of scooping up aluminum cans, Tavon was the first to hear it. He caught Loose Tooth's attention and the two of them crept behind the bushes to get a better look at the scene. Dollar and his boys squared off against Miss Jane and her latest dupe.

Tavon knew Dollar, from another life it seemed. They were childhood friends, having grown up in Section 8 housing back when the Phoenix was still called the Meadows, back when life was all potential. He lived two houses down from Tavon, but they might as well have shared a room for all the time they spent together. In another circumstance, Tavon might have admitted to loving him. Boys never said such things, but they fit, despite how most thought they shouldn't. They liked different teams, different television shows, different music. But they shared copies of *Player* magazine stolen from his dad's closet. They skipped classes together. They ran from the police, after hitting a passing squad car with rocks, together. They played roof tag, diving into snow banks during the thick of winter. Always together.

Dollar gave himself his own nickname, reasoning that it was better to fashion your own legend than

leave it to chance. Soft-spoken and calm, he turned
cold and all the way hard, embracing the quiet un-
nerving certainty of the inevitable. He had an
upper-management resume that anyone could admire: he monitored sales and mitigated product loss
(no one messed up a count or snorted his product on
his watch); he tabulated product (handled distribution); he invoiced shipping (got a package, broke it
down, and re-upped); he arranged staff (set up lookouts, runners, touts); he organized and motivated
staff (often by the barrel of a gun, but mostly by the
implied threat of such); and he oversaw several
branches (ran two corners – here and at Breton
Court – and had his eye on a high rise). And he was
a marketing genius. He was all about brand names,
having successfully launched Widowmaker (it
helped that it had been spiked and killed a few fiends
the first day. Fiends flocked to it the next day, assuming that their dead friends simply couldn't handle
their high); and all the fiends were a-buzz about his
new product launch, Black Zombie (call the fiends
what they were and they would still snatch it up).
So excited, that it led one of the more ingenious
fiends, namely Miss Jane (behind the body of her
dupe) to sell burn bags with the Black Zombie skull
and crossbones stamp.

Tavon had seen this kind of Mexican stand-off before. Dollar – with his roughneck gait, all stiff-legged
and locked jaw – waited wordlessly with his hard
stare. A pantomime of threat, neither side could back
down without losing face, though Miss Jane had a

lot more to lose than face. She and her stick-figure physique had only daring for strength, her implied craziness returning his cold glare. She brazenly stood eye-to-eye, even leaning into Dollar's boy, Prez. A bold tactic for sure, but someone had to pay for this sojourn into Dollar's market.

Dollar gave a rueful nod.

With a rancorous snarl, his boys pushed Miss Jane to the side and sprang on the fool who still held the forged product in his hands. He raised a lone hand, a drowning man beneath a tidal wave of fists. Tavon turned his head from the worst of it, settling for listening to the sounds of weakening frantic pleas and the thwacks of flesh pummeling flesh. Loose Tooth scrambled for a better view. Not a peep from Miss Jane. She was a hard one. When Tavon turned to look again, Dollar had his back to the display. He'd settled into an odd posture, as if resenting his own soldiers. They were the new breed, who enjoyed violence for violence's sake. They didn't care because they had no future, no connection to anyone beyond themselves.

"Don't let me catch you again," Dollar said, pulling on a pair of gloves as Miss Jane scuttled down the alley. She didn't even help her played paramour to his feet, but he nipped at her heels anyway. Dollar muttered, "Dusty-ass heifer."

By all rights, Miss Jane earned a beat down. It wasn't like Dollar's crew was above hurting women, but not in Dollar's presence. Tavon wondered if the rumors were true about Miss Jane and her boy being untouchable.

Dollar and Tavon were the only family each other had, really. Most of the kids on their block regarded Tavon as soft; he always had problems hitting other people. Dollar, on the other hand, loved it. He thought of Tavon as a dog, faithful, following him around only for the beggin' bits he had, or rather, the vials at his disposal. Even if Tavon turned on him, as all bitches eventually did, all Tavon was capable of was the occasional buzz of an irritating gnat.

Dollar dropped out of school to pursue his ambitions, which involved a lot of sitting on a front stoop, running the streets and getting his head up in chronic. Tavon joined him. It was like they ran out of imagination and couldn't see a life for themselves outside of the streets, like they didn't have any ideas about what to do.

"You can come out now, Tae," Dollar said casually. His boys reached into their waistbands, but Dollar waved them off.

"How'd you know we was here?" Tavon asked, Loose Tooth standing silently behind him.

"My alley. You see anything interesting?"

"Naw." Especially not anything he'd report back to the police.

"Good. How about I set you all up tonight. Testers for the new line. Come morning you all spread the word that Black Zombie's the shit."

"For old times' sake?"

"Yeah, for old times' sake."

• • •

Michaela hated being referred to as one of the Durham Brothers. But life was all about marketing and the Durham Brothers was a solid brand. Not that she was ladylike, but she hated being discounted as a male because she rolled harder than most thugs she ran across. Michaela was the elder by thirteen seconds, though it might as well have been a decade the way she lorded it over her brother, Marshall. Neither she nor her brother were attractive in any way, she accepted that, with their pug noses beneath eyes too small for their large heads. Jagged scars, like lightning bolts, crossed each side of their faces. Because of their constant flop sweat, their long hair stuck to their foreheads. They could each stand to lose fifty pounds. A half-dozen deodorizers dangled from the rearview mirror of their Ford Focus. Each of them had drowned themselves in cologne. Incense choked the air of their room, yet a musky, earthy odor clung to them despite their best efforts.

Rarely separated, the Durham Brothers stood equally tall, their muscles filled out their gray Armani suits which they wore awkwardly, not quite comfortable in their latest image choice. Every encounter – other drivers at a stop light, any jostling in a crowded room, little old ladies at church – was taken as a challenge from all around them which usually resulted in a beatdown. Their father was not from around there, so they were told. Their mother was on the slow train to Crackville, which was why they killed her. And ate her.

To be honest, Michaela was surprised when she got the call from Dred. It wasn't as if they had parted on the best terms. To hear Dred tell it, Michaela and Marshall were brood vipers prone to attacking whoever was about whenever they felt underused or underappreciated. The cost of doing business with them, he said. Michaela saw it differently. Dred played his family close, from Baylon to a few other members, keeping them in a tight circle around him. Everyone else he treated like second-class citizens. So no matter how much she or her brother tried to do to demonstrate their loyalty, they were always on the outside looking in. Of course, that was enough to make any man, or woman, snap after a while.

Granted, maybe Marshall didn't need to burn Dred's stash house down or try to spread the man's business on the streets, but Marshall could be less than reasonable once he built up a head full of steam. His was a scorched-earth policy for even the slightest perceived infraction, which often left him ass out because once you've scorched enough earth, you found that you had no place to plant new seed. Sooner or later, they'd have to come crawling back to Dred, all contrite and apologetic, trying to make good, and the cycle would begin again.

They pulled into the school parking lot. A couple of Green's troops played dice at the side of the building.

"What do you think?" Michaela asked. "Should we say 'hi'?"

"They don't look like much."

"No, I suppose they wouldn't. I hear Green's over them."

"Green, huh?" Marshall sneered.

"They look more impressive now?"

"Not really. I've always wondered about Green."

"They say he eternal."

"They who?" Marshall remained unimpressed. His sluggish thoughts flowed toward the mundane of when they were going to eat or where they were going to crash that night.

"I guess they who survive those who didn't outlive him."

"I'd like to test that sometime." He punched his left fist into his right hand, imagining a set of brass knuckles crunching into a jaw.

"I'm sure you'll get your chance before too long."

Omarosa stood in front of the full-length mirror admiring the figure before her, not entirely satisfied with her make-up. Her eyes the color of frost on grass, matted by her cream-complected oval face and crowned by her freshly done braids; she hadn't quite attained her "you can't get with this face" and as such continued her tireless primping. A mix of both woman and fey, she now employed the glamour known as science to accomplish her will.

The time and attention spent by someone who accomplished her business by not being seen was an irony that eluded her. Vanity was an inherited trait of her people as was her gift with any weapon. And she had some serious creep to her. Her twin brother was an assassin of the first order, while she preferred life closer to the streets. Life was all about illusion. She read the streets better than anyone, hoarding intelligence like an information magpie. True pros kept little piles of clothes in the gangway or along the side of the building in case they were going to be out a couple of days or needed to appear in court. The girls were just as invisible as junkies; except with them, instead of a person, people saw a searching dimebag. No one ever saw Omarosa actually take a john, but because she worked the stroll, they assumed her to be a pro. She did little to dissuade them, going so far as to dress in fishnet hose under a blue jean miniskirt. Her cashmere jacket kept her plenty warm.

A warm, breezy fall night, churning the humidity stirred by the low-lying gray clouds threatening a chance of rain. It was as if someone blew hot breath about. Omarosa leaned against the brick façade of the old Bank One building. Though the chain had been bought out by Chase, this particular branch across the street from the Phoenix Apartments building was simply closed rather than renovated. From her vantage point, the comings and goings of the Phoenix opened itself up to her. She absently twirled a set of handcuffs around her index finger then caught them, spinning them with a flourish before "holstering" them. Her inner gunslinger satisfied, she clicked the jaws of one side through, letting the clink of each tooth settle before continuing.

• • •

Hypnotized by her poise, Lee McCarrell watched her. His stomach rumbled as he set up to watch this latest player. Just south of her position, in the rear of the old Bank One parking lot, an open driveway entrance had been blocked off by cement barricades to prevent parked loitering. Folks stole the other one so they could still come and go as they pleased. Situated behind a row of trees, the northbound traffic along Sherman Drive couldn't see him.

On the TIPS line, a woman who refused to give her name claimed to have seen two young black men exchanging a gun. The younger of the two walked toward the back of a man, took aim with the gun turned on its side, and fired. The man, once he realized he wasn't hit, took off running. The shot went through the window of the Walker family. The crime scene unit's investigation had come to a similar conclusion and a hunt was underway for the anonymous woman as well as the man who apparently never saw a thing, but thanked God for a wannabe gangsta's poor aim.

Not officially on duty, he had no business at the Phoenix Apartments – a white boy no less – unless he were out to score. He tired of Octavia pointing out his lack of street intelligence. According to her, he had to learn to talk to people, to read the streets. "A detective is only as good as his informants," and he hadn't cultivated many. Yet he kept watching her, even found himself lighting up a cigarette to help while away the time. A potential john approached her. To his surprise, a sudden wave of

protectiveness for her enveloped him. He forgot all
about food.

Omarosa sensed the man long before he made himself visible. His nervous gait betrayed him, his palms
sweating so much he had to shove them in his pockets. From his approach, she calculated that she could
cripple him six different ways.

"How much?" he asked.

Omarosa laughed both at his effrontery as well as
his nerve. Were she a common whore, she would
still demand someone who'd bathed at least once
this week and who didn't share his clothes with lice.

"How much for what?"

"A debate about politics. What do you think? Say
a half and half."

Obviously her game must be off. Once stationed
here, even the regular girls stayed away from her.
Dealers, fiends, everyone left her alone. Either he
was too high, too bold, or too stupid to live, but she
was in a charitable mood.

Her elbow jutted into his neck with enough force
to render him unconscious before his body hit the
ground. She followed through the balletic turn of her
movement with a raised knee to his groin which
lobbed him into the air. A roundhouse high snap
kick sent him flying into the shadows of the parking
lot.

The lights of a squad car flared to life. Lee McCarrell pulled his car into the lot, his surveillance
distracted by the street beef. Cigarette smoke issued

from his window as it rolled down. Letting him see she was unarmed, she approached with a cautious confidence, and rested her forearms on the lip of the window.

"So what are you, this week's offender, victim, or witness?" Lee asked.

"No problem here, detective. Merely a girl defending her honor against the lecherous advance of someone mistaking her for a whore."

"Guess that makes you the victim."

"I'm no one's victim. My, such an awfully cynical attitude."

"These are cynical times."

"I know. No room for magic in anyone's soul." Omarosa shifted allowing a better view of her cleavage.

"Magic?" Lee's eyes obliged her gesture.

"Everyday magic. Like, say, a chance encounter between a man and a woman who hit it off immediately. That spark, that fortune, that synchronicity of crossed paths."

"The magic," Lee repeated, his voice faraway. Entranced by her beauty. There was something different about this girl. Something enchanting. Intoxicating. The longer she lingered the more she seemed to fill up his mind. Already the hump who had his ass handed to him faded into the mists of distant memory. Lee's standard credo, how anything could happen at any moment on the streets, fell by the wayside, his guard dropping despite himself.

"Exactly. I'm sure this isn't the worst thing you've ever seen."

"Not the worst things I'd seen by half."

Words tumbled out of his heart to this stranger as if they were long-time lovers. "This one time I was called to a scene where a new mother hadn't slept in three days. You could see it in her face, all drawn and gray, even the rings around her eyes had rings. She received no support from friends or family. I don't even know for sure if she had either. Too many people find themselves alone and when a baby comes along, they don't know what to do with this intrusion into their personal space. So she chopped up her baby and left the pile of limbs in the center of her bed. She just stood there, blood all over her as if someone else had come in and did it. She turned to me and said that she still wanted another baby. A chance to prove that she could be a good mother."

"I guess we all want second chances." Omarosa met his gaze. Her intensity made his insides squirm.

"So what are you doing out here if you aren't working the stroll?"

"I'm merely an observer of life's little games. A people-watcher. And the Phoenix gives me plenty to watch."

"Is that so? I always thought that we ought to go in, bust some heads, and send those assholes a message." Lee backed up, suddenly aware of her blackness, despite her hypnotic green eyes. "That's not racist: if someone's an asshole, I'm gonna treat them like an asshole, because assholishness knows no color. It's not my fault most everyone out here's an asshole."

"Most." Omarosa smiled, a delicious curve to her lips. She had watched the detective and his partner staking out Dred's crew for a while now, but she hadn't guessed the gang mess had wormed its way so under his skin that he'd taken to working it on his own time. Or maybe... maybe his partner had gotten into his head. Omarosa was never one to pass up an opportunity. "Now the way I see it, you're a real man. I'm tired of all these wannabe hoodlums trying to play hard. Want to talk that 'whose dick is this?' mess out one side of their mouth and talk about how women ain't nothing but tricks and gold diggers out the other. Like there's any gold to be found in them trifling fools other than in they mouth.

"I need a real man. One who knows how to handle a woman who's been bad. One who can put me in my place, not let me walk all over him like I'm better than him. Who do I think I am? I'm no better than any other of these... well, you know. You deserve better.

"So, you want to ride my black ass? Take me down a few notches?"

Lee's heart thudded so hard it pained his chest. His saliva turned thick, he suddenly found it difficult to swallow. His palms slickened as they rested on the steering wheel. He leaned over, opened the passenger side door, and she climbed in.

# CHAPTER EIGHT

Baylon tugged at his crotch, adjusting the fit of his pants, primping in the mirror. Long sleeves made him invisible. In long sleeves he was straight, a nine to five working man who no one would give a second glance to. Hair cut low, but without flash, no gold, no grill, no tattoos, he could walk into any church or office or restaurant or store and be treated as Joe A. MiddleClassCitizen.

For this meeting, he went with short sleeves. The short sleeves showed he'd been working out, made him appear harder. He scratched the head of his pit bull. Even his dog was more affectation than necessity. His troops needed to see him as the shot caller, second only to Dred in word and deed. As it stood, they begrudgingly followed orders and too often challenged his authority by asking to hear them from Dred himself. It boiled down to how he carried himself. Maybe he would never escape Griff's long shadow.

"Yeah, you still the fairest one of them all,

nigga." Griff sidled next to him, examining his reflection up and down in the mirror. "But you'll
never be me."

"I know." Baylon spritzed on some cologne.

"You don't have the heart."

"I know."

"Your men sense it."

"Then I'll have to make them... respect the office."

The house leaned between two others just like it.
King, Wayne, and Lott observed the comings and goings without a plan. They just wanted more
information. If Michelle had a bounty on her, it had to
come from one of the local dealers. His neighborhood
was under assault and he had not taken notice of it
until now. A young man approached another, neither
out of high school. The one palmed the cash, slid into
his pocket, while he scanned the streets. A smooth,
practiced move.

A group of young boys gathered only a half-block
away. Fixed with industrial intent, they tore strips of
newspaper into dollar sized scraps. They took their
assembled "bills" and fashioned wads for themselves. They'd pull it out of their pocket and peel off
a couple bills to one another. One took his stack and
threw it into the air to the chants of *"Make it rain"*.

And King's heart seethed.

Before he was aware of himself, he strode toward
the men.

• • •

Austere but clean, the brown walls had a greasy film *to* them, like a kitchen with a long history of deep-frying everything. A tinge of smoke in the air mixed with faint fumes of alcohol. A cracked fixture filtered cold light into the room, casting a yellowish pallor. The electric money counter unattended on the counter, they were on the count, their duties interrupted by a tryst. Junie straddled the couch, one leg sprawled over the back. He sat alone, god of the couch, master of all he surveyed. Waiting for Parker to finish. His fatigue pants around his ankles, he was laying pipe to a jump-off girl, pumping furiously in plain view, a voyeuristic thrill heightening his performance. Junie squinted at the girl, trying to place her. These tricks started to blur together after awhile.

Junie loved that boy after his fashion, conjuring vague plans for Parker's future, but also hated him. Hated him for making him see himself. As he was, not who he dreamt he was.

"You bout done over there?"

"I don't give a fuck. You feel me? I don't give," Parker retorted in close to an insulting tone. "A. Fuck." Tall, but skinny. Heartless, he had done had all the life damn near ground out of him. His smile, even his laugh, was joyless. He could shoot or otherwise inflict all manner of cruelty without a moment's hesitation. He was perfect. The secret to enforcement wasn't a matter of the most intimidating body, but the precision of the coldest heart.

Parker carried around his share of pain, let it accrue in his belly until it knotted the muscles in his shoulders. Pain he was all too happy to dish out. Not one for confession, he was one of those mute motherfuckers, just as soon turn to an icy glare and stone lips rather than admit to anything personal or true. Stoic silence was his definition of holding his head up. Of being a man. He'd never admit to anything like abuse. Bitches were abused. Yet when he was eleven, a friend of his mother's came to stay at their house. It was how family did, drop in and board with their people for a minute as they pass through. Every night the woman secretly summoned Parker to her room. Three raps against the wall separating Parker's room from his sister's. Each night. As his sister slept in the next bed, the woman had him go down on her. His first sexual experience outside of nutting off to his father's stash of *Player* magazines. She had no special love for or attachment to him. During the days, she dismissed him, choosing to talk only to adults. Beyond the initial conversation where she told him how special he was, asked him if he thought she was pretty, and asked him if he wanted to prove how much he liked her, they never even shared a knowing wink. The age difference didn't matter. Nor the fact that she didn't let him get off. He was a means to an end. An instrument of her gratification. She taught him everything he needed to know about sex. And put to death the idea of love.

He never told his friends. The bragging of his tryst with an older woman, no matter how he cast it, rang hollow to his ear. All it brought up was the feeling of powerlessness. Of weakness, of being a bitch. He buried it alongside the other memories, like the leather strap of his father when he was due to be punished.

"I just don't give a fuck." The words had become his personal mantra. Half prayer, half braggadocio, he announced his climax not caring that Junie was in the room. Junie tossed him an admiring smile and knew they would fist bump later recalling the events. The money-hungry ho who still chicken-headed in his lap swallowed his seed without complaint. She was faceless, a walking fix waiting to score, a convenient orifice to empty into. Something akin to pride stirred within Junie as he dismissed the girl with the turn of his back and the hitching of his pants.

"We got to wrap this up and turn the count over to the Durham Brothers."

"Them some ugly-ass Samoans."

"You need to learn when to back down and when to step it up," Junie said in a low, warning tone. Parker was an eager student, one who looked up to Junie, and admiration was a powerful intoxicant.

They trod downstairs where the Durhams discussed a matter with Baylon. Junie and Parker waited to the side, not interrupting. Baylon waved them in. Junie wasn't too fond of the Durham Brothers, but respected their rep. Michaela with her purple hair and matching shirt over a pair of blue jeans towered over Baylon. Her brother, Marshall, sported a set of chops which looked like he glued two hedgehogs to either side of his face. Ridiculous appearance aside, their penchant for the most brutal of violence to the human body was well documented. Rumor whispered that they occasionally ate their kill. From Michaela's recent weight gain, he assumed Baylon had them out on assignment.

"What's with the hair?" Junie tried to forage for any humanity in her eyes to reassure him, but found no trace. Her jowly face, the extra waddle about her throat, the girth of her belly failed to make her any less a killer.

"Needed a change in my look," Michaela said.

"I don't think a haircut's gonna do it. Plus, purple—"

"Draws too much attention?"

"I think you've got that covered too."

Baylon made some mild clucking noises. Junie was never fond of him. He had a way about him, let folks know he didn't think much of them. Condescending, like they didn't know nearly as much as he did. His ass never held a gun. His ass never did any jail. His ass never did anything beside talk. He acted awfully superior for someone who was simply Dred's errand boy.

"Damn girl, you packed on a few pounds," Parker said with the brazen fearlessness of youth. Or psychosis.

"It's not polite to talk about a girl's weight." She flashed him an eye warn.

"Since when you so sensitive?"

"I'm a flower. I'm a delicate flower who's gained five dress sizes in the last year and is pretty pissed about it."

"Need to work off a few calories?" Parker tossed

her the taped-down grocery bag full of cash.

Full of hate and wariness, Marshall leaned near Junie's ear. His fetid breath reeked of decayed carcasses. He smacked in his ear with a wet gurgle. "We get called in for special jobs. The man says come up, we come up. The man says make this delivery for me, package gets delivered. The man says handle this here problem, the problem gets handled. Do we have a problem here?"

"We don't have shit," Baylon said, feeling suddenly pressed in. "You got a delivery to make. I got an errand to run."

"You hooking up with Griff?"

"Not that you need to know, but yeah. You two hold down the fort. Don't need any unnecessary drama tonight."

That was the night everything went to shit.

*Griff stood guard while Baylon slipped into the house. He* didn't know who was such a threat to Dred who might have lived out here. One of those transitional houses used for homeless teens to get off the streets. Baylon was hit with that critical self-assessment of living in Griff's shadow. Having no heart, no respect, no gravitas. He skulked about the house, every bit as dangerous as Griff or Tavon or even Junie, but he lacked some essential intangible. The focused will to survive, oblivious to the lives of others, he lacked. The single-mindedness, the ruthlessness. Intelligence and prudence, on the other hand, he had in spades. Out here, if you were going to make it, all you had was your name, your word, and your rep. Without heart, you were nothing. And Baylon needed to show heart.

The first door on the left, a soft light revealed the outline of a door. He pushed it open. A young woman rifled through some cabinets. Under a furred jacket she wore a black Korn T-shirt and had five friendship bracelets on each hand. An acne scar dotted the middle of her forehead giving her a vaguely Indian appearance. Blue jeans – bell-bottoms in his day, flare cut these days – with ragged edges barely covered her ragged Chuck Taylors.

"Who are you?" he asked.

"Who are you?" she retorted, unstartled and without making eye contact.

"Michelle."

Davis. Michelle Davis. Baylon expected a prostitute, maybe a burnout crack whore, someone who had run game one time too often or stolen money and had to pay the final piper. Not some fresh-faced girl no older than his niece. She reached into her rich, furred coat and fondled the hilt of her knife.

"We match." Baylon pulled up his shirt and revealed his knife.

"Where'd you get that?"

"My father gave it to me."

"I never knew my father," Michelle said.

"Not all of us are so lucky," Baylon said. "A pretty girl you. It isn't right for you to have such... teeth."

"I ain't got no choice out here. A girl's got to be

able to take care of herself. I'll carry it until I find someone good enough to take it from me."

"Someone good enough to make you feel safe?"

"Something like that. You know King?"

Baylon bristled at the name. "We go back a ways."

"What's he like?"

"He a'ight."

"Seriously."

"He's good people. Means well. Big heart," Baylon admitted. "But, damn, he has this way about him. Where you always feeling judged. Like no matter what you're doing, he expects more. Better."

"That sounds like a good thing. Someone who believes in you and pushes you."

"Unless you're being pushed off the edge."

"No one doubts your heart. No one other than you."

Her amber-colored eyes pierced him as if reading his soul. No attitude. No stiffness. No fear. She bared her teeth to let him know she could handle herself but let the conversation play out. Baylon found himself intrigued by her. On the flip side, one quality Baylon didn't lack was the fact that he was headstrong. And he had just decided that Michelle was either "unable to be found" or otherwise not going to be killed. At least until he learned what her offense might be. Once he got an idea in his head, he ran it into the ground without looking or thinking. As if he couldn't change course even if it meant his destruction.

"Damn, man, what's taking you so long?" Half out

of breath, Griff poked his head into the room and spoke with a hurried whisper. "Oh, I see. This a private party?"

"Naw man, nothing like that. Let's roll," Baylon said.

"Naw, naw. We got a minute." Griff's eyes were without hope but swam with complete malignancy, shark's eyes. He walked around with so much pain, trying to figure out a way to make it all go away. His shirt loose to hide the gun in his waistband, he closed the door behind him.

"Come on man, let's go."

"Not till your big brother has a taste."

"It ain't like that. You can't..." Baylon put his hands on him to get him out the door. Griff laid a feral glare on him, promising that Baylon, Baylon's kids, and Baylon's kids' kids should line up and apologize for the effrontery. Baylon released him and raised his hands in a "my bad" gesture.

"You always did have trouble sharing."

The strange look on Griff's face, hungry and predatory, made Baylon anxious. Griff touched one of Michelle's tendrils of hair, a gentle caress flush with intent. Her braless breasts pert and at attention, he could trace the curve of her back through her threadbare outfit. Stifling a lascivious grin, he stepped to her, the heat of him wafting off in waves. He grazed her cheek with his finger, an intimate gesture, one too reminiscent, to Baylon's mind, of an owner with his dog. Griff all but let her take in his scent, but she slapped his hand away.

"Oh, it's like that is it?" Griff asked.

"It's like that," she said, too defiant. Unafraid of him.

Baylon winced. Griff had changed over the last few months. Became harder, an impressive feat as he was already one of the hardest men Baylon knew. However, not just harder, but colder. And he didn't brook women telling him "no".

Griff smiled seductively. An icy laugh. He grabbed her arm and jerked her to him. She raked her fingernails across his face and drew her knife. The thing about knives, to Baylon's mind, was they showed more heart than a gun. Any fool could squeeze a trigger and blast. There was a distance to the killing. The death. To use a knife required one to be up close and personal. Angry and intent. They couched together, crashing to the ground. Wrestling over the knife. "NO!" Baylon shouted and jumped in, hoping to leverage the blade. He tried to take it from her or keep it from him. If anyone was to have it, it should be Baylon. She clung to it, desperate that he might hurt her with it. Griff released his hold. The blade pierced her with a soft gasp, driven into her body. Her hand dug into his arm, a lover in the throes of passion, and then released. Warm in his arms. So peaceful. He wished he could hold her forever. Her lifeless gaze not too different from Griff's everyday expression. Her blood smeared his clothes. Stained his hands. Baylon's senses left him. The sorrow hit him like a blow to the chest, his heart heavy with shame and grief.

"Come on, man," Griff announced, a kid whose

dinner had been spoiled. "We gotta get out of here."

Baylon took the knife, the proud owner of a matching set.

Laying naked next to Omarosa, Lee became suddenly self-conscious of how much his bed smelled like ball sweat and cheap aftershave. The sheets were rough and stiff, not fit for a woman like her. Omarosa slept barely making a sound, little more than an observed presence in his bed. That was the only way he could think to describe her. As if he took his eyes from her, she'd disappear, a wisp in the night. So he stayed up watching the gentle rise and fall of her chest. Taking in her scent. Listening for the sound of her slightest stirring.

"I'm awake, you know. I'm not going to disappear on you."

"I'm trained police. I specialize in finding folks intent on disappearing."

"That what you were doing at the Phoenix?" Omarosa asked.

"Nah, I was looking at you."

"Ah, the fates conspiring for us to meet." She curled up, the sheet wrapped around her. A portrait of seduction, her every movement was choreographed to elicit an effect from him.

"Something like that." Lee sat up. He never imagined himself bedding a black girl. His mind focusing on the black part of her description, he rolled the idea around in his head. Not that he bought into the stereotypes of black people's sexual prowess. He contented himself with knowing what to do with what he had. "What do you do?"

"Do you care or is that some residual Protestant guilt rearing its head?"

"Catholic. Very residual."

"Do you even remember my name? No, never mind, don't strain yourself." Her voice little more than a low purr, she made him feel both inadequate and important at the same time. "What do you know about dogs?"

"They bark, shit, eat, and sleep," Lee said.

"They fight, too."

"Not legally."

"How often do you stake out for legal operations?"

"What are you getting at?"

"I just hear tell of a dog-fighting ring."

"Not my beat."

"So you'd think. You gang task force."

"How'd you–"

"I know things," Omarosa said. "Now, who do you think runs the dog fights?"

"I'm listening."

"Lots of rules go into these things so that shit don't accidentally jump off."

"Even police."

"Po-po go where they go. Can't be helped. Cost of doing business."

"So you know where one of these fights is going to be held?"

"Maybe. But I'll take some convincing to give it

up."

Suddenly uncomfortable, he didn't know if he was capable of anything approaching tender.

But the thought of her riding him again rekindled an erection.

Junie didn't know how things got so out of control so quickly. One minute he and Parker chilled in the house, getting their heads up with a little weed, catching up on television. The next, raised voices outside put him on high alert. Donning his professional grimace, he stormed outside to see if there was a problem. Two camps of men squared off, beefing over the corner. He didn't have time to sort through the nonsense. Locked in an aggressive lope, he peeled off a couple rounds. The men scattered.

"Night!" one of them called out. "I got you. Get behind me."

The blood drained from his face. His sallow and wasted complexion reflected in the car window, full of hate and wariness. Oh shit. Did I just fire at Night? The full realization left his legs weakened. He forced himself to a steady gait. Duplicity he learned was in his own nature. With a level voice he called out, "Dred says hello, motherfucker."

He watched his head, making sure he wasn't seen. It wasn't much of a plan, but better the shit not fall back on him. His was already a life of a false resignation. A false life filled with scorn.

Junie knew when he first learned to carry the mix of

rage and shame. In fourth grade, his teacher, Mrs Crider, a bun-haired brunette with a pinched face and aristocratic manner, made him a member of the safety patrol. This was back in the day when fellow students wore white sashes and were given badges and were charged with seeing their fellow students across the streets. This was a matter of high prestige, and short of student council or making the honor roll, only the most responsible or favored were chosen for the function. Junie was neither. Instead, as he could only surmise later, that Mrs Crider attempted to reach him. To give him a connection to the idea of school and his fellow students. It wasn't lost on him, even at the time, that his post was the most remote, where no student or quasi-responsible parent would allow their child to cross, especially escorted only by a three feet tall scrawny black kid with unkempt hair and questionable hygiene habits. Defying all odds, and despite Junie's reluctance, the blatant and transparent manipulation worked. He actually swelled with pride when the safety patrol was dismissed early and he rose as one of the chosen lot, eyes of his fellow classmates on him, to attend to his duties. Nor did he feel ridiculous, lone black boy at the ass end of an isolated stretch of road, barely within eyesight of the nearest safety patrol member, as he waved and returned the all-clear signal. It worked, that was, until like every else in Junie's life it turned to shit and was taken away from him.

As brilliant as Mrs Crider had been getting him to care about being responsible, she had a sizeable deficit when it came to sustaining that limited sense of self-esteem she had successfully fanned to life. One day in class, she called upon Junie to answer a question. Flustered at the sudden attention, he stammered about. Mrs Crider stood there, silent and waiting. The eyes of his fellow classmates pressed in on him. He grew so desperately nervous, he knocked his books and papers to the ground. They scattered with a furious, though unintentional, shower. Springing out of his chair, he fell to his knees to gather up the papers. That was when he heard her, Mrs Crider, laughing at him. He was so perfectly pathetic: lone black boy, white teacher looming over him, white classmates a chorus of open-mouthed laughter and finger-pointing. The words "fuck you" flew out of his mouth without thought, but they hung in the air like the empty echo of gunshot. The two little words stilled the laughter. Mrs Crider's eyes narrowed into an unforgiving glare and she sent him to the principal's office.

He never walked as a safety patrol member again.

Actually, he didn't walk as much of anything again. Whether he realized it or not, that was when the educational system lost him. He went through the motions of school for another four years or so, but he was already done. There was no reaching him after that. He had turned his back on the institution knowing that whatever path for his life he was to chart, it wouldn't be through any hallowed halls of higher learning.

And on quiet days in what passed for reflection for one Juneteenth Walker, he wondered how many Mrs Criders shut down countless Junies each day.

He retreated into the house.

"Any problems?" Parker asked.

"Just some nonsense," Junie said. "Nothing I couldn't handle."

Octavia Burke never lamented her quick rise in the ranks. She didn't have time for political games nor did she buy into either affirmative action or workplace racism. Either were self-defeating traps of a game she refused to play. Like her mother, she was nobody's victim. "You kiss butt, then you kick it." her mother always said, not one to pay attention to firsts either. First black nurse hired at Wishard Hospital. First black nurse promoted to department head. First black nurse elected to serve on the board. Strong and vital, nothing got in her way. Her fierce determination came at a cost. There was always a sadness about her, like she were missing out on something. She was always closed off, a cool aloofness she never intended with her children. Passed onto her children.

So when Octavia's first husband told her that she had trouble letting folks in, it came as no surprise. Nor was she surprised when he left.

She kicked her shoes off at the front door and hung her coat up. The house, silent and dark. A residual flow from upstairs, probably her second husband in bed watching television. Home was her oasis. Away from the madness of the office away from the detritus of the streets who took up so much of her time. She was happy to be home. It centered her and it saddened her that she spent so little time here. She continued her after-work ritual. Shoes, coat, then food. The microwave and oven were bereft of a plate of food. Whatever they had done for dinner didn't include her. The check-in calls of "when will you be home" were fewer and further between, tired of "I'll grab a bite on the way home" or "don't wait up, it's a long one".

Then the boys. Long asleep, she made a point of peeking in on them if only to reassure herself that they were still alive and that she could pick them out of a line-up. To each boy, she'd sit on the edge of his bed and stroke their hair. To let them know she was present and loved them, even if they weren't awake to know. The simple gesture allowed the day to drain out of her, all of the misery and hopelessness and futility of her work. And it was the only time they'd let her love on them anyway. They were getting so damn big.

Their marriage had hit a bad patch. Her long hours, the Job, were worse than having a man on the side. She suspected he filled the void of her absence with… someone. No, that wasn't fair. It wasn't in him. The only thing he filled himself with was quiet, festering resentment. Never going to bed at the same time. Letting the gulf between them fallow.

The television played coolly in the background. He watched an episode of that new medical drama she liked so much where all the oversexed doctors looked barely old enough to drive. It was a show they decided to watch together. Or so she thought.

Without betraying any hurt feelings, she walked into their bathroom to brush her teeth and closed the door. His passive-aggressive point having been made, he turned off the television. She came out wearing an old T-shirt. She slipped into her side of the bed. The same old night-time dance.

Percy watched the whole scene go down. The three men who confronted those soldiers, unarmed except for their bravery and determination. How the other man came out – another soldier, he could tell, but terrified of the men. Firing wildly because the men were true.

His heart soared.

Dred stood in the littered living room of the abandoned house the crew squatted in and used as a stash house. One hand in his pants pocket, he checked his watch on the other, a bored spectator with more pressing concerns. Griff loomed over the dope dealer they'd caught unawares. The man sat up in the ruined couch, its cushions missing and he in his boxers startled from the nap he was taking along its box springs.

At the other end of the room, the cushions were spread as a makeshift mattress, stained in blood, piss, and come, yet ready for business again. Baylon guarded the door, a careful eye on the streets.

"I don't think you hear me. B, are you having trouble understanding me?"

"I hear you just fine, Dred," Baylon said.

"Griff, am I not using the King's English correctly?"

"Like you was born to it."

"Then why is this group of fools operating in my neighborhood? Why do I have to come down here and see to some petty bullshit?"

"Some niggas are hard of skull. Maybe need their ears cleaned out," Griff said.

Truth was, Dred was in a mood to make his presence felt. Sometimes he couldn't resist a little knucklehead stuff. It was the life. He had several stops to make that required his personal touch. And he'd heard some disturbing whispers about Night. Word on the street was that he was setting up his own shop, had crews working on his watch and was lining up his own distribution. That was the only reason Dred's interest was alerted. He had the distribution into Indianapolis locked up. Even the Hispanic gangs came through him. He had tied things up nicely to where, though still new to the scene, little more than a name whispered among the operators – he doubted even the police had gotten onto him yet – he could step away from handling the product, short of major deals. Like the meeting he was soon to be late for. But before he became a complete ghost, he needed to personally rattle a few cages.

"Rent's due, motherfucker. That plain enough for you?"

"I'm just a wrong time, wrong place brother. This ain't even my joint." The man cupped his crotch and draped his chest with his other arm. "I hear you,

Dred. I didn't mean no disrespect."

"Is that a glamour working?" Dred asked, suddenly suspicious. He studied the man, searching for a flaw or telltale giveaway. "You the one been having women coming in and out of here at all times, like that ain't going to draw no notice. What you call yourself doing? Maximizing your resources? Running dope and girls? Hope you ain't fool enough to run guns, too. Griff?"

"I believe we have the night's proceeds." Griff held a paper bag loosely filled with cash. Not enough for Dred's notice, but enough for him to justify the diversion.

"What? We got a problem?"

"Nah," the man said.

"I think we got a problem."

With a strength and ferocity that surprised them all, Dred upended the couch and spilled the man onto the floor. Before the man could struggle to his feet, Dred straddled him, his hot breath steaming the man's face. Dred headbutted him into senselessness, then slapped him like he was a hooker short with his money. The man's nose exploded and covered his face with blood.

"Don't you ever," Dred said between subsequent slaps, "let me see you" slap "up in my territory" slap "without my explicit say so." Slap. "Explicit, motherfucker."

The man fell backward in a pool of his own blood. His heart unmoved, Baylon wondered how many women the man had similarly beaten. The man crawled, a dog in cowering retreat, taking a foot to his side from Dred.

"Dred, man, we got what we came for. If we're going to make that other thing..." Griff trailed off in half a sing-song voice. Griff had leap-frogged Baylon in the hierarchy. Nothing had been openly said but Baylon knew the deal.

The rituals and things he'd seen – things that were never explained nor even talked about – didn't bother Griff. He considered himself a need-to-know soldier. His brutally efficient fearlessness, and lack of questions, caused Dred to favor him in subtle ways. Tended to go to him first when something needed to be done. Seemed to favor his company outside of conducting business. Spoke of him quite favorably when he wasn't around. Things Baylon was certain was never done or said about him. The Ndibu led, it was still business as usual. Folks scurried to curry favor or step on the back of even their brother to get to the next level. There was no such thing as enough: not enough women, not enough money, not enough rep, not enough power. Discontent was its own raison d'être.

As Baylon saw things, Night had his own ambitions, they all did, but Night saw himself as the rightful heir to the throne of the streets and Dred as a pretender to it. Baylon's strategic thinking was what made him valuable to Dred, but not valuable enough. He was being pushed aside, reduced to a consigliere within his own crew.

Dred and Griff turned toward Baylon. After another check of the streets from the slit of the window beside the door, he nodded. Without instruction, Griff led the way, clutching the bag full of cash, knowing to keep money and product away from Dred. To insulate him. Dred followed. Baylon gave one last glance at the dope dealer who moaned as he crawled back onto the couch. Discarded as soon as he was inconvenient.

The dope dealer stared straight at him. "Sir Baylon, this is the boundary of your life. Turn back and you may save yourself." And with that, the man vanished.

Baylon imagined the trajectory of his life as him running. Running through a dark forest, heedless of what lay ahead, knowing that he couldn't remain where he was. His fate chased after him, undeterred and dogged, closing in on him like an inexorable curtain. He fought against the listing hopelessness. He stood on the precipice knowing the time to change ticked away quickly. He closed his eyes and waited, giving into his destiny.

The squeal of car tires shattered the night like a hunting horn signaling the death of their prey. The car slowed to a deliberate crawl. Griff released his hold on the paper bag, whatever warrior sense or maybe just in tune to the scent of violence and blood and death in the air alerting him to action. Without hesitation, he leapt between the approaching car and Dred. For his part, Dred stood there. Not frozen, as if the impending violence caught him short. No, he wore a different face. One of resignation. Of giving in to the inevitable. Of a time coming full circle.

Baylon withdrew his knife. The blade snapped to life with a sharp click.

From the lowered car windows, several gun barrels protruded. The first shot caught Griff before he could reach Dred. The shot caught him in the shoulder spinning him, then a second shot caught him in the side sending him towards Baylon. As Griff's body careened toward him, Baylon – perhaps on instinct, perhaps the knife had a will of its own, perhaps many things Baylon preferred to not think about – brought the knife to bear. It plunged into Griff's gut. His accusing eyes widened in shock, fresh pain atop his bullet wounds. He gripped Baylon's shirt, a desperate grasp which pulled him down on top of him. The action drove the blade deeper into him as they landed. Baylon cradled his head. The blood from the mortal cut covered his front. He peered into Griff's eyes until the light left them, but not before his countenance fixed in a look of knowing. There were no secrets from the dead.

Dred arced his fingers down in a wave. The night seemed to split, carved open with the gesture, eldritch shadows catching the first volley of bullets. A shotgun barrel leveled at him. Its thunderous report caused Baylon to cover Griff as if he could shield him from any further damage. The shrapnel tore through the arcane shield Dred had cast and caught him fully in his gullet. The blast knocked him from his feet.

The car sped off into the night.

Baylon stood, surveying the damage. Not realizing

his cell phone had found its way into his hand or that he had punched in the digits 9-1-1 and babbled non-sensically into it. He folded the knife and tossed it down a sewer grate until he could retrieve it later.

Baylon wondered if he had ever had an honest moment in his life. A time of perfect truth. The ritual of dressing in front of the mirror, the care he took in picking out his wardrobe, the fastidiousness of his look was so much wasted effort. He knew it. His men knew it.

"There it is." Baylon's arms hung at his side. He didn't know how long he had stood there, staring at his reflection as the memories overwhelmed him. "The cost of my sin."

"What sin?" Griff asked.

"Bad luck."

"All your wounds are self-inflicted."

His life was an inexorable spiral leading to a point he dreaded to think about. Somehow not thinking about it made its inevitability less real. Night and Dred. He and King. He and Griff. He and Michelle. There was no warranty on friendships. They began, they ended, each in their own season. And when they ended, the ripples of those relationships spread into the next. A cycle of pain he would continue to pay for.

"Sometimes I feel like it's cursed. Either of them."

"The knife?" Griff asked.

"Yeah. All it has ever brought is blood and trouble."

"The cost of defending yourself."

"But it shouldn't have to be that way."

"You still the fairest of them all… punk mother-fucker.

## CHAPTER NINE

No one knew who threw the first punch and for damn sure who fired the shots that dropped Alaina Walker. Truth be told, even when the video was shown and re-shown on the news later that evening, the mob scene in the park was little more than fifteen to twenty girls wilding, a sea of arms and blurred faces scrabbling in a cluster of aggression. Investigators determined the fight actually started at Northwest High School.

"I need to go ahead and get my GED." Lady G swatted at one of the lazy bees who flitted after her can of soda. A thin trickle of sweat trailed down the side of her face. The heat of the day already fouled her mood and the incessant buzz only furthered her irritation. She tugged at her gloves.

"What for?" Rhianna's small rasp of a voice scraped at her ears. A sweatband with a skull and crossbones insignia on it encircled Rhianna's head. A dozen jelly bracelets choked each wrist. It didn't matter that she never spoke of things on her mind.

She wore them, or rather, they wore her. She shirked whenever men neared, moreso than usual. Chipped nail polish wasted along the fingertips of her ashy hands. Dark circles welled under her eyes.

"I don't know. Maybe go to college."

"Why? What you gone be? A toxicologist or something?"

"Nah…" Her voice trailed, the tan brick walls of the school seeming suddenly formidable. "Just talking I guess."

The park was next to the Jonathan Jennings Public School 109 elementary school, though that didn't stop graffiti artists from tagging the slide or tables with profanities and gang designations, marking their territory like so many dogs pissing over themselves. Nor did it stop folks from coming up here to get high. The pair, along with a few of their girls, sat along one of the two dilapidated picnic tables under the shelter. Rhianna wanted to get her head up a little since Prez hadn't spoken to her since the night at the bridge. In fact, she and Lady G hadn't said a word about it either. It was like if they never mentioned it, maybe it didn't happen. Sure, they'd been questioned by the police and released, but the evening blurred into a haze of half-remembered conversations. Still, the image of the black tarp spread over two distinct lumps of flesh that had once been Trevant haunted her. That and the sight of all the blood. There was no tarp large enough to cover all the blood.

"Come on, now. Beyonce sang about doing for her man 'what Martin did for the people'," Lady G chirped to lighten the mood.

"That song is an earworm. I'm tired of these fools who call themselves singers these days. You see Justin Wiggerlake's ass trying to dis Prince? Come on now." Rhianna scanned the front of Breton Court for any sign of Prez. Prez was alive enough, still selling for Dollar over here at Breton Court, not that he acknowledged them. He certainly wouldn't describe the ineffable dread he felt whenever he thought about being with the girls as fear, but he, too, kept a discreet distance from them.

"You're still talking about my baby."

"I'm just sayin'. You never saw Hall and Oates dissin' Earth, Wind, and Fire."

"Come close so I can cut you." Lady G rolled up her sleeves, in feigned anger, unconscious of how conspicuous her gloves now seemed.

"Shut up."

"Someone hold my earrings." Lady G pantomimed removing her earrings and waited for Rhianna to give into her smile. "Some fools need to be cut."

In order to put on a pleasant face for rush-hour commuters, Breton Court had been freshly painted. The townhouses were two storey, two or three bedrooms depending on the layout. The end cap of the rows were one level, one bedroom. Its landscape was fairly well maintained, as an old Jamaican father-and-son team tended the lawns every Saturday

morning. Life percolated along at its usual rhythms.
A Hispanic family, a grandmother with her two adult
children and a few toddlers, chatted amiably in a
doorway. A few children rode their bikes unsteadily
along the drive. Some teenagers huddled under trees
engaged in the play dance of hormone-fueled flirting
and banter. Green's people loitered on porch steps
or ducked between patio enclaves in order to conduct business.

As one went deeper into the court, the pleasant
façade broke down. A gradual erosion into dilapida-
tion the further away it got from casual eyes. Cars
jacked up, tires missing, windshields cracked if not
entirely knocked out, glass shards still pooled beneath them. The townhouse window shutters
shattered or dangled at odd angles. Chipped paint
and rotted wood made up many patios. A couple of
end condos had the back patios missing entirely. The
siding on the end townhouses missed a few slats. A
patch ran perpendicular to the rest and still revealed
wood rafters of roof. The disrepair from storm damage when a tornado touched down a few years back.
This was where King lived. He removed the 'For
Sale' sign from his front window.

King couldn't pinpoint when he'd developed spiritual eyes – soft eyes some folks would say – able to
take in everything, the full picture, and even feel it
on some level. He was connected to the court and its
people. Up until then, all he'd wanted was to keep
his head down, mind his own, and muddle through.
No, that was a lie. In his heart, his life had always

been one of quiet discipline, despite his circumstances. Reading. Meditating. Working out. Always in a state of preparing for something. Maybe he sensed something was coming. It had to be more than simply knowing that he was meant for something, a purpose, because who didn't have their childhood daydreams fueled by a belief that they were destined for greatness? King sat on the porch of his condo, whiling away most of his days people-watching. Every time he wandered toward the front of the court, Green's crew declared a time-out. Lingering at the front of the court, he had an unobstructed view of the park.

School dismissed barely twenty minutes earlier and those who walked home trickled into the park. A lot had changed at Northwest High School even in the few years since King attended there. Back in his day, before every major holiday break – Christmas, Spring Break, even summer vacation – the school collapsed in a cauldron of racial tension. Too often, the police helicopter circled the school as mini-riots spread throughout the campus, the slightest spark – a jostle in the lunch line, the wrong color boy rebuffed by the wrong color girl – provided all the excuse needed to pit black against white. Now, with the major Hispanic influx, the game had done changed for real.

A white Toyota Corolla, a decade old with a rusting bumper, screeched to a halt in the middle of the road, drawing everyone's attention as a half-dozen girls tumbled out. Alaina Walker just got out of juvey and was not allowed to associate with her gang sisters. The crossroads moment of her life was between a boring-ass life with no friends or risking her probation by standing tall with her girls. Some folks couldn't help but gravitate to chaos. If chaos was all they knew, chaos was their comfort. Chaos was safe. Alaina marched her crew into the face of Lady G. The two simply hated each other and neither, if pressed, could tell anyone why. It was as if the air between them poisoned with a pheromonal hatred whenever they neared each other.

"Perhaps we should, as a community, just put an embargo on bad weaves," Lady G said.

"What are you doing here? Trying to fit in?" Alaina tossed her hair back from her neck, revealing a tattoo that read "Numba 1 Dick Sucka". Her doorknocker ear rings and gold bracelets combined for a symphony of jangles whenever she moved. Most days, Alaina was all right. East side fools tripped so easily when they thought their man was being stolen out from under them. She had two brothers and one on the way, but she was the oldest. A man, especially one with long money, represented the hope of stability and a way out. Even Baylon. That was Alaina's way. Being too desperate and short-sighted to get out was a contagion which led her to choose bad men to cling to. Lady G had seen her too often around the way with too many bruises for the occasional scuffle. But that, too, was Alaina's game and she played it like the soldier she was.

"Pissing off mommy and daddy. You should know about that," Lady G said.

"You want to get down? We can get down."

"I'm telling you, she's Baylon's girl," a girl stage-whispered to Alaina.

"I. Am. Not." Lady G bristled, rolling her eyes at the sudden respect by proxy she was given. She could fight her own battles and didn't need the shadow of Baylon as a cloak of protection. She never trusted the chivalry of men.

A second car pulled up and that's when things truly went to hell. Percy jumped out of the not-quite-stopped car. Standing just over six feet, a buck eighty and change, he could have been a running back on Northwest's sad-ass JV team. A soft-spoken boy who carried himself like he was afraid he might accidentally break those around him, he, Rhianna, and Alaina stayed over at the Phoenix. Alaina's mother had slammed the car into park and squeezed her six month pregnant self out of the driver's seat and waddled quickly into the fray.

"You girls don't need to do this." A sweet, a pure fool, Percy called himself intervening, trying to calm the situation. He had a way about him. Pain didn't become a part of him, wasn't something he marinated in or dined upon like so many others. Like air, he took it in and let it out. Not that he could express such lofty notions himself. Even now, he realized the escalation was a simple misunder-standing, but he lacked the words to communicate it to any of the girls. His hope was that a mother could quell the situation. Poor deluded fool. As if adding maternal estrogen into the mix had any hope of doing anything except fan the flames.

"You need to mind your own," Lady G said.

"Stay the fuck away from him," Alaina reared, rarely letting the opportunity to spray her particular brand of venom pass.

"No one gets to tell me who I can and can't be friends with." Lady G was pissed at Alaina getting loud. She didn't even like Baylon, but the effrontery of being checked by this heifer, well, pride was pride.

"You spread your legs for any trick who'll buy you a Happy Meal."

"Don't hate cause you don't know how to keep a man," Rhianna chimed in. Most people dropped their guard around her. She had an angel's face, soft and round, her toffee-colored complexion seemed darker against her white teeth and gray eyes. With her small frame, no one expected her to be able to scrap like she did. But the girls knew. Lady G knew. And Alaina for damn sure knew.

"You know what? You a nigga and I don't mean that in no nice way!" Despite the three inches Alaina had on her, Lady G neither cut her eyes away nor stepped back. Neither girl was about to be punked, especially not in front of their people. Not to mention that cell phone cameras were already being waved about with nosey folks ready to parade their shit all over YouTube. "He's from our neighborhood. People like you shot and killed my cousin (rest in peace)."

"Fuck you and your neighborhood." Lady G put her hands on her hips in a *now what?* pose.

Sometimes when confronted with situations one couldn't control, instinct dictated either of two responses: fight or flight. The crowd surged forward as Lady G and Rhianna got rushed. Alaina dropped her head and charged Lady G in a tackle. Lady G let her body go slack to take the hit but control the fall to the ground. Her legs sailed over the girl's shoulder. Alaina squatted over her belly, throwing punches into her. Lady G could handle Alaina. A fight wasn't no thing – the cost of doing business out here. Some you won, some you lost; it was about how you carried it afterward and Lady G could carry this and its attendant scars. No matter which way it turned out.

The flutter of panic which tripped her street antennae was the chaos. The fight had degenerated into a mob. Folks were straight up wilding, fighting just to be fighting. She took a kick to the ribs from a faceless body – barely felt beneath her layers of clothes – her focus on Alaina. The fight had become a stalemate. Without room to maneuver, the two wrestled about essentially entangling each other's arms and interlocking legs so that neither could get in a clean blow. An unspoken message between them as the fight was no longer about them. As they strained against one another, each took a second to do a glancing assessment at the scene about them. The vibe was ugly. They flew under the radar of the crowd, largely unnoticed.

• • •

Neither claimed a set – the investigating detectives would later breathe a quiet sigh of relief over that. The last thing they, the neighborhood, or the school needed was escalating gang retaliation. A crowd of looky-loos gathered around, cell phones out to capture as much as they could.

Folks were their own worst enemy, getting caught up in their own foolishness. "You can't lose if you don't play," King's mother used to say. King scampered toward the melee. Fights happened. The way King saw them, they were healthy. So much stuff kept going down, poor folks struggling to get by, frustrated, pissed off, they occasionally needed to vent some of that hostility off or else they'd just self-destruct. The girls wrestled about, caught up in their anger and self-hatred. A slap for the parents who weren't there for her. A punch for the system of poverty that enslaved them. A kick for the teachers who didn't give two fucks for her. An elbow to the gut for her even being in this place. A rake across the face for the police baton across her back. Fights were neighborhood sport as long as you weren't caught up in them and as long as folks remembered to use their fists. Folks were too quick to settle things with guns, escalating things to levels past what they needed.

But King didn't like the… energy… of this brouhaha. There was something in the air, an undercurrent of violence and hate. It looked like a couple ladies beefing, probably over some man, fueled by the need to show out for their girls. But something else was at play. The ground too warm. As if the earth itself spread into the crowd, a cloud of methane waiting for something to spark it. One looked like she had some Mexican blood in her. The other... King's heart tugged at him. The girl, medium-skinned and serious-faced, drew him in, filling his spaces, voids he wasn't aware he had. Not wanting any harm to come to her, he found himself moving toward her. His grim strides turned into a jog.

A strong set of hands grabbed Lady G by the shoulders and lifted her up, freeing her from the entanglement of Alaina. With regained leverage, Alaina unleashed a flurry of punches and kicks. Lady G, prepared to defend against them, clawed and kicked in her direction. The man who held her spun her away from Alaina's assault and took the blows himself as he backed away. Bodies jostled against them, but they seemed to bounce off the man. He put himself between her and them, unasked. Then the shots rang out. He wrapped his thick arms around her, his hard muscles cocooning her as he scooped her along.

"You OK?" he asked, his voice breathy, not from the exertion but from speaking in low, controlled tones as if crazy shit wasn't jumping off all around him.

"Put me down and mind your own. I got this," Lady G said.

"I know you do. I'm worried about them if I let you loose."

The crowd moved like a tangled swarm of cicadas, limbs intertwined and flailing about trying to gain leverage or hold their ground. Girls pulled at each other's tops and hair extensions. Despite the screams and shouts reaching a cacophonous pitch, they couldn't drown out the report of shots ringing out.

The fight degenerated into a storm of scratching and clawing and folks wilding out on folks just for the sake of doing so. Part of her thrilled at this. It was exciting, sexy, and dangerous. And made her feel alive. If only for a few moments, she felt.

Jockeying for position. A hardness in her eyes, she'd quit caring. She held onto the emptiness she always carried inside her. The crowd darted toward her, spilling into the playground, kicking up wood chips in their wake. The mood of the crowd turned uglier. The instant chaos.

No one needed to yell "gun!" The reports scattered the crowd and the people charged from every direction.

Rhianna found herself separated from her girl. The melee was like a riptide, pulling folks caught in the undertow of bodies away from the action. If Rhianna stopped moving, she might have been trampled.

His head lowered, hands raised above it as if he were shielding himself, Percy waded through the bodies. Without trying, he pushed people aside.

Heedless of his own well-being, all he knew was that her bloodless face was etched in pain. Despite no foundation, no lip gloss, no nail polish, no blush, no eyeliner, she was as beautiful to him as ever. He was embarrassed to stare at her for too long.

He stood there, not touching her. Not crowding her in any way. But he remained between her and the danger. He took any blows purposeful or accidental without so much as a wince.

Two bodies were left in the wake of the gun shots. Alaina, one eye a pocket of darkness with much of the back of her head missing; her mother shot in the belly. The news would go on to speak of the violence, the irony of Alaina's mother giving birth to one child as she lost another.

The cops put a knee into Percy's back, dropping him to the ground. Rhianna screamed at them to let him go. Blows rained down on him. Bloodied, but without complaint, he laid on the ground.

"What's the problem here?" Detective Burke said.

"Just securing the scene."

"He's a suspect."

"He was threatening the girl."

"No he wasn't. He was looking out for me."

"That true, son?" Detective Burke asked.

"I'd never hurt Rhianna."

"Let him go." Detective Burke's eyes softened. "But we do need to get control of the situation and secure this scene."

"Yes ma'am."

"And get an ambo up here." Angry and controlled.

Another in a trail of bodies leading back to the Phoenix Apartments, it was like a poisoning of the souls emanating from there. A tension settled on the west side of town, an ugly, frenzied spirit of darkness threatening to smother them.

## CHAPTER TEN

The police questioned everyone for hours. What facts they could piece together from the jumbled statements was anyone's guess. Folks recounted little past fists flying and barely remembered glimpses of faces here and there.

Lady G hadn't left King's side since the attack. Though he towered over her, a tremor of fear ran through him. Instinct fought against the connection he sensed with her. His gut told him to move along – run if need be – that she was trouble waiting to hurt him. Many times he'd encountered women like Lady G. Women who took one look at a darker brother and cast him aside like a lesion best scraped off. But maybe that was him being unnecessarily defensive. There was a familiarity to her, a piece of a puzzle he never knew was missing. Too much of that had been going on in his life lately, like a game was going on and everyone had a copy of the rulebook except him.

"Can we get out of here?" Lady G slipped her gloved hand into his, soft, gentle, and unassuming.

Struck by the mystery of the affection, King didn't know what to do with it. It wasn't wholly unpleasant.

"Yeah, I only live a few blocks down."

Lady G hesitated. She read his tone see if there was the hint of proposition, or worse, the expectation of one. The invitation wasn't what made her uncomfortable. It seemed genuine and despite there being little about his day to justify her feeling safe, she nevertheless did. No, what made her uncomfortable was being seen. Most times, no one saw her. People may have had a sense about homeless folks, the same way one could be in a darkened room and know that they weren't alone. People knew when to walk around them or speed out of the way of a possible solicitation of a handout.

Like hunting deer, one didn't look for the deer themselves, but rather trained their eyes to detect movement or some evidence of presence. With homeless teens, one checked what didn't belong. Like wearing long sleeve shirts on an eighty degree evening. Why? Because it got cool under bridges even at night. Or duct-taped shoes. Or conspicuous backpacks, containing all of their earthly belongings. Nothing definitive, only clues to a greater story, once you know what to look for. If you bother looking at all.

But King saw her.

Lady G hiked her backpack onto her shoulder.

"We ready to go?" Rhianna strode over to them, cutting a dagger-filled glance at Lady G's hand in

King's. Percy, bruised and bandaged, followed behind her.

"Nah, I think I'm all right," Lady G said.

Rhianna continued to study King, wondering – though not having to guess too hard – what this old-ass dude (he was what? Probably twenty-eight or something) wanted with her girl. "Where the spot be at?"

"Round the way."

"So is it just y'all or is there room for a few more?"

"It's tight as it is."

"It's like that?"

"Yeah. I'll catch up with you," Lady G reassured her. "You be at the bank squat?"

"Uh-uhn. I don't want every motherfucker knowin'."

"I know a spot," Percy said.

"All right then." Rhianna relaxed.

"You sure?"

"You giving me a choice?" Rhianna asked. Lady G shook her head. "All right then."

Dismissed, Rhianna and Percy walked toward the bus stop. She turned around one last time to make sure her friend was OK only to spy Lady G leaning into King's casual embrace.

Big Momma sat on a plastic bench with her neighbor from across the way. Freshly coiffed gray hair, Big Momma's sculpted dignity was undercut by her ashy elbows. The slight heft to her gut actually matched her neighbor's. They didn't say anything, merely sat there. The night wind bit at them, unexpectedly cool for an August night. Lady G assumed a posture designed to keep her warm: arms pulled within her T-shirt. A security porch light lit the court of townhouses. They sat in white plastic lawn chairs. Bent over, King slowly rocked back and forth on the cooler that was his makeshift chair – letting Lady G have the last seat.

"Who was that one girl who came up here half-naked?" King asked.

"Who? Alaina?" Lady G felt a pang of regret at belittling her dead nemesis.

"Nah. Some spot girl, strolling on up talking about how she just got through letting another woman eat her coochie."

"Around the kids?" the neighbor asked before taking another drag from her cigarette. That usually signaled a brewing shit storm if she built up a big enough head of steam. She had been married for six years to her high school sweetheart. After the birth of their daughter, their marriage had hit a rocky patch. He had simply had enough at playing grown-up. The lure of whiling away his days running the streets proved easier than holding down a straight (read: boring) nine to five gig, but she had bills to pay. So she put his ass out. And took up smoking.

"Ain't no kids around here anymore," King said. "Folks have to grow up too quick."

"She had to have been high," Lady G said almost to herself, her mind still mulling over Alaina suddenly bugging out the way she did. "Tweaked out on something. She could be bad, but she don't wild out like that."

"She like that?" King asked.

"Just saying. I hear they've got new stuff coming in, got some folks acting up."

After his father, Luther, died, his moms, Anyay, went off the rails. He lost her in degrees, so no one noticed for a long time. She moved out her momma's house, declaring it time further to spread her wings. More to let the streets seep into her, to find a connection to Luther. Love was a cancer which crept into you unsuspecting, and by the time you realize you have it, it had metastasized into every part of you. And Anyay sought her own brand of chemo, breaking her mother's heart. She died not too long after.

Two kids later, from men fueling her chemotherapy, it was a short jump to living in their car. They maintained as best they could: school in the morning, cutting out early so that King could do lawn work and odd jobs to get enough money for hotel rooms at night. King thought that his mother would get her act together if she only had the little ones to worry about. A good woman still lived within the fiend she'd become, she just needed a push. The chance to gain her footing in life and she'd pull it together. He knew she would. So he left them.

She and the kids froze to death that winter, a spike still stuck in her arm.

"Where she stay at?"

"Over at the Phoenix."

"Hmph." Big Momma was a trip. Hers was the only name listed on the lease, her daughter's baby staying with her most of the time so that she could go to a better school. Which was fine with Big Momma. She'd done as much as she could for her own girl. Raised her, put some Jesus in her, prepared her for the world as best she could. But all the good training in the world couldn't trump the ways of the heart and her baby girl kept trying to fill the hole in her spirit with a man. Big Momma was one of those women who had a lot of love to give and hated an empty house. She believed Prez had a good heart but fell in with them boys before she could get a hold of him. She feared she'd lost him for good.

"I hear the police scooped up Prez," King said as if reading her thoughts. He still rocked on his cooler.

"His cousin is bonding him out."

"How much?"

"Two thousand. I hate dealing with him cause now every time I ask him for something, he's gonna be like 'that's coming out of the money to get your boy out'."

"'Your boy'. Like they ain't cousins," the neighbor added.

"OK," Big Momma amen-ed. "Still, I'm lucky that he has that much. The first is around the corner and he could've started crying 'rent's due'. I tell you what though, when Prez gets out, we gonna have a barbecue for the whole neighborhood."

"I guess that means I'm cooking," King said.

"That's why I'm telling you." Though she smiled a rueful grin, she wasn't fond of having her business discussed on the street. Of course, neither did King. "How's Nakia doing?"

King's eyes narrowed, moving from Big Momma to Lady G. Lady G turned toward him, eyebrow arched. His eyes softened as a stratagem of how to play the situation to his advantage sprang to mind. And he wasn't going to give Big Momma the satisfaction of seeing him sweat or scramble. "Let me ask you something. If your baby's momma was with some dude, would you ask to meet him?"

"Yeah. I'd want to know who my baby was spending time around."

"That's what I'm saying. I don't want Nakia up around just anybody, but her momma says that I'm too ghetto to meet him."

"So what'd you say?"

"I said that 'I'm over you, so it's not like I'm gonna fight him or start anything. I just need to meet him.'"

"Yeah, but she's still your baby's momma," Lady G said. She found herself wanting to tease out more information from him.

"So?"

"So… you always gonna have feelings for her." The statement sounded more like a question to his ear.

"Not true. I just need to meet him cause if I see my daughter walking down the street with some dude I don't know, then I'm gonna jump on his face for real."

King couldn't make up his mind who he was mad at the most. His baby's momma for getting pregnant. Himself for dropping out of high school to support her. Big Momma for floating his business. Or God for letting all this mess happen to him.

King always had a path. Too many folks wanted everything handed to them, but he knew what he wanted, but all paths had the occasional bump. King had no reason being with his baby momma, especially for as long as he was. They knew each other from around the way and hooked up for no more reason than they were there. Then she turned up pregnant. King didn't know what it was, maybe the idea of being a father, but he saw things differently. He wanted to be there to hold Nakia, be a part of her life, show her how a man was supposed to be, so he tried to make it work with her momma. Like an arranged marriage, they had nothing in common except Nakia, he wasn't sure they even liked each other all that much. It was a relationship of convenience: he could be with his daughter and his baby momma had someone to pay the bills. Duty held them together. All this "being in love" bullshit was for poets and chick flicks. Real love went beyond the passion and hype and he had real love.

For his baby girl.

Eventually the relationship got old and his baby momma, bills or no bills, came to the point where it wasn't working and threw him out. Despite her getting on his last nerve, he had gotten kind of used to her. He almost missed her sorry ass, though mostly the empty space in his life, and that distant ache he felt was the absence of his daughter.

"Man I wish next Wednesday would hurry up and get here," the neighbor said, trying to change the topic.

"Why? You don't get paid till Friday," Big Momma said.

"Wednesday's the first." Welfare check day.

"I couldn't handle it if I got paid every other week. I couldn't budget right."

"Me either. Had to learn." The neighbor flicked her cigarette butt in the bush just past King's head. "Still wish it would hurry up and get here, though."

With the conversation devolving into the travails of budgeting, King nodded to Lady G and she followed him inside. Big Momma eyed them. Their court of opposing townhouses lived by its own code. Folks minded their own business as long as they were good neighbors. Even drug dealers: as long as they brought no drama to the court and were polite, a blind eye was conveniently taken. Them throwing the occasional barbecue spurred goodwill also.

Dragging his cooler inside, he had a chair. Walls painted white, though they required a second coat of paint to cover the graffiti of folks who'd broken in previous. He left the condo unlocked. The back door and window King secured once he moved in. Upon entering, he locked the deadbolt behind them. The water still ran, but the power and gas had been cut off. King unfurled his bedding to form what passed for a couch. In the corner a stack of books propped up a large, quite full, backpack.

The quaver of sexual ache shocked her. Her pulse quickened at his nearness and it turned her stomach. There was no mystery to boys. Simple creatures that delighted in the friction of lust. Rhianna's constant quest to bask in their attentions baffled her. To be the object of their desire, their conquest, was no difficult feat. She feared that part of her wanted – and feared even more that she needed – their attentions. Her sense of needing to belong. Perhaps to be owned. And wasn't that what relationships were? Two people owning one another, chained by the heart, the genitals, or however they chose to define love in the breathless moments between sheets. The content capture of heat and presence and temporarily satiated need. King must've stood six-six easy, half a foot taller than her. His goatee-framed lips – both pouty and sure – like a confident model. He wore his black shirt with two too many buttons undone, revealing a necklace of Mary and Jesus, except both were black. That was what she stared at when King's eyes caught hers.

"Would you like something to drink?" King asked.

"What do you have?"

"How old are you?"

"Why?"

"Had to know if I only had water and Kool Aid."

"As opposed to…?"

"Beer."

"I can vote, but you'd better serve me some water."

Her contagious smile – a wide, even thing with teeth too small in her mouth – masked the pain just under her face. The pain that formed her skull. That writhed beneath her skin, a living hard thing. But her face hadn't asked for pity. It wore the veneer of an independent woman, quick to show affection in tiny ways if she felt safe. And she rarely felt safe beside any boy.

Lady G wandered around the room, the space seeming that much greater without any furnishings. All of the townhouses in Breton Court had the same basic layout: a great room – the family room/dining room combo – with a small kitchen in the rear. The stairs at the entrance led to the two-to-three bedrooms. Lady G had no interest in a tour of upstairs; however, King's library fascinated her. Marcus Garvey, Malcolm X, WEB DuBois, Paul Dunbar, Maya Angelou, Toni Morrison. The title of a book on film caught her eye and made her giggle. *Toms, Coons, Mulattoes, Mammies, & Bucks.*

King enjoyed her laughter. "I like to know what I'm dealing with when I watch a show. Can't just let folks brainwash you."

"I just try to enjoy a movie. Leave the deep stuff to folks who look for deep stuff."

"You can't just let folks slip anything they want into you."

"That's not what I'm saying. You see, there's two kinds of folks: simple and complex. I'm a simple girl. That ain't the same as dumb. I just don't make things complicated. To me, a movie's a movie. I ain't trying to find any social meaning, not trying to look for metaphors, or any of that other stuff. I'm just looking to kill a couple hours. You complex folks like to burn yourselves up looking for hidden meaning in everything."

Lost in his thoughts, King hadn't realized how angry he always was. The knot that clotted his stomach and congealed in his veins had become such a part of him, he'd grown used to it. If he had to name the source of his anger, he'd be hard pressed. He had grown up with it for so long, it was all he knew. His constant companion. He doubted he would have even noticed how much it defined him until the constant churning leveled. His rage suddenly quelled. The darkness which shadowed the fringes of his life receded. Around her. And the implication frightened him. And the fear was every bit as uncomfortable as the anger. Something new to get used to. The fear wasn't so bad.

Her forthrightness appealed to him. She wore a family reunion T-shirt, though it wasn't for her family, but a shirt she'd gotten from Outreach Inc. The tattoo on her shoulder was what he was staring at when her eyes caught his.

"What are you looking at?"

"The tattoo. BMG?"

"Big Money Ganger." A regretful tone underscored her voice. She turned her shoulder from him.

"A girl like you runs in a set?"

"You have no idea what it's like to be me." Lady G stood by the window. She pulled back the venetian blinds to take in the evening scene.

"True. You do seem to be quite the mystery."

"Forget you." An unbidden smile betrayed her.

"You make a brother work to talk to you." King sat on the cooler, inching it forward but not threateningly close.

"If I don't want to say something to you, don't say nothing to me."

"And if you do want to say something?"

"Oh, you'll know."

He nodded at the tattoo. "This what you saw yourself being when you were little?"

"It feels like my kid life is gone outta me… if I ever had one. I want to own my own salon one day. One without all the gang and drug money all up in it. Baylon must own half a dozen by now."

"You know B?" King's voice grew sharp, not that Lady G acted as if she caught it or the overly familiar recognition of Baylon as "B". They all came with the baggage of the past, not that any of it was his business, so she simply moved on.

"He was trying to go with me, but he wasn't my type. He put that 'L' word in there, hit me too quick with that. I don't play that game. I don't put out signals and I don't read them terribly well. I feel something, I tell you. Problem with the rest of the boys I deal with, is that there's not enough truth in them. They can't just say 'I got feelings for you, I'm digging you. You kind of tight.' They can't admit that they want to treat you dirty. Do better."

"I will," King said as if her "do better" was aimed at him.

"Do you believe that some people are just… connected?"

"What do you mean?" He knew what she meant.

"Like how you can think of a friend and they just show up."

"Or how you can be in need and they just know to come over or have the right thing to say."

"Exactly."

"Do you want to go out sometime?"

"You ask out all the girls you rescue from a fight?"

"Only the interesting ones." He stood up to kiss her, but she pulled away.

"I keep myself to myself. I can give you a hug, though," she said with the crooked smile of a child who'd been caught in a lie.

King saw the little girl in her then. The light and potential, the fragility and strength, that innocent part of her she still tried to cultivate as well as protect. The one who'd been fucked over too often by life along the way. And he felt as if something in his chest was broken, as if just realizing it for the first time.

Both of them stood rigid within the embrace, as if neither knew what to do with the display of affection. He was pissed that he gave up something personal about himself within a few minutes of talking, but it happened right away like that sometimes. When he peered into those damaged almond eyes of hers, however, he belonged to her and she knew

it, too. Their eyes smiled, hopeful despite themselves.

They all had to play their roles.

## CHAPTER ELEVEN

Fall Creek ran through the east side of Indianapolis, non-discriminatory to the neighborhoods it flowed through. As it passed the Phoenix Apartments, a grove of trees lined its banks forming a natural green space that had become popular as a walkway. During early morning hours, many a citizen walked its path for exercise, each armed with a stick or bat in case of emergency. On some evenings, such as this night, cars crowded the rear of the Phoenix Apartments parking lot, sealing it off into its own little world. As people made their way down to the woods, they knew they were entering Switzerland, a "no beefs allowed" zone. Dred's crew, Night's boys, ESG, Treize, Black Gangster Disciples, any of a number of independents, all noise had to be squashed for the evening.

Stands of bootleg CDs (including homemade mixes), DVDs, T-shirts and hoodies (with portraits and quotes of Malcolm X, Marcus Garvey, and Bob Marley), and shoes lined the parking lot. Vendors sold beer from coolers. All the faces wore similar masks: jaws set, faces hardened, no gazes lingering too long. Fight night brought a tenuous peace and it couldn't afford any sparks that came with the fronting of machismo.

It wasn't but the early to mid-'90s when everyone thought it a needed accessory to have a Rott or a Pit. As with any fad, they soon fell into disfavor except among those interested in protection or fighting. Tonight, a temporary ring had been set up, an area of folding chairs nearby, though most people stood, crowding in with money clutched in raised hands.

Dog handlers, bookies, and referees crowded the ringside area. One of the undercard bouts was about to start. Their handlers released them and the two dogs ran to center, two gladiators clashing at full speed. As they were trained, ever wanting to please their masters, they lashed out in demoniac frenzy. Neither made nary a sound, their vocal cords severed, making them deadly weapons when they were at home, not alerting unsuspecting prowlers. Or police. Even though it meant senseless blood and death, the dogs showed more heart than most soldiers on the street.

So Omarosa thought.

Nearly invisible among the trees, she skulked about with a natural ease. Having already secured Lee's eventual presence, she bided her time and buffed her nails. Her eyes, with their perfect night vision, focused in the low light. Soon a couple of runners, no more than eleven years old, tore ass down the hill.

"Time out. Time out, yo." They announced the police's arrival.

About time, she thought, as she prepared to go to work. The grumbles of the dispersing men filled the night. The old hands, nonplussed by the arrival of the police, took the time to finish their drinks, grind out cigarettes under their heel, and collect their bets in nonchalant strides. Those with more to worry about, say a bench warrant out in their name, beat feet in a hail of mutters and curses, showing out to the police for their boys' benefit.

Between the crowd clearing out and the police making their way down, the press of bodies led to confusion, just as she planned. She smelled the gentle scent of the red rose clipped to her lapel which served as her calling card. She always left one at the scene of one of her robberies. Theft was so common, better to do so with a touch of panache. It was in such short supply these days. To her, this part of the game was like playing football: the offense was going to throw a certain look, the defense took its own posture, but the key to any given play was to follow the football. In this case, it meant trailing Dollar as he banked his money. He gave an uptick of his chin as he prepared to jet, a shoulder roll and a dip in stride as he received his package and threw it into the back of his ride. Omarosa, like all of her kind, had a talent for learning the players and their histories: in Dollar's case, he had a tendency to do his counts at his mom's house before making his final drop to Night.

Boys and their moms.

Dred's mother, Morgana, squatted alone and determined, in the filth beneath a bridge. She cradled the full swell of her belly, and resolved herself to the fact that it was time. The scurry of rats in the hollows above her head didn't distract her. The concrete embankment was cold against her back, her legs spread and water long broken. Drops plinked in the distance, falling from the bridge. It had rained earlier that day and the creek had swollen in its bed. The susurrus of the creek as it wound its course served to focus and calm her, but her pain proved too excruciating. *He* saw to that. She pushed and breathed with little more than a few grunts, not giving him the satisfaction of a sob. Theirs was a love – if one could call their bond "love" – forged in war with one another. Lessons taught from his first moments.

Dred fought then and even now, only the battles changed.

Contrary to popular belief, the streets had rules, traditions by which folks comported themselves. Even the young bucks coming up stuck to the rules of the game, those who abandoned them for the sake of making a name for themselves quickly found out there were stern reprisals to be faced. One such rule was parlay. Under the rules of parlay, two rivals/parties otherwise beefing with one another could come together – usually in neutral territory, sometimes brokered by a third party – in order to work out their disagreement. At its core, this was a business. Every now and then, circumstances dictated exceptions to the accepted conventions.

Escorted by Green, Night made a rare foray away from the safety of the top floor – entirely his, a ghetto penthouse – of the main building of the Phoenix Apartments. The more power he accumulated, it seemed, the more its reward was isolation. Instead, he chose to meet Dred at his place of power. Night was diving-suit black, a straight-up thug-nigga. With a low-cut fade, big chest and huge arms, he walked with that survival stride learned from several bits in prison. At one time, he was the chief enforcer for the crew. Not smart enough to set up his own operation, but vicious enough to stage a palace coup at the right time. Backed by Green. It was said that there would be no Night without Green.

Though many knew about Dred's situation, few dared speak of it openly. One, out of respect; two, out of – if not fear of reprisal then – recognition of the fact that nothing had changed. Dred still ruled his crew and would continue until he showed weakness. The wheelchair didn't mean he had lost any heart and many bodies had been dropped to demonstrate that case. As an allowance, however, Green accompanied Night.

Stale air filled the outer chamber from blunts, cigarette smoke, sex, and overturned beer bottles. Baylon sat behind a desk poring over figures and accounts while Junie attended to the mess. Both men hard-eyed Green and Night as they approached. Junie's veins pumped water at the sight of Green. Baylon's chin up-ticked in the direction of the door leading toward Dred's sanctum. Green took up a position outside the door as Night entered alone.

"Pleasure before business?" Night asked as Dred took the opportunity to spark up himself, his marijuana heightened by his own mystical concoctions.

"The Rastafari consider it a sacrament." He wasn't as skilled in the Dark Arts as his mother, but he knew enough to be dangerous.

"And you're what? Ecumenical?"

"All in the game, son. All in the game." After all the nonsense that had gone down lately, few believed the street mantra much. Night's tone was hoarse and weary. He took out a bottle of lotion and rubbed some onto his keloid-scarred arms.

"Damn, boy. You look positively peaked." Dred pronounced "peaked" with two syllables.

"Been running wild lately, you know how it goes. Nothing I can't handle." Not that Night, that either of them, would admit to anything that sounded remotely of weakness. Weakness invited attack. "You're one to talk. You lookin' a might bit rough yourself."

"We got us a situation."

"What?"

"King."

"Not trying to tell you your business, but you telegraph your moves long before you ready to make your play."

"The mage is back."

"He never left."

"Well, they've found each other."

"I don't see how this is a 'we' problem. If King is such a big deal, just smoke the motherfucker."

"It's not that simple. There are rules to this thing. A larger picture to consider."

"Of course there is. You motherfuckers play too many games. He a mark. Just like any other mark. And marks can get got."

"He's coming into his own now."

"What the fuck does that mean?"

"You think Jesus always knew he was Jesus? You think he burst out the womb thinkin' 'Damn, I'm the Son of God. Let me get a little bigger so I can drop some miracles on your ass.' He had to grow into it. I mean, maybe he grew up reading about who the Messiah was. Studying, learning, a nag in his spirit about how it was starting to sound familiar. Then one day it clicks. 'Oh snap. They talking about me. They been waiting on me.'

"I bet he had to sit on that shit for a minute. Sure, he had all the hype. Folks been waiting for him to show up from the jump. Been persecuted, living hard, got all sorts of Romans walking up and down they space. They were looking out for him to show up. Thing is, it also came with a price: the burden of knowing.

"Don't get me wrong, he step up and accept his title, his mantle, his responsibility and BAM... his days are numbered. In the end, he's gonna get got. Everything in its own time."

"See what I mean? Too many games."

"Look here, I'm about business and business can't get done if we're steady beefing. It'd be one thing if there was serious drama, but I want to head things off before it gets to that point." Dred was in the game for the power. When all was said and done, this was a business with margins more thin that people realized. After payroll, houses, cars, and the accoutrements expected for a man in his position – granted, it was the accoutrements which tempted people into the life – not much was left over. However, he provided a sense of family for his men until jail or death caught up to them. Dred didn't know about jail and he had no plans to know about jail.

"Agreed. Agreed," Night said.

"I'm just saying, there's plenty of money to go around…"

"Plenty of that product. You seem to have a steady enough pipeline."

"I get mine direct. No middle-man, no mark-up. You get your supply out of New York, right?"

"Something like that."

Dred's heavy-lidded eyes cast a knowing gaze on Night. They would continue to dance around each other with verbal feints, testing for weakness, and teasing out information. Dred knew that Night was supplied from New York after he split from the Egbo Society to go on his own. Dred's drug connect was locked into him. Dred's name rang out for several reasons. His hands no longer touched drugs, instead he operated a community center by Avalon Park and made sure the park's basketball court always had fresh nets. When he had two able legs, he got to know the neighborhood kids from Haughville to Woodruff Place. For those youths, Dred was a role model of respect. And he gave back to the community, donating to church fundraisers, passing out turkeys at Thanksgiving, buying Christmas gifts for neighborhood kids, and sponsoring ball teams. No charges stuck to him, the police was the enemy; he was the folk hero wronged who kept his head up and stayed true to the game. Kids dreamt of one day being him.

Night hadn't learned the finer points to establishing himself as a folk hero; and if he couldn't be loved, he'd be feared. Dispatching Green for any of a number of perceived infractions or slights to his accorded respect, his name was whispered more as the boogeyman of Breton.

"Say I let you in on part of my package," Dred said. "You let my people ease into some of the Breton Court territory. Off my package and with what you pull in from Li'l Nam, you'll be doubling your profits."

"What's in it for you?"

"Spread in territory. Another revenue stream from distribution through you. And peace. No business gets done if bodies keep dropping and the police come in to grind things to a halt."

"True dat."

This was a temporary measure at best. Once he got a feel for the new set-up, at his first opportunity,

Night would slit his throat and leave his body for all to see as he took over the entire operation. Dred understood that. He also understood that soldiers were trained for combat. So every now and then, there had to be a war.

Fountain Square Mortuary was no stranger to burying the far-too-young. Just the other day, the old man who managed the mortuary had to watch a family grieving over an eight year-old. Those were the hardest on him. Funerals for teenagers, though often just as tragic, caused his blood pressure to rise for other reasons. Jowly with a graying mustache, his body with the contours of a cruller donut, he mopped his beaded brow with a handkerchief. Wisps of his good hair, combed over to cover his thinning pate, clung to his forehead.

The funeral of Alaina Walker was well attended with the requisite friends, family, police, media, and publicity seekers. The mayor gave a brief address decrying the rising tide of violence in what was proving to be the most bloody year in the city's history. The concerned clergy took turns denouncing gangs, hip hop, and Republicans. The newspapers ran columns on the story, but the incident would be forgotten in the next day or so once some famous-for-no-reason would-be actress did something equally vacuous in public.

Everyone would return to their steady state of benign neglect, the numbing consistency of the violence silencing them. With eyes both friendly and frightened, the old man did his best to greet each mourner neutrally, but the ways of this generation eluded him. The mourners came in, most not much older than the girl. Sagging pants. Underwear showing. Untied shoes. Basketball jerseys. Tattoos on any exposed flesh. Piercings in their ears, noses, lips, tongues, and chins (and those were the ones he could see). Gentlemen not removing their hats. Ladies revealing their bras and wearing pants with words written across their bottoms. The art of decorum lost on the lot of them.

Towards the rear, studying each face, the police weren't too hard to spot. The girl must've been caught up in something fierce, though no one could tell from today. Dressed in her Sunday best, she was the spitting image of a lady of occasion. The woman she could have been juxtaposed against the trappings of the woman she was, judging from the flower arrangements made into gang symbols and guns.

King arrived at the funeral escorting Lady G, not that he felt obligated or anything. She wished to attend the funeral and he thought it prudent to accompany her. He recognized few of the people, but all of the faces – set hard with no tears, impassive and inscrutable – were masks of barely checked rage. He stepped closer and put his arm around her. Lady G didn't object to his proximity. It was a non-threatening intimacy.

Regret was a powerful emotion. It gave weight, if not words, to ideas and feelings unable to be expressed in life. Things like mourning the waste of her life. The futility of their constant fighting. The lost opportunity to have been friends. No, these things were sealed behind another layer of armor as she stared, hard-faced. She knew her presence might upset a few folks, but Alaina was... she didn't know what Alaina was, only that they had been connected somehow. She knew that she owed Alaina some measure of respect in death that she never had the chance to give in life.

The graveside service was at Bethel Cemetery. The casket lowered into the ground, another seed planted though what fruit would come of it King didn't venture to guess. He eyed the crowd warily. Car doors slammed shut as most of the mourners departed. An air of unchecked resentment lingered. Word had it that no one knew who fired the shot. Just the same, blood was in the air and demanded more to be appeased. He knew where the trouble would come from as a few boys tarried, pointing to King and Lady G, and laughed.

"He do one of us, he's got to fall," one of them called out, daring King.

King had his fill of violence for one week. For one lifetime, really. One of them caught his disaffected sigh.

"What 'chu lookin' at nigga?"

"I'm tired is all. Not everything is about how you carry it."

"Might be time for you to tip on out," the young one said.

"We will when we're ready. We've come to pay our respect. When we through, we're gone." King had to stand tall or else those chump-ass busters would think he was shook.

The boy, tall and good-sized – barely out his teens, if that mattered at all – stepped forward, inches from King's face, nearly bowling him down with his butt funk. He had some flex in him, but having no fear was easy when you had little to live for. No dreams of tomorrow. For next year.

Lady G let go of his slowly balling fists.

King met his eyes without fear. He could feel the flare of his heated blood. The boy said something to him, but King didn't answer, just hard-eyed him with a hint of disdain. By the code, the boy couldn't back down. The eyes of his boys were on him.

The boy put his weight on his back foot, preparing to throw a punch. When it came, King sidestepped and countered, planting his fist solidly in the boy's kidney, turning him, then shoving him into the wall of a memorial. The anxious squawks of the crowd had suddenly been reduced to mumbles. From the corner of his eye, King spied a light-skinned girl with fine braids, observing the proceedings from behind a nearby tree, then, like a will o' wisp, she was gone.

To Night's mind, wizards were white men with long beards, robes, and pointy hats. For that matter, African witch doctors conjured images of men in large masks dancing around pyres of fire. Neither picture came close to what he practiced. He slumped

within his great wicker chair, exhausted from ma-
nipulating the dragon's breath. At his beckoning, it
poured from the vents of the Phoenix Apartments
penthouse and pooled at his feet, a faithful dog
awaiting his master's command. So he thought.

"What we gonna do about Miss Jane?" Green
stood in the corner of the room, a discreet distance
from the enveloping tendrils of mist, and watched as
they entered Night's nostrils and open mouth. The
distortion added to the ghoulishness of his face.

Night's eye's fluttered, his upturned pupils returning to normal and focusing on Green. "What do you
mean?"

"Her time's about up. She's bound to become a…
liability before too long."

"You mean give me up? She don't know nothing."

"She knows more than you think. Plus, she thinks
she has a trump card to play."

"Percy?"

"Yeah."

"Leave her be," Night said. "He's still my blood and
she's still the boy's mother."

"Not much of one. No disrespect."

"No, you right. But the bug or the blast will catch
up with her before much longer." Night struggled to
upright himself, but his arm muscles gave out. Sweat
scattered like buckshot across his face and chest.

"Are you OK?"

"Just off my game is all." Night wouldn't have
suffered any interruptions or taken any visitors
during the ritual – definitely would not have risked

appearing weak – except in front of Green. Night's T-shirt draped over him, his gaunt face betraying his emaciated body. His dark flesh withered. If Green had seen this before, his thoughts were his own.

"You're using it too much."

Night threw a bloodshot glare at Green. The undersides of his eyelids itched with the scrape of ants crawling alongside his eyes into his skull. The rasp of his breathing choked into a cough. He rolled his tongue across his dry, cracked lips. The ashy pallor to his skin obscured by the waning mist, Night's head was already caught up in the heady throes of the dragon's breath.

"I'm so close to having them all. And beating Dred at his own game."

Marshall rested on his side, stroking the bare back of the hooker sprawled across his dirty mattress. Her flesh cooled to room temperature, her head buried face down into what passed for his bed, staring into eternity. She died during the throes of his climax; that was when it usually happened, though it rarely stopped him from going a second round. Michaela sat in a chair across from them. As much as Michaela hated being referred to as the Durham Brothers, she hated the appellation "The Trolls" even more. All elementals were known to be capricious, treacherous, and, well, hostile. It took them a long time to find a place that suited their needs. An abandoned home which had been gutted, all but the load-bearing walls removed so that new owners could refashion the layout any way they wished. Without power and with the windows boarded, the house was little more than a huge cavern.

"Was it good for you?" he remarked to the corpse, but turned to Michaela to see if she'd give him a polite chuckle. It wasn't the fact that he had to pay for company that upset Marshall, it was that pros charged him at least double. A shadow crossed his face whenever things did not go his way. If Michaela wasn't around, he was often cheated, the victim of a Murphy game or worse, so she always watched over him.

"It's time," Michaela checked her watch. She had similar but different problems. With a measure of wit and charm, she had little difficulty getting a man, when away from the baleful uncomfortable stare of her brother. Unfortunately, she couldn't stop herself from consuming them. When it came to men, she lived with a constant fear that if he got to know her or if he knew her name, he'd either abandon or destroy her. Better to kill them before they hurt her. Dining on them spoke more to her frugal mentality.

"We shouldn't go to work on an empty stomach."

"You're supposed to load up on carbs, I hear."

"Well, waste not, want not."

She stared at the corpse. Her mouth watered as she imagined chewing the fleshy muscle of the woman's upper arm, tearing sinew from bone in large sloppy bites. "I suppose we have time for a quick nibble."

• • •

The metallic squawk of the phone, the din of voices, the pallid haze of fluorescent lighting all faded into background static as Octavia studied the spread of folders before her. Glasses low on her nose, she picked up folder after folder, eyes dancing along each line until the information became as familiar as her own heartbeat. License plate numbers from surveillance of Breton Court Phoenix Apartments activities led to girlfriends, and in a couple of cases, mothers of the players. But nothing on Dred, Night, or Green. They had pictures of Green and a rare shot of Night, but that was it. Social Security, date of birth, assets, credit history, criminal records, lawsuits (not that any beefs were handled in any court other than the streets) – it was difficult to track anyone who had checked out of the system.

The local reverends were up in arms and calling for an open and honest investigation. Apparently the lead investigator being black wasn't enough because blue was blue and police hid behind a wall of silence. The take-home message was that she was window dressing, little more than a House Negro faithfully attending to her master's business. Her unspoken message to them would be that there came a point when talk was cheap, when you had done all you could do to draw attention to a problem and had to come up or join in with a solution. Protests and prayer meetings didn't cut it anymore. Maybe they – the people, the community – needed to do more to stem the tide of violence where they could; bear their share of the burden. Put some "action" into social action, not just stopping at press conferences pontificating and prevaricating until the cameras were finished rolling. But that would be her selling them as short as they were selling her.

Lee was down the hall with the prize catches from his little raid on the dog-fighting ring. Even Octavia gave him silent props on that bust and that was before it yielded a couple of rival low-level players. Mr Parker Griffin, they all but knew that they wouldn't get anywhere with: well acquainted with the system, being far from a virgin with it, he had already graduated from the juvey system. He'd keep his mouth shut and stand tall, but Lee had to go through the motions. Now, Mr Preston Wilcox, street name "Prez", was another story. He was new to the life. Word was he made it no secret that he hated the rules of the game. People whispered that he had no heart when, in fact, what he had was sense enough to realize that it was the needless violence, especially the collateral damage of bystanders, that drew the police down on them. Even so, any perceived weakness, even voiced attitude, could get him dead, except that he was new enough for folks to consider him still learning the rules.

"Do you believe in God?" Octavia knew that she herself hadn't seen the inside of a church since her momma quit making her go. As a detective, it was her job to sidle alongside a perp, get into their head, and become their best friend. In short, her job was to be an actress or at least a professional bullshitter, because who would befriend this worthless lot?

Truth be told, when it came to God, she'd thought about Him and church a lot lately, a beacon in the darkness. Maybe the reverends were getting to her after all.

"I guess."

"No, son, that's not good enough. Either you believe in a Creator that is looking over you, the same God your momma and grandmomma believed in and raised you to believe in, or you don't."

"Yeah." Slouched in his chair not meeting her eyes, Prez studied his hands as they rested on the table. The wan light gave them a sense of… otherliness. All of the God talk made him uncomfortable. It reminded him of more innocent times, when he was capable of believing in things like burning bushes, parted seas, and resurrections. He no longer believed in miracles.

"So you know wrong from right?"

"I guess."

"All right. Now we getting somewhere. You know why I became a cop?"

"No."

"I'm a truth seeker. I believe that there is truth out there, sometimes buried under layers of lies and bodies and secrets and things most folks don't want their momma to know they were doing. But it's out there, right, son?"

"Yeah." Prez squirmed every time she used the word "son". And the word became her knife.

"I believe in God, too. I want to do His work, be a blessing to those around me, especially the neighborhood my mother and father raised me in. But I can't help a neighborhood that won't help itself. We try to uphold the truth, uphold the law though it is sometimes, well, most times too painful. But we do it anyway. Not because of you or your knucklehead friends. You all are in the game. You know the rules, we know the rules and we just play tag with one another. But…"

Octavia pulled out a folder and withdrew pictures of Alaina. Shots of her in the park, her bullet-ridden body on the ground, dead eye accusing any who bore witness. "Most folks ain't in the game. Some get caught up in stuff despite staying as far away as they could. She was a promising athlete and a good student," Octavia risked embellishing Alaina's story a little. "Odds were she wouldn't have gone much further than college playing ball, but she could've been a doctor or a business-woman. She could've gotten out. And this one." She pulled out a picture of Conant. "This one was just playing in his mother's kitchen. Can you believe that? His whole life in front of him. Laughter, love, friends, family all gone because folks playing the game too close."

Prez's gaze fixed on the picture. He held it gently. *So this was what he looked like.*

"Something you want to tell me, son?" Detective Burke relied on her instincts. The light of recogni-tion, the apologetic droop of his shoulder, eyes full of sorrow and regret but not tears. Rarely tears.

"No."

"No? You going to look this boy in the eye and tell me 'no'. Ah, you a street soldier standing tall. No snitching from you, ain't that right?"

"Yeah."

"See? You can say 'yeah' when you need to. And this boy needs you to. Look, I know we have you up in our house – you're free to get up any time you want," she quickly reminded him without breaking stride in her spiel. "But I'm not saying that you had anything to do with it. I just need your help. I need to tell his people something. Every day I get to work and you know what I dread hearing? My phone ringing. Why? Because I know it's his momma calling. Every. Day. Wanting to know if we've made any progress. Wanting to know if we've found her baby's killer. Every day I have to hear her heart break all over again when I have to tell her that no one cares about her baby. No one wants to step up. No one wants to do the right thing. No one wants to stand tall for Conant. Everyone wants to be blind, deaf, and dumb and call themselves being true to the game. Are you blind, deaf, and dumb?"

"No."

"Someone's got to answer for his blood. Don't you agree?"

"Yeah."

She slapped the table. Prez jumped. "Just tell me whatever you know, son. Whatever you know."

"I don't know."

"Don't you care, son?"

"I... I don't know what it means to care." Prez stumbled for a response and latched onto the first thought that came to mind. He didn't think he'd grasp anything so truthfully self-revelatory. The words hung in the air and Prez cast his face downward again. The room suddenly felt too hot.

"I don't believe that, son. I don't believe you're that far gone. I don't believe you're a monster, son."

*A monster.* There were too many monsters, real monsters, running the streets. The kind of monsters not found in bedtime stories or fairy tales. At least not the ones he read. He studied Conant's picture again and held it in those hands (whose hands?) which did things he certainly couldn't be held accountable for. "All right. Maybe I heard something."

"I'm listening. Conant's momma wants to know, son."

"Someone who was there. I'm not saying he did it."

"You got a name for me?"

*I bet that woman had a name.* "Dollar."


The rarely observed fact about 38th Street was that it told the tale of the city. Beginning on the west side, along the picturesque Eagle Creek reservoir, it wound past the Breton Court apartments then Lafayette Square, and traced an area in the throes of white flight. The street crossed White River and then ran in front of the Indianapolis Museum of Art and the Butler University campus, a once mildly decayed stretch that prettied up a bit as it led to the State Fairgrounds.

Passing Fall Creek, now well into the east side of the city, the curb appeal of the street was forgotten once more. Though it continued long past the Phoenix Apartments, that was where Omarosa's journey ended. Not so much at the Phoenix, but at a house not too far south of there.

Rumor had it that this was Dred's mother's home. Rumor had it that Dred's mother had a bit of a falling-out of some sort with her son and hadn't been seen since. Rumor had it that the home was now a convenient bank, under the protection of Dred. His word was like the Roman emperor's seal of old: no one dared break it out of penalty of a death that would be sure, swift, and certain for any who dared trespass on Dred's hallowed ground.

Omarosa's skill as a thief was unquestioned, demonstrated in part by the fact that she didn't even possess a criminal record. Were this a simple break-in, it would merely be a matter of some second-storey work and a few picked locks. But they weren't in the suburbs now and the front door – on top of being the original door which meant real wood of substantial thickness – was probably reinforced. Plywood covered the windows. Weighing her options, she decided on a different plan. She rang the doorbell.

"Look here, shorty." Junie held the door open. "You got the wrong place. You need to step."

"That's cool. Baylon sent me to help someone here relax, but I'll sure as shit save my back the strain." She stepped back to let him fully appreciate the view.

Her hair ran in a series of fine braids. Hoop earrings hung down to her shoulders. An azure cloud framed her eyes, complementing the electric-blue gloss on her lips. A rhinestone dotted each blue nail. A zippered blue jean jacket matched a skirt which stopped along the curve of her ass. Handcuffs looped in front, an ill-fitting belt buckle. Her fishnet-gartered legs ran down to boots with a six-inch metallic heel, the edge honed to a fine bevel.

"Whoa, whoa, whoa. B sent you? He just full of surprises tonight." Junie studied her fine physique for a few moments; the budding bulge in his pants would've held the door open for her on its own.

"It's just you? I was expecting a bit of a party."

"You mean Parker? He down at juvey. Got locked up on some bullshit. Should be back tomorrow. But we ain't gonna let his absence spoil our good time."

Junie replaced the wood plank and metal rod to secure the door. Omarosa thought they depended too much on Dred's aura to guarantee their safety. That was fine when dealing with folks more afraid of Dred than death. Not so fine when dealing with one of the Fey. These fools ran a sloppy operation and left everything out in the open: product on the tables, baggies half-filled, money still in the counter, and only Junie on watch. Junie, a well-known fuckup. With her deliberate stride and revealing the taut muscles of her thigh, her body language deceptively promised sex. She counted how many bones to break in each arm once he touched her. The creak of protesting floorboards gave her pause.

"Well, well, well, look who we have heah." Michaela wiped her hands on a towel as she came in from one of the back rooms. Wearing a white bohemian-style skirt with red ruffles, the outfit only accentuated the heft of her figure. However, Michaela was much more comfortable dressed this way, than in a suit. More in tune with her personality as she saw it. "I smell fey."

"Me too." Marshall descended the stairs soon after her, his awkward bulk causing him to clutch the railing and concentrate on negotiating each step rather than tax himself with banter.

"I smell unwashed ass and wet horse, so it must be the troll brothers coming out to play."

Michaela bristled. "She the one that's been taking off folks' money."

"Matches the description. No sawed-off tonight, though," Junie circled behind her as he appraised. "Don't know where she'd hide it in that outfit."

Omarosa cursed at herself for being too cocky, even for her. As traps went, however, she wasn't overly impressed. Though it demonstrated probably as much sophistication as Junie could handle. The trolls weren't exactly an instrument of subtlety, say like a finely balanced blade. They were more like a war hammer and if they smashed enough, they got the job done. The job was a bust and it was time to cut her losses and make a hasty retreat. They weren't in position yet which left her plenty of opportunity. Time to expose their weak link. She turned to Junie.

"I didn't think I'd need more than a strong pimp hand for your punk ass."

Junie stepped toward her but was met with a side snap-kick to his gut which doubled him over. Omarosa planted her elbow in the back of his neck, then tossed him at Marshall. With Michaela almost on her, she pulled out the .22 she kept tucked in the back of her skirt. Omarosa was never truly un-armed. Michaela grabbed her gun hand, but Omarosa peeled off two shots, one firing wild, the other catching Michaela in her shoulder. Michaela barely grunted, instead she squeezed the hand until the gun dropped and then punched Omarosa in her belly. Michaela's speed belied her bulk. She smashed a meaty fist into Omarosa's cheekbones, then hit her in the nose the same way. Her head whipped to the side. Her blood dotted the wall. Sent sprawling to the floor, the petals of the rose she'd planned on leaving tumbling from her jacket pocket scattered. Omarosa staggered a few steps to her right, position-ing herself hoping her next gambit might work better than her original plan. Marshall lumbered to-ward her, his deliberate pace full of menace. He eyed her long, fine fingers with the delight of using them for toothpicks later.

Omarosa spun into action, a blur of boneless gym-nastics as she tumbled overhead and arced the blade that formed her heel toward Michaela's throat in a movement so improbably fluid, she almost couldn't react. Raising her arms to protect her neck, she re-ceived a thick gash along her forearms rather than having her carotid artery severed. They seemed to move in special-effects slow-motion as Omarosa grabbed the electronic money counter and smashed it into Marshall.

He spun on his heels waiting for Omarosa's next attack. She landed soundlessly, then Omarosa jumped at him, clawing at his face with the nails on those long, fine fingers. He grabbed her hands and pulled her into his headbutt. Stunned, she began to drop to the floor. He reached for her shoulders, but instead caught her ear rings. He yanked them free, holding one in each hand as if he'd just pulled two grenade pins. Her head ringing and blood spurting down her neck, Omarosa punched her knee upward into his balls. A savage look filled his eyes, his face collapsed into a portrait of pain-fueled rage. She tottered to her left in order to position herself. Marshall staggered back a step, then fully enraged, seized with both hands and threw her, despite the cry of "NO!" from Michaela.

Glass shattered, the sound muted by the plywood on the other side of it. Omarosa's body flew limply through, taking most of the bay window with her. The crystalline teeth scraped her flesh, several shards still protruding from her, though nothing major had been pierced. The impact of the frame and plywood took the wind out of her, but she toppled herself over the porch wall and scampered down the sidewalk. People stared as she ran, moving out the way of the beaten and bleeding prostitute that fled the house of Dred.

"Sorry, sis, I wasn't thinking. Should we go after her?"

Michaela put the flat of her hand against his chest. "No. Look at the fear in the people's eyes. See how they turn their heads away not wanting to see too much. No, I'd say the right message has been sent."

## CHAPTER TWELVE

With Halloween came many kids not bothering to put on costumes, going from door to door making the words "Trick or Treat" truly sound like an implied threat. The jack-o-lanterns' faces slumped with rot, soon rat-chewed and discarded as the fall days bled into Thanksgiving and times of family reunions.

An upturned maroon umbrella rested against a back patio. A storm door was propped open. A swarm of large male mosquitos congregated within a stand of pine trees riddled with brown needles down by the creek. Some of King's neighbors still kicked it out on their plastic lawn furniture and usually a good breeze kept the bugs off them during the warm night. Two of them stood off to the side to finish their smokes, even some of the neighborhood kids ran around, despite the late hour, but it was a Friday night and it wasn't like they had a bunch of appointments lined up for their Saturday morning.

As he started toward them, he noticed Baylon beside the large bush that blocked the view from the side street. A skinny white girl with blonde hair – carrying a mixed baby wearing only a diaper – stood close to him pleading her case. Nodding toward Junie, he whistled to draw his attention, and pointed to her. She beamed with appreciation and headed toward them.

"I expect to see you tomorrow," Baylon barked after her.

"You're a real man of the people." Though he wore an open leather jacket over it, King filled out his black T-shirt allowing his muscles to coil and flex beneath it. The word "RESISTANCE" captioned a picture of the '68 Olympians with raised fists.

"King."

"Don't you ever give it a rest?" King asked.

"Capitalism marches onward. A brotha's got to get his."

They stared at each other in a tense silence. King hated this part of the show. The never backing down, never showing weakness, escalating sense of impending violence. It was such a waste. King wasn't sure how to react. Baylon and he had a history and it was clear that Baylon and Lady G had known each other. With Prez being gone, Lady G had been staying with Big Momma, but it wasn't as if she was his girl or anything. Then something else occurred to him. Both Baylon and Green were personally overseeing the corner, and their troops appeared thin. "No harm done. I'm just out here seeing what's what. Been hearing things."

"I just didn't want there to be any... misunderstandings," Baylon said.

"Don't start none, won't be none."

King walked toward the gathered throng as Baylon watched. Lady G slumped in her chair, a sweater slung around her. Any self-consciousness she might have felt under Baylon's gaze, she ignored with a cool aplomb. Big Momma sat between her spread legs, her hair half combed out, half with micro-braids. After a few minutes observing King and Lady G's awkward dance, Baylon moved back to his corner work. One of the neighborhood kids headed their way from the opposite direction of King. His T-shirt had the words "I LOVE ORAL SEX" emblazoned on the front.

"Boy, where'd you get that shirt?" Big Momma asked, the way King's mother used to "ask" when she was really yelling at him.

"It's my dad's. He said I could wear it."

"Then you can wear it, but not around here. Go on back to your house and change shirts."

"It's the only one that's clean."

"Then turn it inside out or something, but you ain't wearing it around here."

"OK." He took off his shirt, revealing his frail frame. He turned it inside out then joined the other kids who had stopped their game to watch the mini-showdown.

"Trifling-ass parents..." Big Momma muttered. "What kind of parents are gonna let their kid walk out of the house in a shirt like that?"

Lady G mm-hmm-ed from behind her.

"Girl, you just mad at the world." King sat down. "You up for some hair?"

"Bout time. Your head's done got all raggedy," Big Momma said.

It was true: for the last few weeks, King had been letting his hair grow out. His frazzled cornrows in need of tightening. It was time for a new look he had supposed. The fact that Lady G did hair in lieu of rent had nothing to do with it. Big Momma, however, had truly taken the girl in and now was every bit the gateway her real momma would have been. Lady G, though she never voiced it, loved it. Her fingertips, the sole part of her hands not covered by her black gloves, danced in Big Momma's hair.

"Boy, what do you do to your hair?" Lady G asked.

"Put water on it then push it back." She took her comb and pulled at a clutched stalk of hair. "Ow. Dag."

"Beauty is pain," she said.

"Who you trying to look good for?" Lady G asked coyly.

"No one in particular," he lied poorly. "That's you women out here who like to act all diva-ish."

"The grass is always greener and some women don't mind mowing someone else's lawn." Lady G parted another section of Big Momma's hair and then planted her comb in the remaining unbraided section while she worked.

"That's what divas do, huh?"

"All I'm saying is that I don't keep too many girl friends, especially around me and my man. One or two close ones I talk to–"

"Like Rhianna," King slipped in.

"A few I hang out with–"

"Like that girl in the park from the other day."

Lady G couldn't help but suppress a grin at the attention he paid to her life. She continued: "But none I tell everything to. They the ones that come back and stab you. You ain't in love or anything are you?"

"I only ever fell in love once."

"Oh, Lord," Big Momma said.

"Your baby's momma?" Lady G asked.

"I ain't talking about her. I forget that girl's name." King closed his eyes while Lady G picked at Big Momma's tangled braids.

"Shameika," Big Momma answered for him. "He was really young, they had a really good relationship. But then she switched to another church, fell in with a new group of friends, and started hanging around with them. It wasn't that he was jealous of her new friends. He wasn't even mad that she had a life outside of him, but he wasn't the type of person to put up with being exiled. First he was in, and then he was completely out. So he turned around and told her it might be best if they chilled for a minute. The worst break-up he ever had."

That was what he thought then.

"That didn't sour you on women?" Lady G asked.

Big Momma answered again. "It was the only time he fell in love. Other than that, all he had was 'girls' like his baby's momma: a girl for a jazz concert, a girl for a movie, a girl for prayer meeting. He didn't want them to get the wrong idea, so he always told them upfront."

"A church boy at heart?" Lady G tugged at a knot causing Big Momma to grimace.

"Nothing wrong with that."

A clearing throat interrupted them. Big Momma, Lady G, and King all turned to find Merle standing there as if he'd been there the entire time.

"What a pleasant scene," Merle said. "I hate to break up such an idyllic moment, but we have business to attend to."

Loose Tooth awaited Tavon on the steps of the porch. On post. Even at night, under the sodium glare, Tavon loved the house. For him, it was almost sacred ground.

"What's up?"

"Same old foolishness," Loose Tooth said with his gravelly voice and a sad, resigned smile. "Miss Jane an' 'em's inside."

Only then did Tavon notice the racket coming from inside. He went around to the rear of the house, Loose Tooth faithfully following, to the basement entrance. He bent the plywood covering enough for them to slide through. If night had a texture, it felt like the black of the basement. Only after their eyes adjusted could they use the residual glow from the street lamps to discern the foreboding shapes around them. They made their way past the rusted-out furnace, an antique from forty years ago. A pile of old window frames, still useable, littered a storage room floor. He blithely slid past the ad-hoc floor joists that leveled the bending floorboards. The rotted stairs croaked in protest with each of their steps. Tavon put his shoulder into the nailed-shut door.

Ship-wrecked lost souls lay about the living room floor. Too many times he came here to find out that Miss Jane had let a whole crew flop there, like a basement party that got smoked out. This time the sprawl of bodies used each other to stave off the cold. Miss Jane quickly explained that she charged each of them a few bucks – a take she was willing to split fifty-fifty with Tavon (which Tavon knew that he'd be lucky to see a tenth of the money) – to partake in the Black Zombie testing.

"Who he?" Tavon asked, nodding toward the lone white guy.

"He's my wigga."

The scrawny burnout with a chest like a squirrel looked like a trailer park refugee. His bloodshot eyes danced like life was one big video game that he was desperately trying to follow. He rubbed his hand over his closely cropped hair. His shoes tied over bare feet and an unfinished tattoo of a dragon rearing to exhale flames glared from above his torn T-shirt. Tavon knew without asking where the money went that was supposed to finish the tattoo.

"I'm just out here trying to school him," Miss Jane said of her latest dupe.

"Yeah, he's my nigger," the burnout said.

The din of the room screeched to an immediate and deafening silence. Fearfully he scanned the room.

"What did I tell you?" Miss Jane asked sternly, stepping menacingly toward him.

"Not too much 'r'?" the burnout answered weakly.

"No 'r'. 'R' means business. 'R' means we obligated to kick your ass."

"My n-nigga?"

Miss Jane put her arm on Tavon to steady herself from laughing too hard. "We just shittin' you. Come on, fool."

Tavon passed out the vials, and played big man and host. He enjoyed the moment of civility, a ghetto tea ceremony.

"You want me to set you up?" Miss Jane asked politely.

"Yeah, great," Tavon said, still attending to his guests. He sat down and Miss Jane snuggled next to him, offering the spike like some champagne toast. She searched out a good vein and with his nod, she pulled back a pinkish cloud then drove the load home. She quickly filled her own and injected it, her head down in a dope-fiend lean, waiting for the blast to hit.

"You know any white Washingtons?" Tavon asked lazily.

"You thinkin' on what that wannabe Muslim be sayin'?" Loose Tooth said with a jaundiced glare from inside his heroin fog. "That fool never met a conspiracy theory he didn't like."

"I'm just sayin', you heard about Thomas Jefferson an' all his kids. George had to be screwin', too. You know all them mugs had slaves. An' Martha wasn't much to look at."

"I guess that makes you practically royalty."

"Well, we don't know our true names," Tavon said with a wan plaintiveness.

"So you want we should call you Tavon X now?" Loose Tooth asked.

"An' give up the smoke? Them Muslims don't play," the disembodied voice of the burnout chimed in from the shadows.

"Shit, he couldn't even give up pork, much less chasing the heroin." The way Miss Jane pronounced it, the word came out "hair ron".

Too much thinking blew his high. Tavon fell silent, but an overwhelming sadness swept over him with the realization that he broke his mother's heart. All of his other siblings went on to college or the military and resented him for the life that he chose for himself. But he missed her, even though he didn't make it to the funeral because he took a charge and did an overnight in city jail. "Life was full of mystery," his mother often proffered as an explanation for their pain. "You can waste your time figuring out the why, or you can let it grow you." She absorbed suffering, especially his, like a sponge and he missed her most during times like this.

He'd been watered.

Why he trusted Miss Jane to be in the spirit of the occasion and not pocket his vial for later, he didn't know. He cursed himself for his stupidity. Turning to confront her, his movement knocked her to the floor. Her eyes rolled into her head. Foam bubbled from the corner of her mouth. Her breaths came in rasps and fits.

"Miss Jane, wake up!" Tavon yelled.

A moan escaped her lips.

"Miss Jane! There's something wrong with Miss Jane!" he repeated to no one in particular. He studied his friends. The burnout had stopped breathing. Loose Tooth still convulsed, his old body dying in wracked spasms. Tavon panicked, flitting from body to body, splashing water on some, trying to get Miss Jane on her feet. Call 911, he thought, letting Miss Jane crumple into a pile. From where? No phones around here. He backed toward the front door. The police wouldn't come anyway. Maybe if he could phone from the KFC.

So he ran.

And kept running.

Wayne slammed the door of the Outreach Inc.'s minivan and tugged on it to make sure it was locked. Street nights were a series of rituals for him. Caffeine was his drug of choice these days. Even as he sucked down a venti caramel macchiato, he thought about the dark places addicts knew. The same sad, scared hole too many folks fell into. Some pushed there by drugs. Some stumbled there due to lack of love. There was always a hole they needed to fill with whatever they could; a need that overwhelmed them such that they pushed their jobs, their school, their friends, their family aside in order to have another attempt to fill it. Wayne knew about the holes and he knew he couldn't save anyone, much less everyone; but he knew what he was called to do. Someone had to step into the gap between the lost and the rest of the world which forgot them. Someone had to push the envelope and risk themselves to go where they were, to love them back to themselves. Someone had to intervene.

That night they went to a wooded area behind the Eastgate Mall. A place he knew well. He knew the temporary tent community that sprung up between police sweeps. He knew the dumpsters that could be scavenged from. A backpack of water, snacks, and socks in one hand and a Maglite in the other didn't seem like much, but with the right team of folks, it was a start. It always came back to who he worked with. Some volunteers were good to mark the location and drop off water. Others truly connected with folks there. Learned their names. Heard their stories. Heard their stories.. Treated them like they were human. Weren't afraid to meet them where they were, in the muck of their lives. A good team, the right team, could venture to the darkest places.

Despite the lateness of the hour, the night always left him energized so he had an evening ending ritual to help him wind down: dinner at Mr Dan's, a twenty-four-hour burger joint with homestyle fries and greasy burgers like your momma would have made. Strains of Outkast's "Bombs over Baghdad" squawked from his cell phone. Wayne sighed, his stomach already grumbling, fearing it would be some street emergency which would delay him sitting down to eat.

"Wayne?" King asked.

"Who you expecting?"

"You didn't sound like yourself."

"Cause I'm ready to find something to meal on and you holding a brother up." Wayne shoved his free hand in his vest pocket and leaned against the minivan.

"Mind if we hook up? I got some things I need to talk to you about."

"Like what?"

"Not over the phone."

Wayne hated these "there's something of cosmic consequence, the fate of the universe hanging in the balance until we talk but I can't tell you about it for a few hours so now you have to spend that time wondering what it is and if you've screwed up some-how" calls. "Long as you don't mind meeting me at Mr Dan's."

"Over on Keystone?"

"Yeah."

"Cool. We'll meet you there."

"We?" Wayne asked to an already dead connection.

Wayne pulled the door to the Neighborhood Fellowship Church which housed Outreach Inc., double-checking to make sure the lock caught. By the time he turned around, Tavon nearly bowled him over. Tavon didn't know what else to do besides ˉˉn, unable to trust anyone at that point, especially considering that his social circle pretty much exhausted itself after fiends, dealers, and police. Wayne was familiar from around the way as one of the neighborhood do-gooders.

"They dead. They dead, man," Tavon stammered.

"Who you talking bout?"

"The fiends that rode that Black Zombie blast."

"Slow your roll, man. Talk to me from the beginning of the story." Tavon's dilated eyes and constant scratching told Wayne a story all right – he was a fiend in need. "Tell you what, I'm about to hook up with some people and get me something to eat. Why don't you come with me and tell us all about it."

Tavon wasn't without compassion, but in the final analysis, fiends did what they did. The need overwhelmed him, pushed aside all other thoughts. A meal here. A ride there. These man-of-the-people types could hook a brother up. Maybe get something he could translate into cash – a bus pass, a gift certificate – and maybe catch the same blast that had knocked the other fiends on they ass. In the end, it was all about getting over, no matter who had to be crawled over.

"You float me?" Tavon asked, suddenly more lucid. "I'm a little light."

"Yeah, I got you."

Lott arrived at Mr Dan's first. One in the morning and he was eating here; his belly and backside would pay for it tomorrow. Actually probably later tonight. He rather enjoyed the simplicity of his life. Having just got off his mandated shift, the gentle skritch of the fabric of his uniform with each step reassured him. He had a little job, was saving a little money, had himself a little place. With no drama and more importantly nothing he couldn't walk away from at any point, he was content within his lifestyle. That was the secret to life, he'd discovered. Folks fell in love with a certain way of living, things they had to have and wouldn't be anything without. That meant they'd do anything to protect it, get all crazy about shit that made no sense. Not Lott. When shit started stacking up, he could cut out any time and set up somewhere else.

Wayne came in next, a fiend trailing behind him. A head nod to Lott, Wayne marched to the counter to place his – and Tavon's – order, not playing when it came to his food. Lott could guard the booth if he wanted. Wayne was still waiting for his order when King arrived.

Lady G and Rhianna pointed at pictures of burgers – though they'd be disappointed by the reality that would show up on their plates later – then joined Lott at the table. Lott seemed to sit up straighter at their arrival.

"He with you?" King asked Wayne, but eyed Tavon.

"Yeah, sorta."

"Always bringing your work home with you."

"You one to talk." Wayne glanced at homeless-
who trailed King. The irony was not lost
dering his line of work versus his

feelings for Merle, but some folks were hard to like. "Extra grace" folks, his pastor called them. Merle always irritated him, as if Wayne was the object of a joke only Merle got.

"I am ever the servant's servant," Merle offered.

Wayne sucked his teeth in response.

"I was hoping we could chat in private," King said.

"You the one with an entourage." Wayne nodded toward Merle and the girls. "I didn't know you knew Lady G and Rhianna."

"It's not like that." King glanced over at Lady G, mildly jealous that she sat next to Lott. "Things been going on and I'm trying to piece things together."

"And I thought 'let us ask he-with-the-wounded-neck'," Merle added.

Wayne rubbed the keloid scar on the back of his neck. "Well, I couldn't leave him alone. I'm trying to get a story out of him, myself. Thought maybe time, fresh air, and a full belly might chill him out enough to be straight with me."

Tavon stabbed several French fries into the gooey mess that was the Mr Dan's Open-Faced Chili Cheeseburger. Gulping down the fries and licking the remaining chili cheese sauce from his dirt-caked fingers, he chanced a peek at Merle and, feeling uncomfortable, he returned his attentions to his plate.

"Curious." Merle stared with mild fascination. "Who are you, my guy?"

"Tavon. Tavon Little." Tavon peered up with distrustful eyes, arm guarding his plate, then went back to mealing.

"Never bring strays where you lay."

"He kinda ain't got it all," Lady G said, more of Merle, not all too sure of Tavon, though fiends she had a better sense for.

"Nah, he good," King said.

"Can I get a new fries? These are greasy." Rhianna pushed the object of disdain away from her, sat back, and folded her arms.

"What you expect from Mr Dan's?"

"Girl, you better eat those fries and be grateful," Lady G said. "It's not like you paying for them."

Rhianna buried her head in her plate like an ostrich.

"What's this about, King?" Wayne asked.

"The gathering of knights," Merle said, ignored by the group.

"I'm not sure," King said. "It's like I have these flashes. Like things aren't what they're meant to be. And I have this feeling like I'm supposed to be doing something."

"Why you?" Wayne pressed.

"He is the dream of a waiting dragon," Merle said.

"Does he ever shut the fuck up?"

King waved off Merle's comments, or rather, Wayne's reaction to them. "Not me. Us. It's like I can almost see the whole story, but when I think on it too hard, it all slips away from me. Merle told me you've all seen something and I thought if we got together, maybe we could sort it out."

"How does Merle know what we've seen?" Wayne glared at him with distrust.

"Magic," Merle said.

"Magic?"

"Magic."

"Bullshit. Chronic maybe," Wayne said.

"In my day, magic was much more commonplace. There's no room for magic in your lives, only darkness. You've forgotten how to dream. To imagine possibilities. All you know is this." Merle knocked on the table. "Continue to make your mud pies and never think to dream of the ocean. Now, some still serve the Old Ways, but there are the Old Ways and ways older still. It is the eternal struggle. The struggle chooses its vessels and we fight where we are. I warn against the beast that sleeps."

"Did that make a damn lick of sense?" Wayne asked.

King steepled his fingers in front of his face and sifted through Merle's words. Like everything else of late, they made sense, an inelegant poem, again, as long as he didn't think about it too hard.

"Sometimes, it seems, we fight the same fight over and over. The players essentially the same, as if light and dark battle to rule each age. The beast changes his form to suit the needs of the age, but the goal is the same: to usher in an age of darkness."

"And the form of the beast?" King finally asked.

"I don't–" Merle started.

"Drugs," Tavon interrupted. "It all always comes down to money and drugs."

"And the sons of Luther," Merle said.

"Sons?" King asked.

"Luther had a second son. Your half-brother. He goes by the name Dred."

The revelation slapped King in the face. It was as if he'd jumped into the deep end of a pool only to be caught in a riptide. He pushed away from the table, suddenly unable to catch his breath. A dark shiver ran along him. His half-brother had lived in his shadow for so long. Everyone continued their chatter without notice.

"Dred? He the one always beefin' with Night," Tavon said.

"OK, someone's going to have to slow this down for me. I can't keep all of this straight," Lott said.

"Shee-it. Any fool knows this." Tavon sat up straight, class suddenly in session. "Right now, the two biggest players in this here game are Night and Dred. Night stays over at the Phoenix. No one knows where Dred hangs his head, but rumor has it that he's been a west side nigga for life."

"So Night runs the east side and Dred runs the west side?"

"It's not that simple. You got to think of the city like a checker board. Dred has the red squares and Night has the black ones. Li'l Nam belongs to Night. Down by where you stay," Tavon turned to Wayne, "that's Dred's. But with all the real estate these two have, they steady beefin' over Breton Court."

"You know why?" King asked, though gripped with a sudden claustrophobic sense about his reality.

"No one knows. No one sees Night or Dred on the streets."

"Egbo. No go. No more," Merle offered. "They are whispers in the nightmares."

"They lieutenants do all the real work: Green for Night and Baylon for Dred," Tavon said.

*Baylon*. The name stung with the familiar pangs of betrayal. King thought that after all this time, hearing the name wouldn't bother him. Yet with the fresh mention, it all came rushing back. All the time they'd spent together coming up. Running through Breton Court with the air of ownership, the young princes of Breton tearing up shit until…

"What about B?" King asked Tavon.

"Who?"

"Baylon. How he fit into this?"

"He's Dred's number two. To be honest, I can't figure out why Dred reached out to him in the first place. It's not as if he had a long resume of overseeing the soldiers, not the way Dred could, even from… his situation. His name rings out like that. Baylon, though, he ain't got no name. He ain't got it like that. Everybody knows he's Dred's errand boy, eyes and ears anyway. Baylon's feeling the heat. Junie and Parker were his people. The troll brothers were called in cause Dred was looking weak."

"Sounds like the shit is building up," Wayne said.

"Yeah, that's the vibe I got," King said. "Like things are about to go to the next level."

"What you think?" Baylon stepped aside so that Michaela and Marshall could view the array unimpeded, the finest merchandise laid out for display along the table. Sig Sauer. Glock. Desert Eagle. Boxes of corresponding bullets stacked like bricks in a pyramid of violence above each. Baylon had even gone so far as to drape the table with a red velvet cloth. Presentation was important. Michaela picked up the Desert Eagle, the light glinting from it.

"They look pretty, but they a waste for us," she said.

"Why?"

"The type of move you talking about making… it ain't a gun type of play. Even if it was, we ain't exactly gun folk. We enjoy getting our hands dirty."

"I'm serious about Green," Baylon said.

"Dred cool with this? I mean, way I see it, we barely got this ship righted. Ain't no one in a position to go after Night's folk direct."

"*We* ain't." Baylon's face grew hot at her "we barely got this ship righted" comment; the insinuation being that he had anything to do with the ship being off-course. "We are taking out one man."

"Green's…"

"Whatever. If you ain't up for it, say the word."

"And Dred?"

"I got this. If we can handle the job."

"You don't know shit about what's what, do you? Got no idea who we are and what Green is?" Michaela squared up against him. She had a few inches on him, worse was her mien of sheer aggression. Close up, he could see each wart, each errant hair on her chin. The frenzied anger in her eyes.

He'd back down if he could and noted his error in directly provoking her.

"Here's what I know and what I need to know: Night and Dred have a truce that will last as long as it takes for one of them to slide a knife into the back of the other cleanly. As I, no, we owe a lot to Dred, we have a vested interest in making sure his is not the back ventilated. As Night owes everything to Green, should he be taken out, Night becomes little more than a shadow puppet. All you got to do is tell me if you can take out Green."

"It'll be like old times," Michaela said.

The booth mates munched in relative silence. Tavon twitched, craving some candy or something else sweet to ameliorate his body's mild trembling. Lady G picked at her food, already full, calculating how to save the rest of her plate for later. King neither ate nor made eye contact with anyone.

"King," Lott began as gingerly as he could, "didn't Green kill your father?"

"That's one story," Merle said.

"What does that mean?" King felt an invisible noose continue to tighten in his life. A wave of nausea swept through him, as if he floated outside of himself while strangers dissected, and then put back together, his life story. Coincidence couldn't explain the players in the game being close enough for them to reach out to him whenever they wanted, yet he be oblivious to their presence. Shadows in plain sight.

"That's all I know, really. One story, the one the streets made legend, had Green slaying the elder Pendragon, but that never made any sense to me. Green had nothing to gain and he never operated without something to gain. Wasn't his way."

"You sound like you were there," King said.

"To you, the arrow of time points in one direction," Merle said.

The rest of the table exchanged sideways glances with one another, not knowing what to make of Merle and Tavon. Bullshit artists of the first degree, probably, like griots of African tribes telling stories for their keep. Lott and King, however, paid extra attention.

"Thing is, Green could and should be running Night's crew," Tavon continued, smacking his mouth loudly as he ate while talking. "He has the name, he has the muscle. He even had the real estate. But he lets Night run things."

"Green prefers the shadows. That's irony," Merle said.

"Green's eternal."

"That's one story. Another goes that for every spring there must be a winter."

"I'm about sick of your riddles," Wayne said.

"We all have our roles to play. I'm only a guide. He's the hero." Merle pointed his dirty-nailed thumb toward King.

"I'm no hero," King said.

"That's why we're here. Heroes, love, and spiritual quests. The story's still the same."

"Any of you know a light-skinned sister, braids, pointy ears?" King asked.

"Thus enter the fey," Merle said.

"You mean Omarosa? What you want with her?" Tavon picked at his remaining fries.

"Seen her around. She fit into any of this?" King asked. The heat of Lady G's body made him all too self-conscious. She continued to eat her fries in silence, making no claim on him. Or any man.

"She's strictly independent far as I know."

"Never accept a gift from her kind," Merle said. "And don't raise the terror of their anger."

No one believed in fairies anymore. With no belief to sustain them, most faded away to the land of Nod, the wellspring of ideas, there to remain forgotten and unmourned. When most folks thought of fairies, the image of gay sprites and winsome pixies sprang to mind. There was the whispered caution to never accept a gift from one, but for the most part, people thought of them as prancing merry-makers. Because few survived to tell the tale of the fey once angered.

On rare occasion, a rogue fairy roamed the land of mortals, engaged in a tryst of some sort, and continued their wanderings heedless of the consequences.

Omarosa was such a consequence.

The Marion County Juvenile Detention Center had grown accustomed to scandal over the years. From their issues with overcrowding to the allegations of sexual abuse (many of those charges were

later dropped, but the stain remained). In the wake
of the ensuing reforms, guards, inmates, and visitors
wore arm bands which could even alert staff when
rival gang members were in proximity to one another. Certain events caused minor cracks in the
system, such as the general scoops of kids in the
wake of the Breton Court shooting. With public
pressure for an arrest, many kids were detained
overnight as the mess sorted itself out. Parker's luck
never was too good. He was merely "spectating" as
he explained to the cracker-ass po-lice who questioned him. As the detective explained, "spectating"
did not explain the vials he was caught with. Personal use became his mantra, a charge to be all but
dismissed by over-worked judges and a crowded
system, and recognized that this was little more than
a charge used to remind him of his place in the
greater criminal justice scheme of things. The hill-
billy cop tried to half-sweat him about Dred and
Night's operations ("who?") with any further questions ready to trigger his Miranda-given rights
("Law. Yer."). So he was put in a cell to give him
time to think about things. A peaceful night's sleep
not worrying about getting got on a corner. That
was the game then.

In the game now, Omarosa stood over the sleeping
Parker, letting an arm of her set of handcuffs ratchet
through the main body.

*Click. Click. Click.*

Parker didn't stir. Asleep, he was still very much a
child, a man-boy, not quite the hardened killer he

wished to be. Asleep, he was someone who could be loved, who'd let someone love him. Asleep, the possibility of dreams, of a better future remained.

Omarosa knelt down and whispered in his ear.

"Parker, your destiny calls you."

He smiled upon hearing the feminine voice, the sound of rose petals against naked flesh; a tease of promise in the night and his dick hardened. A few moments later, his eyes fluttered – he required several moments to be convinced that he wasn't dreaming – not quite making out the form, enough to register that he wasn't alone. Before he could react, Omarosa grabbed him from his bed. She had him in a choke-hold, but adrenaline-fueled panic soon flooded him. He had nothing to flail against besides her as she drew him to the middle of the cell. Her height advantage on him meant little compared to the blood and strength of the fey in her veins. His eyes bulged, his face reddened with his last gasps and dawning realization that he had reached his life's endgame. His arm shot out, grasping at nothing in particular, his other fist slamming weakly into Omarosa's side. Consciousness fled him and his body fell limp into her arms.

Tearing his bedsheets, she fastened a noose and propped him against the bed to let the body fall. The investigation – such as it would be since no one would look too closely for fear of the phrase "dereliction of duty" entering their job performance jackets; and with suicides being more common than anyone wanted to believe – would conclude suicide.

Still, she wanted folks to know that she could reach them anywhere. She placed a black rose on the shelf above the sink. It would be a note in a file somewhere, but it would find its way into Parker's personal effects. And people would know. The fey were not to be trifled with.

You let them go about their business unless you want their terror to rain down upon you.


"Wait," Wayne said, still putting pieces together. "ESG was independent."

"Not that independent. There are a few dozen gangs here and everyone has their ties somewhere. ESG's loyalty was to Night," Tavon said. "I hear the trolls got into them."

"We were there." Wayne shifted in his seat. Lady G and Rhianna studied the napkins in their laps. Wayne told the tale of the trolls' attack on Rhianna's friends.

"And the police didn't do anything?" King asked Tavon.

"Oh, it's hot out there, for sure. Po-po out in force. But what they gonna do? Can't investigate with no body. And the trolls eat their prey. So Prez's boy is just another missing nigga. They wouldn't be looking too hard no ways."

"You know Junie? Him and some young dude he's been rollin' with," King said.

"Junie and Parker?" Tavon asked. "Yeah, I know them."

"I saw them trying to muscle Green."

"Once a fuck-up… Junie and Parker were replaced by the trolls. I hear they been demoted. Out slinging where ESG used to."

Smoke layered the air around him as Junie got blunted up, tripping high on his weed as he took swigs from his forty ounce. When he was up like this, his simple thoughts and false courage turned dark and focused, a cold, sick churning in his head. In the corner of the hovel he called home, sweat trickled down the burnt marshmallow flesh of his grayish face. The life he envied when he saw the likes of Dred or Night roll through the neighborhood in their Escalades with their rims, their stereos, their bling, had come to this. His body ached and he stank of overripe fruit fermenting in a dark, moist place. His scraped knuckles were red and swollen from punching the plaster from his walls. Rumor had hit the wire that Parker was dead. That he'd done himself. Not that the word of junkies and prostitutes was to be trusted, however, Junie knew down deep in his soul that the story had the stink of truth about it.

A bout of sudden nausea sent him scrambling to the bathroom. The sink looked like someone tried to wash their abortion down it. Junie reached into his waistband and fished out the grip of his auto. Stainless steel, it was the most expensive gun they had. He flipped the safety then tucked it in his waist, the tail of his shirt covering it. He'd been punked, and that didn't sit well with him. He needed to come back on Green. He had built the corner down off McCarty

Street into a real spot, had carried his demotion by proving himself. He had earned his way back up to Breton Court. But he still needed to step up, let his name ring out for real by taking out Green.

He had to correct a situation.


"Sounds to me like everything keeps coming back to Breton Court and the Phoenix," King said.

"How you figure?" Lott asked.

"Breton Court seems to be the flash point, but everything seems to come from the Phoenix."

"Like it's at the heart of the web." Lott followed King's thought.

"The dragon's lair," Merle said.

"But what about the fiends?" Wayne asked Tavon.

"They fell out. Sick or somethin'."

"Who?"

"My people them, down in Li'l Nam. We rode the Black Zombie blast. Knocked everyone right the fuck out."

"Except you?"

"I… got watered." Tavon studied his plate, not meeting anyone's eyes. Even fiends knew shame when they got played at their own game. Things didn't get much lower than that.

"They out for real? You call for an ambo or something?"

"Nah, I–"

"So let me get this straight: you got all worked up cause some fiends got knocked on they asses? Shit, I thought you had a real problem."

"I'm telling you, this was different."

"Look, here's my card." Wayne slipped his card across the table. "Outreach has a 1-888 number. Where they stay at?"

"Penn and 24th."

"Tell you what then. You go back there in the morning and see what's what. You got a problem, call 911. Either way, call the number and check in with me. The person on call will get me the message. I'll come out. I don't hear from you, I'm still coming out, but I'll be pissed."

"You smell that, Sir Rupert? He reeks of the dragon's breath."

"What's with the dragon shit?"

"The dragon… he's wide awake now."

# CHAPTER THIRTEEN

Green was on it. There was no getting inside Green's mind. His was the primal thoughts of nature unbound. Elemental. A force of nature. The ways of a dragon were easier to understand. Most people assumed him to be a soldier, a corner boy, a thug in clean vines. Those things they understood. Those things – however violent, however toxic, however shallow and dehumanizing – wouldn't leave them screaming in the night. Green was Green. And Green was eternal. So when the bug-ridden girl – with too-thin arms but whose body wasn't too far removed from the voluptuous beauty she'd once been – ambled towards him, he was unmoved. To the casual observer, it might have seemed that pussy was pussy, easy to get, and thus none especially swayed Green. She could display her wares in the sauntering suggestion of seduction in order to mooch a vial, but it would do her no good. On a good day, he would ignore her with a glare of casual disdain which would freeze the blood in her veins.

On a bad day, well, the streets ran rampant with tales of Green on a bad day. He was on it. If ambitious fiends tried to run game on him, if daring street thieves raided his stashes, or simply if fools just came up short, miscounting money or just losing shit cause they were careless, Green was on them. Eyes on point, never faltering.

There was a time when he enjoyed this time of the morning. The world was still fairly dark, but with the hint of sunrise, the day was still full of promise and imminent hope. Dew, an equal-opportunity shroud, blanketed windshields and grass. His blood afire against the cool of the fading night, he used to be at his most creative, his most alive. Now the mornings drained him. So much work left undone and yet to be done. Those fleeing the dawn's light still left a mess in their wake, and the day served only to remind him that night would once again return.

"Fellas, time to tool up," Green said to the latest bunch of workers he supervised. His was an ancient and dark voice, the sound of twigs snapping like brittle bones. Somehow he'd been relegated to middle management, too far separated from the pulse of the streets, too far from the thrill and experience of life; but he had found ways to make up for it. Supervising from street level, for one thing.

"What's up?" a young, rock-faced soldier asked because he was ready to call it a night.

"Just some business I have to settle. Make sure we have no other surprises."

● ● ●

The gray sky lightened with the rising sun. The street lights hadn't turned off, obstinately clinging to the embers of night. The Durham Brothers pulled into a side street on the other side of the bridge that crossed the creek that separated Breton Court from the rest of housing addition. Their long and ample limbs jutted ridiculously from the Ford Focus which creaked noisily when they exited. Pressing smooth their outfits, one last primp before their engagement, they shambled along the sidewalk, then veered off as they got to the bridge, careful to remain out of the direct line of sight from Green. They cut through the yard of the house they parked in front of, whose backyard opened onto a sloping hillside that terminated at the creek. The bridge wasn't the largest by any stretch, little more than a culvert, but it would suffice.

"He out there," Marshall said.

"I didn't see anyone, but, yeah, I can feel him." Michaela closed her eyes, double-checking the odd stirring in the core of her being.

"You think he can feel us?"

"He Green, ain't he?"

"Yeah, but we're in our–" Marshall started.

"Place of power. True." The bridge became an echo chamber whenever a car rumbled along it. The murky creek water lapped at the edges of the embankment, riffles of current thinned by the lack of rain. Overgrown with weeds, overturned grocery carts divided the channel. The yellow and brown of fallen leaves blanketed much of the embankment, blown under and trapped by the mild breeze.

Michaela shuddered with her own chill. "But Green's outside. It's all his place of power."

"Be a good time to hit him. Late fall. Winter's only technically a few days away. Close enough."

"Not much of a plan."

"We hit. Hard. A lot. What more do we need?" Marshall blew out a snot rocket then wiped his porcine nose with the back of his hand.

"You're right. Ain't no plan at all."

The siblings did a fist bump.

"Let's do this."

Octavia Burke drove because she never trusted Lee's judgment behind the wheel and idly turned onto Georgetown Road from 86th Street. They had opted to grab a bite at the Thai House and then head back to Breton Court to do some follow-up interviews. Georgetown Road was one of those confusing streets. Remaining Georgetown Road until it crossed Lafayette Road, "Georgetown Road" picked up again a street light south on Lafayette Road and the winding street they continued to travel on became Pike Plaza from the corner strip mall for the few blocks until the street wound past a Meijer at which point it became Moller Road. Moller Road and High School Road were the east and west boundaries, respectively, of Breton Drive, the side street leading to the world within the isolated world of Breton Court.

"I don't have to explain myself to you." Lee slouched in his seat, a vacant stare etching the glass of the window. The defensiveness of his voice bit at his ears, though it was too late to do anything about it.

"I guess it's OK to date hookers then."

"She's no hooker." Again his voice betrayed him, raised in too vehement a protest. Part of him wondered about her practiced ease of seduction, not wanting to confront the notion of what a beautiful woman like her might see in someone like him.

"So she says."

"So her sheet says. I don't pay for poon, pardon my fuckin' French."

"She's not a pro, but you ran her anyway. Nice." Octavia shifted in her seat turning as much of her back to him as possible. Some days, she didn't want to even look at him. "Play semantics all you want, just cause demanding a freebie ain't technically paying for it."

"Even if she was a pro, and she ain't, getting a little on the side – as long as no money changes hands – ain't a crime."

"It is if you let her walk rather than bring her in." Octavia fixed her eyes on the road, not deigning to chance even a glance in his direction. Once folks started getting on her nerves, she found it easier to block them out as if they weren't there.

"It's not like that."

"What's it like then?"

"It's like… none of your business." Lee, with his trailer-park features and sensibilities, wasn't going to admit that women who looked like Omarosa rarely took a second glance at guys who looked like him.

Especially black women. And he was tired of the black women he encountered taking one whiff of him and deciding not only that they knew him, but that they were better than him.

His silence told Octavia everything she needed to know.

A call came across the radio about a fight occurring by the Breton Court bridge. Lee sighed. Civvies rarely understood the dangers of a fight, though, in light of the recent shooting, maybe they might comprehend them a little better. When folks closed in on you, it wasn't as if you could just draw your gun and back them down. In the heat of a melee, with hands and fists everywhere, folks kicking and punching with no skill or thought, your gun was only yours as long as you held it. Then the call came in about shots fired as they screeched to a halt at the intersection just prior to the bridge. The intervening silence brought its own ghosts.

For years, Octavia had been haunted by a recurring dream. She would be chasing a perp, his face always a blur, never quite coming into focus. Suddenly, he'd turn to face her and draw his weapon. She fired her gun first but the bullets never hit him. They'd be on target, center mass, but the bullets would stop a foot short and clatter against the ground.

Lee's ghosts were memories that brought to mind the old hates. He remembered his first day out with his field training officer, Maeda Graham, a bear of a man, even then. Everything was so new to Lee, hearing the sounds of the street and the language he'd never heard, from the cops' insider jargon to the hard language of the streets (even the streets he grew up on took on a new, harsh aspect). All of it was confusing as hell, like seeing life for the first time.

It was also how he learned to hate the animals over at the Phoenix. He and Maeda caught a call of shots fired over there. They arrived in the middle of a shootout, so they decided to wait for back-up. Fresh out of the Academy, all Lee could think about was protecting the civilians. As he and Maeda crouched behind their vehicle, garbage started raining down on them. On them. They who were trying to quell the violence perpetrated against the citizens, their community, their children. The guardians got garbage dumped on them. Amidst the chaos, the warring gangs declared a temporary armistice, and turned their guns jointly a-blazing at Maeda and him. Maeda, determined to go after anyone who dared fire on "true po-lice", yelled where to meet him – the intersection of two streets Lee had never heard of – then took off. Being a rookie, he had no idea where to go or if to go, since that meant abandoning his partner. So he squatted low, kept his head down and prayed, holding his gun with both hands praying his shaking alone squeezed off a few rounds. He'd never been so scared in his life.

Until he saw the figure covered in blood lumbering toward him and Octavia, a bloodied rock in one hand and a severed head in the other.

• • •

The three of them stood there underneath the bridge, all hard and eye-fucking each other like a gunfight scene from an old spaghetti western. Except that this wasn't every man for himself. Nor was this like any other bridge. The creek that the bridge spanned was a natural ley line, augmenting the bridge as a place of power for the trolls. Also for Green. The Durham Brothers were essentially one person. His protestations aside, Marshall was a follower; no shame on it since that was the way he was wired. In his size 17 combat boots and Army camo pants, topped by a black T-shirt with a heavy metal band no one had heard of (but the picture was cool, he thought), he needed someone's lead to connect with. His hands balled and relaxed, balled and relaxed, flexing into meaty clubs waiting for the go moment. He turned to Michaela.

"What you going to do?" Michaela asked.

"Probably get my ass kicked," Green said, "but I'll go down like a man. And there ain't no shame in a man being taken down by another man. That shit happens. There's always someone stronger."

Michaela's brown gypsy skirt flared in the slight breeze. It had a way of making her figure more squat than it should. Standing next to Marshall, she seemed like a man in poor drag with her bunched-up nose and porcine eyes. An old myth ran through her head: the Incarnation of Spring, must be slain in winter.

Michaela and Green's eyes met. His laconic glare was nothing but white death, snow-blind eyes staring into a blizzard. Michaela's eyes betrayed fear. Only a hint, not enough for her brother to see. Spit flew from her mouth.

It was go time.

Michaela charged Green, throwing a wide punch. He sidestepped the punch but hooked her underneath her shoulder and dropped her to the ground by back-sweeping her legs. He turned when his mind registered the approaching shadow only to have the full weight of Marshall's punch slam into his jaw, bowling him over.

Marshall dipped his head down and rammed Green in a tackle that pinned him against the concrete wall of the bridge. Marshall held Green up with one arm and punched with the other. Green clawed at the arm.

"Marshall!" Michaela yelled.

From her vantage point she could see what Marshall couldn't: with every slam into the embankment, Green's skin splintered through his clothes, leaves and branches jutting then retreating like an overstuffed garbage bag full of raked fall leaves – his skin knitting itself back under the illusion of flesh. Green turned to her, his eyes aglow with emerald fire, aiming one free hand at Marshall. In an instant, the length of his arm shot through Marshall's mouth out the back of his head. A wayward stalk, a jutting branch which pulled back into the shape of Green's hand as it withdrew from Marshall's skull, still gore-covered, bits of gray matter stuck between his fingers.

Marshall stood there, a fist-sized hole in the back of his head, still holding Green to the wall as if what remained of his brain couldn't process why he was holding the man when, in fact, he should be dead. Green fell from his grasp as the body finally decided to collapse. Limping aside, a mixture of blood and sap poured from Green's wounds.

"No!" Michaela charged him, wild-eyed and unthinking. Green hinged forward, doubled over by the force of her fist in his gut. His eyes bulged out and breath left him. She stepped in and kicked him for all she was worth, stomping on his side like he was a fire in need of extinguishing. He caught her foot, pulled her off balance, and toppled her. He scrambled on top of her and drove his fist into her face. The crack sounded like a tree branch toppling. She elbowed him in his side, the force of which knocked him from her, and staggered to her feet.

The two circled each other. Green held his side. What appeared to be green flames, mystical energy, trailed from his eyes. His clothes a tattered mess, stained with blood and a viscous, clear fluid. Michaela spat out blood and a tooth. Snot ran down her face which she wiped with the back of her hand. Her eyes glazed with the resignation that perhaps it was not close enough to winter. Catching a glimpse of her fallen twin, she stood from her crouch, her legs a buckling mess.

They rushed each other one last time. Green's fingers raked across her face even as her meaty fists connected with his already-wounded side. His fingers dug deeper, finding purchase in her eye sockets and nostrils. His fingers extended into those cavities. Michaela's left eye burst, a mix of bone and blood, the eye dangling free from its socket. Her mouth opened in a silent scream as he kept pulling. He drove the talon-like nails into her face and pulled. Her skull cracked, a slow splitting egg, her expression a frozen rictus of – if not terror – with a sense of understanding eternity. Her head exploded in a rain of brain matter and blood.

Green staggered forward, his fingers slowly withdrawing into the approximation of a human shape. Michaela's body collapsed onto her knees and held that position, a headless supplicant in prayer before tumbling over. Slowly, he climbed the hill leading up to Breton Court. The shouts of his boys were a mishmash of sounds. He saw them running toward him, slowing as he came into their eyesight. His alien – the word their minds would scramble to elucidate was ancient, but to them he would simply be alien – elemental form, the disfigured form they knew as Green, horrified them. They raised their guns toward him. The weapons reports echoed, the flight of bullets whirred past him.

"Get down," one yelled.

Green was about to turn when a slug burned into his back. More emerald flames erupted from the wounds. His skin was like aged parchment sewn together by rough cords which now threatened to tear loose in sheets. He needed time to fully heal. Time that Junie – in his harried amble and eyes a mix of terror and frenzy – was not about to give him.

Anger consumed Junie. To compare his anger to cancer did a disservice to the disease. His anger filled his every waking moment, defined his very core, and seeped into every pore of his body. He wore his anger like a life-preserver, clinging to it because not only was it all he knew, but he was desperately afraid to let it go. It was so much a part of him, he didn't know how to function without it. So Junie had no choice. He had to do what men did. Parker was gone, but he didn't know what to do with the anger. He didn't know who to blame. He couldn't blame God because God had long turned his back on the shit stain he called a life. He couldn't blame Parker because sometimes you got got. They all knew how the game would end for them. He couldn't blame himself for contenting, no, consigning both he and Parker to a life without vision or purpose. But he knew in the shriveled remains of the thing he called a heart that this whole mess had to be someone's fault. He wasn't a particularly contemplative man. He felt. He acted. Had he been of the more reflective type, he would have realized that he raged at the futility of his world. A world he accepted and was complicit with. Anger and blame was all he knew and it twisted him up inside. Burning up all that was good and decent in him until there was nothing left but the rage. A rage occasionally assuaged by drugs.

But Parker was still dead. That boy had potential. Potential Junie knew he didn't know how to encourage. All he knew was this life. He didn't know from books or college or a straight life. He didn't have the tools to get him out. He thought by teaching him the game, by being there, he could protect him. Be like a father to him. He failed at both. Damn it all. Men like Junie didn't love. Love fucked with him or he'd fuck it up. Either way, he didn't truck with no love. He did know about respect. And consequences. Rage was the all-consuming consequence. Once men like him figured out this was all there was to their lives, this was all they'd ever be, a calm would overtake them. An existential peace that came with figuring out something most folks hadn't. And was freeing. Junie was ready to die, a samurai ready to fall in honor to his master. For Junie, the master of his life was the game. His hoodie drawn up, a burial shroud, and the gun heavier than usual in his hand. He recalled the first lesson Baylon taught him: "Don't be caught half-stepping with your gun on safety."

Green stumbled up the embankment, each step a struggle. His clothes ripped to tatters, the man appeared to have been used as a retrieval stick for a rabid dog. He lumbered toward Junie, eyes unfocused, as if unaware of Junie's presence. That was how it had been for Junie his entire life. Even when he was present in the classroom, in the meetings, he wasn't there. No one saw him. No one took him seriously.

He squeezed the trigger and didn't quit pulling it.

• • •

Green was officially pissed off.

Green grabbed a stone from the broken concrete of the bridge and charged toward Junie. His muscles flexed like a bound cord of twigs. His flesh threatened to be rent from him with each step. The eldritch fires seethed in spurts, he barely contained them now. The assault by the troll brothers took their toll on him, causing him to expend more power than he expected. Drawing on the green, the force of life, the elder magicks that held even his current form together, taxed him on many levels. He was tired. This age exhausted him. The effrontery of this mortal intruding on the soliloquy of his thoughts, however, elicited a more than commensurate response.

Junie fired wildly, the courage of the gun waning as his target didn't shrivel and cower but rather ran toward him. He all but dropped the gun to turn tail himself, but Green was upon him before he could move.

"Now we play the most ancient of games," Green said, his voice a fatigued whisper, the sound of dead leaves scurrying across cracked pavement. "Only one has ever bested me in it. You and the trolls have tried your best to behead me, but I still stand. Now, we see how well you do."

Green shoved Junie, face down against the sidewalk, pinning his head with his left hand as he straddled the man's body. Junie feared Green was about to rape him, to punk him out in front of his entire crew. Entreating words pleaded for Green to not do what he thought about doing, to leave him with some measure of dignity. Hot tears scalded Junie's cheeks, ashamed at himself for begging, much less being in this position again. The life had its costs and Junie had already paid dearly during his last bid in prison. Memories he thought he had dealt with, blocked out, and moved on from. Yet they haunted part of his soul and further stoked the flames of anger.

Green raised the rock above his head then brought the edge of it down on Junie's neck. The first blow nearly severed his head clean off, silencing Junie's merlings with a single wet thud. The next three were pure rage. Junie's blood splattered on Green. Heedless of the sanguine shower, Green went about his task with grim determination. His fury nearly spent, he roared with the righteous indignation of spring interrupted by a last blast of winter. The wails of sirens quickly drowned out his cry as Five-O screeched to a halt along either side of the bridge.

A dull roar filled Lee's ears. His mind couldn't quite digest the chaos going on around him, not fully process what he was seeing. Through the cacophony of white noise, he heard his partner yell at the man, if indeed he was a man. A disfigured creature, branches protruding from his face like a man who ran his car into a tree with such force he'd become one with it. Not much of his skin or clothes remained. Octavia ordered him to drop whatever it was he had in his hand and lace his fingers behind his head. All Lee could do without having to think about the sight in front of him was parrot his partner, repeating the command of "on your knees, get on your knees" like a mantra hoping its familiarity would somehow center him. The man, locked in his weary stride, carried himself with a laid-back yet in-control aspect, an ambulatory bush attempting a pimp stroll. Under the mucous, the blood, and torn clothes, he had to be Green. *What was wrong with his skin?* Lee kept asking himself, his brain not leaping to believe what his eyes took in.

The rest of Green's boys scattered without command. The radio car pulling up from the west side of Breton Drive boxed them in. The nervous officers drew their weapons, the scene uncertain, radioing for more back-up. They shot panicked, disbelieving glares at one another before settling on focusing on the straggling – and equally confused – soldiers. The equation of portending violence amounted to four officers (and thus four guns) against two street soldiers and Green, in-between them.

Green stood tall.

One of his soldiers ducked behind the row of cars along the front parking lot. The other ran back and forth between the sheltering presence of Green and the presumed safety of being taken into police custody. His body, if not quite his conscious mind deciding between having Green's back by facing down the officers (he had skidded to a halt mid-jetting out as they slammed their brakes) and darting between the rowhouses in the better course of valor, or turning himself in to be hauled far away from the entire scene. Such decisions were better made without having a gun drawn.

As he doubled back toward the cars, the first soldier popped his head up, gun clearly visible through the car's windshield. Lee fired the first shot. Dropping his gun in reflex, the second soldier hit the ground, spread-eagled before the officers nearest him could fire. He held his hands up, deliberately and quite visibly away from the gun, but kept his head ducked. The former soldier opened fire, heedless to Green being in the way. One of Lee's rounds hit Green in the shoulder. Green staggered backward, wavered for a moment, then toppled over the bridge railing. A heavy splash soon followed.

Lee eyed the side of the bridge, preparing for Green to sneak up the embankment. The ambling mass never arrived. Distracted by the thought of being taken unawares – from all that he'd learned, Green never backed down from anything, no matter the odds against him – Lee stepped out from the shield of his car door. Due to more luck than skill, the shooter caught him in his leg. Collapsing in a hail of profanities, Lee's world had been reduced to pain. He didn't know from where, couldn't even tell which leg though his body knew, and he clutched the wound. He only knew pain.

Octavia darted out from behind her door, presenting herself as a more immediate threat. The soldier turned to draw a bead on her. Too nervous and untrained, his aim faltered. Hers did not. She hit him twice in the arm and shoulder. The gun fell from his hand.

"Lee, you all right?" she yelled in his direction but didn't take her eyes from the perp. She eased over to him and kicked the gun away. With a nod, she had the uniform officers secure him.

"I'm all right. You get him?"

"He's down. Don't you move, motherfucker." As one of the officers pulled the first soldier's arms behind him, locking him down in cuffs, she began stomping him in his side with a flurry of kicks. "What. The fuck. Were you thinking? Shooting at police?"

The flashing lights of the radio cars tinted their faces red. The blood on the pavement looked like spilt red Kool Aid. Plastic number placards dotted the scene like a game of connect the shell casings. Whispers coalesced into a dull susurrus of background chatter: "… could he have been set up?" "… came out blasting… " "… don't know what to think…" "… Glock 17…"

"Losing blood here," Lee whined. "I think I'm gonna pass out."

"How is he?" Octavia asked to the ambulance driver.

"I've seen worse paper cuts," the attending paramedic joked. The bullet had passed through the fleshy part of Lee's spindly leg, missing any vital arteries.

"Any sign of Green?" Lee asked, struggling to sit up in the gurney even as the paramedic tried to load him into their wagon.

"Nothing. He went over the side and then vanished," Octavia said.

"He looked bad. Not quite…" he wanted to say "human" but his mind still wouldn't let his thoughts go there.

"Like Death eating a soda cracker."

"What?"

"Something my grandmother used to say."

"We've got to go," the paramedic said.

"I'm B+, if anyone needs to know," Lee started up again. "Get me to Community North. Don't try and drop me off at Wishard. Wishard's for homeless people and welfare cheats."

"Get him out of here," Octavia said, her smile a matter of relief that her partner would be OK more than any actual affection for him. It would be a long day and she feared they hadn't seen the last of it.

# CHAPTER FOURTEEN

The sun bled on the horizon with night quickly stanching the wound. Tavon anxiously rubbed his hands together, blowing into them only to see his breath pour though his fingers before shoving his hands deep into his pockets. He needed a new jacket. Eyeing the house from down the block, it drew him in, a black hole of guilt. The hunger brought him home, he'd abandoned his friends. His hands trembled. His skin itched as if centipedes scurried beneath it. The desire threatened to consume him and he needed to get well. Soon.

Li'l Nam was jumping tonight.

The occasional scream distracted him, but as soon as he turned to find the source's direction, gunfire erupted. Deciding to mind his own business, he lowered his head and marched to his spot. No, the ambulances or police had shown up. Wherever they were, they weren't in Li'l Nam. He could almost hear Knowledge Allah go on about no one caring about the plight of the black man, and it exhausted him.

More automatic gun bursts.

Leaning against a tree, its bare branches stretching toward the night sky, Tavon wondered if it was worth going in. Nausea snaked through his system. His palms itched. He felt fingernails scrape along the back of his skull. Only when the wave of sickness ebbed did he notice the door ajar. He cautiously lumbered up the steps, pebbles scattering with each footfall. The slow creak of the heavy door shattered the still of the house. The street light filled more of the room – boards had been ripped from the windows – though the night still left deep pockets of shadow. The room smelled of stale sweat, piss, and unwiped ass. And spoiled meat.

He vomited, wiping the vestiges with his cuff. From what he could make out, the house appeared as if a frenzied work crew had gutted it. Holes dotted the wood slats that lined the walls, like a fist punched through a rib cage. Creeping through the debris, he noticed that many of the walls thrown up to divide the house had been torn down, leaving only exposed wiring (much of it cloth wiring patched into newer) and plumbing (smashed PVC). A staircase, much of the original woodwork intact, stood revealed like a body in mid-autopsy. He feared what the basement might look like.

Tavon staggered back out of the mess. A hand landed on his shoulder. He whirled only to be greeted by Dollar.

"Damn, you trying to give a nigga a heart attack?"

"Could say the same about you," Dollar said, his

heavy-lidded eyes studying the scene. He pulled in more in a couple of months than a cop in a year. Only spending money on clothes, he wasn't too flashy, not like his boys. For a young lieutenant, he primped worse than a woman, taking a razor to his head every morning.

"I know I don't look well. I'm sick. Could you hook me up with a blast, just to get right?" Tavon asked.

"How sick are you?"

"How sick I need to be?"

"I mean… have you seen any of your crew lately?" Dollar asked him.

"Naw. I got watered out of those testers you gave us. Then they got to feelin' bad. Real bad. I thought they was OD-ing or something, so I took off. For help. I had just come back to check on them when you showed."

If Dollar spotted all the holes in his tapestry of near-truths, he was too polite or too preoccupied to say anything about it.

"It was a bad package," Dollar said.

"Bad like Widowmaker?"

"No, not quite like that. Night got up with a new supplier and then got word that the re-up was tainted," Dollar said evenly. He rarely got to meet with Night or any of the higher-ups. Being dispatched to the corner left him feeling like an errand boy. "That's when *we* decided that *I* needed to come down here and check things out for ourselves."

Tavon followed Dollar out the door. His boys stood on post on either side of the porch. A few gunshots echoed in the night. Like an approaching storm, more thunderclaps erupted a lot closer. Not sure if he bought his earlier story, and rather than regale Dollar with tales of his guilt and cowardice, Tavon spun an account of going out to visit his sister before scraping together a couple of dollars to try and get a taste. The hunger wrapped its tendrils around his mind, needle pricks in his eyes. Seizing Dollar up, he wondered if he carried any vials on him and if he could snatch them and get past the rent-a-thugs.

"You holdin'?" Tavon asked, praying that his voice didn't waver suspiciously.

"Damn, fiend. Ain't you been listening? The package was bad. And it did something to anyone who rode it. Have you seen any of your fellow fiends?"

Tavon never expected to see any of them upright again. Once he thought about it, Dollar never held. His boys might've, though. "Told you, I ain't been around."

"They dead."

The statement snapped Tavon out of his hunger lust, if only temporarily. "Dead? But I ain't seen no ambos."

"Ain't gonna be none. Even death can't keep a good fiend down."

"What you mean?"

"They tearing up shit. Attacking folks. Breaking into houses. What you think all that ammo's been about? Niggas got guns. They ain't putting up with the foolishness of some fiend that don't know when to quit."

"D?" one of his men said, street-sharpened instinct on high alert. He gestured for silence.

Everyone made their way to his end of the porch. They heard it, too. Something stirred, like the rustling of dead leaves across a floorboard. Both the guards drew their guns. The boards of the house next door shattered, baseheads poured out of the window frames or ran out the front door. Dollar and Tavon ducked behind the guards, landing hard on the concrete. That white burnout leapt onto the porch, a feral gleam in his eyes, slashing at the throat of one of the guards. He took three bullets to his chest before another shot sprayed the back of his head along the porch stones. The fiends fell on the guard, tearing at his clothes, shredding his pockets. Not satisfied, one held him by the back of his head, his fingers digging into the sockets of his eyes, then bit into his skull. His body danced, as if caught on a live wire, then slumped. The other guard never even got off a shot. Overwhelmed by the scene, he just stood rooted with both guns drawn. The fiends dragged him down, without a cry, knocked a gun from his hands, tore out his pockets, then took turns scooping out bits of gray matter with their fingers.

Dollar scrambled for the loose gun.

"Come on," he said, waving him inside. Tavon spied a couple more fiends coming from the other end of the porch. Whatever fiends that remained converged on the house.

Dollar and Tavon rushed into the house and lifted the plank into place. The plank normally served to stop any impromptu police raids. The scale of the problem dawned on Tavon. The house had over twenty windows, plus four doors, not including the basement entrance. He heard a crash from the back of the house – the kitchen – then a thudding from behind him. Fists pounded against the basement door as if the house itself had found its heartbeat. They pushed against the door. A creaking shudder came from the great room. Tavon chanced a peek around the corner. The already-weakened floor gave way. Miss Jane pulled herself from the hole, paying no mind to the jagged floorboards tearing a bloodless track through her thigh. A bone protruded through her flesh, yet she tried to walk like she still had wares to sell. There was no residual spark, no light of recognition in her eyes.

"Shit, they ain't even bleedin'. Don't look like they even feel pain," Tavon squealed.

"We gonna have to go upstairs. Get them when they come up one at a time."

As soon as their weight left the door, hands – craggy masses of picked flesh – wrangled through, desperately grasping after them. Tavon scrambled up the stairs first, followed by Dollar who took each step one at a time, aiming his gun at any movement. When the crush of bodies started shambling up the stairs, he let them step near enough to pop them in the center of their foreheads. Couldn't have been more than a few dozen fiends taken out by the package, Tavon hoped. Judging from the daylong gunfire, there were maybe a dozen of them laying siege to the house.

Tavon heard a scrabbling along the roof.

He stared along the vaulted ceilings, then opted to check the three bedrooms. The first bedroom had once been its own apartment. Someone had torn the kitchenette from the wall and pulled a door from its hinges. Inside what Tavon originally thought was a closet was a bathroom that had been nailed closed, its cracked ceramic bowl bled thick urine. A pile of crap sat in the corner. All the boards remained intact on the windows, so Tavon shut the door.

Dollar let the bodies pile on the stairwell, the obstacles proving difficult for the walking decay to navigate. Even as one climbed over the half-dozen bodies' sprawled limbs, he'd shoot them, adding to the stack. Tavon closed off the second room before slipping into the third. Piles of split boards and plaster were scattered in the room. Three windows on one wall, still boarded, but cracks of light revealed an odd shape to the middle window. Tavon stepped nearer. It wasn't a window.

It was a balcony door.

The door splintered open. Loose Tooth hung from the gutters, having swung down from the roof through the door. Tavon hit the floor, shielding his face from the flying glass shards and bits of boarding. Loose Tooth was slow to get to his feet after a landing that left his legs bent at odd angles and him laying on his back. Still, he pulled himself together, heedless of the glass teeth of the broken window that ripped into him. With the shamble of a hit-and-run victim, he shuffled toward Tavon. Stinking of fetid mud, his vacuous face eyed Tavon hungrily. His mouth moved in an approximation of speaking. If Tavon didn't know better, he would've sworn Loose Tooth tonelessly voiced the word "Blast".

Tavon grabbed a board and swung it, breaking it over Loose Tooth's shoulder. He barely flinched. His mouth opened and closed, long ropes of saliva streaming in thick gooey bands. If you couldn't bring the mouth to the curb, bring the curb to the mouth, Tavon thought. A jousting knight, he charged with the board. The board plunged into his friend's mouth, then he used Loose Tooth's neck as a fulcrum and snapped the top of his jaw. He still twitched, his arms pining toward him in loose spasms.

"This way," Dollar yelled, only glancing at the pursuing fiend. "There's too many of them and I'm almost out of bullets."

They ran into the back bathroom. A cast-iron tub took up most of the space. The white-tiled walls looked relatively pristine, though the stench of the long-unflushed toilet gagged them. Stool steeped into a muddy tea. They shut the door and sat against it.

"I think they after you," Tavon said.

"Why me?" Dollar asked.

"They need a fix. A fiend is a fiend." Tavon glanced at the gun. "How many shots you got left?"

Dollar pulled out his clip. "One, with one in the chamber, left."

Tavon thought about his last blast. A taste would sure go down good about now. If he didn't have much world to begin with, handling the end of it wasn't a stretch. The door lurched, the fiends pushing forward. Hands pressed in from all sides, searching for purchase. Dollar held the edge of the door. Another burnout squeezed his head between the opening, the skin of his face pulled taut. He craned his neck and bit into Dollar. Dollar pulled back and fired into his skull. His body fell into the other fiends, giving Tavon the moment he needed to get the door closed again.

"I'm done, Tae." Dollar clutched his arm. Tavon moved his hand to see the wound.

"It's only a scratch. Ain't nothin' but a thing."

"He took a bite of me. They're like rabid dogs, Tae. I can feel their poison working its way through me. It's warm, almost tingly." Tavon knew the feeling, but said nothing. Dollar continued. "It's only a matter of time. And I don't want to go out like them."

Before Tavon could stop him, Dollar put his gun to his head and pulled the trigger. A crimson trail filigreed the tiles. Tavon opened the door to an explosion of skeletal hands. They pulled Dollar's body through. Tavon listened to the terrible wet chomping sounds. He couldn't believe that it would end this way. He did the deeds, a soldier in the game. They all were. He expected to die on the front lines, but with some sense of dignity. Not to face sickness in that place where beetles crawled and centipedes squirmed. He prayed that Dollar, or whatever they found on him, might sate them, at least for a little while. But he knew better. The friends he knew were gone.

Only the desire remained.

# CHAPTER FIFTEEN

Watching the natural ebb and flow of the neighborhood, King sat on his porch step. An unusually cool night, the wind caught the storm door of the vacant condo next door and produced a series of crashes and grinding metal squeaks with each gust-driven clang. A smoke-hound on a bicycle peddled up and chain-smoked cigarettes until Prez came out to greet him. A handshake-cum-transaction later, and they parted company. Prez with the bike. Either Prez had impeccable timing, or he was a call-ahead/curbside-service drug dealer. He eased his new bicycle away from the front door of his condo and rode it across the grass before ducking into the condo for a few furtive minutes. Nodding to King, he rode off to run his errands. King still liked Prez, a young brotha not so far gone as to give up on him, but that was quite a bit aways from saying that he respected him. Having dropped out of school, Prez was one of those no-account niggas: no job, no car, no responsibilities beyond servicing his dick. Prez now crashed at one of the neighboring condos rather than at Big Momma's. With several of Green's boys crashing there, the condo proved to be an oasis of temptation for Prez. King wondered, how you could you tell your momma you were working, leave for "work" every day, within two weeks make up some elaborate scenario detailing how your boss was a racist or simply out to get you and thus you lost your job... but never bring home at least one check? Prez was probably setting up a break-in or some side-ass quick-money gig or buying weed to pass his days.

Dollar and his crew set up under Green, flashing their easy money. Weed for days with women coming and going at all hours. Other than the occasional humble charge from the cops, from which he'd already been released, life was pretty easy being Prez. Still, he thought it best to avoid the corner for a few days until things sorted themselves out between Dollar and the cops; so he pedaled down the block toward the dirt path separating the rear of Breton Court from one of the strip malls which girded it. Way out of the eyes of Green who had taken to overseeing the corner personally, though none had seen him for a minute.

Several condos had Asian and Hispanic families crammed into them, so it wasn't merely the presence of the Hispanic man stumbling towards them that caught their attention. Sometimes fifteen to a house, wall-to-wall mats, most of them were in need of some sort of citizenship papers. They worked at the Chinese and Mexican restaurants that littered the area. No, the man hiked up his red shirt across his shoulder like a sling. Wearing a white shirt underneath covered in blood, even his blue saggy shorts were doused in it. A spray of blood speckled his white shoes. As if stanching a bloody nose, he held his hand to his face, a face smeared with caked blood stains. His hand had a gash deep enough to reveal his white meat.

"You the weed man?" he asked King.

"Nah, you got the wrong brother."

"He around the corner," Prez said.

"What happened to you?" King asked.

The story went that he got jumped outside of Kroger, by the Eagle Terrace apartments. He assumed it was because he claimed being part of the Treize set. Not that they truly cared. Apparently, they pummeled him anyway, fiends out of control. Supposedly he got a knife from one of them and stabbed them, but they just kept coming. Clawing and biting at him, he was lucky to get away. Now he simply needed a wash cloth and some weed.

"What you need is some stitches," King said.

"You got weed? I'll buy weed for everybody," the man said. He danced from side to side as if looking for a partner or someone to take him up on his offer.

"Now you talking," Prez said. King simply hated seeing smart brothers like Prez turn to drugs, but once school was out as an option, a brother's chances slimmed for any legitimate work. Prez didn't have the patience to start at the bottom of a gig and work his way up.

The man left and promised to return for some weed. However, the next time they saw him, he had changed outfits and gotten into a car with his buddies, probably to go roll on those anti-Treize fiends.

Such was life at Breton Court.

Dogs barked in the distance. They always barked, but the tenor of their barks drew King's attention. A lone figure walked an American Pit Bull Terrier. Baylon prowled about.

Late into an Indiana fall could be hard on a body. In the course of one day it could go from raining in the morning, snowing by noon, to a late afternoon blue sky and bright sun that left no hint of either. The cold had a way of stilling activity in Breton Court. A neighbor occasionally stepped out on their porch for a quick smoke and a wave, a groundhog checking their shadow, but for the most part, his neighbors kept indoors. All except Baylon. No, Baylon was out walking the flesh-and-blood weapon that he called a dog, a brown and white Pit Bull with splotches of pink around her mouth. Keeping her chained in his back patio when he wasn't putting her through her various paces, he abused her regularly and called it training.

"What's up, King?" Baylon called out. He pulled the leash taut, halting the dog. The distance between him and King charged with antagonism, challenge, and even a forlorn sense of regret. A sad anger.

"B," he said, more out of politeness than anything else. His momma raised him to be polite, lessons he'd kept close to his heart no matter what life brought.

"Dog looks a little rough."

"I'm gonna fight her on Sunday. Got to get my bitch ready."

"You ain't busy enough?"

"I'm what they call a Renaissance man."

"Been hitting them books, too?" King asked.

"Yeah, nigga. Now I'm the scariest kind o' nigga: *educated*. Anyways, as I see it, life's about finding your niche."

"And philosopher. How do you find the time to do your soldiering?"

"That's what I mean. My niche is strictly heroin. That there's a gentleman's operation."

"Just so I have this straight, you just a misunderstood gentleman and scholar."

"Exactly. My clientele is stable. And competition? Hell, we like Wal-Mart up in this joint. I'm like the grocery department. Prez and his coke, they like the electronics. Green an' 'em can keep his crack on the corner, like the toy department, far away from us. That draws too much attention. See, we just one big store. No need for beefing."

"Except for the random shooting."

"You think they coming out here for a couple caps and no body? Shit, bet they didn't even brush the donut powder off they uniform."

"Green's boys' caused more than a little ruckus the other day. I heard tell they even left one of your soldiers a little... light-headed," King said.

"I'm a low-key nigga. Straight cheddar, baby, that's all that I'm about."

"I don't think you feeling me. That shit's got to stop. We got kids running around."

"By who? You? You planning on going incog-negro on me?"

It would be easy to drop a dime on Baylon or Prez. It wasn't like they weren't already under surveillance. That had to be the second biggest open secret in the neighborhood, second only to the fact that folks sold drugs on the corner. They were the elephant in the room that no one – no politician, no police of rank, and no reporter – wanted to mention. Everyone knew, but no one wanted to do anything about it. Folks made the most of the opportunities afforded them and played the hand they were dealt. As long as they proved to be good neighbors, how they made their living was no one's concern. Alaina Walker was long forgotten. Conant Walker was a faded image on the occasional T-shirt. And no one wept for Juneteenth Walker.

"Do I look like some played-out punk? If I got a problem with you, I step to you. Like a man." King wasn't a snitch and didn't care much for the insinuation. Snitching wasn't a long-term career move. Exhibit A: the house down the street that to this day hadn't been rebuilt since it was torched and had the word "snitch" spray-painted on the ruin.

The dog flared its teeth, a rattler warning of its strike. Baylon stroked the fur along the dog's neck.

"Better watch yourself. My bitch don't like people stepping up on us incorrect." Baylon spit on the ground. "It's about being the man. This here's a...

how they say it?… a consumer-driven market. They come to me. I give them product. They give me cash. No muss, no fuss. I ain't some Jehovah's Witness going door to door with the shit trying to convert nobody."

"I just don't want it done in my neighborhood."

"You want to be the king, you got to take the king."

Baylon turned his back to him, with a casual dismissal, and walked into Prez's little play condo. This was the life they chose. Empty, but free. The prospect of big money versus the lack of flash of menial work: that was the problem with too many brothers: they felt owed, as if the act of being born entitled them to instant coin and high living. That was what they saw on television and was how they thought they were supposed to live. It was stupid and short-sighted, but King understood it. But he had pride in his neighborhood. He lived with good people, good neighbors, and he wasn't going to see it ruined by the likes of Prez. Or Baylon. Or Green. Good men had to stand for something.

"I hate to break up any internal soliloquy you got going on," Merle said, "but you've got company."

Merle was worse than a repo man and King hated the way he appeared and disappeared whenever he wanted. An umbra tent, Merle's black jacket wrapped around him. His aluminum foil hat teetered on his head, extra layers having been added since his last visit. He smelled of day-old fish wrapped in spoiled vegetables, flecks of food trapped in his red beard. Terribly lucid eyes focused on the pair approaching them, Wayne and Lott.

"Yeah, I was expecting them," King said.

A contrast in dark and light, Wayne had a bucket of Popeye's under his arm. A white down vest covered a blue zippered sweatshirt, his jeans had a picture of a phoenix, an eagle, and a crown reminiscent of a crest, along their sides. His big-boy girth made his belt superfluous. His stylized Yankee cap tilted on his head at such an extreme angle, it defied the laws of gravity by staying on. Lott, with his light complexion, seemed almost white when next to Wayne. His FedEx uniform like layers of blue armor.

"We gonna do this?" Wayne said between bites of a chicken leg.

"We still have to figure out what exactly we gonna do," King said. "What do you think, Merle?"

"I think you need to check with the lady." Merle pointed to the woman standing at the end of the row of condos. A nest of micro-braids crowned her cream complexion. With ears not quite as pointed as that dude from Star Trek, she wore an opened fur-lined hoodie over a T-shirt with the word "Babe" across her chest. Fur-cuffed jeans topped her fur-lined Timbo boots which had pom-poms dangling from them. Walking with the easy stride of a large cat on a hunt, she approached them.

"Hell-O." Wayne admired the fashioned beauty, trying unsuccessfully to not ogle her chest.

"You are seriously fucking up my shit." Her piercing green eyes narrowed, focused solely on King.

"I don't even know who you are," King said. Her beauty enrapturing, he straightened his posture. His palms moistened with nervous sweat.

"Omarosa."

"So *you're* Omarosa," King said with too much lilt to his voice.

"Of the fey," Merle said, with something short of an elbow to his mid-section. A gentle reminder before the worst instincts of the Pendragon spirit carried him away in a torrent of lust.

"Stay out of this, mage." Omarosa stared down at Merle, but whatever rules of intimidation she played by were lost on him and his distant musings.

"That's exactly what I mean," King said to Merle. "It sounds like there's some shit between y'all that we are caught up in."

"*Shining Star for you to see/What your life can truly be*," Merle sang.

"How exactly am I 'seriously fucking up your shit'?" King asked, returning his attention to Omarosa.

"I don't know what you did, but somehow you've got Night and Dred pulling out every trick they got beefing over this little stretch of real estate. It don't even take in enough to make it worth my time, but they steady squabbling over it. I don't even know if Night knows why, but because Dred seems to want it, he's fighting for it."

"It's getting bad out there, King." Wayne suddenly sounded weary. "I tried to get up with Tavon earlier today, and seems the brotha was onto something.

Half the smoke-hounds out there have been dropped by a bad package. The other half is wildin' out for real."

"Night gets his package off Dred's consignment and think he's safe over at his place in the Phoenix," Omarosa said. "Dred spiked that shit. Fool fake Jamaican motherfucker."

"Damn, girl," King said.

"Nigga plays both sides and then fucks the middle. I don't know if even he knows why he does things besides the fact that it amuses him."

"From the way he behaves, you'd think he was a half-caste fey," Merle said.

"Have you seen Mab lately?" The fey were well aware of Merle's long-time feud with his mother, despite the fact that she had long passed through the Veil, remaining in Nod while he still roamed the mortal plane in his pursuit of the true king. "I'll have to remember to give her your love next time I see her."

"Damnable bitch." Merle adjusted his tin-foil hat. "I'm going to bake you a cake. I like cake."

"Things are jumping so much, a girl can't make an honest living," Omarosa returned her attention to King.

"Ripping off both sides?" King asked.

"A girl's got to earn."

"I'm surprised you ain't taken him out." King leaned toward her, not threatening but crowding her space. "Isn't that how you operate?"

"Taking out a drug dealer, that's biting the hand that feeds me."

"Sounds like you're part of the problem to me."

"What did you say?" Omarosa's eye arched curiously. There was a royal charge of offense to her question.

"It's bad enough we've lost so many to this nonsense, but you, you're the…"

"Carrion feeder," Merle helped.

"No, I'm a predator among predators. I'm higher up on the food chain." Omarosa was fey and it was a terrible thing to raise the temperature of her blood. Worse still to be the object of her rage. Worse further to be caught in the throes of history, a pawn in a game, fated to misfortune. She admired and pitied this one, but they all had a role to play. Omarosa handed him a heavy box. "This is for you."

"What is it?" King reached out for it.

"Your legacy. A client hired me to… procure it for you."

"You shouldn't accept gifts from her kind," Merle warned, though his eyes recognized the runes on the box.

"It's no gift. I'm returning something rightfully his. I've been watching you for a long time. Not much slips past my eye. That's a quick way to get dead in my line of work." Omarosa studied the man. "Haven't you tired of playing the reluctant hero? You don't wear it especially well. You need to embrace your calling. Play or get played. But that's not your biggest problem. Do you know what it is, King?"

"What?"

"You *give* a fuck." With the curt dismissal, Omarosa turned on her heel and walked away from them. They stared in appreciation as she left for what good it did them. At the first shadow, the darkness enveloped her, or she merged with it, and disappeared. She'd accomplished what she came to do.

King turned the box to face him. It warmed in his hands. The strange lock nearly popped open on its own as he barely brushed against it while still examining it. He opened it with great care. Merle sighed.

"What is it?" Wayne asked.

"Twin 9mm Springfield Armory custom-ported stack autos, with the frames, slides, and some other parts plated in 24K gold, and gold dragons rearing up on the contrasting black grips," Merle said, without so much as a glance into the box.

"Twin? There's only one of the… Caliburns?" King picked it up. In his hands, he didn't know how to describe it, but it felt like more than a gun. It was magic. He knew he was meant to wield it from the moment he first touched it. No, from the moment he laid eyes on it.

"Caliburns? I've never heard of it," Wayne said.

"Privately made," Merle said. "It's time for the hero to act."

"I'm not much of a gun guy." King returned it to the box and closed it. "What do you think?"

"I think we've talked enough. We've come this far and we're ready to follow you to the next level," Lott said.

"And you?" King turned to Wayne.

Wayne studied the shadows for any hint of Omarosa. "I love her like a big-tittied play cousin at a family reunion."

Despite his comment, the moment remained tense. Their assembled little band stood in silence. King, its leader-apparent. Wayne and Lott, his most loyal troops. Merle, his advisor. They were the core, though of what, they didn't know. They were a sword in search of blood to draw. There was one place to begin their journey.

"You know who we are going to cross before this is over with?" Lott asked.

"Baylon," King said.

"You sure you just not looking for an excuse to beef with him?" Wayne asked.

"Nah." *Yeah*. History built up between them. Too much unanswered for. A debt of blood and broken promises. "He handles the package. He'd know."

"So much like the father," Merle said. "Now look, the gang's all here."

Lady G handed Big Momma a glass of red Kool Aid then walked over to the collection of swinging dicks. She could always spot when men were up to their "men things", ready to prove themselves to whatever fool or fool notion crawled up their behinds to gnaw on their insecurities.

"What you fellas up to?"

"Nothing," Wayne said.

"We're going to the Phoenix Apartments." King stepped to her. Whenever he neared her, he felt he could do anything. He didn't know if it was because he needed to prove he was the man he wanted to be for her or if the power of her faith in him charged him. "Put a stop to some of this nonsense once and for all."

"Not without me," Lady G said. "Rhee stays up in there."

"You'd take a bitch into your mess?" Baylon exited onto Prez's porch. He cold-eyed Lady G who sniffed in his direction then sucked her teeth in disgust. Between her obvious disdain and his own growing irritation, Baylon was in a mood to push things. The Durham Brothers. Junie. Parker. No one heard anything from Green or Tavon. With Night buying on consignment from Dred anyway and both sides weakened, Baylon saw an opportunity for consolidation. Perhaps head-hunting the top talent in order to make a move of his own. With their troops getting thin, Prez had risen up the ranks of foot soldiers. Baylon no longer had the luxury of traveling with a retinue of any sort. It was too late to recalculate the strength of his position now staring into the ranks of King's crew.

"No, I'd take a woman who could handle her business to clean up your mess." King glanced up from his perch to the porch step and stepped between her and Baylon. Although the idea of her anywhere near danger didn't sit well with him, he'd respect her decision.

"What you doing over here?" Lady G asked.

"Checking on some business. I had no idea you stayed here if that what you thinking," Baylon said.

"Some niggas need them high-drama bitches. They need the bang, the rush. Not me. I need a straight bitch. One that can handle her, and my, business. Say what you will, and Lady G's no joke, but she ain't needless drama."

"Careful now." King squared off against Baylon. A spirit of over-protectiveness commingled with a surge of jealousy. His face grew hot.

"What? You don't like it when I talk about your 'friend' like that?" Baylon asked, stepping down to meet his stare. His Pit Bull leapt to the screen door, all thunderous scrapes of paws against glass. It mimicked growls as best it could through its severed vocal cords. "Oh, I see. That's it isn't it. I don't think I like the way you be looking at my girl, dog."

Lady G wasn't his girl. She knew of his… whatever he was feeling, and never accepted his overtures. She was something he desired that he didn't own and couldn't control. He didn't even know her beyond whatever idealized idea of her that he had built up in his head. Nor was she especially flattered by the pissing contest going on between these two, neither of whom had any particular claim on her. Her affections were hers to place wherever she wanted.

"How's that? With respect? Like she's a person?" King knew he had crossed a line. He'd called Baylon out, in front of the neighborhood. There was no backing down for him now. Honor, if he could call it that, demanded that Baylon answer this upstart's challenge. No one could afford to show any weakness.

"It ain't shit to be loved by a saint. Saints have to love everyone. You might as well be a dog. But we devils, nah, we ain't got to love anyone but ourselves. So when we do love a bitch, shit, they know and they ain't going nowhere. Me, I'm straight-up gangsta now, not the boy you grew up with. Gangsta recognizes gangsta... and you lookin' kinda unfamiliar."

Baylon threw a quick hard punch with his free hand and caught King off guard with a punch to the kidneys. King doubled over at the impact, leaving his head perfectly poised to receive another crashing blow from Baylon. As the roundhouse arced downward, King stood into it, deflecting it. His back slightly turned to Baylon, King thrust his elbow into his belly then stepped to the side to hit him.

That was the last clean blow landed.

Fights rarely worked the way that they did on television or in the movies, nor lasted as long. Baylon scrambled from his awkward stance and charged King, wrapping his arms around him. The two of them bowled over into the front lawn. A flurry of movement meant to be the exchange of punches followed, neither one of them doing much more than pushing into one another while entangled.

Wayne and Lott rushed over to break them up, with Lott holding back Baylon. King glared at him, unflinching. This time he was ready in case Baylon decided to start something again.

"Let go of me." Baylon shook him off. "This fool just got it in his head to try and step to my girl and I ain't the one to get played out, like some punk bitch."

"What the fuck?" Wayne asked King. "All the stuff going on and you reduce it all to a jealousy beef?"

It was all slipping away. Lady G. The crew. The Egbo Society. The world he knew raced toward entropy, decaying from the outside in. Soon King's name would be ringing out in the streets. Baylon could sense the momentum change already. For now they were a small band, but they stood true. Should they come out the other end alive, they would be well on their way to becoming legends. Sometimes survival itself was the stuff of legends. He had no plays left here that would have him save face. Except one. Maybe.

Baylon slipped the knife into his hand. He lurched forward in a stumbling gait, like a wino tromping through an alley trying to steady himself. He thought of Michelle. And Griff. The history of blood and misfortune on this blade. And he determined that King was the rightful inheritor of its pain. With a flick of his wrist, the steel tooth snapped to life and in a fluid movement, he arced the weapon at King before he could react. A searing pain lanced through King's side. The problem with knives was that once they were drawn, the user depended entirely on them. Baylon, off balance and startled, made an easy target. Stunned for a moment at the utter futility and ridiculousness of the attack, King landed an uppercut that snapped Baylon's head back, even as his momentum sent the two of them tumbling onto the lawn.

"King. Oh shit." Lady G rushed to his side. "He get you?"

"I don't… I think so," he said, slow to get to one knee before giving up and supporting his weight with an arm then slumping back to the ground. King raised his hands so that he could see them. Blood stained each of them.

"Don't move. Don't move," she said.

"It's all right. It's only a flesh wound. Seriously."

Baylon didn't move, but instead released a low groan. King stooped over him and snatched the knife he still desperately grasped. He rotated it in his hands, examining it as if its touch told him everything he needed to know. He tossed the blade to the side.

"Just… just stay down. I'm tired and I'm not here to beef with you. If there's gonna be a fight, I'm gonna take it outside of the family."

"Time grows short," Merle warned, his eyes studying the mood of the day.

"What do you want us to do?" Lott stared at the still-stunned Baylon.

"Leave him." King clutched his side and stood up. "We go to the Phoenix."

# CHAPTER SIXTEEN

Winter had arrived and few had noticed. Like the previous few years on memory, the temperatures were chilly but not too cold, in the mid-40s. The wind didn't rob the body of warmth, not in that deep bone-chill way of the harsher winter of childhood memories. No, these days it more often rained than snowed, not that anyone complained. Had it been cold enough to turn the rains to snow, the blanket of snow would have settled six feet if an inch.

The six-story complex ran over two city-blocks long and one block wide, a veritable prison of inexpensive accommodation. To the east, past the back parking lots, Fall Creek wound its length, the thin grove of trees separating the apartments from the rest of the city. To the rear of the buildings which formed the Phoenix Apartments, a gravel trail – overgrown, as if something once stood there – led through a canopy of trees. Brown leaves pooled against the base of the black chain-link fence which circled the outer boundaries of the apartments. Cans of Budweiser littered the playground. Concrete slabs, a desert of cracked pavement choked with weeds and broken glass. Nobody wanted to be here, all equally prisoners in a compound of liberal well-meaning benevolence. Along the sad array that passed for a playground, the ladder of the slide held more rust than paint. One of the swings looped around the top of its frame. The yellow school bus jungle gym had been tagged. RIP Alaina. RIP Conant. A few more RIP notices, names no one recognized.

The Phoenix Apartments were once central to one of Indianapolis' top neighborhoods, its construction greeted with optimism. One mile east of the state fairgrounds, near 38th Street and Sherman Drive, Edgemere Court ran through the heart of what used to be called the Meadows. In the '50s and '60s this was the place to be as people claimed their pieces of the American Dream, with restaurants and shops crowding the area. But the area saw the ownership of the apartment complex change hands several times over the years and the initial optimism soured. Folks were shuffled into there, the city not wanting to inflict poor black people on their white neighborhoods. Huge swathes of vacant land isolated it. Dubbed too dangerous to patrol by the police, the layers of fencing only further added to the sense that folks were being imprisoned rather than being given space to live.

By day, the apartments had the thinnest veneer of respectability. The red bricks seemed clean and fresh, distracting from the bedspreads which shielded most windows. The decay was there, first seen in the trees. Wine-colored leaves interspersed with green ones, jutting from dead branches. One tree a stark, unnatural shade of white, gnarled and neglected, with green leaves still sprouting from it. Now, with ninety percent of the tenants on Section 8 housing, and crime, poverty, and hopelessness combining for a cauldron of pain and anger, life in the Phoenix Apartments had been reduced to relentless decay and a cesspool of warrants. Churches nestled densely around the property, a bulwark against entropy. Immanuel Baptist. Church of the Living God. Pentecostal Assembly. Nazarene Church. Temple of Praise. Indiana Missionary. Living Water. Their church signs promised passersby "Don't worry, God is still in control".

The engine cooling, the five of them sat in the Outreach Inc. van. Wayne drove with Merle riding shotgun, his window slightly rolled down to cut down on his odor. Lady G sat between King and Lott in the back. King watched the denizens shamble back and forth, the silence conducive to his thoughts. They had bandaged his side and taped it as best they could. King refused to go to the hospital, preferring to end this terrible business that night.

And then there was the matter of the gun.

"Has anyone wondered 'Why us?'" Wayne asked. All eyes fell on King.

"Why not us?" King leaned forward to better see them all. "I don't know about you, but I'm tired. Tired of people having no expectations of us. Tired of not bothering to dream because I don't think I'll be around to see it. Tired of not being able to walk down a street without part of me fearing a brother walking my way.

"Ain't but a few of us here, but even a few good people banded together in the right cause can make a difference. I have to believe that or what's the point of even going on? Good people have to stand for something."

"Damn, man," Wayne said, "I didn't say go all 'Win one for the Gipper' on us."

A brooding silence enveloped the apartment parking lot. Dead leaves skittered along the cracked black pavement on a desolate, cold wind. The silence was as pervasive as it was unsettling. Even during colder temperatures, the Phoenix brimmed with activity because fiends and knuckleheads knew no rest. Despite the appearance of a few bodies in the yard, an eerie stillness settled on the apartments. No cars idled, no music poured from speakers, no loud voices claimed the night as their own. Separated like sentries, though locked in their heroin leans, the bodies became more animated as King neared. Some moaned in distress. One man appeared to be attempting to shave the color off his eyeball with a razor blade.

"It's you. They're reacting to you," Merle said to King.

"How can you tell? They can't even see me."

"Exactly."

"Look at them," Lady G said, "They look–"

"Dead," Lott said. "Remember what Tavon was saying about the fiends falling out?"

The weight of guilt bubbled in Wayne's belly for losing track of Tavon. Some faces looked familiar to Wayne and Lady G especially, having encountered them during their street lives. However, the people they knew were gone. Some shambled about with shorn limbs, some having obviously taken gunfire and ran out of blood, yet still stood. The drugs consumed them a piece at a time, but now it was as if their souls had been snuffed out.

"Got anything we can use as weapons?" King needed the comfort of having some sort of weapon.

"You have the gun," Lott said.

King waited impatiently for the facts to settle in his head. The familiar weight of the Caliburn nestled along his spine. "I know, but... it doesn't feel right. Not yet."

"You'll know when to use it," Merle reassured.

"I have a crowbar, a baseball bat, and a golf club," Wayne fished through the trunk of the minivan.

"A golf club?" Lott asked.

"What? I'm a civilized motherfucker."

"Fine, you the next Tiger, but only one?"

"Shit, I ain't made of money," Wayne said. "Figure I just keep hitting shit till the ball gets in a hole."

"Sounds like a plan for this here game, too."

"You sure?"

"They're already dead."

Lott grabbed the crowbar, then grabbed a couple of the screwdrivers which rolled along the floorboard and shoved them into the sides of his jeans. King opted for the baseball bat, leaving Wayne with his precious golf club. Hardly masked by the slight wind, the smell of rotting meat hit them. The trees loomed, strange fruit dangling from their low-lying branches. As the band approached, the forms coalesced. Small bodies, the flesh peeled back or knotted in chunks hung like ornaments. Birds. Rats. Squirrels. The cloud-occluded moonlight gave the illusion of their tiny jaws still moving. The sight of the squirrel bones especially unsettled Merle.

The copse of corpses had been dead for nearly a two days and slowly made their way here to this place of power, this place that beckoned them. To wait. Though the fiends had to have ridden the same blast within a day of each other, some were wasted in such a way as to have been dead for months. Even the freshest among them had meat falling from them in clumps. Their tattered clothes starched with mildew, the rot of their flesh infested their wardrobe. Vacant eyes – a condition not entirely unfamiliar to the fiends – tracked the approaching skulkers. Folks held hostage terrified to leave the building now noiselessly under siege. As long as it was quiet – because indeed, no bullets rang out – the police considered it secured. Loitering was one of those law violations enforced in lighter neighborhoods.

King took point with Wayne and Lott in lock-step behind him forming a wedge through the heart of the milling bodies. Using the bat more like a staff, King jabbed the hand grip into the gut of the nearest fiend, doubling it over as the action forced air from its insides. Its rancid breath choked him. The fat end of the bat smashed into the jaw of one attempting to sneak up from behind. The creatures amped back up, and found their legs again. It seemed easier to think of them as creatures. Stay down, his eyes pled, but the creature stirred. With the sickening accompanying sound of splintering bone, he planted the bat firmly in its skull.

Wayne took no joy in his task. His goal was to keep the creatures at bay from Merle and Lady G, more a distraction until Lott finished them with a severing blow to the back of the neck or a curt ram through an eye. Distracted by the approach of the first body, three fiends collapsed on him from the shadows of entranceways before he realized they were organized enough to create a feint. Stumbling off the broken curb, Wayne kicked the first one, his foot collapsing the chest of it, then getting stuck on the jagged bones of the shattered ribs once the creature juked. Wayne toppled to the ground, and disappeared under a crush of fiends as they pounced on him. Tavon's face suddenly peered down at him, his open mouth a siege of rotting teeth.

Swinging the crowbar like a sword swung with skill and precision, an exuberance to the grim task thrilled Lott. Black ichor, more than blood, poured from the slit throat of one. A decomposed fist slammed into his skull, the warning cry of "look out" from Lady G arriving seconds too late. Lott staggered to the floor; the creature's desiccated arm lashed out

and lifted him from the ground before he could retrieve his crowbar. Its strength flowed from
somewhere else, because its brittle arms didn't hold
enough muscle to swat at a passing mosquito. Whatever animated them also burned them up. The
creature held him up, waiting for others to see his
prize and come tear him apart. As if catching his scent
from upwind, some undead striders stopped in mid-
movement and ambled toward them. Lott fished into
the side pockets of his jeans and pulled out the screwdrivers. Plunging the twin daggers, he rammed the
screwdrivers into each of its eye sockets, exploding
what was left of its eye and piercing what passed for
its brain. Landing as the creature collapsed, Lott
tugged at the screwdriver which was stuck in the
bone of the eye socket. As he yanked it free, it flew
out of his grasp and tumbled to the ground. As rav-
enous for a blast as it had been in life, a fiend fell to
its knees, grabbed it and jammed it into its arm.

Wayne, his foot still caught in the chest of the
fiend who didn't know enough to drop dead,
dragged his leg bringing the creature with it. The
body crashed into the others, which allowed Wayne
to roll through the grasp of one of them. Tavon's
rasping fingers found purchase in his side and his
side burned as the fingers clawed through his flesh.
He grabbed Tavon with both hands and headbutted
him. Wayne whirled the body like a shield, shoving
the fiends back. He threw Tavon to the ground. Any
trace of the man he knew was gone, so Wayne
stomped on the back of his skull, smashing its jaws

on the sidewalk. A hole opened up among the ranks and he waved Merle and Lady G through it. He chanced one last look at Tavon's still form and told himself that he had to do what he had to do.

Loose Tooth scuttled toward King. In death he seemed to have put on weight. The former old man had renewed vigor as his mouth, his jaw barely attached, dangled open and snap shut as he entangled King in his embrace. Contempt filled his hollowed eyes. King pulled as far away from the chomping teeth as he could, then forced the bat's hilt upward into its gaping maw. A sound, rather like gagging, preceded the creature's arms slackening enough for King to escape. With a hefting swing, the bat connected with the creature's neck, the head held fast by a skin flap of rent flesh and spidery sinew. The creature's eyes followed him. Its mouth moved, tongue black and swollen, words voicelessly formed on its lips though without air enough to express them. In the throes of the brief loss of self accompanying a swift punch to the belly, King couldn't swallow and couldn't breathe. For a moment, King studied the still form, thinking he should feel something more, a vague sense of satisfaction or even vindication. But he felt nothing. Only the hollowness, the sense of waste that came with a pointless loss of life.

Only Merle knew that King had avenged the death of his father.

King waved Lott after him, following the path cut by Wayne. When they got into the main entryway doors, they ran the bat and crowbar through the door's handles to keep it wedged shut.

"That was easy enough." King gulped in the dry air, his strength rushing back to his numb limbs. His skin flushed hot to the touch, a battle fever rushed through his system.

"Knock on wood or something." Claw marks covered Wayne, chunks of flesh torn from his body. Blood coated his jeans, an ugly gash along his leg seen through his torn pants.

"No need. That was hardly its best. Merely its squires called home," Merle said. "The creatures were half-dead when we started. It was like they'd already done what they were called to do."

"Like attack whoever got in their way?" Lott tottered on his feet, hands pressed against his thighs to steady himself until he caught his breath.

"Were they keeping us out or going for Night?" Wayne echoed.

"They were pawns used by both sides until they were used up. Look at them. They aren't even pursuing us now." King reflected on what Omarosa had said, about Night getting his package off Dred's consignment thinking he was safe here at the Phoenix. Taking out a rival in a way that might bite the hand that fed him, but moving others to complicate and disarm or possibly just distract his rivals; now that opened up all new realms of possibility. It created a sea of uncertainty. *Change the players, change the game.* "Dred's playing both ends against a useless middle."

"What?" Wayne asked.

"Just piecing things together," King said. "All of this feels like a distraction, misdirecting us from the true objective."

"You're learning," Merle said.

"Never a true shortage of crack fiends no ways," Lott said.

"We need to grab Rhee and get out." Lady G tugged at King.

"Yeah, we need to keep going," King said. "We cut this off at the source and hope this whole nightmare ends."

A bank of mail slots lined the foyer wall of the Phoenix Apartments building, each slot large enough for bills, collection notices, and subsidy checks. With the layout of an old elementary school and the design sense of a detention center, two hallways branched from there, each leading to elevators each with signs which perpetually read "out of order" and stairwells whose lights had been busted out. As they essayed further into the building, King noticed bizarre symbols carved into the walls and seen within the swirls of graffiti letters to the discerning eye. The symbols were reminiscent of, though not exactly matching, the ones on the box which held his Caliburn. In the last vestiges of light, the tags for ESG had been spray-painted over with the letters "ICU" within a circle.

A tremulous silence enveloped them, the palpable shadows thick as curtains. The dank odor of piss and sweat mixed with mildew hung cloyingly in the air.

With so little light, the walls were cancerous with fungal growth. Women avoided walking the stairwell alone for fear of the shadow denizens grabbing and attacking them. Their nerves stretched like fine catgut, ready for a symphony of terror to be wrung from them, Lady G clutched after King's hand. Wayne stumbled in the darkness.

"You ain't got no kind of creep to you," Lott whispered to Wayne.

"You know what the cops say?" King said.

"What?"

"It's like an underground world over here."

"Hades," Merle added.

"Everyone knows everyone," Lady G said. "So folks trying to hide can always find someone to let them in they apartment."

"Always jumpin'," Wayne said.

"Got to learn to sleep through that mess," Lott said.

King cocked his head in the direction of a sound he thought he heard. The darkness pooled all around them, a living thing in its own way, distorting sound and even their sense of balance. Their voices drifted apart, no one able to determine the location of another, though King's hand tightened around Lady G's. Again, the idea of sound tickled King's ears. An odd, indistinct skritch in the distance.

"Sh!" King said.

"What?"

"What part of 'sh' didn't you get?" King leaned toward the deepening shadows. "You hear that?"

A whir, similar to the hum of current through a power line, thrummed along the walls. The croak began as a whisper. Had they still been outside, they would have seen the mouths of the remaining fiends moving in unison. The shadows swirled like a rushing wind. The apartment foyer, casket-dark and desolate, called out in a mouthless whisper.

"The endgame approaches. Good. So hungry. So tired."

"What do you want?" King shouted at the darkness.

"We await the Pendragon. Alone." The voice, ancient and weary, reverberated through them like a passing foul wind.

"Who are you?"

"I am what was. What won't be again. The Devourer of Dream. The Umbra Spirit."

"The dragon," Merle whispered.

"Show yourself!" King yelled.

"Prove yourself worthy of my attention. Be careful with my little squires."

"Squires?" Lady G asked. "You think he means them fiends?"

"I don't–" King's words were cut short by something hard falling and bouncing from his hand. "What the...?"

A small pellet of some sort landed in Lady G's hair. When she went to swipe it away, it scuttled off on its own. She craned upwards. The shadows churned along the ceiling, brief shafts of light penetrating the wall as if a shifting dark sheet covered the light fixture. When she was about to proclaim her observation, a cockroach fell in her mouth. Its antennae brushed against the roof of her mouth as she gagged to expel it. An undulating wave rippled through, dislodging the insects all at once.

A shower of chitinous shells rained down on them, cockroach bodies pelting them where they stood. Millions of tiny legs created a cacophonous scratching, the bugs scrabbling over one another hitting the group in an obscene wave. Stiff hairs itched along Wayne's body, the soft crunch of bodies underfoot reminding him of treading on vials in alleyways. In his hair, in his clothes, he closed his eyes and covered his nose and mouth as he waded through the sea of roaches. In the wake of them skittering down the stairs, he still felt the sensation of bodies crawling within his clothes.

"It's toying with us," King said.

"You know," Lady G concurred.

"It will get worse from here," Merle warned.

"I can't do this. Not with you here," King told Lady G. He squeezed her hand and let her go.

"I won't leave you." Her voice, full and low, resounded with a grim finality.

"I wouldn't ask you to. But I need to be able to do what I have to do, be who I have to be. I can't face him, whatever he is, and worry about you. And I don't know if I want you to see me be... what I must." King turned to Lott. "I'm trusting you to get her out of here and keep her safe."

"You got it," Lott said, then gave him a fist bump.

"Uh-uhn. You don't get to pass me off when I get inconvenient. And you don't get to sweep me under a rug. I'm not some doll you get to hand off or fight over." Lady G caressed King's face and held her hand along it for an extended moment before letting him go. Chiding herself for being selfish, she wanted to support him, not distract him, but this was her fight, too. "So I'll tell *you* what: I'm going to go make sure Rhee is OK and get her out of here. If Lott wants to come, that's on him."

King stared at her, seeing her for the first time. "You got it."


Percy squatted at the Phoenix Apartments at the insistence of his mother. She had an arrangement of some sort with Night and his people which allowed them to stay without having to pay rent. Percy thought she had to do bad things with the men who worked for Night, but Miss Jane insisted it wasn't the case. He believed her since she was so open about who she did the bad things with. Night's men secured the building, discouraged visitors, and kept order. Altruism was a side effect. Order allowed them to conduct business, without Five-O or social services crawling up their insides. So when fiends fell over them like a wave of barbarian hordes at the gate, most of the foot soldiers scattered. The scene grew too hot with the prospect of ambos and po-po. However, the emergency services apocalypse never materialized. The fallen fiends circled the apartments and attacked any who entered. Or tried to leave. The remaining tenants were effectively cut off from the outside world. Cell phones wouldn't even work. It was as if a force interfered with their signals. A force that bided its time.

Percy checked on the folks in his care. He wore an *Evan Almighty* T-shirt stretched over his bulbous frame. Grungy, unwashed for days, he'd pulled it from one of the piles of dirty clothes. Fast food wrappers separated the piles. Mattresses spread out in the back rooms, bodies sprawled over them. Two boys slept with their light on and their door ajar. The first laid face down on the bed in Buzz Lightyear pajamas. The second had only his face visible; his hair wrapped in a bandana.

Rhianna stayed on his couch. Despite the "boy funk", she'd kept herself fastidiously clean. She began her day by running to a cousin's place to shower. Today she wore the same clothes from the previous day. She jumped at the sound of a distant thump.

"Percy, what's going on?" The rasp in her voice thickened with the onset of a cold.

"If you want, I'll go check." Percy loved the long-time smoker's timber of her voice, though the bruises about her neck told him that smoking was not the cause. Part of him secretly hoped she might get sick, not too sick, but just enough to slow her down and depend on someone else. Just enough so she'd let him watch over her properly. He just wanted a chance to prove himself.

"Don't leave me," she said, then quickly corrected. "Us."

"We can't just wait here. If nothing else, things might have changed. It's OK. I'll be right back." He smiled a brave smile as he opened the door. He held his breath and rushed out.

The hall was empty, but smelled of burnt crack, vomit, urine, and BO. His heart thudded, his pulse throbbed at his temple. Blood rushed to his ears, a roar of oceans that muddled his thoughts. The linoleum, bubbled with age and cracked underfoot. Thinking he heard something, he tilted his head to the side. Someone tried to skulk toward him. A figure came into view, with the quiet scrape of a hesitant shuffle.

"Momma?"

Miss Jane held a fiend lean, defying gravity as if caught up in her high. After a few moments, her head at impossible angles, she snapped out of her revelry and staggered toward him. Clumps of matted hair nested at one side, the rest mere wisps which hadn't been pulled free. The corners of her eyes leaked a yellowish fluid, like formaldehyde tears. Dried vomit stained her clothes. Her shirt flapped open, revealing rot across her chest and leaving one sore-riddled breast exposed, ready for him to suckle.

"There's my baby boy. All grown up. Almost a man," she said, her foul breath nearly making him gag. An ancient rasp, her voice wasn't her own, almost like another one laying on top of hers, as if her own back-up vocals. The Miss Jane thing shambled toward him with the gait of someone who had every bone within them broken, yet remained propped up.

"Momma, you all right?"

"If I'm not, what are you gonna do? You so simple. I should've smothered you when I first saw those big doe eyes of yours. I knew then that you didn't have the sense God gave you. No heart whatsoever. Not your daddy's son."

"Don't say that, Momma." Percy clumped as if wounded, a big man deflated which made him appear that much smaller. He wanted to reach out and hug her, to feel the heat of her against him and have her protect him against the world. That was the mother he remembered. The mother before the drugs, before the bad things, before men, life, and need used her up and left this withered thing behind.

"Sh, baby, it's true. Look at you. Ready to cry. Chasing after the Pendragon. That's your destiny, you know. But not the life I'd have chosen for you. I've never been the best mother, but least I could do is put you out of your misery."

She lunged at him, arms outstretched in an eager embrace. Flesh worn soft, her clammy skin pulled from her bone like perfectly cooked ribs. Her putrid breath worsened as her jaws snapped open, her teeth anxious to rend into his neck. He pushed at her as they grappled, not letting her get her balance or purchase. Her spindly frame no match to his girth, he charged her. He kept running until they crashed into the wall next to the stairs.

"Give Momma a kiss." Miss Jane's lips pulled back over cruel teeth.

Percy pivoted and then flung her down the stairs into the maw of shadows. All he heard was the sickening crack of splintering bones.

"I'm sorry, Momma," he said into the darkness. Through the window the remaining fiends shambled toward the building. Events tumbled toward an endgame. Turning to return to his room, a cloud swirled at the end of the hallway. Not smoke. The mist seeped from walls and had a knowing quality to it as it slipped to the ground in an intelligent trawl. It worried him more than his errant mother. He rushed back to the room and stuffed clothes at the crack of the door.

"What is it?" Rhianna asked.

"Precaution." Percy slumped onto the couch.


A smoke alarm dangled from the wall, the light from the previous floor fading with each step along the stairs. The next floor's light had long burned out. Wires hung from the ceiling. In the residual light, they could make out a final graffiti pronouncement along the stairwell: "A city of refuge in a time of great tribulation." Though none dared voice it, all were bone weary. Merle hadn't spoken in so long even Wayne missed his spouted gibberish. Wayne trundled on, vowing to exercise more when this ended. The keloid on the back of his neck ached. King walked point, unfazed by the intermittent light and the peculiar dance of shadows. Each ascending stair step, despite the sense of climbing one's own gallows, was a minor victory as their feet became heavier and heavier. Their ragged puffs reverberated louder than they wished in the stairwell echo chamber. King was the first to turn the corner leading to the final floor and thus was the first to spy Green.

An impassive sentry, he stood there with a burnt brown suit over a burnt orange shirt with a matching orange and brown tie and pocket kerchief. A chinchilla coat rested on his shoulders. No expression crossed his face. No recognition, no resignation, only a flat affect of business. King came to an abrupt halt with Merle and Wayne bumping into him.

"Fallen so far?" Merle began. "An exercise to experience what we experience."

"*We* now, is it? You consider yourselves one of the mortals, do you?" Green said, his voice the sound of rotted bark giving way. "This, at least, was my choice."

"You were always about choices. How is dear old Morgana?"

Green said nothing.

"What's the matter? Winter got your tongue?" Merle pressed. "I heard a story once. Of a man transformed to exist only as the adversary to the court of chosen knights. Some people knew him as Bercilak de Hautdesert, some as the Green Knight. Part man, part vegetation elemental, he challenged any man to strike him with his ax if he would be allowed to return the blow a year and a day later. One knight took the challenge. But when the appointed time came, the Green Knight barely nicked the chosen one, as said knight had passed all of the tests, made the right choices, set before him. What say you?"

Wayne's keloid on the back of his neck flared with the blazing intensity of a sunburn. He rubbed it but found no solace. The hot pain ran to his core and unsettled him with its sudden familiarity.

"There were many knights. As the age changes, so do its players," Green said.

"So we begin anew. The eternal cycle."

"I got this," Wayne said.

"No." King grabbed him by the arm. "It's my responsibility."

Merle put his hand on King's arm. "No, the first assault belongs to the good Sir."

Without another word, Wayne strode into a sprint, taking the stair steps two at a time. Green remained rooted to his spot. Wrapping his arms around him, Wayne ran through the room and slammed him against the wall. A window shattered behind some cheap venetian blinds. Wayne held him aloft with both arms, attempting to squeeze the life out of Green's trunk-like neck. With a baleful glare of calculating malevolence, Green clapped Wayne's ears, breaking his grip and sending the two of them tumbling to the ground. When they got up, the span of two bodies separated them.

"My turn," Green said simply. His first blow knocked Wayne from his feet. His neck jerked forward and suddenly his mouth filled with the taste of his own blood. The keloid on Wayne's neck burned. Green cried out as vegetal shoots sprouted from his mouth. Leaves blossomed from his nostrils and ears. With a huge sweep of his arm, his fingers became branches, bare limbs of hate scourging King and Merle. Weeds erupted through the floorboards, the mildew spoors given new life: first trapping their feet then, kudzu-winding up their bodies, the roots squeezed them. Turning his attention to Wayne, a jutting spear of a branch impaled him in the shoulder.

"Winter is finally upon you," Merle choked out.

"Senile old fool. Age has addled your magics as well as your mind."

"You see how well you handle it if your mind ages one way while your body ages the other." Merle said. "Still, I have enough left for the occasional spark."

Merle raised his hand, his gaze fixed on his palm. At first, a single ember, little more than a gnat of light, circled in a tight orbit. Soon, a swarm gathered, each light following its own path until they coalesced into a comet of flame. Merle blew on the ball and it leapt from his path landing on the trail of growth leading to Green. Unfortunately, the flames also crawled back toward King and Merle. "Hmm, that might not have been in my best interest."

Green reared back in a frozen rictus of terror, his mouth a blackening maw. His form morphed behind the curtain of flames, until the knots and whorls became the screaming mouth of a scorched tree. Once the flames subsided, the grip of the vines slackened to where King could escape and rush to his friend.

"You all right?" King cradled Wayne.

"Hanging in there. I got me a splinter to end all motherfuckin' splinters, though." Wayne's bravado didn't match his concern at the pooling blood.

"Can you do anything, Merle?"

"A little. But time runs short." Merle plucked an unscorched bud from one of the remaining branches. "For all of us. I fear the bloodwyrm will not take well to us daring so deep into his lair."

"Bloodwyrm?" King asked.

Lott banged on the door, constantly scanning each end of the hall, his imagination afire with all manner of possible attacks. As long as no rats came charging down the hall – because it'd be just his luck for there to be rats – he thought they'd be OK. A lone eyeball flitted across the peephole before the door opened a fraction to double-check what it had just seen. Rhianna opened it fully to Lady G rushing her with a hug.

"What the hell?" Rhianna exclaimed.

"Girl, folks done lost their minds out here, for real," Lady G said.

Their voices faded to white noise as the two caught each other up. Lott again checked the hallway before he made his way in and bolted the door behind them. The dull, shit-colored room reeked of benign neglect. Bullet holes circled the window. Ill-fitting Plexiglas lodged in the frame. A mattress was propped up against the sill. Percy sitting on the couch having paused his Nintendo game at the banging.

"How you holding up?" Lott asked.

"I'm her knight in shining armor," Percy said, lowering his head as if embarrassed at the admission. "That's what she said."

"Yes you are," Rhianna reassured him, not with the voice of someone with romantic intent. The tone, however its raspy delivery, was unpracticed and didn't carry easily from her lips. It was gentle, serious, and true. A rare attempt at vulnerability.

"Are you one, too?" Percy asked.

"I'm hers." Lott pointed to Lady G.

She turned with a smile. A pang lodged in his heart at the sight, though he didn't want to admit to such feelings. Regret, jealousy... longing. King would be a lucky man if he was to get with her.

Percy sang softly to himself. "*Jesus loves me this I know, for the Bible tells me so.*"

"The bloodwyrm formed from a primordial void, the embodiment of all things uncertain," Merle intoned. "In its veins runs the fury of both chaos and creation. They have always been with man, haunting them. This is your journey."

"I know. I've always known, I guess. Part of me anyway. Not the specifics, but a sense of things and how they ought to be." King squatted on his haunches and drew absently on the ground, tracing idle patterns with his fingers. "Take Wayne and get him treated."

King turned his back to Merle and continued into the antechamber to which Green had stood guard.

He waited for Merle to get clear then passed through the chamber opening. The grand penthouse he expected dissolved behind the mists swirling about creating a dreamy haze. Journeying inward, King had the sensation of leaving the physical plane of the apartment complex. Feeling his way downward, he descended into himself, the ancient memory of mankind. Through seeming endless darkness, only the occasional soft crunch under heel broke the silence. Sweat buck-shotted his chest through his shirt. The living mist recoiled at King's presence; however, his Caliburn warmed in his waistband.

*Plink. Plink. Plink.*

"I... no..." he said to no one in particular.

The sky bled and spun gray clouds against a matte the color of a clotted wound. His face flashed with heat, but not the kind usually brought on in temper. Scorched with the nearness of the sun, longing for the cool of an errant stream. His Caliburn. The weight of it so pure and right, yet it was incomplete. Pallid, bloodless faces, the faces of his people hung from poles. Wayne. Lott. Merle. Lady G. Baylon. A few faces he didn't recognize. Flies crawled in and out of their mouths and gave their lips the semblance of movement. Holes replaced their eyes, holes that bore into his soul with the knowing of failure. Phantoms. His Caliburn. The desire to plunge his hands into the fetid earth and make a grave to crawl into. To heap the dirt onto himself. To leave no mark of his passage.

*Plink. Plink. Plink.*

The room took on the aspect of a cave, the gentle plinks of dripping water not too far away. Scattered gold coins along the dirt-floored pit, the remains of a once-hoarded treasure. A spire of rocks, a cage of stalagmites, ran the length of the rear of the prison. The temperature spiked and sweat dotted his forehead. Only then did he realize he could see, the room lit by the glow from eyes and the gentle phosphorescence of the creature's body.

"Here, there be dragon-slayers. Is that what you are, Pendragon stripling?" Its open maw revealed the constant flames that warmed it. Large unblinking yellow eyes, wholly other, tracked his movements. A spectacular ruin, its scaly body bisected by a row of dorsal spines, the bloated beast was soft-bellied, not sleek and armored as he had imagined. It sank its talons into the earth, shifting its posture as if leaning up in bed after a disturbed nap. Its leathery wings folded underneath it. "You come at last, O Prince of the City."

"Who is the Pendragon?"

"You are, Little Dream."

"Then who are you?"

"Be careful with your name, Pendragon. Knowing a person's true name can give one power over them. The Tempter in the Garden. Níðhöggr, the serpent that gnaws at the World Tree. Such is my line and I am weary. Long had I slept, my home built around until I found myself caged. Once feared by man, I have become its vassal, to power petty dreams. So I awaited your arrival."

"You're the genie in the bottle. What do you expect me to do?"

"Kill me, of course." Immense boredom settled in its slitted eye pupils. If it were ever young, it dreamt of massive hoards, gold coins, and gems falling from the folds of its wings and skin whenever it stirred. Its mighty wings cramped in its lair, longing for the freedom of the skies to stretch out and soar. It dreamt of swooping down upon an unsuspecting farmer's livestock – nothing but swords and spears, maybe the occasional bow to deter him – gobbling down a juicy cow or succulent sheep within its snapping jaws. A carefree youth. While the elder beast enjoyed the security of an enclosed lair – a fortress in which to sleep, to protect the various things he treasured – somehow security exchanged itself for imprisonment as the years went on. But the creature was only ready to die if the death was worthy. "Or I'll pick your bones clean."

The elder beast shifted its weight, not used to such movement any longer. Its wings, cramped for so long, unfurled with the slow creak of an arthritic spasm. Once proud and mighty, its long neck reared up and revealed several piles of the skulls of innocents. Too many skulls were entirely too small. As the creature stirred, King's footfalls crunched underneath him. A bolt of flame spewed from its vile mouth. King scrambled out of the way of the initial blast; the heat of it scorched his backside. Steeling himself against his fear, King withdrew his Caliburn though he felt awfully small before the immensity of the dragon.

The dragon's head blurred past him. King leapt to the side, the creature's neck bashed him in mid-air, sending him into the wall. The wind knocked out of him, King closed his eyes to focus past the jarring ache in his bones and move before the dragon could take aim for its next strike. The dark passage was more deep dungeon than cavern. King wedged into the passage of stalagmites and ran. The beast coiled for another blow, its slitted eyes tired, and snapped its jaw shut, gnashing its sword-like teeth. The great horned head turned then smashed the columns in its swipe.

The oozy smell of a rotting hole assaulted King. The scales of the creature had been ground to sores. If the dragon hoped to feign even the shadow of its former glory, its body betrayed it. Talons that once ground stone to dust barely held it upright. The Caliburn warmed in King's hands, ready for use. King took aim at its thick hide and fired into what he guessed to be the heart of the creature. The bullets glowed, tracing a path straight inside. The dragon howled, the tenor of its screech changing from one of pained surprise to melancholy relief.

"Like the knights of old. It has been so long. So very… very…" The dragon began to hum, a melodic sigh, serenading itself. Perhaps the last of its kind, the dirge continued for nearly half an hour – heard like the rumbling of a fierce storm for hundreds of miles around – a great song wasted on deaf ears that didn't understand what they had lost. King stood watch until the last note echoed in the chamber and the beast collapsed into the waiting pool.

*Plink. Plink. Plink.*

With its passing, the chamber resolved itself into the penthouse proper. Suspended on a web of smoke on the far side of the room was Night. His emaciated form held aloft on tendrils of mist. Reed-thin arms raised in objection. Open sores oozed, bloodshot eyes of turgid flesh, he stank of putrefaction. His ashy skin parched with a filigree of veiny cracks and pock-marked by abscesses.

"It is finished." Night's eyebrows whitened. Wrinkles etched his face.

"Was it worth it?" King asked.

"I took what I had to. In this world, you only have yourself to depend on. You can't wait around for folks to give you what you want." A side of Night's face drooped, a palsy of withdrawal, his face appeared to melt. Perhaps the dragon's death severed some connection, the echo of an empowering presence. The vile odor of spoiled offal scourged King's eyes and nose and brought to mind images of maggot infested beef. Fungus crept along Night's skin, a slow parasitic digestion no longer kept in check, devoured the way rust consumes steel.

"Dress it up any way you want. You were a bully and a punk who fed on your own."

"We all live in service to something. Turn on the television and see all those commercials promising what should be ours. Taught to want and get from the time we learned to flip the remote." Night coughed. His wizened arm lifted in protest, but then lowered. Reflective eyes focused on King. "I started at the bottom of a crew, worked my way up, eventually set up my own stand and franchises. I am the American Dream. You can turn your back on me and forget I exist, but I'll feed in the shadows. I'll always get mine."

The battered body gasped for breath, the coils of smoke slackening their grip on him. King finally answered him. "At what cost?"

"My coach once talked about how he couldn't retire from coaching. About how it was all he knew what to do and couldn't leave it behind. Athletes. Coaches. Us. Anyone who is about the game. Once we're done, we die. Or we die and we're done."

With a last gasp, Night's emaciated husk, fully desiccated, toppled from its fading perch and smashed into bits when he hit the ground.

"Yeah," King said. "It's finished for now."

# EPILOGUE

Despite the cold evening, the neighborhood was jumping. Police lights bathed the rows of condos, red light reflecting from all the windows. The police loaded some fool into the back of their squad car. Not just some fool, he was a frequent flyer of foolishness. The family was obviously new to the neighborhood and hadn't quite divined that this neighborhood wasn't quite the same and didn't play by the exact kind of ghetto nonsense that they were used to. The whole mess started a week earlier when the matriarch of the family, all of twenty-five, needed new plates for her car. Indiana license plates were more inexpensive thanks to the tax on the poor that the state called Hoosier Lotto, but they still cost more than the nothing she wanted to pay. So she removed the plates from Big Momma's car, taking the time to crawl into the car and help herself to any spare items, which amounted to spare change, a few CDs, a Bible, and a child car seat. She then proceeded to place the license plate in the back window of her

own car. The main flaw in her plan was that her car
was two parking spaces down from Big Momma. Big
Momma, who also knew the price of a license plate,
immediately recognized her plates and raised a
ruckus. The lady denied it, of course, but King had
Wayne back the Outreach Inc. van up to block the
lady from simply taking off. They all stood guard
until the police came to settle things.

"Let this be a warning to all the drunk uncles trying to pop, lock it, and drop it at the next family
reunion," Merle said.

"Big Momma scraps like she has cerebral palsy,"
Wayne laughed to himself then winced as the movement tugged at the stitches in his shoulder. "I'm
scared of her."

"I'm done with women." Merle plopped on the
sidewalk. "I'm not saying I'm ready to suck a dick or
anything, I just don't want to be in a relationship."

"You know what that heifer had the nerve to ask
me?" Big Momma asked, more rhetorical than anything else, on the verge of a full-on rant.

"What?" Lady G played straight-woman.

"Would I take care of her kids while she was gone."

"No, she didn't," she said with mock shock.

"I hate her monkey ass."

"I ain't mad at you." Lady G high-fived her then
collapsed in a squeal of laughter.

"No. I mean hate." Big Momma played to her au-
dience. "Oh, Lord, I want to paint her picture on my
windshield so it looks like I'm running her over all
the time."

"That's some hate," King interrupted. His T-shirt had the portrait of Malcolm X painted within the shape of the letter X.

"I'll see you, girl." Big Momma stood up, preparing to head inside. Some unspoken message passed between her and Lady G, but King was not a member of the estrogen club, and thus couldn't divine its meaning.

"You looking good." Lady G planted her comb in the half of his hair that remained unbraided. King plopped between her open legs. He brought his idle-too-long hands up on both of her calves, running them up and down. She tensed, a panicked freeze, then relaxed, radiant and poised.

"I'll be back." Merle admired the gathering, but couldn't tarry. Lott and Rhianna would soon join them and the circle would be complete. He still had one last errand to attend to before then.

Dred nervously chewed on his tongue, the movement compounding his throat's swollen veins, thick as serpentine coils, and threatened to stop his breath. The power rippled through the knots of dead muscle. The pain might have killed another man, but his body had been trained by years of abuse. The drugs. The women. The violence. The hate. His blood was the venom of the streets, concentrated succor, and he savored its pulse coursing through him despite its burn. His chair rattled as he convulsed in it, his fingernails digging into the vinyl arm rests. His scream the sound of a soul raped, then cleaved from its body.

Baylon rushed in to check on him, faithful to the end. The umbra tendrils knotted around Dred, their foul energy like black lightning. The unfocused slits of his eyes turned toward Baylon. Dred spat a tendril at him, an ebon tongue lodging on his mouth, the two locked in a dark kiss. Baylon back-pedaled, his body skittering from beneath him as the leeching strand smothered his inhuman cry. It scorched holes into his skin, searing it like tissue paper over a match. Like digging out chunks of his face with shards of glass, the pain was his desperate night of the soul. His muted screams reduced to a dull lowing, his large eyes embracing the inevitable. His flesh reduced to red chaos, puddles sopping under the tread of the wheelchair. Hate his only coping mechanism against the pain.

Dred hyperventilated, choking on the stink of hot blood, trying to find meaning in a meaningless world arriving only at the pure white depths of his loathing. The plasma screens of his televisions flickering to life. With a wave of his hand, the cable spread of channels all shifted to the same image. King.

Psychosis. Self-annihilating violence. Sociologists only guessed to make themselves feel better and justify their own useless existence. They didn't know what it took to survive on the streets, where the rules of the civilized world didn't apply. Where polite society had turned its back. They wouldn't keep him away, sealed away in this chamber, away from the game. His back spasmed. He knew when it all went wrong. He could hear the manic screams of people as he unremembered the pain of the bullet ripping through him. Devoured whole by the shadow and absolved from what he would have to do in the name of his holy cause. His left leg kicked out, wracked with exquisite pain. The metamorphosis happened quickly now, much like giving birth to himself. The throes of labor pain, with Baylon's vitality as a mystic Pitocin. He regretted that King couldn't be here to witness it, nor know the hand he played in his rebirth. A phoenix rising from the ashes of his own body.

"I am…" His mouth opened and closed around the syllables letting the word break in the echoing emptiness, a stillborn child given voice. An awful laugh of a broken soul knitting itself back together. The laughter of the damned. He wiped flecks of Baylon's blood from him.

He rose from his wheelchair and stood. Walking stiffly on undead legs, he shuffled to a shelf and the box that sat in the middle of it. Opening the box, he lifted the gold gun. His Caliburn.

Soon it would be his time.


"None of it was real." Prez scratched at the frayed edges of the peeling wallpaper. Some pieces pulled free in strips, lifting patches of drywall with it. Still, he continued to channel his nervous energy focused on the last bits of paper. A distraction to break the tedium, he wanted to dig his fingers into something real. Most of the homes on the block stood abandoned, boarded-up windows proving little deterrent for a body looking to get out of the cold. Stacks of stuff waited to be hauled out, the previous owners prepared to take everything not nailed down. Clay tiles from the roof. Iron grates from vents. Pile of fixtures. Door knobs and jambs. Cabinet handles.

He sat down on a couch, in direct eye line of a mirror. To wear his game face, as affectless as a Noh mask, all day every day. He washed it, shaved it, presented it in every way, treated it as his own until it became the only face he knew. He scraped behind his ear at an itch of the greasy build-up hidden there. He stank of unwashed armpits and a sweaty crotch.

"Ain't no one up in here but niggas. Niggas can't get a job, got no place to be. You want to be black? You want to be African American?" He emphasized the "can" syllable of each word with a sarcastic bite. "You need to move your ass to the suburbs."

He thought he knew what life was about. He thought he knew what he wanted. Gold-capped teeth. A fine whip with fresh rims and a bumping stereo. Gold chains were still chains. And a blast was still a good high. The idea of life and success putrefied in his mouth. His past a horror of broken promises, his present bleak, his future one of dying dreams, he threw a cabinet handle and shattered it. Putting flame to the blackened bulb, he sucked on the glass dick. Prez let the smoke issue from his mouth. The tendrils slowly swirled around his head.

"Me? I don't want to feel nothing." Tears burned down his face. Angry that they'd come so easily, he lacked the will to wipe them away. "I don't want to feel nothing…"

Only history could tell you certain truths. Puddles of shadow darkened the streets from failed street lamps. The truth was people were slow to learn, if they ever truly did. A stiff-necked bunch, the lot of humanity, destined to repeat their follies, re-live the same hurts, and need the same healing.

The Indianapolis Metropolitan Police Department announced that it would soon open a command center within the Phoenix Apartments. Captain Octavia Burke was put in charge over it. The recent spate of tragic deaths awoke the city to the forgotten blight within itself, where poverty and crime had been given free rein. There were talks of organizing crime patrols and offer job training and mentoring programs. Community leaders applauded themselves, joined in choruses of a community coming together and staying together.

(120 Degrees of) Knowledge Allah's gait dipped with each step of his limp. The pain bothered him more when rain threatened. No clouds dotted the skies but he knew a storm was coming. The mathematics of circles. The sidewalk stopped abruptly giving way to a worn-down-to-the-dirt grass path which cut in front of the beginnings of a construction site.

To little trumpeting, the mayor announced the ground-breaking on a new set of apartments. A high-rise with an emphasis on security. Camlann. The Camlann Apartments.

Though not a playwright himself, with no gift for words or even the subtleties of speech because those sprung from understanding the human condition, the human heart, and he'd stopped trying to be human long ago. But he understood the gift. How writers often stood outside of their own lives, watching people, the intricacies of their interactions, the interplay of bodies and language as they danced around certain truths. Observers in their own lives, unable or unwilling to live them, contenting themselves to scribble their accumulated elucidations in lieu of having to participate in the messy thing called life. And he pitied them.

Merle saw things with the double vision and distance of a writer. He saw the here and now, but he also saw the story being played out and the characters, the roles, they played out. He knew his part in the greater scheme of things and he pitied himself.

Merle withdrew a bud from the inner pocket of his coat and dug his finger into the earth. A squirrel ran up to him then stopped, scratching around for an acorn.

"Sir Rupert. Where have you been? The days were dark and dangerous, not the time to be running around willy-nilly."

The squirrel rested on its haunches, turning its head left and right on the look-out for predatory eyes.

"We must take care of the old ones. Preserve the ways as best we can." Placing the bud within the hole, Merle gently folded the pile back over it. It was his seed to plant, but he hoped the next age treated Green better than this one had. He thought of King and his brethren with a pang of regret as he understood how things had to end.

That was the way. The streets had their own legends, their own magic.

# ABOUT THE AUTHOR

Maurice Broaddus is a notorious egotist whose sole goal is to be a big enough name to be able to snub people at conventions. In anticipation of such a successful writing career, he is practicing speaking of himself in the third person. The "House of M" includes the lovely Sally Jo ("Mommy") and two boys: Maurice Gerald Broaddus II (thus, he gets to retroactively declare himself "Maurice the Great") and Malcolm Xavier Broaddus. Visit his site so he can bore you with details of all things him and most importantly, read his blog. He loves that. A lot.

Maurice holds a Bachelor of Science degree from Purdue University in Biology. Scientist, writer, and hack theologian, he's about the pursuit of Truth because all truth is God's truth. His dark fiction can be found in numerous magazines, anthologies, and novellas.

*www.MauriceBroaddus.com*

**Coming next in the
Knights of Breton Court trilogy:
KING'S JUSTICE**

## Prologue

The ebon hole of the storm drain some called Cat's
Eye Tunnel. A thin stream of water trickled down
the center of the concrete tube. Its sides not quite dry
to the touch. Ignoring the faint smells of algae and
waste, the boys crawled for what felt like quite a
ways in the damp, dark pipe. Their ears strained
against the shadows, past the faraway plink-plink-
plinks of water dripping somewhere further down
the line. Nor was there any mistaking the skritching
sounds.

"Rats!" a voice yelled in the dark.

"Oh, snap!" another called out.

Gavain and his younger brothers scrambled on all
fours, sloshing through the brackish water, rushing
towards the light of the opening until they tumbled
out of the pipe. Piling onto one other, they formed a
twelve-limbed beast that writhed in its own laughter.
Gary and Rath were practically twins; the way their

momma raised them. It was easier on the budget and it simplified fights if they both wore the same outfits. Gary, six, bright-eyed and innocent, idolized Gavain. Though a little bigger than Gary and only five years old, Rath had a potty mouth that sailors envied. Both had the scrawny physique of angry twigs. Their youngest brother, Wayne, stayed home with their mother. Sick again.

"Get your butt out my face." Gary shoved Rath.

"Who yelled 'rats'?" Gavain asked.

"Gary."

"Get that bad boy," Gavain said, knowing full well that it was actually he who had made the scratching sound. "Let's kick his li'l butt."

Gavain scooped Gary up and tossed him easily over his shoulder. He smacked his little brother's butt a couple of times, over Gary's playful squeals of "no" and "stop", before letting Rath get a piece. Gavain, nine and a half, felt a generation older than the other two. Tallest in his class, with the same weedy thinness of his brothers, Gavain loved both of them, but – in his heart of hearts, in that shadowed place where all secrets lay fallow – he admitted to being partial to Gary. The boy's unquestioning, unflinching idolization helped, but it was more the simple, no, innocent way that Gary approached the world. Gavain envied him his purity and wished just for a moment he could reclaim any sense of his own.

After letting Gary tumble from his grasp, Gavain leaned back against the grassy creek embankment to stare at the clouds. The thin creek divided their housing complex, Breton Court, from the rest of the neighborhood. Some days, the creek was the same sad stretch of trilling water serving as a receptacle for collecting trash. Other days the creek seemed to stretch out into infinity, an event horizon of adventure and mystery. Today it was both.

They laid on the grass of the sloping hill. The rear fences of houses caged Dobermans and Rottweilers, who barked incessantly at their presence. From their hillside vantage point, they could see all of Breton Court. Gavain liked this spot, the wide creek separating Breton Court from the residential neighborhood. He'd been chased by bullies through the court, his rare black face in the area too tempting a target for the white thugs. His speed kept him out of harm's way for a long time. Then, nearly cornered, he turned and dashed toward the creek. He leapt its breadth, landing flush on the other side. It was as if he crossed a border check and the bullies didn't have their papers in order. A natural dividing line.

"Look what I found." Rath held up a bent piece of discarded metal pipe.

"Here's another piece." Gary first held his pipe to his eye, scanning the neighborhood like it was a telescope before mounting it on his shoulder, like a bazooka. "Boom."

"Yeah, c'mon, we've got to kill our enemies," Rath declared.

Gavain watched the two of them scamper toward the overpass the creek ran under. Stifling heat thickened the air making it akin to breathing steam. His brothers pantomimed shooting at the unsuspecting cars as they drove past. He meandered after them, just in time to break up the inevitable. No matter how much or how little money they had, no matter what school they attended, no matter which doors opened and closed for them in the maze of opportunities life afforded, boys would be boys.

"I said I was going to blow that one up." Rath swung his pipe at Gary.

Gavain separated them. Forgetting who he was for a moment, they turned at him with a feral grimace. "Don't hit me with that," Gavain said in an unmistakable, no longer playing, tone. "F'real. I ain't playing with you."

The sternness of Gavain's voice shocked them back to their senses. Rath slunk a short distance away, pouting, before contenting himself to shoot at more unsuspecting cars, unhindered by his distracted brother. The dreamy, distant stare – which so often filled Gary's eyes – signaled him drifting into his imagination. Whatever thoughts occupied his mind in that moment would find their way back to his little stack of "his papers" at home. Not quite a journal, more like a collection of stories and day dreams that he chronicled, such as his comic strips with doodles in each corner that depicted two super-heroes fighting when he flipped the pages.

"'Mother, may I go out to swim?'/'Yes my darling daughter./Hang your clothes on an alder limb/And don't go near the water.'" Gary sang, dragging the length of pipe behind him.

"You little bitch," Rath chased after him, in his half stalking lope which indicated a mood to bully or get into mischief. He knew he was the tougher of the two. He hated the softness his brother had and hoped to toughen him up. It was either that or spend the bulk of his days as his brother's shadow protector. Which, all told, he didn't mind too much.

"Watch your mouth!" Gavain yelled.

"Alright... Preacher."

*Preacher*. The word spat at him with the venom of an ill-considered epithet. Gavain loved going to church, especially Sunday School. His class was small, so the teacher lavished extra attention on him; easy to do with an eager student. So at his instigation, the brothers often played church, building blanket cathedrals in the living room. Gavain recited his favorite Old Testament stories (Noah, Moses, Jonah) and led songs while his brothers Amen-ed and sang along, happy just to be playing any variation of forts with him. They all knew it would only be a matter of time before his friends claimed him and he spent his days running around with them instead of spending time with his little brothers. At nine, the called of the streets beckoned with its siren song.

"Momma used to sing that to me," Gary said.

"Cause she thinks you're a girl. She still tucks you in too," Rath said. Gary lowered his head, with a splash of shame as if hit with too close a truth, obviously too sensitive to play insult games with Rath. He always took them too personally and hated the idea of hurting people for amusement.

"I know where we can go," Gavain changed topics, speaking more under his breath than to anyone in particular.

"Shut up." Gary had pretty much exhausted his comebacks in one shot.

"No, you shut up," Rath retorted.

Gavain stage-sighed. "Forget it. I'm going without either of you. I don't have time to baby sit, no how."

It didn't matter who said what, the apologies rang with the same cheery melody, a chorus of "Wait up, Gavain" and "Yeah, we're sorry." Whenever they turned on him, or even got too out of line, the simple threat of abandoning them was usually enough to straighten things out. Gavain reveled in the adulation that bordered on respect and the power that accompanied it. He smiled a wan, yet victorious, smile.

"Where we going?" Gary asked.

"To the lake," Gavain said.

"But that's so far."

"We're almost there already." Gavain's tone didn't invite debate.

"Quit whinin', you can't come anyway. You too little," Rath said.

"Momma said I could go with you," Gary whispered.

Their momma's parting words slowed Gavain's steps. Look after your little brothers. "Fine. C'mon then."

The trio followed a trail known only to Gavain. This marked the first time he had taken them to his special spot. He retreated there to read, and think, be by himself, away from his brothers and the responsibilities of them. Though they only lived two miles from the park, Gavain had deemed his brothers too young to make the trip before; but now they walked along a creek bed, its low flow revealed slippery rocks under the late afternoon sun.

Across from the Indianapolis Colts training facility, Eagle Creek Park, a national reserve spread out in open invitation. A brief traipse through the woods allowed the boys to by-pass both the main gate (with its honor box: 50 cents for walk-in visitors to the park) and the ranger stations along the main roads (police, even wanna-be police, was still police). When they reached the old rusted-out fence, he knew that they neared their final destination. Long gashes, wounds of age and curious teenagers, marred the evenness of the links. Gavain pushed back the torn bit of fence barring their path. Flecks of rust painted his hand orange as he pushed through the low-lying branches occluding the dirt-worn and matted grass that served as their walkway.

His spot was a natural alcove of shore and trees, as if a giant mouth had taken a bite out of the park forest and backwashed sand. Dark sand, far from sun-bleached, lined the small inlet as waves lapped against it. The tree line dropped off sharply at the water, skeins of roots revealed by erosion. A tire on a rope hung in forlorn innocence from an old tree whose branches shaded a good chunk of their spot. Constructed to launch canoes before it dawned on the bureaucrats running the park to do so near the main beach and charge people for the privilege, the rickety boat launch bobbed on tires. Testing its mildewed boards, Gavain imagined himself walking the plank of a dilapidated pirate ship. The sun glinted from the water, its shards of light held Gary and Rath in rapt attention.

"You sure it's alright to be here?" Gary asked in an almost awe-struck whisper. "We didn't bring any clothes to swim in. Or towels."

"Damn, fool. You know momma wouldn't let us go swimming." Rath said.

"Just swim in your underwear. It'll dry out on the way home," Gavain reassured him with a smile.

That was all the encouragement the boys needed, shucking their clothes over near the tree roots and running to the water's edge. Warm gusts of wind blew towards them; tiny, lazy waves sloshed against the shoreline. The alcove lay around the bend from the main beach, like a forgotten part of the park, fenced off (or fenced in) to keep people from wandering off. With the occasional boat horn belching in the distance, he knew they weren't alone. On such a beautiful picnicking day, the beach proper had to be crowded and all the shelters full.

However nary a sound drifted into their alcove.

A strong breeze rushed off the water. It was downright frigid in the shadows where Gavain watched the boys play. They wobbled on slick rocks, their arms flailing to steady their balance as they acted out king fu movies. Gavain already regretting letting them watch *The Five Deadly Venoms*. Discarded in their frolic, the branches piled at the dock. He feared that he'd have to confiscate their improvised weapons, especially if it occurred to them to battle any unsuspecting underwater enemies. The last thing he wanted was some sort of light saber duel in the water. Their private hideaway did its job, enchanting the boys. It wasn't often that they played near anything that wasn't concrete or plastic. They had some relatives that owned a farm or something down in Jeffersonville, but they were their father's side of the family. Momma never quite fit in with the family.

The innocuous chattering of the boys strained Gavain's nerves, but only in a bemused-by-the-familiar sort of way. The boys beamed, amusing themselves, and that gave him time to read. He pulled a tattered copy of Danny Dunn and the Smallifying Machine from his back pocket, surprised by how much he enjoyed the ludicrous series. There was a quaintness to them that he liked.

Then something at the back of his mind nagged him, an unscratched itch. He searched for a word to describe the feeling. The water mesmerized him. Breathing in the loamy smell of leaves, the stiffness of the breeze, he realized what the feeling was that he couldn't shake. The weight of eyes followed his every movement. Someone watched him, exactly the way the little Korean beauty salon owners watched him when he bought stuff for momma. Someone on a rock down the beach, barely within sight; a body, light as bleached bark, nearly white in the furtive sun and slight of build, a woman perhaps, watched them.

Making sure those children didn't cause any trouble, he thought. He'd been on alert for indignant park rangers, full of their authority, coming to scare them off. The possibility of a chase gave him a thrill to look forward to. Not that he expected anyone else to be here: it kind of ruined his illusion that only he knew about the place. The woman stole away into the trees.

"Hey, did you see her?" Gavain asked.

"See who?" The boys answered in unison. Sand somehow managed to dust both of their fresh faces though neither was even up to their knees in the water.

"The woman over by the trees. She was staring at us."

"Probably a park ranger," Gary turned from Rath as if the two of them had to caucus before deciding the proper response.

"Then why didn't she come chase us?" Gavain asked.

"Probably one of those sun bathers then."

"Was she naked?" Rath finally chimed in.

"Don't listen to him. There probably wasn't no woman. He just trying to scare us again." Gary's eyes widened in a tacit plea to not taunt them anymore.

"I wasn't, but that does remind me of a story." Gavain squatted over an overturned log, drawing in the sand with a twig, waiting for the boys to come over to him. They did, they always did. "You remember that nursery rhyme you were singing earlier, Gary? Do you know what it's about?"

"No." Gary searched for his own twig and began to draw in the sand.

"There was this old witch without a name but folks called the Lady of the Lake."

"I don't believe in witches," Gary said, not quite looking into Gavain's eyes.

"Do you want to hear this story or what? Anyway, you see there was a woman who lived by a lake much like this one. One day she goes out for a swim, but the water…" Gavain trailed off, making his voice sound haunted, for good effect, especially if he wanted to frighten the boys into caution around the water. "Water can be a powerful thing, scary, but they don't make movies about it. It's not something that puts on a mask and chases you through an old house. It's deep. Strong. Mysterious. And things live in it. Things that scientists don't know about or can't explain. Maybe the Lady of the Lake got caught by one of those things. Maybe she became one of them. Maybe she was the mother of all of those creatures. All folks say is that she drowned, but every seven years, she comes back to claim a life, a life that should've been hers. Sort of a guilt offering. She comes for those who wander too close to the water's edge, grabbing their ankles with those long arms of hers, and pulls them to her, draws them to her underwater kingdom. And you don't want to see her in the water. Her skin is slightly blue and puffy from being drowned and all. She has long hair, greenish like it's wrapped in seaweed or somethin'. And she greets them with a kiss, a kiss full of her long sharp teeth. She stares at you with those big dead eyes of hers. She couldn't help herself. It was in her nature. They're the last thing that you see before you take your last breath...

"BOO!" Gavain yelled and jumped suddenly.

The boys reared back and screamed before hitting each other and laughing.

"Bitch done wet hisself," Rath said.

"Boy, I ain't gonna tell you again." Gavain tossed his stick at him. "Watch your mouth."

The boys scrabbled off, unphased, splashing into the water.

"You comin' in?" Gary turned and asked. Gary had a way of asking for things that sounded not only like a command, but as if his whole life depended on you giving into him.

"Yeah, in a minute," Gavain lied. "Hey, if you can't stand up and be above the water, you need to come back closer." He didn't want to have to get wet if he could help it. His brothers might have bought the idea of their clothes drying out on the walk home, but the idea of wet, bunched-up underwear rubbing against him for an hour didn't appeal nearly as much to him as it did them. Visions of having to swim after one of the knuckleheads caused his fear of deep water to rear itself again. He wanted to spend more time in the water, but the shore was as close to the water's edge as he dared go. He shielded his eyes with his hand to better study the deceptive calm of the flat surface of the water. Gary jumped into the water. Not used to the acoustics of the woods, Gavain thought he heard a second splash a little further away. It might've just been an echo. He scanned the periphery anyway.

The water exercised a strange fascination over him. He lost track of time, idling his minutes away, not really reading his book but only holding it in front of him while he studied the water. The splashes of his brothers grew faint. The book fell from his limp grasp. The lolling waves lapped against the sheltering embankment. The swishing sussurus made it easy to ignore the rising uneasiness that washed over him. The sobering shimmer of light, the dispassionate gaze of the deep, the sibilant call of the waves, held him in a spell that reached to an ancient, yet familiar part of his soul. The seaweed, like trees helplessly caught in a strong wind, unfurled, forming a chain that pointed toward the deeper part of the lake. The brown murkiness of kicked-up lake bottom swooshed about, as if something stirred to life. The water. A war waged within the waves, breaking the smoothness of the water.

That was when he noticed that Gary was in trouble.

Gary slapped at the surface, his head cocked up at an odd angle, as he fought the water rather than swam in it, spitting out mistakenly inhaled gulps of water. Rath was nowhere to be seen. Gavain clambered down the embankment, each bob of Gary's head an eternity whenever it ducked under the waves. The drooping branches whipped at Gavain. He stumbled over an exposed tree root and fell face down into the wet sand. Lines of smallish footprints criss-crossed the dark sand. They could've been the boys' footprints, but there were so many. Gavain stumbled to his feet and waded frantically into the water. Not a strong swimmer; he swam well enough to get where he wanted to go, but had no technique beyond his floundering variation of the dog paddle. His lungs burned as he took in gulps of water. He splashed about in near panic and tried to reach Gary who seemed only a few yards away from him. Frustrated tears stung his eyes. The water flowed thick and heavy, the painful rush of it towed against him like bottled-up rage. He strained against the water, but made little progress. The tide, too strong, swept them further out into the lake. Gavain thought that he glimpsed someone. A woman.

"Help them! Help them! They're drowning!" he cried out.

Gavain swam across the sucking, parallel to the shore; it was all he knew to do, desperately fighting against the watery vacuum that threatened to yank him under. He scanned for any sign of his brothers. Gavain stretched out his arm, almost within reach of Gary's outstretched hand. Gary's face turned toward him, blanched and exhausted, like a boy who'd seen a ghost, but was too tired to run.

"Gary." Gavain dug his arms into the water, his measured strokes like swimming through quicksand.

He reached out toward him, spotting Gary's terrified eyes, his body seized in some invisible, powerful grip. The water climbed higher along Gavain's chest. The tug gnawed at him. He shivered, suddenly aware of how cold the water was; too cold for such a day. The water seemed so dark, murky. A cloud covered the sun and created deeper pockets of shadows beneath the waves. No, this shadow was small, heading towards him just out of reach.

Rath. Eyes bulged out, his face frozen in a rictus of panic.

Something scraped against Gavain with the bite of coral, like the sharp, thick nails of a large hand. The splashing ceased. Gavain searched for any sign, any shade, that could've been Gary. Nothing. The waves, its anger spent, subsided. Gavain imagined how his brothers spent their last moments. Their arms outstretched, fighting for air, their minds wondering where he was. Where was their big brother? He was supposed to look after them, protect them from bad things. Bad people. That was when he knew.

She had come for them, with her yellowed sinews, black blood pulsing through her veins. The Lady of the Lake, her belly bloated with the rage of the sea; head lolling from side to side, caught in its own current. He remembered something like hands brush against him. Like hands, but not hands.

He never forgot the hands.

# CHAPTER ONE

King James White had spent his entire life on the west side of Indianapolis. Despite being funneled through Child Protective Services, in and out of homes – more out that in by his teenage years – he'd attended schools #109, and #107 (transferred to be a part of their advance placement curriculum because his high intelligence was noted despite his efforts) for his elementary years, #108 for Junior High School, and then Northwest High School for the couple years he could stand being in high school.

The rhythms of this side of town were as familiar as the constellation of razor bumps along his neck. Exiting on the 38th Street ramp from I-465 – the highway loop that circled Indianapolis proper – he expected the same rotating cast of panhandlers. The homeless vets who couldn't quite pinpoint what war they were veterans of. The folks who needed money in order to get home, who turned down rides to said home. They swapped time with a woman whose sign told the tale of her being pregnant and homeless.

The weather faded backpack and mottled teddy bear wrapped in a blanket were nice touches, but she'd been "pregnant" for over two years now. When off shift, her or the vet or the lost couple were picked up by a van. Begging was just another way of life in the hustle.

Turning east off the ramp took one to the corner of 38th and High School Road. Three of the corners of the intersection had gas stations on them. The fourth – the north-west corner – was a collection of store fronts. The Great Wok of China's kitchen caught on fire a few months back, the timing of which worked out well for the lingerie and marital aids store next door. The owner had been embezzling money and the new ownership was in place and was planning on relaunching the store with basically the same name with the letters jumbled, familiar yet different. The adjoining Karma record store would be down for a month or so. Folks would have to get their drug paraphernalia somewhere else for a time. The lot behind the store fronts was a deserted concrete slab built on a hill nicknamed Agned for reasons no one any longer remembered; enclosed by a Dairy Queen and a Shrimp Hut, thus free from casual prying eyes, especially so early on a Sunday morning.

Though it was still Saturday night as far as Caul was concerned.

In a North Carolina Tar Heels jacket, Caul stood a bulky 7' 5", towering over both King and his best friend, Lott Carey. Under a thicket of dirty hair, his eyes gleamed red in feral madness. A jagged keloid ran down his left cheek. His thick lips drew back to reveal teeth painted black within his wide mouth. Curiously, he had neatly trimmed fingers, except for the nail on his pinky which jutted out an inch and a half.

"It's over, Caul." King cold-eyed the giant. Tall, though still easily a half-foot shorter than Caul, King wasn't overly muscled like one of those swollen brothers just out of prison. The sides of King's head was shaved clean. The top of his head in short twists, almost reminiscent of a crown. King let the wind catch his leather coat, allowing the handle of his golden Caliburn to be seen. A portrait of Marcus Garvey peeked from his black T-shirt. Skin the complexion of burnt cocoa. His eyes burned with a stern glint, both decisive and sure. His lips pursed, locked in a mission, as he focused on the task at hand. He stepped defiant and sure, confident without issuing a challenge. Though prepared to meet one if need be.

"It ain't over, you Morpheus-looking motherfucker. You ain't po-po. You can't arrest no body."

Lott had told King he thought the sunglasses were too much. The weather was getting too warm to justify the leather coat. Still, King liked the look. Lott lowered his head to conceal and "I told you so" smirk.

"I'm telling you to go." King put both his hands up, signing for everyone to just calm the hell down. He pitied the thugs he ran across more than anything else. Social outcasts masquerading as the definition of loner cool, no one would have them, not school, not family, not friends, not relationships. They didn't know how to connect and in their loneliness, they turned angry, little more than sullen children destroying what they couldn't have. In Caul's case, he terrorized the elderly during their grocery store runs, jacked people at ATMs, and harassed women going about their business. The final straw, he threatened King's girl, Lady G. King and Lott took a personal interest then.

"You telling me something now? Don't think I didn't notice that you brought your boy."

"Boy? I'll climb all over you like a spider monkey." Lott checked his watch to mark the time before his shift was due to start at FedEx. He hated to wear himself out before going to work, but when King asked, explaining the threats made to Lady G, his face went hot and he knew he'd call in sick if he had to.

"Don't think that I can't snap your back over my knee and fuck the stump of you right here," Caul snarled. The keloid arched upward as if waving at King.

"What is it with you people? Always talking about 'fucking' other dudes then say how they ain't gay," Lott said. "How player is that?"

"It ain't gay if your eyes are closed," Caul said.

"Is that how it works?"

"A hole's a hole."

"We don't want any more trouble. We just need you to move on–" King began.

"Or what? You think I'm scared of you? Or your little gun? I've had guns pointed at me before. Been shot more times than I can count."

"I'm thinking there's not too hard to get to," Lott said.

Caul's world turned red. The heavy-lidded gaze of the fiend snapped to full fury. He hated when people assumed he was stupid. That just because he was large, he was also slow. His teachers had always treated him like the large simpleton taking up precious classroom space until the jails caught up with him. At some point, he bought into their beliefs about him and it angered him. But he stuffed that anger back onto itself, allowing indo smoke to chill him out most days. Today he needed to wipe that "better than you" grin off the tan-skinned one's face. With his FedEx uniform as if that made him someone. Caul snarled and charged Lott without further comment.

"It wasn't my fault," Caul said as he swung, to the ghosts only he knew.

Skin the color of burnt butter, and with the delicate features of a male model playing at being thug, Lott danced out of the way of Caul's lumbering charge. True to his word, Lott skittered up Caul's back, wrapping his legs around the brute's chest while attempting to subdue him with a choke hold. Caul cantered backwards, slamming Lott into the wall of the China Wok. The air escaped from Lott with a sudden gasp.

King's vision blurred the scene before him shifting, merging, with another scene as familiar as memory. Caul lumbered toward him, stumbling from the shadows of a massive cave. Past two great fires he strode toward King. The giant gnawed on the bone of a human clutched in one hairy hand. Blood smeared about his lips like barbecue sauce after a ribs repast. The dreamy déjà vu sensation annoyed King, like weed getting his head up at the most inopportune times. King shook his head to clear it, then jumped back barely avoiding Caul's thrown punch.

King ducked under the clumsy attack, cursing himself for an ill thought-out strategy with no end game in mind. The fact that he and Lott's blood got so roiled at the idea of someone menacing Lady G was all but dismissed by the pair. The threat of the Caliburn was just that: an empty threat. King was loathe to draw the weapon if the situation didn't warrant it. Ever since the Glein River incident. The weapon called when it demanded to be used. On its terms, any time else was an abuse. King threw a couple of quick jabs into the man's kidneys which seemed to annoy him more than anything else. What did he hope to accomplish? His only plan was to beat this man's ass under the guise of asking him to move on.

The mistake most people made – it occurred to King as he stepped out of range of Caul's massive swipes while leading him away from a shaken Lott – was to use the same weapons against all enemies. There was nothing to be hoped for going toe-to-toe with Caul. That was fighting a superior foe on his terms. No, the only weapon against strength and size was smallness, stealth, and speed.

As if reading from the same battle manual, Lott charged Caul, tackling him at the knees. The giant collapsed to his knees catching himself before his head hit the concrete. Scrabbling for purchase, he hoped to wrench Lott into his grasp.

King withdrew his Caliburn. The gold glistened in the early morning light. Lott's eyes widened. Caul turned, following Lott's gaze, his sight landing on the gun. Shifting his grip, King swung the weapon in a low arc, clocking Caul just above the temple.

"So what do we do now?" Lott asked.

"Call the police?" King examined the unconscious giant.

"And say what? Where I come from, snitches get stitches."

"Self-defense."

"Trouble just seems to keep finding you."

The morning had barely dawned.

A pair of New Balance tennis shoes – gray and mottled with mold – dangled from the overhead phone line. A schoolyard prank gone awry to the casual passer-by; an advertisement, or ominous warning and cause for alarm, to those more in the know. King sucked his teeth in disgust and wondered how long they had been there and if it were too late to stave off the attempted infection of his neighborhood. His philosophy was simple: if a community didn't take control of itself and one guy entered who could think, the community would have a problem. If people in the neighborhood took control, however, that guy knew he had opposition. Most times before he stood against opposition, he would leave for an unprepared, less resistant neighborhood. Now, in LA or Gary, they might go toe-to-toe with opposition. Not here. Not in Indianapolis. Not yet.

"Back it up." King waved the Outreach Inc. van back a few more feet then held his palms up for it to stop. Armed with a broom, he jogged around to the front and hopped up along the hood to the roof in a limber movement.

"This is stupid," Wayne said. Brushing back a few of his long braids which had fallen into his face, he turned all the way around, revealing a scar on the back of his neck. A tight knit shirt stretched across him, showing off the stocky build of a football player, with the light gait of someone who knew how to use their size should the necessity warrant. A quick smile broke up what otherwise would have been a hard face. "You better not leave any shoe prints up there."

"A little work now prevents a huge, pain-in-the-behind worth of work down the road."

Breton Drive separated the assemblage of townhouses of Breton Court from Jonathan Jennings Public School #109. The school was designated a zero tolerance zone and once Night's drug crew had been dismantled, it was one in deed as well as word. King stared at the shoes as if they personally mocked him.

"It's a pair of shoes."

"It's a *declaration*," King said. "Says someone intends on dealing out of here soon. It's a set-up notice. Well, message received. Now we're sending one back."

"Yeah, throw up a pair of tennis shoes and see how many brothers it takes to take them down."

"Two. One to do the work and another to wear his ass out with complaining about it." King waved the broom handle about, a blind conductor directing an unseen orchestra. Eventually one of his haphazard swings connected with the shoes and they tumbled free. "There. Now they know. You try to set up shop in this neighborhood, there are folks around here who care enough to stop it."

"Uh huh. If you close your eyes, you can hear your applause."

"Come on." King gathered the shoes, holding them with two fingers well away from him. "We going to be late."

**The quest continues in**
**KING'S JUSTICE**
**THE KNIGHTS OF BRETON COURT II**

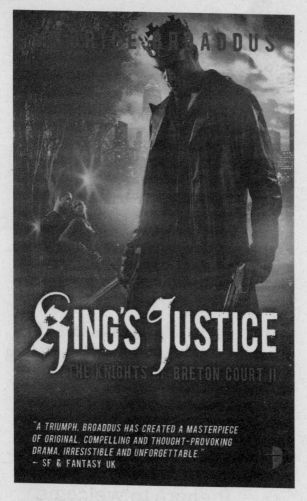

King's quest takes a darker turn in
the explosive sequel to *King Maker*.
Coming very soon from Angry Robot.

w w w . a n g r y r o b o t b o o k s . c o m

ANGRY
ROBOT

Teenage serial killers
**Zombie detectives**
**The grim reaper in love**
Howling axes **Vampire**
**hordes** Dead men's clones
The Black Hand
Death by cellphone
**Gangster shamen**
**Steampunk anarchists**
**Sex-crazed bloodsuckers**
Murderous gods
Riots **Quests Discovery**
**Death**

Prepare to welcome
your new
Robot overlords.

**angryrobotbooks.com**

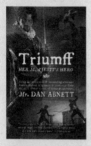